THE SPECTRE & THE RAVEN

Ned Ward

The Spectre & the Raven

Copyright © Ned Ward 2020

Cover Design Copyright © Emily Foster 2020

This novel is entirely a work of fiction. The names, places, characters, and events portrayed are of the author's imagination. Any resemblance to actual persons, living or dead, events or locations is entirely coincidental.

All rights reserved. No part of this publication may be reproduced, stored in a retrieval system, or transmitted, in any form or by any means, electronic, manual, photocopying or otherwise without prior permission from the author.

For Claire and Connie,
my mother and sister.
The warriors in my life.

Prologue

An era ago, All-Mother Zohya, a goddess of great power and beauty, had fought and overthrown the Eternal Giants who had oppressed the world. Zohya planted a tree at the centre and named it Nhivaliurn, the tree connects the realms of life, death, reality, and time.
The All-Mother was weak from war, however, and created a council of magic to see her plans fulfilled. Her creations, the Vayshanaa were powerful sorcerers, which each embodied an element of magic.

The Vayshanaa were each given a task, and a tool for it:

The Vayshanaa of Emotion was given a ring, for the world would bleed and cry, yet sing and dance through their hands. It was named Embasha.

The Vayshanaa of Creation was given a hammer, for they would strike against the anvil and forge the first beings. It was named Caereth.

The Vayshanaa of Life was given a staff, and from it, seeds that would grow into trees, would be planted from it. It was named Dr'arenth.

The Vayshanaa of Death was given a cloak, for they would use it to cover and transport those who had died into the next realm. It was named Ortharlia.

The Vayshanaa of Time was given a sword, and it would be used as such, but also as a key. It was named Sciraria.

Another artefact was created, a crown, which was hidden among the first tribes of the world, for they would need it, should the giants ever return. They never did, though, and so, the crown became lost to a legend that was rarely told.

The Vayshanaa went on to lead the tribes of the world and created a book to store their history before choosing others to take on their mantle.

The Calitreum was made, in part, by each Vayshanaa together; a living book that exists between reality and out. It is upon these pages that the life and story of the Vayshanaa are placed.

Chapter One
Cold as Stone

The title 'Vayshanaa' came from the Language of the First, a term rarely used these days. It was the language spoken by the first Vayshanaa, the language of magic. Vayshanaa means 'Master of Words' for to be a Vayshanaa is to speak two languages. One of words and one of magic. To each Master of Words, the magic is but a different pronunciation. – Calitreum, A Vayshanaa's Oath, Page 1.

Rain. It was always raining here, or at least it seemed that way. Dark, ominous clouds seeped across the sky from the very first glimpse of sunlight, masking it as though ashamed of its attempts to bring light and joy. Joy had long since been forgotten here, in the marsh-surrounded villages, for it was a place where fear ran through the rich soil more than roots of any plant; contagious and poisonous. A man, riding on a tall silver-brown horse, made his way down a muddy track that led towards the small village of Porthna. Porthna had one been a fertile land with long blades of grass that stood like carved strands of emerald, the water once a magnificent blue that reflected the sky's honest intention, and a gentle breeze would carry the smell of lemon-blossoms for miles around. Now, however, it was a murky, miserable place. The rivers overflowed and flooded the grassy soil creating deep marshes, and the clear blue skies were replaced with sheets of black and grey. Cold droplets of rain splashed into the fine hair of his horse and tumbled down the smooth skin of his cheeks and coarse stubble. His saddle was old; torn, scratched, faded leather with fraying straps, and his long, green cloak was grubby and damp. The thick cloth had a matted and rough feel, it may once have been of fine quality, but now it had lost all its colour and shine. Upon his back was a bag, filled to the brim. A sword was concealed between his cloak and bag, hidden as best he could. Pale brown grass ran the length of the track and into the surrounding world as far as the eye could see. The grass was home to thousands of vile rats as large as cats. Snakes burrowed deep in the soil, slithering through the towering plants only to feast upon dogs or people that had lost their way. A white raven flew above, passing over the field, keeping an eye out for its next meal. The Bone Marshes: these fields were called.

With a gentle nudge the rider encouraged the horse to continue forward and small huts surrounded by a makeshift wall, which stood only a few feet tall, came into view. Rain continued to hurl from above and thunder now roared across the sky, closely followed by lightning bolts that dashed over the clouds, like the antlers of a great stag. Upon entering the small town, the rider headed towards the stables, muddy trade faded out and was exchanged for a red-brick road, although it was clear that little or no maintenance had been paid after the first bricks were laid. The road was dotted with holes and the earthy mounds to the sides had slumped, spilling dirt and pebbles across the cracking bricks. The stables, much like many of the buildings in Porthna, had been left to rot. The roof was a weed-thatch, but rain still seeped through, splattering onto the muddy-straw floor. The walls creaked in the slight breeze. Regardless, the rider dismounted, tied the horse to a post and swung a blanket across it from inside his bag, he snapped a carrot in half and fed it to her,

"I'll be back soon, girl."

Across from the stables was what appeared to be an inn. What had once been a signpost, hung proudly as a city trophy now lay in the ground, submerged in filth. 'The Horn and Crow' it read, just visible to a keen eye. The rider strolled over, turning his coat up and pulling his hood forward, blocking the rain. The door creaked open when pushed, the candles and lanterns inside flickered and many heads turned. A bar lay directly ahead and there was a fire to the right, a big dog sat next to it and watched the rider as he strode forth. The floorboards creaked with every step he took. The barkeep turned away from him when he took a stool at the counter while others, sitting on a table behind him whispered to themselves. The rider caught glimpses of conversation; 'outsider', 'turn him away'. The rider took a pouch from inside his coat, dropped it on the counter and addressed the barkeep,

"Can a man get a drink, maybe ask some questions?" His voice was deep but smooth, the barkeep turned to him, scowling,

"A drink, perhaps. What questions would they be?"

"I'm looking for someone. A woman. Tall, dark skinned, with bright eyes."

"We don't serve your kind here, dark-skin! Hit the road!" A drunk man yelled at him from behind, sitting on the table with others who nodded.

The rider stood up and faced the drunkard, who stumbled backwards at the sight of him. The rider was at least two feet taller and even though cloaked; it was clear that he was strong.

"You can have that drink and we can talk." A different man spoke, behind the bar, standing behind the first one who looked at him with deranged eyes.

The second barkeep poured ale into a horned cup for himself and the rider, beckoning to a table by the fire. He was tall and thin, with straw-like blond hair and brown eyes. He sat down and gestured to the rider.

"Please."

The rider sat down, dropping his hood to reveal murky brown skin and a chiselled jaw with a stubble of black bristles. He had a patch made of coarse leather over his left eye, his other one, a wild-green that one might see in the crystals of the deepest sea caverns, splashed with shards of grey. He had a sharp, keen nose. A scar stretched from the bottom of his right cheek to the top of his nose. He had short, shaved hair that was slightly rough around the edges where the blade had been held at an awkward angle. He reached out to grab the horned cup, three of his fingers were bandaged, stained blotches of red.

"Eyes as bright as day. Skin as cold as stone." The barkeep spoke softly.

The latter of the two phrases was only known by those working with Rayna for her mission here,

"You were her contact?"

"I am... I was... I don't know, I've not heard from her in a while. My name is Drayn" He continued, while taking sips of ale. "What is your name? Who was Rayna to you?"

The rider lifted the cup to his lips and sipped. The ale was warm and fruity. The liquid had grains and seeds from the fields. It was probably brewed right here in the town, maybe in the basement.

"My name is Athias. Rayna and I go way back." Athias sipped his ale again before pressing on, "Can you give me any information on where she may be? Where she was heading?"

"In her last contact she mentioned a place called Ly…" He was cut off by the clang of the door bursting open and a woman scrambling over the threshold.

She hastily tried to cover her head but not before everyone in the room caught a glimpse of the brown, furry ears atop her head. The barkeep who had first greeted Athias took steps back in horror and the men at the table by the door looked to each other in disgust.

"Help me. Please help me! They're coming for me!" One of the men at the table tripped her and she fell into the bar, knocking dishes and cups over the edge, he sat back down laughing with his companions and swigging ale.

Athias went to stand up but Drayn grabbed his wrist.

"Don't. It'll cause more trouble; this town doesn't need that. It's barely standing as it is."

The barkeep sneered at the woman who knelt against the bar, soaking, and trembling,

"You don't belong here, half breed."

"Please!" She started crying.

Sobbing and shaking she stood up and ran to different people in the inn, begging them for help. The door crashed open again. Five burly men stepped inside. The men were wearing the same attire; iron cuirasses worn over gold and red coats. They each had a rapier at the waist and a flintlock rifle strung over their shoulders. One of the five stepped forward, eyeing up the woman. He was fatter than the others with dirty brown hair and saggy cheeks.

"Well. Look what we 'ave 'ere boys. Vermin." He chuckled to himself revealing rotten, pointed teeth, "what you doin' all the way out 'ere, half breed?"

"Please… please don't. Mercy. Please. I can't go back there." The woman sunk to the floor, her hood had fallen off her head revealing the ears of a wolf and the starts of whiskers on her face.

"Who said you're going back? We've 'ad a long day looking for you. You're coming with us."

The woman swung round, looking from person to person at the inn, frantically searching for someone to help before the soldiers grabbed her and dragged her to the door.

"Help me…" She screamed.

The ringleader approached the bar and lay a few gold coins on the counter.

"The captain thanks you for your support against these savages." He snorted before turning back.

The woman started to sob. A soldier hit her across the face with the back of his hand, the thud echoed around the room and the men at the table laughed, egging them on. Athias' grip around the tankard tightened and it cracked. He slowly got to his feet and Drayn looked to him and shook his head frantically. Athias looked away and turned towards the bar.

"There's a saying where I grew up." He addressed the entire room as it slipped into silence. "Kalvae vau'lomo dellata." He slowly placed his bag and sword, still wrapped in leather, onto the bench he had been sitting on. "'Raise your sword for those who cannot.'" Athias began to walk towards the soldiers who looked to each other, smirking, "it doesn't look like I'll need it, however."

"What do you care about this half-breed, outsider? Do you want a good thrashing too? The dogs haven't been fed for days…"

"Well… We'll have to give them something to eat then, won't we?"

As soon as the last word had leapt from Athias' lips he had grabbed a tankard from the counter and slammed it down onto the barkeep's hand. The rough, jagged edges sliced through the flesh and cracked the bones. One of the soldiers let go of the woman and swung the rifle from his shoulder, pointing it at Athias who closed the gap and pushed the barrel to the side. A crack rang out through the inn as the rifle fired. A drunkard whelped, falling back off the chair. Athias delivered a deafening blow to the side of the soldier's head, buckling him. He swiped a knife from the bar and threw it into an eye of the soldier holding onto the woman, who fell to her knees and ducked under a table. Athias then jumped and grabbed a soldier by the neck. He swung down over a table, cracking the soldier's spine. He turned to the other two, one lunged towards him while the other, the ringleader, loaded his rifle. Athias blocked the incoming punches, thrown by an amateur in a frenzy and took hold of his head, smashing it against his own and then swung him around to face the last. Athias slid across the floor, kicking out at the legs of the last, who fell, his head smashed into a bench and his jawbone fissured. Athias drew a long, thin knife from his sleeve and threw it into the soldier's face, he then grabbed the hilt and pushed the blade into the flesh further. The soldier's screams echoed throughout the inn and even into the fraying timber of the walls. A vessel ruptured and blood cascaded from his eye, surging over the broken craters in his face, as a river would over rock.

"Wait here." Athias joked to the soldier and opened the door, disappearing into the storm. He reappeared moments later, three enormous dogs on the end of a chain. He tied the chain to the door handle before looking to the woman who was hiding under the table.

"I can't." She showed him a collar around her neck.

Athias strolled to his bag and sword to see Drayn lying, motionless, a bullet wound to the eye. He shrugged, drew a small knife from the bag and headed back over to the woman. He leant under the table and sliced through the collar.

"You've got no reason to fear me. This kill is yours." He said to her and she nodded.

She looked to the dogs and her eyes turned white. The dogs started to snarl and bark at the captain who looked up to Athias and whimpered.

"P... please."

He then looked on in horror as one of the three dogs opened its mouth and began to speak. The voice echoed over the inn, amplified as though it was being shouted by a giant.

"Please?! You dare to ask forgiveness from me?" The fire flickered as a wind swept through the inn.

The barkeep hid behind the counter as the pots and pans rattled above him. The men at the table next to them scarpered through the door, looks of pure terror upon their faces. The dog continued to shout the words of the woman's thoughts,

"Me. Who has watched you torture and murder my people. My brothers and sisters. You dare to ask?!"

The solider looked on in horror. As he opened his mouth to plea, the dogs pounced. Plunging their long, jagged teeth into his chest, snarling as they sliced across his legs with sharp claws, pulling out his throat out and digging into the wound. The barkeep took this moment to look over the counter and was greeted by a splatter of blood. He scrambled to his feet and leapt for a pistol on the behind the bar. Athias clocked this and jumped the counter, kicking the barkeep over. He grabbed the already fractured hand and brought a swift about to the shoulder, breaking that too. In a howl of anger, the barkeep grabbed a butcher's knife, and swung wildly at Athias who took a calculated step back and with the thin knife, lunged into the barkeep's neck. Athias lay the barkeep down before observing the room, the dogs were eating the corpse and the woman was now sitting at the bar opposite him, shivering. He picked up two tankards and poured some ale into them, placing one in front of her. He nodded and took a huge gulp of his own. Sitting down next to her, the dog that had been by the fire was now sitting next to her, its head tilted and ears back as she scratched its neck.

"My name is Athias. You have nothing to fear from me. I am not like them."

The woman sipped the ale, before dipping her finger into it and letting the dog lick it. She turned to him.

"You're not frightened of me?" She asked, looking into his eyes.

"What is there to be frightened of?" He asked, rhetorically.

Her expression brightened, she smiled and blushed.

"Thank you and thank you for helping me."

"Let me have a look at your face."

He put the tankard down and gently lifted her face a little towards the fire's light. It was cut across the cheek and beginning to bruise. He withdrew a vial filled with liquid from his bag and scooped some ash from the fire. Mixing the ash with the liquid formed a paste. "May I?" he asked her, gesturing to the paste and she nodded. He brushed two fingers around the bowls, and then across her cheek. He smoothed it over gently.

"You may feel a slight numbing sensation but it'll only last for a few minutes. You're soaked, let me find you some clothes." Athias stood up and proceeded upstairs to search the rooms of the now-empty building.

The woman went and sat by the fire with the dog, its shaggy fur entrapped the heat and it warmed her hands as she ran them over its back. Athias returned after a few mins to see her standing up by the fire, she had taken off her sodden coat and was wearing a thin blouse with brown cotton trousers and tanned boots. She had various belts and straps around her thighs and waist, and the wolf-ears and whiskers had disappeared. She was tall for a woman of her age, which must have been mid-teens and she had pale skin that shined like sand in the desert. Her hair mirrored the golden-brown of fallen leaves in a new autumn and her eyes; a flare of brilliant orange speckled with brown, reflected the dancing spikes of flame.

"I found some fresh clothes upstairs, first room on your right as you climb the stairs. I didn't know what you would want so I laid them all out upon the bed."

"Thank you, but shouldn't we be going? What if others come back?"

Athias looked to the soldier's mauled body, the dead barkeep, the other dead who lay in the inn and then to his sword,

"I think we'll be all right for a while. I'll go and find another horse for you. I will ride with you to Icaria. It's safe for coarans with the Syndicate. We can rest safely there."

"I can't thank you enough." She said, quietly to which he nodded to her.

While she went upstairs to change, Athias carried Drayn's body over his shoulder and went outside. He went around the back of the inn and sat the body against the tree, laying both of his hands flat against the soil. He scraped a handful of soil up and scattered it across both of Drayn's palms. Rain still poured, beads of water slid down Athias cheek and neck. He stood and looked down to Drayn. The white raven that had been flying over-head swooped down and landed on Athias' shoulder, it cawed twice before perching.

"Mother Zohya. Accept this sacrifice. Protect him in the next life of tree, and salt, and rock." Then he lay his hand on Drayn's head before finishing, "Eyes as bright as day. Skin as cold as stone."

Chapter Two
The Lair of Icaria

Coarans are the largest population on Brineth, after that of humans. They are a truly fascinating race. I have split their characteristic differences into a term called 'echelons'. Those of the first echelon may take on traits of animals, such as claws or wings. Those of the second echelon may turn themselves fully into animals, and third can, miraculously, become animals while communicating with others. I hope to find out more about them as I study this great world. – Calitreum, Dar'ien's Research, page 408.

The pair rode out of the town, Athias fastened the sword to the saddle bag while the lady settled into the saddle. The dog from the inn sat up on the horse behind her, laying on her clothes. Rain still descended from the sky, it carpeted the land as far as the eye could see as though the sky was crying, grieving an awful loss.

"You know my name, but I do not know yours. May I have it?" Athias said, slightly tilting his head back over his shoulder.

The woman sped up the horse, so she was even with him and looked to him,

"My name is H'Khara. "I'm seventeen years old and was born in Harthorn during the war." She looked solemn again "my father was away when I was born, fighting, and my mother was killed in a siege when I was three." She then looked to the raven that was still perched upon his shoulder.

"I'm sorry. Where did you go?" Athias said, quietly and noticing the glance, turned to her. "This is Gralnor. My spy, my friend."

"I was taken in by my aunt, a human, and I was raised a human until my sign began to develop, that of a wolf. When I turned twelve, conditions were worse than ever for my aunt and I, our lake was polluted, and we ran out of food. Someone alerted a nearby camp and they came for me. My aunt was murdered in front of me and they hunted me. Ever since then I've been moved from camp to camp with the others like me."

"Which camp did you come from today?"

"Acre Farm. It's a few miles that way." H'Khara pointed to her right.

"I can't imagine what it's like for those who live it. Icaria has a sizable resistance force now; another contact of mine is there with the Syndicate currently. I promise you, if he and I can do anything for your friends in Acre Farm, we will." He reached into a pouch on his horse and withdrew a carrot, snapping it in half, feeding one half to his horse and another to the dog on H'Khara's horse. He reached into the pouch again and withdrew a piece of bread this time, holding it out to H'Khara who snapped it up.

"Why would you help me like that back there?"

"I know what it is like to live in an unknown world, away from family or friend. The world's beings deserve to be free." He nodded to her and she smiled.

The thunder had stopped entirely, and the rain had decreased to a gentle drizzle. White, fluffy clouds could be seen above, mixed in with the grey and black. A slanted post lay ahead of them. The post had a sign atop which read Icaria, seventeen miles.

"A day's ride. We should make it to Icaria tomorrow, we'll rest up nearer the city and I'll send word to my contact then too. Is there anywhere you need to go before we get to Icaria?"

H'Khara shook her head before leading her horse into a canter and then a gallop. They sped forwards towards the city, passing hundreds of fields of forgotten, rotting crops, while crows soared over head. They rode all day. People were scarce in this part of the land, the occasional farm or town was seen in the distance, but the main road was unhindered by traffic. Athias and H'Khara stuck close to the forests and long grass on the side of the road anyway just in case they should have to hide as they approached the city. Icaria was one of the biggest cities in Brineth, roughly fifteen miles across and was the industrial capital. It was built atop the cliffside of Icaria Lake, from where the city's name came, as did the rock for the huge, stone walls that reached forty metres high and ran around the city. The cliff also doubled as a mine and a port, and steps ran from the docks to the entrance of the tarpits and then into the city. Most of the city was a wooden, towering, slum. Thousands upon thousands of homes ran alongside canals, built atop each other, where murky, disgusting water ran through the city. Small bridges and tunnels connected the districts that were in fact mountains of homes, hospitals, churches, and courtyards. A thick layer of dust and smoke covered the area of the city that sat next to the mine, any long exposure to this left many ill, and many more dead. Icaria saw the highest slave labour force in the world, with hundreds dying every day due to the toxicity, only to be dumped in the canals and replaced.

The city stood ahead of the pair, to their left was a series of farms and to their right were the cliffs, a beach and cove. Athias looked to Gralnor, handed him a silver coin, and raised his arm. Gralnor clutched the coin in his talons, spread his wings and took to the skies, heading up and towards the city.

"We'll make camp there, just over the ridge." Athias said to H'Khara who sat, motionless in her saddle, watching Gralnor fly up into the clouds. She was mesmerised.

"So, about the white raven? I thought they were extinct."

"I thought they were too. Gralnor found me when I was in a place that no-one should ever be. He's never left since." Athias directed his horse to the right, off the track and onto a beaten path leading towards the rocky cliff.

H'Khara followed him, cautious but eager to sleep. Riding was a tiring way to travel, especially for those who were unfamiliar with the roads. Athias found a clearing in the rocks with a sandy-earthy floor. He had clearly been here before. Athias took the bag from his back and unpacked a rolled-up bear pelt, which he lay down on the floor. Then he pulled out another pelt, this time of deer, and placed it over his horse. The clearing they were in was sheltered from the breeze that came in across the lake, and partially covered from the rain by over-bearing rocks.

"We'll stay here tonight." Athias said.

"I'll make a fire, dry out these clothes." H'Khara spoke up, she was much more cheerful now. It was probably because of being away from the stench of Porthna.

"I'll find us some food." He took his sword and climbed up the rocky formation before heading towards the clumps of trees by the water.

H'Khara pulled down a rock from the earthy ledges at the base of the clearing. She put together a fire of twigs, leaves and grass, and set it alight with two flints. She took off her scarf and coat, laying them on the dry grass next to it and then she sat against the rocky ledges. The dog from the inn curled up next to the fire, gnawing on the carrot from earlier. Not long after he had left, Athias returned with three rabbits. He sat down opposite the fire and started preparing them, placing each on a stick. He rotated them occasionally until they were all done. He stood, and slid the first rabbit off the rod, dropping it in front of the dog who sniffed it and upon H'Khara's gesture, took it and chewed on it.

"You've developed quite a bond with him already."

"I've always preferred dogs to any other animal. There were plenty of animals at Acre Farm and I used to imagine myself as them, running wild through the hills. I had my first collar at the age of thirteen, but you never forget how to connect."

Athias smiled, he handed one of the two rabbits to H'Khara and the pair began to eat.

"My contact will be with us shortly I imagine; we should get some sleep." He said, after finishing his rabbit. "You can take the pelt; I'll stay here by the fire. He glanced to his sword which was back on the saddle.

H'Khara, sitting on the pelt, addressed him again,

"You keep looking to that sword. As if it might stand up and vanish. Why?"

Athias came and sat next to her, looking to the sword again, only the hilt was visible.

"It belonged to someone very dear to me. A friend and my teacher, he gave it to me before he disappeared." He lay down onto his back, staring up at the sky. H'Khara did too. "I've carried it for twenty-six years; its name is Spectre though it had a name before that." Spectre was a beautiful silver-blue longsword with a hand and a half grip, made of winding black leather. The pommel was an elegant, curved-diamond made from steel, and the cross-guard was thicker at the end than in the centre.

"Who was he?"

"That's a story for another time." He said gently before closing his eyes and drifting to sleep.

He dreamt of fields filled with ruby-red flowers, and a small child, a girl. She was running through the flowers with her hands out, the pollen smudged against her dark skin. He awoke by the tinkle of a small bell that he had tied across the path behind him. Turning around he saw H'Khara still fast asleep. He took the sword from the horse and crept towards the path. Athias popped his head up to see a man in a long black cloak embroidered with a raven. Behind him were two more men, cloaked, with bows drawn.

"Tristan." Athias stood up and the archers lowered their bows.

"Come this way." Athias beckoned to them and pointed towards the clearing. They walked down into it and Athias brought up the rear.

Athias knelt by H'Khara and nudged her awake,

"We're going." She sat up, surprised of the people behind him.

"Don't worry about them, this is Tristan Banner. He's my contact here, he's with the Syndicate." He gestured to Tristan.

"And these two Herne and Calda. They are my friends." He said to her, reassuringly. They bowed their heads to her. Then he turned to Athias "you didn't say there would be another, the boats really only take one extra."

"It was unexpected but don't worry, nobody is going to see us."

"What are you up to? If we get caught, we will hang, the city-watch have doubled their patrols in the last week."

"I just told you, nobody is going to see us" a hint of impatience on his lips "we're going to need to link. Join hands with me and each other."

He went to the horse that H'Khara had arrived on and cut it free, it snorted and tossed its head back before galloping off. The rest of them linked together and Athias drew Spectre from its sheath, pointing it upwards.

"Tristan. Picture the place we're going. The people, the walls. We need a clear bind."

Athias placed his lips against the steel of the blade and whistled. The melody carried over the steel which glimmered in the light of the stars, it flew up and into the sky. Athias then pointed the blade up, high, outstretching his arm. Gralnor was circling above and suddenly he dived, hurtling towards them. Faster and faster until he was moments from the blade. Athias closed his eyes and in a split second, Gralnor spread its wings as its talons touched the blade tip. In the same moment, a blinding white light filled her eyes and then, when the light disappeared, they were inside and surrounded by people. The walls and floor were stone and brick, behind them was a large tank of water with grates in the wall, and tables, chairs, beds, and a makeshift counter was set up around them. The room had several doors leading to other places. The people around them stared at them for a second or two but then returned to their own business and conversations. Tristan stood in front of them.

"Welcome to the Lair of Icaria. Home to the Syndicate. Litha, see that they're fed." He spoke politely and calmly to a lady ahead of him, he then took Athias' horse and went through a large door, other horses were glimpsed as it swung shut.

"Why didn't you do that as soon as we arrived outside the city?" H'Khara asked Athias.

"I've never seen this room, neither has Gralnor. He can only bring us to places where someone in the binding has been before."

The beings here were all different. Multiple species, humans, coarans, liavos, even the occasional trinata could be spotted, their scaly skin shimmering in the light. They ranged from simple sailors and farmers, to liberated slaves and gladiators, to soldiers that survived the war camps.

"Various types of magic exist in this world, some of which we will never understand. Some, we do however, and it used to create and to destroy." Athias said to H'Khara as they sat at the bar and ate their first proper meal. H'Khara rubbed her neck, scars from the collar she had been enslaved with lingered on her skin.

"Whatever you hear about magic, and magical beings such as yourself, remember this. You are as much a part of this world as are the great forests and far-reaching oceans. You belong here."

Tristan returned and clapped a hand down on Athias shoulder,

"May I steal you away for a few moments."

"Of course," Athias looked to H'Khara who nodded, smiling,

Tristan bowed to her,

"Thank you. May I say that your eyes give you away, but you have nothing to fear from any of us down here. The coarans are brave and brilliant people, we certainly would not have this place" he gestured to the room around himself "without their efforts."

Athias stood up and walked away with Tristan, they proceeded through several doors and corridors into a room with maps spread out across the walls and table. The shelves were stacked with other rolls of parchment, letters, maps, documents of the city. The Syndicate in Icaria had been running interference throughout the city for years, utilising the tunnels beneath the city for a base, stumbling upon them while fleeing the Emperor's legions. This room was bustling with activity. Many soldiers baring the symbol of the resistance, a gold raven in flight, were crowded around tables, drawing up plans. Tristan and Athias passed them all however and came to a small room. Inside was just one table in the middle, with one stretch of parchment across it. Upon the parchment was a drawing, a design of something and written across the top of the parchment were several letters and numbers along with some symbols. Athias stopped next to the table and hunched over it, observing it, while Tristan scrambled around the room, lighting more candles, throwing a log onto the fire and setting two scrolls down next to Athias. They both bore the wax-stamp of the golden raven, its wings outstretched,

"These are from Riltord, and Hicasus. They too are of a design like this one."

He stretched them both out, he then took string and connected parts of the designs to each other, showing similarities. The design showed cylinders and tanks of liquid.

"Mother Zohya…" Athias muttered to himself.

"The Emperor is building something. Something terrible, that could halt our rebellion once and for all.

"Where is it?"

Tristan stood up and walked to the wall behind them, taking a map down from the shelves. He pinned all four corners open, revealing a map of Icaria's tunnels and substations, then he put another pin in the centre of the top-right quarter of the map.

"Here. About sixty metres directly above us."

Chapter Three
Crystal

There are some that walk upon the grass to the west, while some burrow deep into the hot sands of the east. Some once walked in the sunlight but now swim, and dance, beneath it. – Calitreum, History of Old, page 277.

Back in the hall that they had all arrived in, H'Khara sat at a table alone, her hands warm from the bowl of stew. She admired the room and its occupants, bustling with a sense of organisation. A man approached her, a curious expression across his face.

"May I sit with you?" He asked, she glanced to his face and neck, which also had scars on his neck from where a collar had once sat.

The room was busy around them, nobody was staring at her or pointing and laughing, it was a weird feeling, having grown up being the spectacle of amusement. H'Khara smiled and gestured to a seat at the bar,

"Please."

They sat down and the man poured two cups of water. He was a similar age to her, give or take a year or two. He had long brown hair that ran the length of his entire back, and orange eyes much like hers, a trait common in most coarans. His skin was an oak-like colour, although specked with scars and burns, and a sharp, small nose was pressed into his thin face. His green cloak and brown boots were dirty with soot.

"I recognise you from Acre Farm."

"My name's H'Khara, I'm sorry, I don't recognise you."

"That's okay, a lot of us went through those gates. My name is Dalto" He smiled, reassuringly. "May I ask… What echelon are you?"

"Third. My animal is a wolf. How did you get out of Acre Farm?"

Dalto smiled again, he looked impressed and happy.

"I was part of a small rebellion in which a few of us escaped, although many did not." A solemn look passed. "I am third too although bear is my animal. I rarely meet more thirds, there are a few here but mostly seconds, a few firsts too. All are welcome here though, coaran or human or other alike. May I introduce you to a few more like us?"

H'Khara stood and she nodded but Dalto could tell she was nervous. He held out his hand to her, it was scarred and blackened in part, some bruises never healed, as she knew herself.

"I promise, you have nothing to fear. This place is home to all who have no home elsewhere." Still cautious, H'Khara hung back while Dalto walked over to a table where many men and women sat, playing cards. A few of them turned their heads as Dalto addressed them. He waved to her and beckoned to a seat that he pulled out from the table. She walked over to the table. Dalto pushed the chair in as she sat down, many faces greeted her; dark skin, light skin, blue skin, scales, they all nodded and smiled to her as she sat down. They all donned green and black cloaks like Dalto, some with hoods and some donned eye patches, while others wore masks.

"Do you know how to play Prison? A woman asked. Her light blue skin with splashes of silver turned her shapely figure into a beautiful painting of deep waters. She had green eyes, and a sharp face. She was a vadoran; the water-dwelling race, who originated from the Spryte Islands. Her voice was slightly hushed, almost like a snake's hiss.

H'Khara shook her head,

"No, sorry."

She chuckled "Half these idiots don't know how to play either and they've sat here most nights with me for over a year." She waved to the table and many of them laughed. "My name is C'k'rian, but this lot call me Crystal." Although sitting, H'Khara could tell that this woman was a fighter, her curved, sweeping shape sat upon a muscular figure, her skin was smooth but worn.

"How do you play?" She pointed to the various cards on the table, before continuing, "my name is H'Khara."

"I… I don't know." She replied, quietly, kindly.

"Well it's very easy to learn." Dalto boomed as he sat down opposite her, "the idea is to escape prison, which we are all in at the start of the game."

C'k'rian dealt four cards each to the group, excluding H'Khara so she could observe. The people around the table picked up three which were black, and left one, a blue one, faced down on the table. Dalto continued while C'k'rian demonstrated as he talked,

"You're dealt four cards. Three will have a picture on and the aim is to collect a full set. Three of the same type. However, the fourth is a simply a trick card."

C'k'rian then shuffled what was left and placed it in front of her, before shuffling another stack and placing it next to the first.

"There are two stacks in the middle of the table, the one to your right are arcane cards aka the trick cards, and the one to your left are picture cards. Each turn you choose a card; arcane will give you an edge over opponents and the pictures will aid you in your quest. You must always have a picture card, so when you draw, you must also discard. You may keep up to two arcane cards on the table and use them on your turns. Each arcane card will have a spell, some are for protection and others for attacking."

C'k'rian showed her arcane card and so did a man to her left.

"If your spell fails then you are blocked from your next turn. If you claim to have a full set, and upon being challenged it is revealed that you do not, you are blocked from your next two turns. The aim, simply put, is to escape from prison while ensuring the rest of us do not, or as many as you can. For if others were to escape, you would bring your secrets with you." This was greeted by a light chuckle.

"Okay, I think I've got it. What happens if you lose?"

"You buy the next round." Dalto smirked.

"I don't have any money." H'Khara said.

"Not yet, but if you're with the Syndicate, they treat you well."

Abruptly, C'k'rian stood up, knocking the table a little. She grinned and left the table, H'Khara spun her head around to see her and Athias embraced in a gripping hug.

"That's Athias. I've only met him once, briefly, before I came here." Dalto said, off hand as though he did not think about it.

"I know. He's who I arrived with, he helped me escape from Porthna."

Dalto's tone and expression also changed abruptly.

"What's it like, travelling with a War Born?" The table fell silent. They were all eagerly awaiting an answer.

Athias and C'k'rian went back to the bar. H'Khara spun her head round, back to the table.

"A 'War Born'?" She asked.

"The War Born were elite soldiers for the invader, they were taken at birth and raised to be warriors who practiced in the dark arcane." Dalto said in a hushed whisper.

Another man jumped in,

"Tales have it that Athias broke free from the Emperor and killed all his fellow students, and his teachers. He fought for the old king against the tyrant and when the old king died, he disappeared… like a ghost."

"What's he like?" Dalto asked.

"Why don't you ask Crystal? She seems close to him." H'Khara joked, hiding the concern in her mind.

"Crystal… is Crystal. She's honest, loyal, and friendly almost all the time but her relation to him is something she never talks about." Dalto sighed.

C'k'rian returned to the table, she looked serious now.

"We're going up soon." She pointed to the ceiling, and then she addressed the whole room, "Second Ravens! Meet me back here in one hour. Dress for a fight."

Everyone at the table minus H'Khara stood up and disappeared through different doors and hatches, the room's occupants followed suit and the scraping of chairs and stools was the only thing to be heard. Athias and H'Khara were the only ones left in the room.

"What's happening?" She asked him, deciding now was not the time to question if he was in fact, a War Born.

"Something's being built here, something powerful. It could destroy everything the Syndicate has worked towards. We have to stop it, destroy it if we can." He reached his hand out to her. "Will you join us?"

"I will." She shook it.

"We've got four hours. The second regiment here are going up in an hour, we're joining them after the first stage is executed. Tristan has found a room for you so rest up."

"Thank you, again."

"Someday I will be the one to thank you." Athias showed her to her room. It was pleasant enough with a small bed and table with a chair. It had some shelves above the bed with a candle lantern and some books. The bed was straw and feather with pelts and cotton throws across. H'Khara hadn't slept in a bed as nice as this for many years, she sat down, slipped her boots off and fell asleep as soon as her head pressed into the pillow.

The streets of Icaria were beautiful once, an exotic place. Cobbled stone had run the length of narrow canals that spread across the city. Now, since the mining had begun, the city was a festering cauldron of chaos. Thick coils of smoke poured out of the factories, swirling through the streets much as the gigantic river snakes did around their prey. The Courtairs, those who were deemed to be of high birth lived, looked down into the sweltering, disgusting city from up high in their solitary courts. Slaves as good as did not exist in the world for the emperor and his malicious government of overseers publicly condemned the very word but behind closed doors where coffers spoke more than sense, slaves were property by the thousands. H'Khara woke to Athias nudging her awake. There was movement from the hallway as soldiers marched hurried past, many carrying bows, and others with swords beneath their cloaks. H'Khara glimpsed a few rifles too.

"It's time." Athias said gently, he pressed a cup of hot nettle soup into her hands. "I'll be outside."

He left the room and slid the door back across. On the table were two small knives in scabbards, roughly eight inches long. Over the chair was a black, hooded cloak with the golden raven embroidery. Black boots stood by the chair and a leather chest piece, a clean tunic, and buckled trousers lay over it. Athias was wearing a black cloak too with Spectre on his waist, instead his back. He had polished his boots and added some smaller knives to a belt, the cloak was tight to his arms and it revealed the sharp edges of pauldrons that accompanied his chest armour. His hands also bore metal rings and his two right fingers were covered by armour. He held two masks, grey with little concern for facial details.

"All Syndicate soldiers wear these on missions. Many of the people here are linked to the emperor, so their faces can't be seen. The cloak suits you, looks like it fits well. Did you take the weapons?"

H'Khara nodded and slipped on the mask. It gripped to the top of her face and chin with curved clips. Her breath was warm, gathering on the surface of the mask for it only bore a small meshed grid where her mouth would be.

"We received word from C'k'rian and her regiment above ground. They've successfully disrupted the city guard, luring them away from our target. Me and you will accompany Tristan and a small group of soldiers. We will journey up and then into the workshop where the machine is being built. We'll be quiet but be prepared for a fight."

Athias led the way down the corridor and into a cave. Dozens of small boats were tied to rocks and loose decking. Tristan was already in one with a group of six people, Athias and H'Khara climbed into another and they set off. The rocky walls were misshapen and poorly cut, as though they had been formed in a hurry. Many smaller tunnels ran off the main ones, H'Khara looked into the piercing black and felt the eyes of others, creatures maybe, staring back.

Chapter Four
To Be Remembered

People have thrived upon Brineth's rich soil, the land is soaked in sun and the moons control a tide which laps, playfully upon the shores of my evening walks. People are not alone, upon these bountiful shores, I met another type of being today, and another the day before last. All walks of life, all souls, and beings of Brineth are but one, together, under the stars.
– Calitreum, Dar'ien's Research, Page 401.

"These tunnels spread across under the entire city, for the most part." Tristan said. Even though he was speaking quietly his voice still echoed, bounding down every tunnel they passed. "Most run into dead ends or into troll nests but a select few come out in Ol'Brick." A soldier at the head of Athias' boat whispered.

"Ol'Brick is the lowest part of Icaria. Those that live there are mostly criminals or simply too poor to be of service to the city, and so, are abandoned by it. It's a dangerous place for most, but especially for the city's new soldiers." Athias whispered to H'Khara.

The small boats slowly made their way out of the tunnels and into the dock-town of Ol'Brick. Most buildings were boats that had been built on, some though were tiny man-made island constructed of timber and rope and cloth and the only source of light were the lanterns dotted across this place, hanging from walls or on the fronts of boats. The group headed for a building in the middle, it must have been the only one made partially of brick, and roughly three stories tall. Long ropes joined the building together and it to other boats. Upon arriving, Tristan and Athias got out of their boats and stepped onto the small, floating tower. They knocked four times and the door opened abruptly as soon as the last tap ended. A thin man stood in the doorway. He had long, spindly fingers and wide eyes. As his mouth opened, they saw the yellow, rotting teeth and filthy tongue. He scratched his neck as flies circled him and peered at their faces.

"He who doesn't laugh but smiles at night." He jeered at them.

"Is he who does smile at death." Tristan replied, in a collected manner.

The pair of them were let inside. The interior wasn't really an improvement from the exterior. The walls were damp with visible cracks in the wood, moss had seeped in from outside, while the walls were covered with ropes that joined each adjacent wall. A small work bench sat in the corner, while rusty nails sprung up from the floor. The thin man retrieved a scroll and handed it to Tristan who slipped a few gold coins into his hand in return before swiftly leaving and returning to the boats that dipped under their weights.

"According to our source the machine needs to be kept cool and they're doing so with water pipes from the canals, taking water down to the laboratory and then the excess amount is drained into this lake itself. That's our way in."

As the boats drew closer to the cliff face at the southern end of the lake, columns of smoke became visible along with the clang of bells and distant sounds of gunshots and swords clashing together. C'k'rian and her soldiers had truly engaged the city guard, scrambling all unoccupied units to keep the city under control. Distracted from this, H'Khara noticed that the pipes were enormous. Her head nodded as she counted how many men could fit between the sides, a dozen at least. Tristan reached down and threw a grappling hook up into the pipe, he was counting on the idea that the pipes wouldn't be maintained or regularly enforced, and sure enough the hook stuck into the metal that had been softened exposure to distilling salts. One by one they climbed up into the pipes and edged their way across it to the maintenance stairs at the side and rats now ran the length of the pipe, scurrying over each other trying to flee from the those now climbing up. Up above them, a grate could be seen.

"Could you…" Tristan asked Athias, his voice trailing.

Athias drew a line of string from his cloak, he wrapped it around his left hand and muttered,

"Inco'delato"

The string lit up, appearing to spark and fizz, it illuminated the pipe around them.

"Light that is only seen by those who use the spell or are connected to those who do." Tristan whispered to a perplexed H'Khara who stared in awe at the illuminated string, the first spell she had ever seen.

Athias stepped forward and took the lead with the others falling in, two by two behind him and after climbing what had seemed like a thousand steps, they reached the top. A hatch sat next to an enormous grate that measured nearly fifty feet across, wider than the pipe they had climbed up, it was bolted from the other side but Athias stepped back and two of the soldiers with them stepped forward, a short dagger and hammer in each hand. They unscrewed the bolt, and then the hatch, and slowly, carefully, lifted the metal door before pushing it across the floor. Athias shut off the light and Tristan peered out, checking for threats. He ducked down again and nodded.

"All clear. Let's go."

Athias and Tristan jumped up, helping the rest as they came. The group remained crouching, hiding in the shadows.

"Let's split up. We have a greater chance of finding it that way." Tristan said while looking around. The workshop was at least three levels high, with various labs spread throughout it. Scaffolding and pipes covered the outside of the labs and the floor they were situated upon was covered in rolls of cloth, tables, lifts, and cranes. "Follow the large pipes and you will come to it. You'll know it when you see it."

Athias stood up first, he pointed to H'Khara and a handful of soldiers,

"With me. Quickly." They stood up, waited for the guards to pass and sneaked off down a corridor while Tristan and the rest took another corridor.

After a few minutes of searching records in a scroll room, Athias found the design, the logbook next to it indicated that it was on the second level, being kept in a water tank. Knowing that they would be harder to find while in smaller groups, Athias instructed the soldiers accompanying them to stay at the scroll room and carefully, quietly, destroy every document, then to make sure the corridor was clear for they would return this way after destroying the engine. The second level was extremely quiet, much more so than it felt it should have been, even with many of the guards above ground dealing with the Syndicate disruption. Athias and H'Khara crouched low, keeping to the wall, and edged their way down the corridor while peering into labs as they passed. Sure enough, after some time, they found the lab in question with enormous iron-bolted doors and a small circular window in the centre. Inside was a pathway and bridge that led over a huge water tank, that stood next to a large window and they noticed chains dropped from the ceiling into the tank.

"Wait here." Athias whispered to H'Khara.

He stood up and moved to the end of the corridor, edging along the wall again. When at the end he disappeared through a door, there was a clang and screech of steel and then he returned. In his right hand was a key on some string, and his fingers dripped with blood. He turned the lock in the door and the double-bolts slid across. He and H'Khara pushed the door open, locking it behind them.

"Over there." H'Khara pointed to a series of levers while crossing the bridge and Athias walked briskly. H'Khara peered into the water, she was unable to clearly see what was below the surface although it looked to be grey in colour and box-like.

"Take this." Athias said to her and handed her a chain, "connect it to that lever." He held his own and connected it to a lever in front of himself, as she did the same.

Then Athias pushed down on a panel and it clicked into place. The chains in the ceiling began to retract, pulling up whatever was being kept below the water. Clinking slowly as the metal links pulled through the wheel.

"So… if you don't mind me asking. How do you and Tristan know each other?" H'Khara asked, hesitantly, trying to distract the rising anxiety in her heart.

"In the war. We fought against each other and he gave me this." Athias replied, almost instantly, as if he knew she was going to ask it. He took off his mask and pointed to the scar on his face.

"He was a soldier for Ziath?" Deciding not to ask if Athias was one like she had heard.

Athias nodded "but he defied orders. Ziath started his conquest over Brineth in the major trade routes along the south-east coast, taking key positions crucial to winning a war. As time went on, however, he sacked defenceless villages and towns, hospitals, and monasteries. Tristan was part of a company with orders to attack a garrison, only the garrison had moved on and the village had been left undefended. Tristan was ordered to kill a man and his young boy, for the man would yield to Ziath's conquest." Athias sat down on the steps to the bridge. "The next time we met, we fought side by side at the battle of Gralows Field. He's a good man, a long-lost brother."

"At the lair… they think…"

"That I'm a War Born. An elite soldier turned sorcerer. I've heard many stories about my life."

"Why don't you correct them?"

"Sometimes the stories are more interesting than the real thing. It gives them a purpose, who am I to deny that?"

The chains clunked away, slowing down as the box beneath the surface drew closer to the ceiling but suddenly, it stopped. The box hung, just above the level of the water and something was not right. Athias looked at the box, it had no cylinders like the designs he had seen and there was no generator or pipes attached. Athias caught a glance of a hinge that began to twist.

"Wait. No!"

Abruptly, a whistle sound teared through facility and the top of the case slid off. Three riflemen stood up from inside and fired. At this same moment, Athias raised his hands and muttered something before a blast of power leapt from his hands, passing over the bullets that spun slowly in mid-air and over the riflemen who appeared to move in slow motion. Moving away from the bullets, travelling slowly towards them, Athias pulled H'Khara and the pair sprinted across the bridge. Athias slammed a lever down and the water began to bubble as heated jets sprung to life. He pulled Spectre from the sheath and swung at the chains that suspended the case and it plummeted into the now boiling water as the spell broke. He looked down from the window to see Tristan and his soldiers fighting guards.

"How did they know we were coming?" H'Khara questioned, over the dim screams of those in the case.

Athias did not answer, he had brought H'Khara here for her to be safe. He pushed this from his mind, preparing to act.

"Come on, we need to go!" Athias spoke out.

He and H'Khara sprinted from the lab. Downstairs they came across the bodies of the men and women they had brought with them, and a few guards too. Ahead of them were more guards, waiting, poised. Spotting the pair, the officer raised his rapier towards them. The group of guards knelt and pointed their rifles down the corridor. Athias went to cast another spell but H'Khara barged him to the side. She began to undergo a change as the bullets hurtled past, narrowly missing them as they hid behind some crates. Her clothes ripped, revealing fur beneath them. H'Khara felt onto all fours and claws began to sprout from her hands which were quickly shaping into paws. A tail grew from her back, ears grew from her head and her mouth was now a snout. Athias stood, now beside a large wolf, almost as tall as him, with silver-flecked, black hair. Her eyes shone orange, as they had when a human. H'Khara let out a ghostly howl and leapt forward, she jumped into the line of soldiers and Athias looked on to see limbs fly while hearing the terror as they shrieked or tried to run. After less than a minute, the carnage stopped and H'Khara stood, licking blood from her paws. Wasting no time, the pair of them burst through the doors and jumped down the stairs. Ahead of them was the workshop, and in it, Tristan, on his knees. No one else had survived; Syndicate soldiers lay around him, bloodied. Athias caught Tristan's eye and he slowly, shook his head. Athias and H'Khara kept to the shadows, ducking behind some crates, listening to what the soldiers were saying. An officer addressed Tristan,

"Tristan Banner. I thought you were dead." He spat on Tristan.

The officer then addressed the soldiers around him,

"This 'ere is 'Captain' Banner. One of Ziath's Soulstalkers themselves. His elite." He turned to Tristan. "You betrayed us and over what? A farmer? Ha."

"A better man than you." Tristan smiled.

The officer struck Tristan across the face with the hilt of his sword. Tristan coughed and spat again, this time with blood. Soldiers behind him grabbed him and brought him back to kneeling.

"You always were funny, weren't ya?" Karr spat at him.

Behind the crates, Athias and H'Khara were sitting up.

"Get to the hatch where we entered and get out of here. I have to help him." He said to H'Khara and she whined a little but bowed her head and slunk across to the hatch, keeping close to the shadows, her black fur unnoticed.

"I wonder if you'll be laughing when the Black Guard are through with you!" Karr sneered at Tristan who's looks suddenly dropped. "You see, they don't interrogate traitors for knowledge, although I'm sure you will give 'em what they want. No, 'ey do it for fun." He plunged a knife into Tristan's leg and Tristan winced, coughing again.

Athias stuck his head up and looked to Tristan again. Tristan was bloodied and broken, blood trickled from his leg and his chest. Athias drew slowly drew Spectre and nodded to Tristan. Athias muttered another enchantment while sliding his hand along the blade of Spectre. He then stood up abruptly and Karr and the guards turned to him.

"Seize him!" Karr screamed.

Athias swung his sword so that the tip of the blade scraped along the floor and the workshop filled with light. Karr and the guards froze, completely motionless. Athias walked over to Tristan who was motionless too, he reached down to him and pulled him up. As if breaking free of a mould, Tristan coughed and sighed.

"We're getting you out of here." Athias said and went to lift Tristan up, cutting the restraints.

"No, *we're* not. You are."

"What are you saying?"

Tristan looked up to Athias, a tear in his eye.

"Kill me. Do it and take this back to Crystal." He said to Athias, reaching into his pocket and handing a letter up to him, it was addressed to C'k'rian, although the letters were smeared with his blood.

"No, we can get you out. Don't make me do this."

"Come on!" Tristan implored to Athias. The time fracture around them was starting to fail, time was beginning to move slowly again. "As soon as you draw blood the fracture will break. This is my only choice."

Athias knew Tristan was right. His heart dropped as he pieced it together, and the fracture began to break, Karr's hand slowly reaching for his rapier."

"Dying a martyr isn't the worst thing." Tristan let a tear go from eye.

"A hero. Not a martyr."

Tristan knelt down again, his hands together in prayer "Mother Zohya, keep me close. Grant me a place in the next life of tree and salt and rock." He looked up to Athias who stared down "Goodbye, brother. May the mother keep you."

A tear trailed down Athias' cheek as he swung the sword. Blood sprayed up, and across the floor as Tristan's head toppled, rolling across the floor. As the sword struck, the time fracture broke and time returned to normal. Athias sprinted before Karr and the guards had registered what had happened, he locked the hatch again and slipped the letter into his pocket.

Chapter Five
A Painless Place

Mother Zohya taught the first that there was but a place after death, a place of neither light nor dark, a place of only peace. Wherever this place is, whatever it feels like, I wonder if the dead see us? Do they hear us? Do they walk by us? – Calitreum, Story of the Vayshanaa, Hathael's Entry, Page 404.

Shots rang out above them as the soldiers learned what had happened. Athias and H'Khara jumped from the stairs and onto the pipe. The water carried them down, throwing them into the murky, dirty water of the lake at Ol'Brick. The boats were gone, they had probably been pinched by the locals, Athias thought. They swam to the shore, coughing up icy water as their hands fumbled on rocks and pebbles. In the main city above, towers of smoke still trailed high although the clang of bells had stopped. Athias and H'Khara climbed up onto some decking that ran the length of the lake.

"Can you change back? Navigating this place will be a lot easier as two people. I'll go and get some clothes." Athias whispered.

He pulled himself up onto the muddy lakebed and crouching, pushed towards a cluster of small buildings with clotheslines connecting each. He grabbed a dress and coat, then hid behind a corner as a couple of drunks strolled past. He spotted a pair of boots, they were worn and slightly ripped but he took them too and left three silver pieces where they had been. He returned to the decking and passed the clothes and boots to H'Khara. The coat was large, too big for her but you'd be lucky to find a comfortable fit here, the sun's light peered over the tops of the city walls and Athias knew they had to be back underground soon, their ally of night faded fast. The pair of them edged their way along the decking, making their way to a jetty in the distance. Many doors around them were bursting open and the habitants of Ol'Brick were pouring out, some already had tankards in hand. Athias pulled his hood up and loosened his cloak, he took off the armour on his fingers,

"May I hold your hand; we have a better chance of getting to that jetty if they think we're just a drunk couple." Athias asked H'Khara, politely and quietly.

H'Khara took his hand. She looked up to him, he was only a head or so taller than her and she could see his right eye clear. He was holding back tears, she could tell.

"Do you know any local songs?" She asked him, "drunk people sing, or at least the guards who got drunk at Acre Farm did."

Athias smiled, it had been a long time since he had sung. He started to sing, yelling out the occasional word louder than the rest and the pair of them swung their arms up and around, throwing off any attention in an odd fashion. The sun's light was seeping down into Ol'Brick now as it rose, prompted by this warning, Athias set about untying a boat and he clambered in, helping H'Khara in too and the timber groaned under their combined weight. Athias plucked a hat from their feet and placed it on H'Khara's head. She smiled and pulled it down.

Athias and H'Khara left the boat as they entered the tunnels, sending it back with a push towards the bay. They then continued along the rocky edge of the tunnels, wading across the shallow ones, and navigating back towards the Syndicate's base. A boatful of soldiers greeted them in the main tunnel back to the base.

"Who goes there?!" One of them shouted.

"Athias, I was with Tristan Loro, commander of this outpost." Athias stood and directed the golden raven on his cloak towards the light.

"Let them pass."

Athias and H'Khara wade through the shallow water towards the dock they had set out from not hours ago. Athias then walked with H'Khara into the hall where before they had been playing a game of cards. Silence fell upon the hall as they entered. C'k'rian stood up from a bed, where Dalto lay, injured. She rushed to Athias who embraced her.

"You made it. I was so worried. They knew... Athias, they knew we were coming."

"I know. Us too."

"They waited for us to assemble in the streets and cornered us, what should have been a quick distraction turned into a war zone. So many... so many died. We did all but narrowly survive, taking charge of a factory and holding for as long as we could." She stopped abruptly, looking at the pair of them. "Where is he?" She was on edge. "Where is Tristan?"

Athias looked to H'Khara, and then back to C'k'rian. He took the letter from his pocket and pressed it to her hand, unsure of what to say, what to do.

C'k'rian looked to the blood-stained, damp, torn letter in her hand and back to Athias who looked around the hall, the benches and tables had been cleared away and now instead, hundreds of beds covered the floor. Blood and water were splashed across the concrete and patches of straw and cloth had been laid over bodies. C'k'rian's eyes brimmed with tears, and her voice growled with frustration.

"How many did you go up with?" He asked her.

"One hundred and sixty-three." She sobbed. "Less than half returned. Those that did, barely did."

"The machine they are building, it wasn't there. They lured us into a trap and then they snuffed out the light." Athias said, as softly as he could, for he was battling the urge to cry too.

H'Khara knelt beside Dalto's bed. Half of his face was bandaged, with blotches of scarlet dotted across its vanilla colour. His chest was also bandaged and where three of his left-hand fingers should have been were now stumps, he reached up with his right hand and she took it,

"I'm glad you made it back… I was about to go back out there to find you." He said, gasping for air, trying to laugh.

H'Khara smiled at him,

"I'm back, yes, and I'll stay here while you rest. Sleep now." As she finished talking, he closed his eyes and drifted off into a dream.

H'Khara looked to Athias who caught her gaze. A tear rolled down his cheek, it glided over his stubble, navigating the rough skin like a small vessel would around trees in a marsh. He made his way into an old armoury and locked the door. Outside it he could hear the frantic footsteps and the screeches of the medical trolley wheels, the cries for bandages and salt. Athias drew Spectre from its sheath and lay it, flat, on the table in front of him and he investigated the tainted silver. Tears rolled down his cheeks and splashed onto the table and blade. His skin tightened, pushing the knuckles up and his veins bulged as the oak table frayed under hand. He let out an almighty cry of anger and sorrow, and the wood beneath him started to crack and bend as he gasped, panting for breath under the weight of tears. The look upon Tristan's face was etched deep into his mind, it was all he could see. The echoed shouts in his voice of those last moments rang through Athias' ears. He knew he had a job left to do, it was haunting him, for he did not know if he could face Tristan again. Athias took a long, deep breath and wiped the tears from his eyes. He stood up straight and took hold of Spectre's hilt, pointing the blade down.

"A bridge standing taller than any peak, a spectre stood upon it, ready to speak" Athias struck down with all his might. The blade sunk into the slabbed floor and all around him disappeared with a flash.

Athias let go of the sword and looked up. Ahead of him, far in the distance, were towers and an archway, comprised of pure light. Between him and it were a dozen figures. The bridge was made of a grey-white stone, as though shards of cloud and ice had been thrown together. The figures ahead shone bright with purple light, as though their bodies were lanterns, recently set ablaze. First ahead of him was a farmer, who Athias had put to rest instead of waiting for the cold to take him. Next was a young girl, maybe thirteen years old, and ahead of her sat a soldier. Athias stopped and spoke to them all in turn, a pain conversation for all, but none more so than the one approaching. Right at the end he stood, tall and proud as he had been when Athias first met him, he was smiling.

"It's good to see you, Athias." Tristan said softly. "I wasn't sure what this place would be like but it's nice, a painless place. I can hear the waves lapping against the salt-bed and smell the honey glazed rolls that my father used to make."

Athias started to cry again. He smudged the tears as they travelled down his cheeks, the water dried almost as soon as he touched the skin.

"You saved me, Athias. You saved me."

Athias nodded and snapped back to it,

"C'k'rian doesn't know how you died. I can't tell her." He said to Tristan who smiled again and sighed simultaneously.

"The empire killed me. You know that, and that's what you tell her if she asks." Tristan laid a hand on Athias shoulder. "You look after her, now I'm gone. Not that she needs it."

The pair of them chuckled, Athias placed his hand on Tristan's opposite shoulder so they were interlocked,

"I'll be waiting for you, my old friend. We can have that duel, settle it once and for all."

Athias nodded once more. He outstretched his arms and Tristan hugged him.

"Now get back there." Tristan said as if instructing Athias, "Kalvae vau'lomo dellata."

"Kalvae vau'lomo dellata" Athias repeated. "So long, brother."

Athias let go and marched to his sword, looking back one last time. He twisted Spectre and one by one, the beings on the bridge faded from view. Athias returned to the room he had been in before he left, to the exact same moment. He sheathed Spectre and walked from the armoury back to his room. C'k'rian was in her room, cradling the letter, unopened.

"What's going on?" She asked him.

"I thought it best to be with you." He spoke, quietly.

"I'm fine…" She started, while tears brimmed in her eyes. "You go and be with H'Khara, make sure she is okay."

At that very moment there was a light tap on the door. Athias stood up and slid outside into the corridor, in front of him H'Khara stood, trembling.

"Dalto… Dalto's gone." She murmured, sobbing. She did not wait for his reply before wrapping her arms around him and crying into his chest.

Athias felt broken, he had been sure that the Syndicate's home would have been safe and a good place to leave H'Khara. It was turning out to be quite the opposite, more so in this turn of events.

"We'll leave soon. This place is not what I thought it would be." His voice was heavy.

She did not speak; she did not even look up. Athias picked her up and carried her inside the room where he lay her on the bed next to C'k'rian who was now asleep, the letter that Tristan had given to her was clutched in her hand.

Athias left the room again, he made his way to the kitchens and taking advantage of the chaotic environment, took a sack and threw some bread rolls, carrots and two rabbits inside. He deposited the bag of food inside his own bag and took some parchment and quills from the table. Suddenly there was a loud crash followed by a rumble. The ceiling and walls trembled, and dust fell from the bricks. Not a second after, another crash, an explosion, louder this time and bells rang out in the corridor while figures, dressed in hoods with bows, arrows, swords, and shield hurtled past. A woman appeared at the door, soldier from C'k'rian's unit. She spoke fast, agitated, and afraid.

"The City Guard are here!"

"How long?" C'k'rian asked, she was wide awake, sitting up in the bed.

Before the soldier could answer there was a deafening roar from above. The walls and ceiling shook, bricks fell from the ceiling, and the floor quaked. The northern tower, the main entrance into the Syndicate's lair had fallen. Soldiers would be pouring into the tunnels from above.

"To the northern gate! Everyone that can stand, we must defend that gate." C'k'rian barked at the soldier who bowed and left, relaying the orders to any that could hear. A different type of bell rang out with a different tempo.

C'k'rian stood up, she tucked the letter into her cloak pocket and placed the mask down on the table.

"I want them to see my face as I take the life from theirs."

H'Khara had woken up too,

"What's happening?" She asked, tears still fresh in her eyes.

"They found us." C'k'rian and I are going to help secure the northern gate while those who are injured are evacuated."

"I'll help." H'Khara stood up and brushed the moisture from her eyes.

"Okay, when you're ready, come back here and take the bag. Head to the southern steps. Go up right to the top and climb the hatch, wait there for us. We will be along." Athias said while walking out the door. C'k'rian had already left, running back down the corridor with other soldiers.

Chapter Six
The Cliffs of Icaria

Icaria, a place of prosperity, a place of fortune. I wonder what runs inside the tunnels that lie beneath it. Maybe nothing, maybe something. – Calitreum, Architects and Archives, Page 73.

Athias left too and hurtled towards the northern gate, H'Khara pushed the bag into the corner of the room and under a blanket before leaving. She went into the hall where the injured now lay, she began to help lift the wounded and carry them towards a southern entrance that left the city, a few small ships were waiting at the lake. Back at the northern gate a sizeable group of Syndicate fighters had gathered. The northern gate was never intended to be used as a line of defence and it would not hold for long, even with the reinforcements. It was originally used to slow incoming cattle, forcing them into a smaller line, and so, bore no real defences. A rumbling sound leaked under the gate followed by the unmistakable march of hundreds of riflemen. The Emperor's soldiers would surely be upon the gate in a matter of minutes. They would break down the gate and chaos would ensue. The Syndicate had but one advantage, their side of the gate was a winding corridor so the soldiers' rifles would have little affect here. The Syndicate widely regarded rifles as a tool and product of imperial industry and thus, rarely used them. In this tunnel, behind this gate, the array of melee weapons would be an advantage for the fighting would be thick and fast.

The rumbling march of the approaching monster that were the riflemen on the other side of the gate grew louder and louder. Brick and dust fell from the ceiling with each fateful step. Athias ripped off his cloak, revealing his leather and hide armour underneath. He took the sheath off his belt and tied it to his back, Spectre's silver-blue glint peeking from inside. The Syndicate's fighters barricaded the gate and Athias kicked a box forward and stood upon it. Facing the soldiers gathered around him he spoke out.

"I know I am not a leader. I know that most of you know of me only by story or tale, but I am here now, with you! We must hold this line for as long as possible. If we do not, all those who cannot fight will die." Silence befell those gathered around him. "There's a saying, where I grew up. Where I am from." He continued as cheers rang out. "Kalvae vau'lomo dellata. It means 'Raise your sword for those who cannot' and today we will do just that. We will fight them for as long as we can." The marching grew louder and louder still. Athias stepped off the box, kicking it across the floor to wall.

The soldiers gathered around him took up a defensive position. Archers behind spearmen, crouching behind a makeshift wall of broken furniture. Athias and C'k'rian crouched with them. Athias drew Spectre from the sheath and ran his palm along the blade, whispering an enchantment once more. The steel of Spectre's blade began to shimmer as the marching monster outside the gate stopped. There was a scurry of feet and sounds as hooks were placed into the door, followed by creaking as the gates tensed, splintering as the ropes tightened more and more. The old wood cracked and bit by bit, holes began to appear. The Syndicate's forces remained deadly still, crouching behind the barricade, archers poised, each with an arrow in their bow.

The gate slacked but only briefly before it was pulled apart in one final effort. As the wood fell apart and the gate crumbled, an officer shouted over the ruckus and the riflemen fired. A hell breath of steel balls flew, soaring into the makeshift barrier ahead of where the Syndicate waited. Athias stood up and threw Spectre like a spear into the ground ahead. As the blade sunk into the stone floor a bright light shone out, blinding the riflemen ahead.

"Now. Fire!" C'k'rian shouted at the same time and a flurry of arrows released, hurtling into the riflemen's lines. "Charge!" She followed up and dozens of Syndicate fighters jumped the barricade and charged headstrong towards the colours of the emperor. Athias jumped the barricade too and ran forward, he leant down and grabbed Spectre as they ran, swinging it upwards and decapitated a soldier in front of him. C'k'rian was to his left, pulling curved knives from sheaths on her waist and throwing them into the lines ahead. The archers aimed up and fired another volley and arrows flew overhead and into the soldiers, behind the initial fighting. Athias removed his eye patch and grabbed a soldier, looking deep into his eyes. The soldier began to scream and claw at his own face before Athias plunged Spectre down his spine. The first wave of soldiers had almost fallen and then, suddenly, a sharp crack echoed the hall as the second wave had released a line of gunfire. Many soldiers with Athias fell, blood sprayed into the air and bodies began to pile up as another crack echoed and more fell beside him.

"Pull back! Back to the barricade." C'k'rian shouted to those left standing, slicing the throat of a soldier on his knees in front of her.

Smoke from the rifles had hidden them from view and they had time while the rifles were loaded. Athias, C'k'rian and their soldiers ran back towards the barricade, but another crack whipped through the air. The riflemen were firing, blindly into the carnage ahead. Soldiers next to Athias collapsed as they ran, jumping the barricade, Athias and those left crouched as another storm of shots rattled through the air.

"Fire at will!" C'k'rian shouted out and the archers let loose another volley of arrows. Their total numbers were dwindling now but they had to hold for a little longer. A fire of rifles, and another. The barricade was starting to wither under the punishment. C'k'rian revealed two vials of pink liquid, one was bubbling.

"On my signal we're going to pull back." C'k'rian shouted over the constant barrage of gunfire, "cease fire and launch a final volley on my command." They waited for a moment of silence between the lines of rifle fire.

"Now." Her voice was oddly calm. The archers fired one last volley and C'k'rian followed by throwing the two vials of liquid. The one that was bubbling crashed into the ground first and on contact with the air, the liquid changed to foam and spread out across the floor. The second vial crashed into the foam and created a torrent of water which hurtled towards the enemy line, stopping the advance for a few moments. Upon this the Syndicate's forces took their chance to retreat and dashed through the winding corridor. The distant sound of water that had masked their escape had ceased.

"Get out. Get above ground and out of the city." C'k'rian addressed those standing with them, now only a few dozen in number." She sheathed her blades. "It has been an honour to serve with you all. Make for the eastern territories and cities, where the Syndicate is still strong."

The group dispersed, all heading to their rooms and setting fires, destroying all information there. Athias and C'k'rian made their way to the southern steps, a tower of spiralling stairs with various doorways leading off to exits around the city. Right at the top was a hatch that led to the white cliffs of lake Icaria and as planned, H'Khara was waiting with their things.

"Let's go. Quickly but quietly if we can." Athias spoke in a tired, hushed voice.

The hatch was heavy, having been untouched for years and the rusted locks creaked open slowly. The air that greeted them was cool, and the top of the cliffs were overgrown with black thorns and flowers. The trio made their way through the overgrowth, looking for a path to follow down to the lake, Athias moved some shrubbery and found a thin, winding path heading towards the cliff face. Sunlight spread across the lake below, creeping forward towards the rocky cliff. Athias led the way, gently jumping from ledge to ledge, making sure the other two made it down. Several explosions and rumbles followed, and looking back, the three saw columns of smoke towering above the city. The journey down the cliff face was long and the three were bathed in sunlight by the time they reached the base. To their left the cliff curved round and entered the mining bay and to their right was a small shipyard.

"The shipyard will be sprawling with imperial soldiers. We should stick to the back roads and forests." H'Khara jumped in, to which Athias nodded.

"I could just swim or walk through the lake and meet you around the other side." C'k'rian's nostrils flared as she spoke, raising her voice.

"I know you're angry, but it is not the time." Athias said, his hands raised, peacefully.

C'k'rian pushed his hands away and pushed him back. H'Khara went to intervene but Athias gestured not to.

"Angry? Anger doesn't begin to cover the feelings flowing through me! He's gone, don't you get that?! He's gone and he's never coming back!" She pushed him again, forcing him to take a step back.

"I know. I am sorry. I'll miss him too."

"You don't get to miss him! You disappeared. You left! You left us here to fight and fend for ourselves against them." She drew her blades,

"Athias the Vayshanaa. With his enchanted sword. He can do as he likes. He can leave with no regard as to what that means for the rest of us!" She swung recklessly at him and he dodged.

Athias made no advances to attack, he only parried with his gauntlets and dodged. C'k'rian lunged once more with both blades and he sidestepped, kicking her feet out as he went. She fell back but Athias caught her before the ground and C'k'rian dropped her blades, they fell against the grassy floor. H'Khara walked forward slowly, she crouched and placed her hands around C'k'rian who turned to her and cried again. Through the sobbing she whispered to Athias.

"I'm sorry."

"Don't be, please don't be."

C'k'rian nodded, she wiped the tears from her eyes and cheeks and stood up.

"I guess two becomes three, hey?" Athias smiled as she finished.

"When do I get a sword?" H'Khara joked, trying to lighten the mood.

Sure enough, the shipyard had a stable before it and it was filled with horses. Sneaking in and acquiring three horses was no trouble and the three of them rode out and towards the pebbled road that followed the curvature of the lake, they wanted to put as much time and distance between Icaria and themselves.

The rest of the day was long and tiring, H'Khara had not slept well for almost four days and she was starting to slump in her saddle, nodding off. The road had steered away from the lake now and into a thick forest. Thousands of thin pine trees scattered across their horizon, behind, and to all sides. The pebbles of the road had been replaced by coarse dirt, pinecones, and roots that grew carelessly, sprawling across the land around them with no regard for those which traversed this land. Many creatures lived in the forests here, wolves in packs, bears, and gruffons too, so the stories said.

"We need to stop soon, H'Khara is almost falling off."

H'Khara jolted awake,

"No, what? No, I'm fine." Fighting her eyes' desire to shut.

Athias looked back to H'Khara and then to C'k'rian and nodded. C'k'rian sped up to H'Khara and stopped, taking the reins of both horses, and bringing them to a standstill. Athias stopped too, he dismounted and led the horse to C'k'rian who took the reins, before heading into the forest. Before long he returned and said he had found a clearing whey they could set up camp.

They tied the horses to a tree and C'k'rian began to chop up some logs and sticks for a fire while Athias unravelled the bear-pelt rug and draped it across some branches to create a canopy. He carried H'Khara to the rug and rest her down on it, slipping a satchel full of feathers under her head. He then dragged logs from nearby trees to the canopy, creating a sheltered sleeping area while behind him, C'k'rian had started a small fire.

"I'll go and get us some food. I'll be back shortly." She said, slinging a bow from her horse over the shoulder and taking a few arrows.

Athias nodded and went to sit by the fire, he brought with him a lump of wax-stone, a selection of small knives, and some pieces of armour. He sat in the light of the fire and began running the wax-stone over the metal, then he turned the stone over to reveal the waxy texture and brushed it across, back and forth. This not only shined the metal but also added a layer of protection, stopping rust and damage. Looking through the trees Athias could still see the plumes of smoke and the daring, white cliffs of Icaria. H'Khara lay fast asleep, deep in dream; undisturbed by the cracking logs and spitting flames but Athias mind wandered back to those cliffs, he thought of a time, years ago, when he and Rayna would sit upon them and throw stones out into the lake, and then he thought to the Lair which would now be buried in fire and smoke, and, too, that the cliffs themselves would surely collapse, burying the lair and all memories of those stones that threw from the cliffs. C'k'rian returned to the encampment, bringing his thoughts back to reality. She carried a bunch of weasels tied together by string, she slumped them down on the floor by Athias, returned the bow to the horse and then sat next to him, skinning them, and removing their heads.

"Athias... I'm sorry for what I said before, by the lake."

"Don't be... I'm the one who should be sorry. I left as you said."

She cut across him, eager that he listened.

"I do not hold any resentment towards you leaving. I was angry earlier, angry at my loss, angry that I could not be there to save him or fight by him." She cut the head of a weasel off and ran the blade of the knife down its spine, "Tristan knew the risks, we all did."

"This war has taken a heavy toll on us all." Athias said, sincerely. "We will take the time to mourn later."

"What happened to you two, did you get to the design?"

"We…" He faltered, "It was gone when we arrived. It was all a trap." Athias sighed. "We need a weapon of our own, magic isn't enough anymore. Your home, Vadoran, it holds an ancient weapon, one that the Syndicate will need if we are to defeat the imperial forces and this new design." Athias spoke softly, as to not awaken H'Khara.

"I know of what you speak, a secret of the seas. I can tell you now, Athias, we will not be greeted with open arms. I haven't been back in years." C'k'rian said, sharply.

"I have a thing or two that will get us a meeting with the Elders. I've been busy on my journey."

"Let's hope so, because it doesn't look like we have much choice."

C'k'rian finished skinning the animals, went to the horses and back, bringing over two spit-roast sticks which she skewered the animals with. She slowly turned the sticks as the flames licked the flesh. Athias decided not to wake H'Khara, she was finally getting the sleep she needed days ago.

"We should get her a sword, you know. We're bound to be together for a while now, I'd say." Athias said, nodding to the shelter where H'Khara slept and C'k'rian showed the first smile that Athias had seen since they arrived at Icaria.

The weasels were charred and smoky, Athias and C'k'rian dug into them. The smoke had provided the meat with a salty aftertaste which the pair washed down with water. C'k'rian looked to Athias and then to the shelter, and back to Athias. He looked back, confused.

"Have you told her yet? Have you told her who you're looking for?" She spoke sharply.

"No. She's been through enough the past few days; she shouldn't be burdened by that knowledge too."

"She deserves to know. She cares about you, I can tell."

"Maybe she does but for now it's safer not to know."

Chapter Seven
A Mother's Kindness

Magic speaks to us; it is all but as alive as you or I. While some know how to yield it, others know how to see it, and some, a few, know how to teach it. – Calitreum, The Fundamentals of Magic, Page 619.

A few hours passed and sunset approached, although the treetops were thick and their bodies dense, the sun's light passed through in beams of longing light. Athias and C'k'rian sat by the fire and looked up through the thick treetops.

"May I ask what the letter says, the one that Tristan gave to you?" Athias asked C'k'rian who was leaning against a tree a little way from the fire, toying with pinecones.

C'k'rian took the letter and held it to him. The letter struggled against her skin, longing to stay and as he started to unfold the parchment, C'k'rian left the warmth of the fire to check on H'Khara, she disappeared into the pine-branch walls. Athias unfolded the parchment carefully, it was torn at parts, bloody too and blotched with sweat and ink from when Tristan had written it.

"My dear Crystal. My light in the dark.

"If you are reading this, then I have fallen to the fate that has pursued me all these years. You were in my final thoughts, because it is only you. I am sorry for the hardships my death will give you, I wanted to grow old with you as we talked about in a land far from here. Far from war.

"Look to the skies each night, look for the six-point star. I will see you there someday, we will have that life. That beautiful life. I know these words will be hard to read for I wish I was alive and had no reason to tell you, but you must live on, my beautiful Crystal. I will always love you, I loved you from the day we met, all those years ago. A warrior of heart. A light in the dark. A crystal among stones.

"Yours forever, this life and the next. Tristan Banner."

Beneath the writing was raven drawn in ink. Athias blew gently upon the parchment and the raven flew up, spiralling before disappearing past the top of the page and slowly fading into view at the bottom again. Magic was as much a part of the world as the people, the trees, the oceans, and the sky. It was that which gave everything life, and many knew how to harness its beauty, some as master sorcerers and some as simple tricksters. Tristan preferred the latter; simple enchantments rather than studying the magical arcane.

Athias folded the letter up, making sure to preserve as much of it as he could, and turned to see H'Khara and C'k'rian appeared from the shelter, he began to cook the last weasel, turning it over the fire. H'Khara was wrapped in a pelt from C'k'rian's satchel. H'Khara sat down on the same log as Athias and rest her head against his shoulder, he handed her a weasel and she started tearing the charred flesh. As C'k'rian sat down too, he also handed her back the letter, offering a smile that he understood.

"I've been meaning to ask, Crystal, how can you... breathe above water." C'k'rian asked between mouthfuls of smoky meat.

"Well, you see, much like the coarans have variations among them, so do we, vadorans. Many of us can breathe and live above water as well as below whereas others only come above the surface for a short while, and a very few, the elders, cannot at all for the sunlight would burn their skin."

"I've always wanted to visit Vadoran. What's it like? I can't wait to see it."

"It's beautiful. The water of Oceans Reach is clear and cool to the touch, and the stone that built the great city is gorgeous; smooth and elegantly carved. C'k'rian rolled up her left sleeve to reveal a piece of body art, a crown of sorts that sat upon a mountain. "This is the mark of my family, the mark of Rian. My family ruled Vadoran many years ago, long before Ziath arrived. The people of land respected us, and we them."

"Where does the name of Vadoran come from? I'm sorry for the questions, I never learned in the camps."

"Not at all, I find the history of this world fascinating. Vadoran comes from the words 'Vald' and 'Oron' which mean 'Bright Peak' together in the common tongue. Vadoran is a city that once stood proud upon the side of a mountain but in a tragedy, the mountain exploded almost three hundred years ago. Over half of the city fell into the ocean and many of the people who fell also died that day but the ones who survived became gained variation through exposure to rare stone on the seabed. It was named 'Oceans Reach' for Vadoran is not but hundreds of tiny islands; the land around it looks as though the mainland reaches for it." C'k'rian stoked the fire as she told the story, the logs cracked and fizzled, flames reflected in her eyes,

"That's amazing." H'Khara sat in awe as she finished off the rabbit. Her lips were salty and dry, she reached for the tankard of water next to the log as Athias did. As their skin touched there was a jolt, as though a spark of lightning had jumped from his hand to hers, and her heart climbed into her mouth. She sipped from the tankard, feeling bashful.

"I'll take the first watch." Athias said, abruptly, to C'k'rian, adjusting Spectre on his back and taking a bow from his horse. "Plenty of wild bears around and many make this forest their destination."

C'k'rian nodded, she stood up and beckoned to H'Khara who took her hand. The pair of them went back to the shelter as Athias kicked sandy earth over the fire and poured what was left of the tankard over it. The horses had sat down, resting their heads on each other. Athias pulled put the blankets from under the saddles and lay them over each animal. He pulled his cloak and hood up and then he set out into the woods, preferring to keep an eye out from afar. Inside the shelter H'Khara and C'k'rian lay, sharing the pelt.

"How will me or Athias breathe in Vadoran?" H'Khara whispered.

"Athias will have a spell, he's very resourceful."

"Where did he learn magic and to use it the way he does. Was it with whoever the sword belonged to?"

C'k'rian paused, unsure to how much she should say.

"Yes, it was she. He was one of many who taught him the ways of our world. Although I should say no more for it is his story to tell." She rolled over and stared into the pine's overhead, cautious that she might have already said too much. "Goodnight H'Khara. We will find you a sword soon enough."

H'Khara smiled and closed her eyes, drifting off into a deep sleep, still exhausted from the travels. C'k'rian also fell asleep, although she tossed and turned, struggling to drift off as quickly.

The forest was mostly peaceful, from what Athias could see. Gralnor was circling over the forest, scoping out the vast terrain. Athias' stood motionless and focused, his mind jumped from his body, and looked through Gralnor's eyes to see for himself. The forest was broad, seemingly boundless. The paths inside it swerved and curved for miles on end. Many souls walked among it, many creatures and their young sheltered in caves and dens, a thin mist rolled in off the ocean to the southeast and within came flocks of birds. Athias left the bird's body and walking through the forest, he stumbled upon a pond that caught his eye. It was almost circular, more man-made than natural, and a statue had sunk into small island in the middle. The grey stone was mossy and had been mostly forgotten, from the looks of it; the earthy floor around the base was covered in pines and dry leaves. The water was jet black straight from the moment it touched the land around it and all the way to the island, a body of darkness. Athias had seen these ponds before, an age ago, they were ancient graves. The water had been enchanted, and it lay protection upon the bed of the pond, the water turned black after the body was placed beneath the statue in the centre and any who drank from the sacred water would suffer horrendous vision, visions that said to show the future for some, and a darker, twisted fate for others. Athias examined the statue as he walked around the pond, making sure to keep their camp in sight he proceeded deeper into the forest. He drew some more string from a pocket and set it alight once more with a spell.

"Inco'delato"

The string, which was wound around his hand lit up like a torch, illuminating branches and trees around him. A sad, low, grunt caught his attention, coming from over a ridge. Climbing to the top, he looked down into a dried gully, and at the bottom lay a bear. Beside it was its cubs, they were nudging their mother and crying as bears do. Athias sunk down into the gully, keeping low, and close to the shrubs. The bears noticed him and cried in fear, trying to disappear under their mother's paws and the bear tried to stand but fell and they nuzzled against her side, pawing at her. Athias broke the string and the spell faded. He slung the bow over his shoulder and raised his hands to the bear family, showing his palms and fingers wide. The bear tried to snarl, protecting her young.

"Hush" he whispered to her as he approached, his heartbeat rising.

He edged forward and approached the injured animal. The mother bear was bleeding from the neck, and her skin was torn by slashes, trailing down her back; plenty of wild creatures more ferocious than bears lived among these trees. The cubs sniffed Athias as edged closer, they nuzzled him and pawed at his legs, crying as a roar of thunder echoed across the sky and a few moments later rain splashed down into the dirt around them. Athias rolled his sleeves up and lay the mother bear's head on his arm, his hand under her neck. He stroked down her face and snout and brushed her ears. She purred and took in deep breaths, comforted by his soft brushing, and he whispered up into the sky as he did, taking off his eye patch.

"Mother Zohya. All Mother. Creator and protector of the world. Planter of Nhivilaurn. Guardian of truth. I speak to you to ask for your mercy upon this creature. She is a mother like yourself, a mother with cubs, a family of her own." He held his left hand up, palm flat, fingers outstretched. "Grant me the spell I need. I know it is of time, that I am bound, but grant me the words to heal what is broken. Acog'dael tirin dothou."

For a few seconds nothing happened, he sat still, his free arm raised and his other under the bear. The rain crashing down around them, surging over the leaves, and splintering over branches, carving tiny canals in the mud. Suddenly, the water converged on Athias' location; a mind of its own, pouring down the gully and climbing it from the other side until Athias and the bears were sitting in a swaying puddle. Athias' hand began to glow, he placed his arm into the water, it began to shimmer too. The water started to rise and form, guided by Athias, he shaped it with gestures from his submerged hand and it covered the mother bear's wounds, supported her head. The water raised the cubs on platforms as it surged with light. The colours mixed and swirled over the bear, warming her and healing, her fur began to steam from the warmth and her breaths became less staggered, and then, almost as abruptly as it had started, it stopped. The rain continued to pour down from the skies, splashing over leaves, trailing down branches and following the gully; droplets racing each other. Athias ran his palms lightly over the bear, her fur was bushy to the touch and warm. Athias got to his feet and took a few paces back as the bear got to her feet while the cubs ran between her legs, her shaggy fur sheltering them from the winds. She let out an amiable grunt before turning and walking up the other side of the gully. One cub, however, stayed back and approached Athias who held his hand out, palm open, the cub licked it and then scampered off to be with his mother again. Athias smiled, he looked to the skies and nodded before placing the patch over his eye again and donning a hood, making his way back towards the others.

It was peaceful, strolling through the forest amidst the rain and roaring thunder, the water splashing down from the trees. On the journey back Athias passed several old tombs like the others; covered in moss and foliage, and saw other animals making their own way on journeys in the distance, through the forest or back to dens and caves. Lightning cracked across the sky like a whip and a volley of thunder shook the air to follow as the rain poured harder. Athias made his way, circling slowly around the camp before returning. Gralnor, above, spotted a group of travellers on the road that they had left, they were dotted with lanterns and a few carriages. Athias spotted them too through the thick trees, they had left the tracks and were walking towards Athias' camp. He crouched low and made his way to the shelter, sneaking inside. He tapped C'k'rian awake quietly and gestured to the direction of the travellers. C'k'rian peered from the shelter to see a group, no more than five, walking away from their lantern lit carriages and towards the three of them. They were cast in shadow but carrying rifles; the shape was unmistakable. C'k'rian gestured in the air, dragging two fingers across her palm, and then clenching her fist against her right shoulder. Athias shook his head and made a similar gesture. The pair of them had used hand language before in the past, it was rarely called for but a notable skill to have. C'k'rian had asked if they were imperial and Athias had replied that he did not know but it was likely. Forests like this were commonplace for all kinds of travellers, from imperial supply lines to pockets of Syndicate soldiers or mercenaries. It would be impossible to tell who they were until right on top of them, the fire had gone out and all light now came from the moons above. Suddenly a whistle blew out, sharp and high pitched, and the five outside ran forward and positioned themselves around the shelter, peering from behind trunks or crouching behind fallen trees.

Chapter Eight
The Hidden Crown

There is power here, and there is peace. It is rare, if not impossible, to have both. – Calitreum, Story of the Vayshanaa, Athias' Entry, Page 416.

"You are surrounded, show yourself." A loud voice rang out. "You have ten seconds!" Their fronts were still cast completely in shadow. "Ten, nine, eight," he began counting down.

"Alright. We are of no harm to you." C'k'rian shook H'Khara awake gently, "we're going to step outside." She whispered to her.

Slowly, carefully, the three emerged from the shelter, brushing the pines from their faces. The riflemen held a lantern high, illuminating C'k'rian's face, blinding her. As C'k'rian stepped into the light the group around them looked to each other, in turn. The last nodded to the rest and they lowered their rifles, uncocking the trigger and pointing them at the floor.

"My name is Captain Lain. Formally Third Battalion of Eastport Station." A man, seemingly in charge of the rest, stepped forward and lowered his hood. His face was tired, sporting a long scar from his forehead down over his nose and below his chin, pale blue eyes were just visible in the light, and brown hair. His skin was pale but covered in dirt and paint, a camouflage.

"My name is C'k'rian of Vadoran, this is H'Khara from Acre Field, and Athias from Carrine" C'k'rian gestured to them each in turn.

Captain Lain bowed his head briefly to all,

"I'm sorry for the alarming entrance, this forest is teeming with imperial soldiers and spies. You can never be too sure." He paused, resting the rifle in his arms like a baby. "May we rest with you tonight?" Captain Lain asked.

"Of course." Athias said without hesitation.

Captain Lain nodded, smiling, and whistled and two short whistle blows followed, from the carriages by the road. Shortly after, a few carriages made their way into the clearing, circling round, and from them came a few dozen more beings emerged, some men and women, different races, clad in cloaks and hoods too. Athias noticed a few liavos among the humans, their singular eye unmistakable in the shape of their faces. The sound of crunching leaves also announced a handful of soldiers from behind the pine branch shelter, each nodding as they slung their rifles over their shoulders and stepped into the lantern light. C'k'rian and Athias helped the Syndicate travellers manoeuvre their carriages into a ring around the trees so that they circled the old fire, which was replaced by a new one, larger and with a roasting rack. There was about thirty with Lain in total, with a few young ones too. Several came from the carriages with pelts and firewood, while others carried a boar down ready to cook and after an hour or so the travellers had set up, three of them stood guard at points around the encampment and the rest sat around the fire on logs, against trees or the wheels on their carriages. Athias and C'k'rian sat among them at the fire while they roasted a boar and cauldron of brew over the flames.

"What brings you through this forest? It's unlike small groups to travel down this road." Said Captain Lain as he stoked the fire and turned the boar.

"We came from Icaria; the Syndicate lair fell. Now we're heading to Vadoran, staying off the High Road." Athias said, passing a tankard of water around the fire.

"We saw the fires of the cliffs from miles away. It's a shame. Eastport fell too just a few months ago, that's where we all were. It was horrendous, one of the most vicious days of my life. We've been roaming between cities and territories ever since, disrupting the imperial reign as much as we can. We're all that's left of the Third Battalion." He raised his own tankard and those in his company did so too.

"You use rifles." C'k'rian spoke out, abruptly. "Why?"

"Sometimes to fight fire, you have to become fire." Captain Lain said, over the cackling fire. "The imperial troops up north aren't like the ones here. They've adapted to our bows, our swords. They use stronger armour and employ ruthless tactics." Not three days ago did we encounter the Black Guard themselves. Nasty bunch."

"The Black Guard? This far from the capital? What on Brineth were they doing?"

"Ensuring his highness' workers meet deadlines." The captain shuddered, closing his eyes. "They're dead now though, 'ey took a dozen of us with them."

"Where are you heading now then?" Athias asked, curious.

"Acre Farm. Porthna has become a wretched ground for farms and camps, more and more coarans are taken there each day." He looked around to the many nodding their heads around the fire. "We're going to set Acre Farm free." He got up, shared out some roughly cut plates, and cut a slither of meat off the boar. He dipped his cup into the brew too and sat back down. The rest of the soldiers, and Athias and C'k'rian followed suit.

The boar was delicious. A herb paste that had been spread over the thin flesh had seeped into the skin, the smoke had riddled the meat with adventurous taste, it ripped clean from the bone and left a salty, tangy, smooth feel on the lips. The stew was hot and steaming, and that was rare to come by while on the road. Athias had studied much of the world's herbs and spices, many were used in magical enchantment; potions, and dream-medicine. H'Khara appeared from the shelter, she was wrapped in a pelt again but also sporting one of Athias' cloaks, taken from his bag which had been moved inside the shelter. Captain Lain stood and bowed.

"Would you like some boar? Some brew? The boar is much better than the brew."

"I did my best." A voice cried out from behind.

"Stick to the shooting, private."

H'Khara nodded,

"Yes please." She went and sat next to C'k'rian who put an arm around her, huddling her closer to the fire.

One of Lain's soldiers handed her a cup of brew and plate with a few thick pieces of boar. She dug in, looking much better than before, the sleep had clearly served her well as the dark patches around her eyes and cheeks had faded away and her eyes shimmered. Another woman across from Athias kept looking at him, he caught glimpses of her golden hair as it tangled in her hood. H'Khara chirped up after a bite of the boar.

"You're from Carrine, your companion said? Were you there when it fell?" Captain Lain addressed Athias, who had a mouth full of boar.

He swallowed, pardoning himself, before replying.

"I left when I was just a boy, so I was saved from that at least."

"Saved indeed. I fought with many others at the battle, many managed to flee into the forests, ahead of the imperial attack."

"Excuse me, did I overhear that you were going to Acre Farm?" H'Khara spoke, abruptly, turning her attention to the captain.

"You did, M'lady. We'll be there within the next few days."

H'Khara smiled but also traced her nails over her neck where the collar had once been for so long. Lain looked morbid, shaking his head.

"I'm sorry, I didn't realise."

"It's okay." H'Khara mumbled, making sure to keep eating so that she wouldn't have to speak of it, for if she did, she felt as though tears would pour from her eyes.

"Well you have my word; all of those insides will be free once more." Lain said, boldly, and the accompanying travellers cheered in unison.

After taking their share of food and drink, many of the travellers dispersed from the fire, setting up beds around it; folding out parts of the carriages and draping fabric over tree branches while others took plates laden with boar and brew to the lookouts. Athias wandered to the edge of the carriages, looking out into the cold, bleak night. C'k'rian and H'Khara were still sitting by the fire, sharing conversation with a few travellers that remained, he heard H'Khara laugh, it was sweet. The woman of golden hair, who had been sitting across from him, appeared at his side as he leant against a tree. She had waist-long, golden hair that shone like the sun, he could see now that her hood was down. Her skin was fair and freckled, deep, dark blue eyes that beckoned for sight with treacherous envy. She had donned a cloak over a hazel coloured dress that engulfed her, the fabric coursing around her shape like a river would around clay.

"A cold night" She spoke in a soft tone, the words brushed over the air.

"Much colder than usual. The name is Athias." He replied, gently.

"I know who you are, Athias. I have heard your name."

"What is your name? Where are you from?"

"I take many names, and I am from a world not unlike this one, far away. I've travelled with all types of people; I show them what they want to see." She ran her hand along Athias' jaw, slowly gliding her smooth skin across his coarse stubble and chin. "I sense a strong future in you, and a dark past. A bolt of lightning amidst shadows, Vayshanaa."

"You're a visioness?" He asked.

"Perhaps." Her voice was rich and velvety, enticing with every word.

Athias looked into her eyes and felt longing. He saw the sea rise and fall and felt fire under foot. The woman placed her other hand on his cheek and looked dead into his eyes and soul. He felt the moonlight upon his skin, though it was far overhead, and heard a rustling of leaves as a strong gust of air travelled in behind him.

"The sixth will be revealed. The hidden crown uncovered. Placed upon their head they will climb the world and raze all upon it." She whispered as the gust of air became strong. "I can see it coming undone, the secrets of the world. They will stand upon the frozen fire and bring forth the wrath that swarms beneath. The world's skin will peel and burn, life will fall to ash and dust and the roots of energy will rot and die." She said again, removing her hands from his face.

"Why will this happen? Tell me why?" He demanded, though his voice was tremulous.

"It may not, yet. The future is not set in stone, it changes, and our future that is to come has not been decided. The stone has not been thrown and the song has not been sung. This is merely a warning, a vision of what may come to pass."

Athias, alert, looked up to the sky as Gralnor flew down and landed in a tree above him, cawing at him, signalling something. He turned back around, and the woman was gone, she had vanished into the air. His eyes were wide as he searched for her hair.

"Athias, are you alright? What are you looking at?" C'k'rian approached, speaking quietly, curiously.

He dodged what she asked, his hair on end and mind wandering.

"It's a cold night, can you feel it?" Out in the forest, pines and leaves danced as the breeze swept through it. "Out there, far from here, a storm is coming."

"I can, it's unlike anything I've felt before." C'k'rian's words were hushed.

Athias joined C'k'rian back to the shelter once more and Gralnor perched in the tree above it, watching over them, a constant lookout. Athias lay his head down in the now warm, enclosed area and shut his eyes. Athias slept well that night, an almost dreamless sleep. He had a short vision of a young child running through reeds this time, not flowers, and then it faded to black again.

The next morning was calm and fresh, the fire smouldered and branches swayed around them in a light but cool breeze. The travellers were getting ready to leave, packing away their pelts and blankets, feeding their horses and fastening them to the carriages. A few were sitting on a log and playing cards, the children were throwing handfuls of leaves up and prancing through them as they fell. Athias brushed the wall of pines aside and stepped out, stretching. The sun had peered over the horizon not long ago and now it was ascending higher with each drawn breath, casting a warm, welcoming glow over the frosty earth. Captain Lain, who was organising the group, marched to him.

"Morning. It's quite spectacular here at this time of the year, is it not?"

"It is. The frost and light are in equal harmony. The bird song and cries of icy wind are in unison." He shook Lain's hand who nodded.

"Thank you for letting us stop here last night, it is a better night indeed when shared with friendly company. We've left you fresh supplies from our store; water, milk, pelts, and meat."

"I must refuse, kindly." Athias smiled.

"Not at all, I won't take no for an answer. You welcomed us around your fire last night and now we will repay the kindness, after all, we can find more."

"Thank you, Athias here is not used to such generosity." C'k'rian spoke, emerging from the pine shelter and holding out her hand too, which Lain shook.

"Where will you three go next? I only ask for there is a checkpoint to the southeast, just over a day's ride from here. They will restock you once more, if you wish."

Athias nodded to him and shook his hand once more. A child from behind Lain ran towards C'k'rian, holding a little carved statue. She turned red upon meeting C'k'rian's gaze, she stopped running and edged over to C'k'rian, bashfully.

"'Scuse me, miss?"

"Yes, dear?" C'k'rian said, gently. She smiled and dropped to a knee, so that she was eye level with the child who turned bright red.

"I… I made this for you." Holding out her hand and opening her fist she revealed a small wooden horse. The animal had been loosely carved, it showed various dents and scrapes where the scalpel and rocks had been used to roughly draw out a horse from the log or piece of park it had come from.

"It's beautiful. Thank you. My name is C'k'rian."

"C… C'k… C'k'rian" the little girl mouthed as she spoke, trying to pronounce the name. "My name's Elana." She said back.

> "That's a beautiful name. You would be a wonderful friend; will you be my friend?"

Elana looked bashful again, her cheeks bright red, her fringe hiding most of her face from view. She looked up to Lain who smiled and nodded back,

"Go on." He said, gently.

Elana did not speak, she simply nodded and hugged C'k'rian, jumping to her, before standing again and running back to play with her friends.

"Precious." C'k'rian whispered, cradling the wooden horse before slipping it into her cloak pocket.

A whistle sounded behind them and they looked to see the convoy ready to move.

"This is where we leave you, friends." Lain said, firm but friendly. "Maybe we'll meet again, on a road far travelled." He nodded, bowed, and marched back to his horse next to the front carriage.

The wheels of the carriages bumped over the roots in the road and the horses neighed to one another. Sitting in the back carriage was the golden-haired woman, she smiled to Athias as they faded from view behind the winding trees, and then disappeared again as the carriage re-emerged. Athias proceeded to feed and saddle the horses before loading the saddle bags, now full of supplies. H'Khara had joined C'k'rian now and was helping to put away the pelts and blankets. They grouped together at the horses, Athias helped H'Khara onto hers wrapped a cloak around her before climbing onto his own horse, C'k'rian followed suit.

"Where do we ride to today?" C'k'rian asked.

> "A place which does not want to be found. We have one more stop before onto the shores of Vadoran." Athias replied, carefully.

Chapter Nine
Life

It is an ancient art to serve and sow life. Few possess such a patience, for you must be calm to tend to life, to plant it and watch it grow, to nurture it, and to feed it. – Calitreum, The Fundamentals of Magic, Page 622.

The forest they rode through, famously titled 'Weeping Woods' was one of the larger ones in Brineth, stretching for tens of miles in each direction. As soon as the world beyond the trees faded from view you were entrapped in almost another world entirely and hundreds of weary travellers had lost their lives, or worse, their sanity as they had dredged through the sprawling roots of the undergrowth and tried to navigate around the countless writhing trees that stood, mysteriously, much as fingers would of a partially buried hand in unforgiving soil. Thorns coiled around tree trunks while rogue pebbles and submerged stones harassed the soil beneath the horse's hooves, and far from the path, shining streams surged through the soil; the water draining memories with every beckoning sip. Forests like this made you forget the war that surged across the world. The forest was a dangerous place but friendly to those who kept it.

"The Greenseekers are an old society of people who tend to the Weeping Woods' needs, they care for it and all life in it. They were first appointed as the caregivers of this forest almost six hundred years ago. Back then they numbered in the double figures but now, with their cause mostly forgotten, their reach over the Weeping Woods dwindled with each sigh of a falling sun." Athias spoke out to the group as they pressed further into the forest, the sky disappearing almost completely. "Hathael has studied the ways of the living world for almost a century, she is the last Greenseeker and a dear friend of mine." Gralnor cawed, seemingly in agreement with Athias.

"Where does this Hathael live then?" C'k'rian remarked.

"It is not that simple. Her home is that of mystery, beyond this realm. A tree that grows inwards with branches of clay and stone. It is a place that nobody can see unless she wants them to see."

C'k'rian stared around, bewildered, for nothing around them even remotely looked welcoming. Thin, haunting trees spread around them, engulfed in mist. Ravens flew above, their cries and the sound of their wings flapping, echoing throughout. Before long they reached an old bridge with a tower that had long since been abandoned; cobblestones clustered together with paste, now covered in moss and damp and beneath the bridge ran a river, shallow but wide. Athias led the way, taking his horse down to the river and travelling downstream, following the cold water as it splashed up over the rocks that stood in it. Dozens of ravens perched on branches of trees overseeing the river, staring intently at each rider as they passed.

"Stop." Athias muttered.

The ravens cawed and exchanged looks with their small, gleaming eyes. Athias held out his hand with a key that hung on string from his fingers. The key was wooden, with lines of green stone flowing over it. He jumped from his horse, splashing into the river as he landed, the cold water pouring over his boots.

"That's a lot of birds." H'Khara observed, all the branches surrounding them were covered in sleek, shining ravens.

"Messenger and Gardner, Greenseeker of old. We stand in the river of memories past, we beckon you. Care for us as you would your garden, for your garden holds us home." Athias spoke out, boldly.

A raven, slightly smaller than the rest, flew down to him and perched on his fingers where the key hung, Gralnor looked to it with beads of black and calmly tilted his head. Athias lifted the key and the new raven took it in its talon, the others cawed around them again and again, becoming frantic, they were beating their wings and hopping. Suddenly, black smoke began to pour from the raven on Athias' hand, shrouding it, and feathers fell from its back. The raven hopped up and extended its wings, still surrounded by black smoke that fell to the floor like a cloak, and then before them was an aged woman, clutching the key. She stood to reveal a woman of pale green skin and jet-black eyes with plaited hair that swung down to her feet. She was clad in a cloak of white, black, and grey feathers and clothes made of plants, joined with vines and leaves. She was clutching a staff; a long, winding branch of silver-grey bark that curved at the top, ending with three finger-like ends. Each end was embedded with a stone that resembled a raven's eye. She had a thin face with a long-crooked nose with thin lips, and long, narrow ears.

"Athias." She nodded, a sweet smile on her face.

"Hathael." Athias shook her hand.

"You're far from home, old friend."

"We" Athias gestured to the others "are traveling to Vadoran but I seek your council first and I have a message I wish you to hear."

"Well you better come inside then, hadn't you?" Hathael proposed while C'k'rian looked around, bewildered once more for there was nothing but thin trees and the river around them.

Hathael took the key and brushed away some vines over a boulder to reveal a keyhole.

"Come, come." She said, inserting the key and the rock face disappeared, C'k'rian and H'Khara looking on in amazement.

The three led their horses down through the tunnel and a cavern. In front of them was a garden, stretching for miles. Hundreds of colours burst from the seams of the grass that was luscious and tall. At the centre of it all was a tree, growing downwards; its roots spreading out across the top of the cavern and its branches spreading out over the floor. The ceiling of the cavern was hundreds of metres high and the roots of the tree were dotted with crystals, where leaves should have been. Behind them the tunnel closed and disappeared entirely.

"What is this place? How has nobody found this?" H'Khara looked around in awe, stunned.

"There is nothing to find, my dear child. This is my mind. Every blade of grass you touch is a memory. Every stone you see is a thought. The Greenseekers' homes were fortresses of life and love, and passion. Now it is just mine that remains." Hathael had a soft, kind voice. It skipped over the air, much as music did as it travelled to the ear. "Please, go, find water and drink, find bread and eat. There is plenty here for those who need it."

H'Khara and C'k'rian wandered off, leaving their horses tied to a tree while Athias and Hathael ventured inside the tree in the middle. Hathael brought forth a pair of branches, controlling it with her hand. She placed her staff into the ground and let it stand.

"Before you ask your question. No, I have not seen her." Hathael said. "I can see your agony as you search for her, but I have not seen Rayna since you and she left my care. She will be found if she wishes it. But remember, if she does not, she will not."

"Hmm." Athias nodded. "I was given a message; I wish to know your thoughts."

"Well come, lay your hands upon mine." Hathael stretched her palms out and Athias placed his own, down onto them.

"The sixth will be revealed. The hidden crown uncovered. Placed upon their head they will climb the world and raze all upon it. I can see it coming undone, the secrets of the world. They will stand upon the frozen fire and bring forth the wrath that swarms beneath. The world's skin will peel and burn, life will fall to ash and dust and the roots of energy will rot and die." Athias spoke slowly, calmly. "This was the message. What do you know of it?"

Hathael sighed and muttered to herself,

"It can't be. No. Surely not."

"What? You do know of it, don't you?" Athias questioned.

"Yes and no. My boy, it is impossible; the thing of which you speak. The hidden crown."

"What does it mean, Greenseeker?"

Hathael shut her eyes, as her hands began to glow. A bright orange shimmered from her fingers, flowing down into her wrists and then through her arms, into her neck and eyes. A book appeared in her hands, it was wide and thick, and larger than when Athias had last saw it.

"Do you remember what this is, Athias?"

"The Calitreum." His head bowed; a sense of nobility seeped from his face.

"Indeed. The book where history is kept, and the teachings of magic are stowed. The Calitreum will be with you forever, had you forgotten how to summon it, or perhaps of its use?"

"My mind has become shrouded, old friend, I had not forgotten though I did not seek it."

"Well remember, Athias, you or any who are bound to the Fate of Magic can summon it to you." Athias nodded, appreciatively. "You learned from this book just as I did. It will continue to teach those after us, as it did before, for we record everything in it. As it did another, once."

"Who?"

"A flame in the night. A warrior. A great, great warrior of old. Her name I know not, nor her land of home. She created this book, and the magic that the Greenseekers used to protect this world.

A beautiful warrior destined to lead. She betrayed her sisters and buried them under the branches of the sacred Gaerlwood trees, a hidden grove deep in this very forest. The tales talk of a sacred crown, a gift from the All-Mother herself that holds immense power to those who have the power to use it. The tale says that her sisters sought this crown to destroy her, because she herself sought not to lead the world but to remake it." Hathael began turning the pages of the book. "The Forsaken Crown, it is called, made of Gaerlwood and the feathers of a white raven. Enchanted by magic, cursed magic." Athias looked to Gralnor, cleaning his own white feathers and then back to Hathael. "The tale says she will rise again, the crown atop her head, and with her will come the end."

Athias sat back, stunned.

"The Crown is the sixth? The sixth artefact?" Athias looked to the sword on his shoulder, to Hathael's staff.

"The most dangerous one at that. With power to transcend the other five."

Athias stood up, extending his hand to Hathael, "We need to tell our kin, the other Vayshanaa." Hathael nodded, a solemn expression upon his face. "I ask if you would take the horses for there is no need or use for them in the cities of Vadoran."

"All creatures are welcome here. I must offer you a cup before you go, old traditions, old times."

Athias nodded and whistled to the others who came back. H'Khara had the smudge of red currants around her lips and C'k'rian's skin sparkled in the light, it was a healthy, healing place. Hathael led them to a stone bench underneath a slumping tree. A small, purple-flamed fire stood ahead of them, though it had no logs beneath, and frogs of all colour hopped and scuttled around them, behind them, upon the tree and into the grass.

Hathael began to mix a pot of liquid over the fire, conjuring and stirring it via gestures from her hand, and noticing H'Khara's look of amazement and awe, Hathael sneaked in some harmless powder that made the liquid foam upwards but not spilling from the pot, it climbed higher and higher, like a fountain.

"Excuse me, err, my Lady?"

Hathael smiled and chuckled,

"I am no lady of titles, my child. My name is Hathael Stona. I am the Greenseeker of this forest, last of my kind."

"Can you tell me about magic, Mrs Greenseeker?"

"I can, but should I?"

Athias smiled, Hathael had always been a mysterious woman, even when Athias was just a teen. He looked out to the grassy knolls that spread for miles and remembered back to when he stayed here, learning the ways of life and nature. He would hide among the long grass and Hathael would find him holding frogs and lizards, examining them as they stared at him.

Still stirring, she threw her cloak up and the entire surrounding went dark.

"Magic is as much a part of the world as you are a part of the world, and I have a tale to tell of it, and of you, but we shall start at the very beginning.

"Long, long ago, our saviour and protector, Mother Zohya, clashed with the Eternal Giants that ruled the Endless Sands... Oh how they stretched for an eternity; how they burned. The Giants, led by their king, laughed down at those who lived in the burning sands, they mocked them and so Zohya challenged them, but they laughed, staying high on their misty mountain tops." Hathael bewitched the tree around them and its branches swayed and twisted, forming the shape of a woman, climbing a mountain. "Mother Zohya climbed the rocky paths, coming to the first giants, which she defeated in a game of wits. From her victory she was granted knowledge, above all. At the second tribe of giants, she defeated them in a battle of agility, and from this was granted magic. At the third of the giants, the king himself challenged her. The giants were monstrous, tall and burly, towers of rotting flesh as hard as stone. Zohya challenged the king to a trial of time, combing magic, skill, and wit. He accepted and fell to her trickery, turning against his own kin as she influenced his mind, then she climbed his rocky arms, up to his head and sliced through the neck. She defeated the giants and lay their corpses down into the great oceans, she tied them together with ancient spells and enchantments and from it, she created our world. The great mountain passes are their shoulders, the monoliths of the eastern shores are their teeth, and the forests are their hairs. The great lakes are their tears, and the caverns and tunnels that spread far beneath the soil are their veins. So, the legend says.

Right at the centre of the world, a place which nobody knows. Mother Zohya planted a tree by the name of Nhivilaurn. With roots longer than the journey of time and a height that dwarfed even the great mountains of old. This tree gave the new world life and from its roots sprouted the seeds of life that would spread far out into the world to become… you, all of you." The tree's roots and branches shaped again, revealing the shape of Brineth and spores of life, blooming. "The tree is the magic and life of the world. Many beings can harness the power of magic as the roots that birth it wind around them, going with them as they walk. There are many studies of the arcane. The study of time, the study of life, emotion, creativity, and death. But there are other ways that magic has seeped into this world, it's in your blood, my dear coaran. It's in your blood, my dear vadoran. It's in the trees that resist the storm, and in the water of the darkest tempest. The roots that direct our world's magic wrap around who and what they see fit. The world is magical, and the magic comes from the world.

Of course, there are some who serve other gods, and their stories of who forged the great world are different to ours, but all the stories. All of them. Involve Nhivilaurn."

The area lit up once more and Hathael stopped stirring as the pot was filled with a bright liquid. H'Khara looked at her in complete awe, her mouth ajar.

"I am a vessel of life. That was my chosen practice. I care for and protect the forests around us and the life inside it." Hathael said while conjuring four cups and filling them with the liquid. It was a colour like fire-baked clay and topped with a thin layer of pink foam. "I am a child of the forest, a position I have held for almost one-hundred and sixty years. The forest gives me life, as I do it."

She handed the cups out to each of them, they were made of wood but riddled with tiny stones. The instant the cup was placed into their hands, they felt the warmth spread throughout their body and the flavours of the drink swirled in their throat and danced like a jester to a song, in their bellies. The foam floated around their teeth and then drifted down their neck, a chewable like substance. It left their mouths feelings both tangy, and clean, refreshed.

"What's in this? It's good." H'Khara pondered.

"Protection, and a little spice." Hathael replied, kindly. "Will you be leaving now?"

"I'm afraid so, old friend. Thank you for everything you have done for us, for me." Athias stood and hugged Hathael.

"It has been too long. My child."

She walked with them to the middle of the tree, and inside, there was a flat stone protruding from the bark.

"Where do you want to go. Think it. Wish it. This will see you make it." Hathael said.

Athias placed his bare palm upon it and envisioned the bright shores of Vadoran waters. The others placed a hand upon him, their bags all laden with supplies. Hathael walked to her staff, still standing where she had placed it. She removed it from the ground and walked to another flat piece of stone, directly behind the three.

"Do you wish it?"

"I do." Athias whispered.

"Good." Hathael spoke boldly. She turned the staff clockwise into the stone and it began to swirl, unfolding as though a slab of melting chocolate. "Go now. May we meet again, Athias."

The surroundings began to spin and merge together too, with the colours of the trees seeping into each other. Then came a flash of orange and it all disappeared. They had gone. Athias opened his eyes, his hand still outstretched, only ahead of him now were clear waters and the gentle sound of the sea lapping against the cobbles on the beach.

Chapter Ten
Sapphire and Stone

The seas are as much as home as the soil is, in Brineth. Once polite and proud hosts, the Vadorans now patrol the deep. Who better to keep the storm and watch the tide, than those who worship nothing but the depths? It is theirs, the depths, and the creatures with it. – Calitreum, History of Old, Page 283.

The landscape around them was so vastly different from where they had come from, even before entering the Hathael's home. The thin, spindly trees standing upright in dusty soil had been replaced by dazzling views of mountains across fields of crop, deep greens, and bright yellows. Turning, they were greeted by the vast seas while water brushed against them, smoothing over the sand which shone a brilliant colour. Pebbles and shells peppered the shoreline, taking turns to be wished away into the sea with every wave that dragged in and out, as though the sea was a being itself, breathing steadily. The water itself was warm and sparkled as the minerals of the seabed soared over the current to the surface. On the horizon were more mountains, and the monoliths that Hathael had mentioned; mounds of earth and smooth stone, dotted across the curvature far away. Closer was another mountain with a flat peak, buildings sat upon the hills of it and ran from there, down to the beach and then further, descending into the depths. The mountain of Vadoran was as mystical and wondrous as the stories had said, even the air was warm, said to be so from the fires of the volcano that warmed them, and the taste of grounded salt hung over their lips.

"We're really here." C'k'rian whispered, "It's been a long time." Her voice was heavy, she took a step forward into the water. "I don't know if I can do this, Athias. My father… my mother… the way I left…"

Athias nodded to her,

"Take your time. We don't *have* to go there at all, but the odds of our success would be improved, if we do."

C'k'rian nodded. She slipped her shoes off and traipsed her feet over the pebbles and shells, partially submerged in the sea. It was said that the water had healing properties. C'k'rian knelt and dipped her hand into the water, she brushed it over her skin and washed her face, she was humming to herself as she did.

"How are we going to breathe, under the water I mean?" H'Khara asked Athias.

"The people of Vadoran practice ancient magic, magic that offers protection to those who they deem worthy of it. He replied, making sure he had a few scrolls; unravelling them, checking and putting them back into his pockets. "We will send a message into the water, one of old magic, a key of sorts, made of sapphire and stone. Combined, and blessed, these two substances form the base of vadoran culture. Upon receiving the message, they will come to the surface. Hopefully."

"Hopefully? We're pinning this on hope?" H'Khara's voice trailed off, lost.

"No." He lowered his voice, "We're pinning this on her." He pointed to C'k'rian who was still washing her hands and arms in the water, while staring out to sea.

Seventeen Years Earlier

C'k'rian opened her eyes slowly as they ached and stung. She felt a searing pain in her side, it travelled from her ribs at the front to her spine at the back and up to her neck. Her ribs were bandaged, as were her left arm, wrist, and fingers. The bandages were leathery, they were thin but waterproof and the water swirled around as she released the clamps on her side which had stopped her drifting away in her sleep. Her chambers were larger than you would have thought for a child of Vadoran. The walls still sparkled as much as they had almost five hundred years ago when the city was built, before it fell. Now though, most of the city stood beneath the waves, upon the reef, while a small part of the city still stood above the water as if mostly for show. Now just a watch tower and trading outpost for the rest of the world. As the city had fallen all those years ago, the Elders enchanted the very water that surrounded it, hiding, and protecting it, and the people of Vadoran adapted to their new home. They made materials that resisted the pressure of the depths and used the secrecy from the outside world to advance their own causes.

C'k'rian was the second child of Elrith Rian and her husband, Ce'ron Rian. They were among their generation of elders, responsible for the welfare of the city and those who lived in it. Vadoran culture was mysterious and the people were powerful; they commanded one of the finest armies in Brineth. Because of this, all children from the ages of six and upwards were conditioned to fight and study for war and C'k'rian was no different, royal or not. Her mother and father were cruel, stating they were preparing her for the future of their world but pushing her far beyond the boundaries of any nine-year old was capable of. Every day she would be subjected to gladiatorial combat with her older brother and younger sister, and this day was no different. C'k'rian sat upright on the bed as her door opened. Before her stood her father, dressed in white robes that billowed around him with the water, with a teal sash from his waist to shoulder, and a crown made of crystallised octopus tentacles. He was bald and had blue skin much like her with a small beard, dark green eyes, a sharp nose, and ears that pointed downwards.

"Come, daughter." *He held out his hand and she walked to him.* "Faster." *He barked at her, so she walked faster, wincing and took his hand.*

Ce'ron dragged her more than walked with her, he took her to the library where she was to study with a tutor. She slipped as they ascended the stairs, falling and crying out as she did, her bruised ribs lurching.

"Get up, daughter." *He snapped at her again with a snake-like voice. She flinched and started to get up, but he grabbed her hand and pulled her to her feet.*

"Ow! You're hurting me. Please stop, father."

"Silence, daughter of mine. You bring shame on this family."

A teenage boy approached them and took C'k'rian's hand from her father. He hugged her and she clung to him.

"Elra. Let go of your sister. She is weak and your softness only makes her weaker."

"Why are you so hard on her? Why don't you see that she doesn't want to fight, that there is honour in more things than strength, father?" *Elra tucked C'k'rian's head into his chest. He was taller than her, although just a teenager.*

Ce'ron fumed and pulled C'k'rian from her brother, carrying on. At the library they were greeted by the tutor. A pompous man, tall and well educated. C'k'rian's father handed her over to him and nodded to her, the tutor nudged her forward and she walked ahead of him, passing her mother who sneered at her as she walked. The library of Vadoran was revered across the city, it had once been a place where thousands would visit, coming from all over the continent. It was an enormous building with a stained glass ceiling, thousands upon thousands of books were kept here and before the volcano erupted all those years ago, the Elders had cast spells upon everything inside, the water that spilled into the great hall passed over the pages leaving them intact. There was a book for almost anything you could imagine in this library, from the darkest corners of magical practice, to recipes of herbal remedies. C'k'rian was here to learn of war again, to learn the ancient fighting styles of her parents, and their parents before them, and beyond that, dating back to even before the city was built for once they had been a people of land just like any other. Vadoran warriors were fierce and loyal, proficient in fighting with swords, spears, axes, and bows, not to mention the other weapons in the vast armouries of Vadoran; tridents, saldrins, viantors, kn'olnots and more. Their weaponry, like their medicine were advanced. Since the city had sunk, they had harvested crystals and minerals from the seabed, using them in their forges, adding to their weaving of clothes, to their mixtures of crop. Vadoran had survived and flourished, its population booming, and if Elrith and Ce'ron had their way, it would stay isolated. However, an invader had landed on Brineth' shores a few years ago, an invader who brought large armies of smoke and death, burning all life that stood before it, and Vadoran had committed a sizeable force to the king, in hopes of repelling the invader.

A lady was sitting at a table in the library, C'k'rian's nurse, committed to her at birth. Her name was La'io and she cared for C'k'rian day and night when not in a trial of combat. La'io was the only real friend C'k'rian had, other than her older brother, and looked forward to their time together.

"Professor D'zha. Let me take C'k'rian to her bath. Those wounds are still healing." He went to interject but she cut across him, for although she was a nurse, she was not a servant and being the nurse to a royal child was a high honour. "I insist."

"Fine." Professor D'zha spoke out. He had a deep voice, it echoed around the hall.

La'io took C'k'rian's hand and gently walked with her towards stairs, through a corner room of the hall, which ascended to the baths. The bath chamber had been drained of water, bar the foamy water in the bath of the floor that sat in the middle. This room was used for healing; water with a thicker consistency, much like jelly, topped with a foam. It healed broken bones, cuts and bruises in a matter of minutes instead of weeks or days. La'io carefully lay C'k'rian into the bath, resting her head down gently and upon contact with her skin the entire bath heated; special minerals in the water reacted to the salts and oils in the skin. The water from the taps shaped around her arms and ribs, massaging her fractured bones, soothing them as they healed. It was warm and comforting.

"This will all pass, dear child, but for now you must rest." La'io whispered to her as C'k'rian fell asleep, partly submerged.

Present Day

The thoughts of that day passed through C'k'rian's mind like a wildfire, scorching everything it touched. A tear dropped down her cheek, falling and crashing into the wandering tide, losing its identity, and becoming a soldier in the great body of the ocean. She remembered the pain of her ribs that day as clear as if it had just happened and traced her nails across them and over her other hand, over the exact lines of the fracture. She rolled her sleeve up to where the body art of her family lay, imprinted upon her skin, and above it another that she had not shown to H'Khara, a symbol of curving ice through a shark. She hastily rolled the sleeve down, as though ashamed of it, and turned to walk back out of the ocean.

"Alright. Do you have it?"

"I do." Athias spoke calmly. He withdrew a small stone disk; it was marbled in colour between white and murky blue. Athias approached C'k'rian and placed it into her hand, firmly.

C'k'rian nodded to him and he smiled back, reassuring her. She let down her cloak and it slumped on the sand and pebbles beneath them as she took off her boots. She swam out into the sea, a stone's throw from the shore, making sure the bed had disappeared beneath her and keeping her head above the surface she lay the disk upon the water. It had a small gap in the middle and C'k'rian took off her ring and placed it, crystal side down, into the disk. The disk began to lower slowly into the sea, glimmering as it went and C'k'rian swam back to the shore, to stand beside the others.

"Now what?" H'Khara asked.

"Now we wait. We wait for as long as they want us to." C'k'rian spoke with heavy words.

An hour had passed and the three still stood upon the beach, looking out over the sea. H'Khara was playing with the pebbles beneath her feet and Athias was counting the islands far ahead but C'k'rian was standing bolt upright, her back perfectly straight, a mixture of courage, honour, and fear, and it was hard to see which of the three was most prominent in C'k'rian right now. Athias had made a nest for Gralnor in a small gap in a rocky wall, it was warm in there with the bags, and Gralnor had nestled into the cloth where he would stay until they returned. Abruptly, a whirlpool opened ahead of them at the exact point the disk had sunk. Out of the whirlpool rose two sharks with soldiers atop of them in saddles, and next to them was a horrific creature; a monstrous beast resembling that of a shark too, only the size of a whale, with teeth larger than a grown man and horns atop its head and neck. Standing on top of the beast stood a magnificent throne tent and a smaller chair over the neck with lavish reigns connected to the monster's jaw.

"Is that...?" Athias whispered to C'k'rian, stunned.

"A Drahk'alar. The Dread Beast."

The soldiers on the sharks sported light armour made from crustacean shell, bound together by hide. Truly little of the body was covered; one shoulder, a helmet, shins and chest guards were all they had. The sharks were also sporting light armour, in the form of the same crustacean material and smooth plate metal over their noses, teeth, fins and tail. The Vadoran Royals loved to show off their prowess, Athias had read countless tales of their grandeur and prowess. One of those on the Drahk'alar signalled to a guard who shouted over to the shore.

"Who sends this message? That of Sapphire and Stone?" Holding up the disk with the ring in it.

Athias went to step forward but C'k'rian stepped across him.

"C'k of Rian. Daughter of Elrith and Ce'on Rian. Bearer of the Fifth Mark, Heir to the Steps of Vadoran and the eleventh reign!"

She was met with silence. A long, terrible silence. Then, another beast submerged, carrying a room-sized shell, although this one was empty. The door fell, revealing a bubble of sorts around the edges and lanterns inside revealed a series of chairs with colourful curtains at the windows.

"Come." One of the robed vadorans said calmly. He spoke quietly, yet they heard him as though he was at arm's reach.

The drahk'alar sunk down beneath the water, the door to the shell closing, and the shark mounted soldiers followed. Athias looked to the others who looked back, C'k'rian marched into the shell and Athias followed, with H'Khara joining them last. Inside, a woman was sitting in a chair ahead of them, completely cloaked and hidden by shadow.

"Please, take a seat." She gestured to the chairs that were dotted around the room. "For the safety of Vadoran, I must inform you that you will not remember how we arrived in the city, not even you, princess." She whispered softly, looking to them all in turn and arriving at the finish with C'k'rian, "Sleep now, let the currents take you. When you wake, you must drink the potion you see beside you, less your skin burns, and your mind lose itself."

C'k'rian picked up a sweet scent in the air, like freshly bloomed flowers and spices. Athias felt his eyes closing and his mind falling into a dream and the more he fought it the stronger the urge to sleep came. C'k'rian felt it too, it took longer for her to drift off than the other two, who slumped in their chairs, but she did feel it, the motions of the beast as it swam, sending her to sleep. When she awoke, the first of the three, they were in a room void of water. Three potions, ones she recognised from her alchemy classes, stood beside each of them on a table. C'k'rian woke the other two, nudging them from their slumber and Athias left the bed immediately, going to the windows and looking out at Vadoran, the magnificent underwater city from his childhood books. Buildings, multiple storeys high, and temples and walls made the city, built into the reefs and corals. Vadoran and creature, manta ray and dolphin, swam side by side through the city and the bright, brilliant sandstone shimmered as the sunlight from high above, beamed down through the water.

"The potion, I presume it protects us from the water and the pressure?" Athias examined it.

"Yes, and the magic of this place too. Even I must drink it, for it has been years since I stepped foot here."

One by one, they took large gulps of the potion. It surged down their throats just as fire trailed over leaves, it left the feel of both freezing ice and scalding burns on their tongue and their eyes began to water as their knees buckled, it felt as though a wolf's set of teeth was being dragged down their arms and up their legs. It was in their fingertips and it was in their spine, a writhing snake with jagged edges. Then it was over, the pain fading gradually. The three stood up straight again, examining their hands, arms, and each other. A robed man entered, walking through a bubble, he was wrapped in orange and black. He snapped his fingers and two guards at the door came forward, bringing him a staff which he tapped down on the floor at their feet, before turning and leaving.

"Now what?" H'Khara looked to the other two.

"Now we go and see my parents." C'k'rian said, calmly.

Chapter Eleven
Beyond the Throne

There are two thrones of Brineth. One sits in halls of marble, gold, and sleek wood. One sits in halls of reef, and bright coral-stone. I am sworn to neither, yet I am sworn to both. – Calitreum, A Vayshanaa's Oath, Page 16.

The Steps of Vadoran, that is what they called it. A glimmering, fantastically beautiful throne room of reef and lavishly decorated stone. Jewels and corals ran the length of the room, and steps had been carved into it, elegantly. It was here, upon the steps, that the thrones of Vadoran sat, their designs intended to mirror the tremendous creatures that roamed the untamed oceans; the manta ray; the drahk'alar; the shark, each throne in the creatures' image glimmered, carved from fine marble and black reef. Seven chairs stood, the thrones, and sat in them were the Queen and King of Vadoran, accompanied by council: the elders. Elrith and Ce'ron sat upright in their thrones, backs straight against the shining stone. They looked out over the hall, where magnificent pillars stood holding the beautiful stonework up and long tables made of a similar reef ran the length of the hall. Dozens of enormous lumu lanterns lit up the hall from above. C'k'rian led the way, marching into the hall and up towards the thrones with H'Khara and Athias behind. As they drew closer a deep, toneless voice rang out across the empty room.

"So, you have returned. After all this time." It echoed around the room, as though they were all in a deep cave, not under the sea.

"I have." C'k'rian replied, bold and steady.

"So, daughter, what brings you back to our glorious nation?" This time it was a woman's voice, slightly higher pitched but toneless like the first.

C'k'rian gestured to Athias and H'Khara to stop where they stood, at the first platform. She climbed more steps and stood in-front of the seven chairs, and those seated in them.

"Mother, father. Elders. I bring a traveller with words for you to hear, words of the future."

"You dare?! You dare talk to us of the future when you, daughter of Vadoran, were so quick to leave?" Her mother hissed, looking down at her. "After what you *did*."

C'k'rian hung her head.

"Look at me, girl. Look up at your father." Her mother's words seared C'k'rian's ears and she looked up, a tear in her eyes. "Pathetic. You always were."

C'k'rian looked directly to her mother and father. Her fists were closed, and she was trembling.

"Look at her." Ce'ron laughed and the other Elders hissed and laughed. "Frightened. Weak. Just as she was all those years ago."

Abruptly, C'k'rian let out a howl of rage and leapt forward, drawing a dagger from her boot but it was met by the blade of a spear, ahead of her father. C'k'rian looked to the guard and took a step back in shock. Nahli, a woman who was once a girl like her, stood before her. Nahli Balhu, the same Nahli who had ventured up to the surface with C'k'rian, and who joined her at the secret vaults as they snuck out of class, who she sparred with and studied with. She was much taller now with shaved hair at the sides and a ponytail at the back. An Amazonian figure sat well on her thin body. She had mercury-red lips and her blue skin gleamed in the light with flecks of oyster white. The armour plates on her shoulder, waist, and chest were tight, clinging to her every move. Her pteruges swayed with every poised step she took, and her shin and wrist braces shone.

"S... sister." C'k'rian said, quietly, still in shock.

"Not anymore, C'k." Nahli barked back, lowering her spear and placing the shield back on her back before returning the thrones.

Elrith and Ce'ron were grinning, a flicker of malice on their faces.

"Now. Who is this traveller you have brought to us?"

"My name is Athias." He had seen enough, stepping forward and speaking in a bold voice.

"Athias? Athias who?"

"I am a Vayshanaa." He said, sharply. He looked to each of the Elders and the guards in turn. "I'm here to make a deal."

"A Vayshanaa? Pah! The Vayshanaa were a myth, one I would tell my silly little daughter as she stirred in her bed. You arrive here with a traitor, my 'daughter' if I must call her that, and you think you can barter with us. You are but a traveller and we are the power of all Vadoran."

"Laugh at me again and it will be the last laugh that leaves your cursed tongue, oh *great* King." Athias stood up straight, his hand ready to draw Spectre from its sheath.

The laughter stopped, and the room fell into silence. The guards that stood beside the thrones stepped forward; spear tight in hand, the other on swords that sat on their waist. It was so silent that the lumu fish, trapped in their illuminated prisons, could be heard fluttering from side to side.

"You dare." Ce'ron whispered, his spindly fingers clutching the throne's arm.

"I dare. For I have seen a warning of what is to come. A storm that will tear the world asunder, that will dry the oceans and pull down the mountains, a storm to end storms. If you do not speak with me, your world, this *great* nation, will die just like the ones above it."

His words were met by hushed whispers, the guards took a step back away from the thrones and the elders, the Queen and the King conferred, looking to each other and to Athias.

"Very well. You will venture with us into our chambers and we will hear what these words are, this warning." Elrith and Ce'ron stood, then did the elders. "Surrender your sword, traveller." They warned Athias and waited while he unhooked the sheath, laying it down on a table where H'Khara sat.

Athias joined the elders as they skulked from the Steps, down and through a door behind the thrones. Inside the smaller room with no windows, sat a circular table and a dozen chairs around it. Sitting down, he was across from Elrith and Ce'ron, and they stared to him, all the elders did.

"Make it quick." Ce'ron hissed.

"A warrior is coming. With her she will bring the end, in the hands of the legions of damned that accompany her, they will burn and break all. The warrior will return and bring with her, also, new powers that defy gods and kings. The reason I am here is to talk to you of the Stormbinder. I have told C'k'rian that I have come to strike a deal so that we can use it against the emperor, but that is a half-truth. The full truth is that we will need it to defeat this warrior as she comes." Athias made careful not to divulge of the crown.

"You wish to take our most powerful weapon, because of this 'warning' of yours. I think not, you could use it to unseat us, our rule. No doubt C'k'rian would like that." The more Ce'ron and Elrith talked, the more they sounded ill, an evil writhing inside them.

"It is C'k'rian's birth right to yield the Stormbinder, is it not? Athias snapped.

"Ha, she lost that birth right when she lost this family, when she cast it aside."

"If you do not let us take it, to defend the world, from the emperor and what comes next, you have doomed yourself."

"That is enough!" Elrith screamed at Athias. "You are but dirt under the great tidal wave, yet you come here to scare us into relinquishing a great weapon." Elrith stood, slamming her hands down on the table, her crown teetering on her brow.

Athias sighed, staring her in the eye. Back in the throne room C'k'rian and H'Khara were sitting on the table, waiting. She glanced at Nahli who stared dead ahead, unflinching. C'k'rian got to her feet and H'Khara placed a hand on her wrist.

"Where are you going?" She looked ahead to where C'k'rian was staring, right at Nahli. "Don't, please. You've been through enough over the last few days." but C'k'rian shrugged her off.

She strolled up to the steps before the thrones.

"How could you? How can you stand there after what they did to us?" Her voice was brittle, a tear rolled down her cheek as her ribs pained, like they had all those years ago.

"This is my penance. I will stand in the place your brother should have taken."

"Don't... don't speak of him." Tears brimmed C'k'rian's eyes, she felt the rage of all those years rising inside.

"Elra should stand here, 'stead of me. This should be his spear, his shield, his helmet." She pointed to each.

C'k'rian drew her daggers again and sprinted forward,

"Don't you say his name!" She shouted across the hall, the words echoed throughout it, gliding through the water like a creature.

Eleven Years Earlier

The surface air was cold in her lungs. She gulped it down and panted, gaining her breath, swinging her bag of supplies down onto the pebbly shore. The words of La'io strong in her mind from earlier that morning.

"When the sun sets to sleep and the moons take their watch across the oceans, you must go. The guards will take an hour's leave tonight, for I shall take them to a place of secret. Swim out and to the great stone house, the tower upon the surface. Make from here to the vaults and through them, up towards the shore."

She had made it; she was free of her wretched parents and their life of brutal hardships. Pulling herself from the water she slumped against a tree, pulling her scarf up around her cold face and looked out over the night, the water at peace, reflecting the stars and moons above. Just as she went to close her eyes, she heard the pebbles slide and woke to see a figure clad in black lunging at her. She ducked, and their spear crashed into the wood, splintering bark. C'k'rian pulled daggers from her boots, though only a few inches long each, she fought with them as though part of her hands. She swung up and down and the assassin's shawl ripped, they rolled and caught her arm, bringing it down to their knee, and breaking her grip on the dagger. She swung down with the other, but her hand hit a gauntlet, the metal bruising her arm. She felt a foot behind her leg and fell back.

The assassin was over her again, and the spear crashed down. She rolled and kicked their leg back, pushing them down to a knee. Rising to her feet she was met by the assassin who slashed forward with a sword but C'k'rian caught their forearm and quickly, ducking, picked a dagger up and drove it upwards into the assailant's neck. The sword fell, clanging on the stones and C'k'rian took a step back, wheezing, out of breath. The being ahead of her collapsed to their own knees, clasping at their throat and drops of blood trailed over the pebbles, entwining into the sand. C'k'rian pulled her scarf down, taking large gulps of air again and she heard a voice gasp as the assassin looked up at her. She ripped the bandana from the face and her heard sunk. A sickness rose in her stomach as she looked helplessly into her brother's eyes. He was gasping for air, clawing at the blade in his neck, opening his mouth to let the blood trickle over his cheek.

"No." *She trembled, her hands shaking.* "Why you... Why did it have to be you?" *She slumped in the water; the tide brushed around her, but she felt nothing.*

"I... I didn't..." *She pushed Elra's body up in her arms and his head hung back.* "I didn't... know it was you." *His voice trailed off as his body fell limp as the breathing stopped and his hands fell, down from his neck, onto the stones.*

C'k'rian sat with him, rocking back and forth, clutching him tight as though she could bring life back to his eyes.

Present Day

"Don't make me do this, C'k." Nahli pleaded with C'k'rian, getting to her feet and wiping blood from her nose, taking the shield from her back while C'k'rian ran at her. "You may have been better at this when we were younger, but now, I will not lose."

"We'll see, won't we." C'k'rian turned side on, her knives pointed outwards in her hands, her arms straight. She leapt up and folded her arms ready to strike.

Meanwhile, Athias was deep in conversation with the elders, impatience lingering on every word, he and them both pounding on the table.

"When the time comes, will you not send your legions to the surface? To fight for salvation against destruction?"

"Perhaps, and what will you give us in return?"

"Years ago, you sent soldiers out with the Ashgrath, did you not? I saw it raised high amidst battle. It was lost too, and those who took it, lost too."

"How do you know of this?"

"For I know where it now lays, the flag and its monument. I will return it to you so you may raise it high above the seas and return Vadoran to secrecy once more."

"Fine. Traveller. You have a deal but now, be gone, for our halls and take our wretched daughter with you."

He stood up and left. The meeting dispersed and they travelled back to the throne room. Inside, ahead of them was Nahli lying on the floor, her shield dented and C'k'rian standing over her. She stepped forward towards the thrones, towards Athias and her parents.

"Maybe there was promise in you after all, maybe not. Either way, you may leave this place for it is no home of yours."

Athias passed H'Khara who joined him very willingly, he took Spectre from the table. C'k'rian pulled the helmet from Nahli's head and followed them out from the hall, not looking back.

"Did you get what we came for?" C'k'rian said. Her voice was cold and emotionless.

"Not entirely. Your parents will send the legions of the deep when we call, but the Stormbinder? We will have to wait and see."

"It's over now anyway." She clutched the helmet tightly as they made their way to the harbour, running her nails over the scratches above the right eye.

The harbour was not like those above the surface. It was a tree-like structure made almost entirely out of the coral reef, while some parts had been excavated; spiralling tunnels that spread through the reef, with windows made of crystal and attached to the ends of these tunnels, which looked like branches, were various transports. Some were small, barely large enough to hold two, while others were as large as whales. The ships were of stone design, and shaped like sea-creatures, from fish to sharks and whales, and they were powered by repulsors at the rear, collecting minerals from the water and turning it into propulsion. The guards at the harbour entrance stepped aside as C'k'rian approached, lowering a bridge to the vehicle, which was cosy and small, and a console at the front was scattered with pebbles that hovered above. Athias dragged his hands over the stones, which turned, twisting in the air, and the repulsor powered up as the door shut, the water draining from inside. Athias sat back in his chair, mulling over the conversation he had undertaken while H'Khara was thinking of Acre Farm, how she opened it would be liberated soon, C'k'rian rest the helmet she had taken on her lap, it was a dark colour with spikes running from the forehead to the neck, she slid it over her head. It was comfortable and snug, the narrow eye slits revealing all to be seen of her face. Athias turned to C'k'rian while she took it off again.

"What happened to your brother?" He said, quietly, as to not wake H'Khara.

C'k'rian glanced back at H'Khara who was fast asleep to which she was. She took a deep breath a few times and began.

"You know of my childhood; how I was forced to fight day in and day out against my elder brother and my younger sister, it is how our nation was, to prepare warriors for a time of war. I wanted to be a nurse, I wanted to raise children and be a healer but my mother, my father, they wanted me to be a warrior, like my brother especially. When I was fifteen my brother, Elra, who was eighteen, had been accepted into the Tempest Guard. The highest honour a soldier could ask for." A single tear rolled down her cheek. "He was an elegant and skilful warrior. Better even than you, maybe." She cradled his helmet. "My brother loved me dearly and he tried to persuade my parents to spare me the fighting, to let me become the healer and live in peace, but they didn't heed it.

When I was seventeen, my nurse arranged for me to be taken in by a group of fishers on the surface. La'io cared for my life far more than my parents ever did. The plan was going well, she had given me time, and I had escaped the city. My parents found out and sent an assassin for me and I got lucky, he made an error and I was lucky, that's all." Tears brimmed in her eyes, rolling down her cheeks, she brushed them off. "I finally had become what my parents wanted me to be, I had finally beaten my brother." Her eyes brimmed and she clutched the helmet close, holding it up to her face. "I'm so sorry, Elra." She whispered, her voice wavering with every word, as she kissed the helmet, looking into the eye slits.

A few hours later they reached the surface. The craft came to a slow halt in the shallows and the sun was beginning to set, bathing the sea in an amber glow. Athias departed with H'Khara and C'k'rian one at a time, laying each down in the warm sand by the wall where their things were kept. He made a small fire from some driftwood and uncovered Gralnor with their bags, the bird was deep in sleep too. He thought to himself, how surreal it all was, the scale of Vadoran beneath the sea and imagined what it would have looked like all those many hundreds of years ago; the brightest city in the world, so the stories had said. He imagined the magnificent towers and the palace, the plentiful shipping docks, and the children playing on the very pebbly sands he sat on. Athias removed a roll of parchment from his bag and placed it down, a map, and he sat up all night planning their route.

Chapter Twelve
A Life Now Lost

To be a Vayshanaa is more than to be a champion of magic, it is to be a champion of the unknown. Some lessons cannot be taught to those who have not lived a life, and some cannot be taught to those who have. – Calitreum, Gilen Abbrath's Entry, Page 427.

The landscape became increasingly eerie as the trio travelled, each day that went past revealed more and more haunted places while thousands of stars shimmered up high every night, blissfully unaware of the terror below. Gralnor had spent most of his time sitting upon Athias' shoulder, leaving occasionally to scout ahead and observe the landscape. He would jump into the air and climb higher, soaring through the air, disappearing into the clouds. They had been moving for a few days, sleeping in caves and setting up makeshift shelters each night, following a rough river, shaped as though a giant had scraped its hands through the earth. On the third day since leaving Vadoran, the three came to an old, abandoned mine, ringed by a small wall, while a cabin sat in the centre. Outside lay three graves, a small stone had been placed at the head of each and each of those bore a small triangle; etched into the smooth flint. They were bathed in a pale pink light as the sun behind them.

"Plague." Athias spoke out, holding his arm out in front of the rest. The entrance to the mine now blockaded.

"I heard stories… I didn't think they were true…" C'k'rian whispered, she sounded defeated.

"Stories?" H'Khara asked curiously.

"When these lands were regularly kept and nourished, they were a beautiful, peaceful place. Now, since Ziath has cast a shadow across it, plague has spread unchallenged, through the wildlands. It came from the mines, something was discovered and spread poison through the air." C'k'rian pointed in every direction. "After much debate, the mining community agreed that four from their number would leave and seal the mines, before sending word to the nearest city or town, they would then take their own lives in a trench, with fire, after setting fire to the mines.

Their ash would be buried by those who arrived later, from the town or city."

"But there's no trench" H'Khara looked around, wildly, back and forth in every direction.

"There is not." Athias pondered, approaching the entrance of the mine, the wood across the tunnel was blackened from within, burned and charred.

Looking around, a glint of silver from the cabin caught his eye.

"Ambush!" Athias shouted at the others and withdraw Spectre, as gunfire cracked over the air.

The windows of the cabin smashed, and the door fell with an almighty clang. Figures wrapped in cloaks and masks sprang from the shadows within. C'k'rian slipped on the helmet and drew the blades from her boots meanwhile H'Khara fell onto all fours and began the transformation into wolf. Athias met one of the attackers swiftly, raising Spectre to his axe, catching the blade and the man holding it swung round for another attack. Athias knelt, narrowly dodging the blade, and rose, cutting across the back of the attacker's leg and driving Spectre through his chest. The attacker fell with a thud and a grunt, and another ran at Athias who raised Spectre up and in a flick of silver, cut across the attacker without so much as a thought. Another rushed forward, clutching a chain, tipped with a sharp head which he swung at Athias while a woman behind him cocked a rifle. The rifle cracked and Athias felt a breath of hot air from behind as he dodged, knocking the rifle up. He pulled it from her hand while bringing Spectre round. Her head toppled as he brought the rifle round, crashing it against the other's face, who let out a howl, his face blooded. Swinging the chain furiously, Athias muttered a spell and shot a blast of power from his hand, knocking the assailant off his feet before finishing him off, driving Spectre down into the ground, through him. The bodies around him all bore a similar look; red paint from their foreheads to their chests, flicking over their eyes to resemble horns: the mark of the Beastmaster.

Behind him, H'Khara had pounced into a group of attackers that had climbed from the well, and C'k'rian stood beside her, fighting with fury. A huge burling man swung a sword at Athias who caught it with Spectre, it slid off the enchanted sword's blade. The monster that stood before Athias was huge, so large in fact that the cloak upon him was bulging and hung at least two foot from the floor. His hood fell and Athias was met by a huge balding head and gigantic eyes separated by a dented nose. He too had the streaks of red paint and his head was covered in scars. The monster of a man wildly swung his sword again with wild, lumbering arms. In a flash of silver, Athias brought Spectre up in front of him and the blades collided, the attacker's shattering.

The brute grunted as the blade smashed, seemingly unable to comprehend what had happened, "I 'ike your wittle blade" he leered, foul breath dancing around Athias' nostrils.

Athias cut across the savage's chest and he stepped back clutching his belly, the layers of muscle and fat entwined into one, and no blood seeped from the wound. He stopped and suddenly looked up, directly at Athias who stared back, surprised.

"Me likey that bladey." His voice was gruff, and his teeth were the same colour as his tongue.

The brute charged Athias like a bull, picking Athias up and holding him by the throat, dangling him at least a foot from the ground before slamming him into the cold, rocky earth. Athias wheezed, he felt dizzy and turned over onto his front to spit out a drop of blood as every bone in his body felt the shudder from the earth. Meanwhile the brute lumbered over to Spectre and picked it up. The hilt barely fit into just one of his enormous, troll-like hands and he toyed with it.

"Calan de'cantro" Athias whispered to himself, clambering to his knees, then to his feet.

"What you sayin'?" The brutish man shouted at him while eyeing up the blade's colour and shine.

"Hae'ruma cralsto." Athias continued, his voice growing louder.

"We got us a wizard ere!" Another of the attackers spoke. A tall thin woman, sporting a silver armband, the leader presumably. "Lago. Put it down." She pointed to Spectre, "and seize him!" Pointing to Athias who was taking steps backwards, slowly.

"No!" Lago said, much as a child would after stealing another's toy. "It mine. It is!" He held the blade up high, out of reach of any of the rest.

A different woman hurtled towards Athias, two knives in her hands. Athias met her with open hands, breaking her wrists against his armour and sending the knives flying. He cracked her face on his knee and kicked her legs out from beneath her, before muttering to himself once more. H'Khara whelped as a thick net closed around her and C'k'rian fell to the floor.

"Shut him up!" The blonde-haired woman screamed at the others. "He's a sorcerer!"

"Volostrau Intarya." Athias continued to talk, his voice growing into a shout. "Volostrau Intarya!"

As he shouted the spell, Lago let out a billowing yelp of pain and Spectre's hilt sparked, burning his flesh, as electric bolts jumped from the blade.

The sword then disappeared with a whoosh. Athias opened his palms, arms wide, and the sword appeared again in his hands as electricity surged through the earth, it burned the few running towards him to a crisp. The air around them thickened as a strong breeze flew in around them all and Athias' cloak flowed around him, rippling, and thunder rolled over head with dark clouds amassing. Athias stood tall and straight while sparks flew from Spectre, bridges of brilliant lightning from the stony floor to the blade. His uncovered eye glimmered in the sparks' light and the clouds rumbled above, as the ground trembled beneath him. The Beastmasters stood in shocked awe as coils of electricity sprung from the sword and Athias' palm and trailed through the soil like roots at an accelerated rate.

"Idiots! Seize him, now!" The apparent leader shouted at the rest of them, spitting in rage.

The Beastmasters howled and shouted while hurtling towards Athias. He let go of Spectre and it hovered a few inches above the ground, slowly rotating. He could see everything, it all moved in a slower time around him, the fox burrowing a few feet beneath the soil he stood on, Gralnor and the other birds' miles high, the beating heart of the woman and her brutes ahead. They were almost upon him, a dozen fanatic fighters. Athias wrapped his palm around Spectre and lifted it, it was as light as a feather and yet as heavy as a bastard sword. He stepped forward and effortlessly parried the first few attackers, with every strike upon them he charred their flesh and felt their pain in the same instantaneous moment. A bolt of lightning shot from Athias as he struck another and it chained to others and they slumped to the ground, their skin black as night. A crack echoed over the hills and an iron ball hurtled towards him but was obliterated by a bolt from Spectre, which had come alive, awakened by old magic. Athias walked forward, effortlessly, his eyes a storming tempest; black, white, grey, and pale blue all battling for dominance. Still they came, and he killed every one of them until it was just the lady left. Around her lay dozens of charred bodies, barely recognisable anymore. She did not cower; she did not kneel. She stood, her spear in hand.

Her head fell to the floor with a dull thud as quick as she had raised her spear, and Athias stood still, a static field around him. He looked to the sword and then to the sky before collapsing. Athias knelt, resting on Spectre before passing out into darkness, H'Khara and C'k'rian's cries becoming fainter and fainter as they leapt towards him.

Twenty-Nine Years Earlier

Athias found himself in a memory, hiding behind a statue in a narrow, cold corridor; slabs of grey stone pathed the floor and made the walls around him. He sat behind the beautiful stone body of a warrior, hidden in the shadow behind.

"Word has reached us, Ziath and his armies landed on the coasts of Brineth not months ago. He has brought a destroyer fleet and our king's own lays in ruin at the bottom of the sea. He has come to conquer the land of Brineth and build his own kingdom." *Tutor Abbrath spoke in hushed tones, while Tutor Vilcor leant closer. Athias, in the shadows of a statue just feet from them listened intently, his small figure hidden perfectly behind the curvature of stone.*

"It is a sign. The message his brother gave us when delivering Athias into our care. The message of a child with orange eyes?"

"He is not ready! He cannot be sent there yet. Athias is still but a boy." *Tutor Abbrath pleaded.*

"A powerful boy, he is skilled in the arcane already at the young age of twelve, no? He is a warrior, a fighter with significant prowess in the arts."

"He is a boy! He was delivered here so that we may protect him, I will not send a boy - skilled or not, into a war of such reckless hate."

"Gilen. If we do not send sorcerers to aid the king, the war will be lost."

Athias rarely heard Tutor Abbrath's first name, it was always a shock when he did, and he crept as close as he would dare, eager to hear more as the Tutor's voices descended into whispers.

"I know. I know." Tutor Abbrath sighed. "And so, we will send sorcerers. Orgon will go with his apprentices."

"Athias is far superior in skill and temperament than any of those apprentices..."

"Of course! However, have you considered what might happen if he was caught and killed, or worse; turned? He is not ready and that is final!" Abbrath hissed. "We will not remain secret here for long, we must make the most of these years while we can." Tutor Abbrath bowed and Vilcor bowed also.

The two went their different ways down the corridor and Athias clung to the side of the statue, masked in shadow, as Abbrath passed. Athias crept forward towards a painting opposite, he prized the painting off the wall and proceeded down the passage behind it. Being a boy of just thirteen years old he was nimble, able to proceed down the passages hidden in the walls without any hindrance. At the other end was a fireplace, he pushed it forward and slunk out before shutting it and tiptoeing towards the bed, which stood, lonely ahead of him.

"How much did you hear?" Tutor Abbrath stood up from where he had been sitting in the shadows of the moonlit room.

"Who is Ziath?" Athias deflected and Abbrath sighed, letting forth a deep breath.

"A conqueror of many worlds. Once a fair king but now, a monster, hellbent on destroying magic for it took his daughter from him, in a land far away. He has arrived on the shores of Brineth to unseat our king and destroy the ways of old, bringing smoke and dust and death with him."

"I want to go. I want to fight."

"I know, Athias. But..." He sighed again.

"I'm not ready. I know." Athias finished the sentence. "Will you tell me when I am ready, Tutor Abbrath?"

"I will, child. I will."

Chapter Thirteen
Old Friends, Old Tales

Brineth is a beautiful land, yes, it is. I wonder, though, what the other isles around it are like. I wonder if I will ever see them, experience their land, their life. I should wish to, one day, at least. – Calitreum, Story of the Vayshanaa, Eifig's Entry, Page 451.

Athias jolted awake, bolting up. He was covered in furs and pelts, on a makeshift bed of stretched leather. A small fire crackled to his side and a boar was roasting above it. He heard muffled voices and then clear.

"He's awake."

He turned his head to see H'Khara and C'k'rian sitting next to two men, and a third sat to Athias' side, keeping watch. Around them were small trees and bushes, the soil was rich and warm.

"Calden." Athias smiled.

"Hello, old friend." One of the men by the fire stood up and walked to Athias. He was tall and lean with short hair; brown but with a red tint, he had a small beard which hid the sharp lines of his face. He lay a plate of meat on Athias' lap and stood tankard of ale beside him. "I'm sorry we were late; we saw the storm skies converging above you." He gestured to C'k'rian and H'Khara, Athias nodded to them and they smiled back.

H'Khara piped up, she had been sitting quietly until now, wrapped in pelts and blankets but still shivering.

"Are you okay? How are you feeling?"

"Hungry." Athias barely finished speaking before picking up the plate and tore off pieces of meat to eat.

"This brings me back, all of us I bet. A campfire, the travelling between locations, the terrible ale." One of the men laughed, looking repulsed by the swig he had just taken, his hair swayed though in a ponytail and he pulled a scarf down to reveal a stubble around sharp cheeks.

"Yep, and there it is the icy wind, right on schedule." Athias sat up further, a strong wind billowing around the small fortification of trees where their camp sat.

"What do you miss more? Fighting with the king or travelling with us?" The one to Athias' side spoke.

"Why travelling with you, of course, Calden."

"Like wise, my old friend." Calden patted Athias shoulder, keeping the rifle steady in his arms.

"Hold on, did you just say, 'the king'? You fought with the king?" H'Khara said in awe.

"I did, I fought by his side on multiple occasions. I was in his guard, a most unusual position for someone like me." His voice trailed off before snapping back. "Calden, Bejarn and Roran, these three, they were united by the war and they then, in turn, united with me."

"What do you three do now?" H'Khara asked. Behind her an ice-tipped wind billowed around them.

"We survive. We take recruits to Nhorrin Dam, a place of freedom for those who need it." Calden trailed off.

"Now we make a life for ourselves." Roran said, standing and taking more meat off the boar, handing it to H'Khara who was still shivering a little.

Roran had pale green eyes that shone bright against his fair skin and his face somewhat resembled that of a cat, rounded with a small nose. He was hunched now but when he stood, he was tall and proud, a strong man with a burly chest.

"How long was I out?" Athias asked, swivelling his feet around to the floor, it was comforting, feeling the soil under his toes.

"Three days. Gralnor has gone too, no doubt he'll be back though."

"That's longer than last time." Athias muttered.

"Every time you access Nhivilaurn's source, it takes a longer effect on you. That's what you told me all those years ago." Calden's voice was brittle, like the last frost before spring.

"I'm sorry" C'k'rian was bewildered, "did you say Nhivaliurn? The 'tree that gives the whole world life'?

"He did." Athias said to her. "The tree does more than give life and sustenance, it grants magical knowledge and power to those who seek it, those who study it."

"What you saw in the valley, that was Athias tapping into its source. It's Powerful magic. Dark magic." Roran spoke ominously while Athias faced his plate, purposely not looking anyone in the eye.

C'k'rian looked to everyone present in stunned confusion, concerned that this was clearly such a common topic.

"I… What?" She said, imploringly.

Athias did not speak while he finished his food. A stronger breeze swept in from the East behind them, the fire flickered and birds flew up from trees all around them. The hushed sound of voices flitted through the camp, dancing up and into the air over the fire.

Bejarn glanced to Roran and then to Calden,

"What is it?" C'k'rian murmured.

"Did you lay the dust around us?" Roran stammered to Bejarn.

Bejarn rummaged through his bag and drew a jar of bronze dust, his stature slumped a little.

"Oh, Mother." Roran spat. "Everyone, get up." His voice changed to a whisper as the sounds of moans carried over the wind. Long, eerie moans.

"What is it?" C'k'rian demanded again, her voice tipped with frustration as nobody would answer her.

"Etharans." Athias whispered, his pupils dilating as he spoke. He saw she still looked confused and this prompted his ushered response, "the souls of lovers, bound by magic upon their deaths. They are denied a place in the next realm but cannot be here in their physical state." He got to his feet, as did the rest of them, quietly.

"Come here, away from the fire; they can't be seen in the light. Stand together, facing outwards." Calden hissed.

They moved quietly, Calden poured water over the fire, making sure not to make a sound. Athias stood next to H'Khara and Calden, and they backed into a circle facing outwards. The moans suddenly stopped and were replaced by sinister shrieks and harrowing screams which echoed through the low trees. Between the screams was complete silence, not even the sound rustling leaves, no birds nor the swaying of branches in the wind.

"They're close. I can feel them." Calden said and raised his rifle up, scanning the shadowy tree line ahead with the scope. H'Khara and Roran knelt, ready to transform while the others drew their weapons and pointed them outwards.

As if transitioning through a veil, pale blue wisps appeared ahead of them all. Glimmering trails of smoke made up bodies with long, spindly fingers and necks. They floated forwards, their voices lost in shrieks and moans.

"Steady now… do not strike until I give the word." Calden spoke in a hushed tone, his voice barely heard over the sizzling fire.

The spirits gilded towards them; their hands outstretched.

"Easy… easy now." Calden said, his rifle still raised up.

Athias looked to them and then to Calden, and the others. He leaned out and slowly pressed Calden's rifle down.

"What are you doing?" He hissed.

"Look." He nodded ahead "Look at them." Athias' voice was peaceful, calm.

The Etharans glided forward, they lowered their hands as the group stowed their weapons and H'Khara, Roran stood up again. The Etharans drifted past them and all stopped in front of another, their sounds now a gentle lullaby. Athias' group moved back and sat down by the embers of the fire, each looking out towards the meeting now taking place. The spirits danced with each other, many came from the east and many came from the west, they met in the middle and paired, hand in hand.

"Look at them… they're so peaceful." H'Khara admired.

"I've never seen them that way." Calden sighed. "I've only ever experienced the damage they can do." He briefly touched his shoulder before slinging the rifle over it.

Athias buckled and fell to his knees again, panting. Calden and Bejarn raised him up and carried him to the stretcher, laying him on it.

"You need to rest." Bejarn insisted. "We found her, Athias. Rayna's at the dam but we can't go unless you rest." he whispered, hiding his words from the rest, while handing him a small vial which Athias sipped begrudgingly.

Athias closed his eyes, gulping too fast and the liquid scolded his throat, filling his mind with smells of lavender and spices, like the potions that helped him sleep as a boy. As he drifted off to sleep the others sat facing outwards, all looking on at the Varans as they swayed, dancing with their loved ones. All apart from Bejarn who lit a small lantern and hung it over a low branch, Calden then stood up, touching Bejarn and Roran as he passed to take watch again, looking out at the mountains and valleys where the small forest joined. Roran turned to H'Khara, he had noticed the collar marks on her neck when they had first arrived and found Athias collapsed, they had faded a little, but marks of the scars remained.

"You're a Coaran too, yes? I noticed the marks when you crouched with me. What animal are you, and what echelon are you?" He was curious and spoke in a quiet, comforting voice.

"I'm a third, my animal is the wolf. I've been drawn to dogs from a young age, I discovered my abilities when I was three, playing with the family hound and I saw everything, smelt everything, felt everything from its perspective. It was surreal." She looked bashful. "Sorry, I'm rambling."

"Not at all. Those two are the greatest brothers in the world, I wouldn't want to be out here with anyone else but… but they don't understand it for, how could they? You do understand." He moved closer and put his hand on hers while they sat. She hadn't noticed his strong jawline before, for it had been hidden by his long, brown hair. "I'm a second and my animal is a bronze cat." She looked puzzled, "They're indigenous to the small peaks of the north, as tall as a horse. He made great gestures with his hands, before setting them down and she moved hers under his again.

C'k'rian looked over to see H'Khara and Roran sharing a pelt. She stood up and walked quietly over to Calden who was still taking his turn on watch. Before she reached him, he slid to the side on the fallen tree where he sat and slid his pack off, gesturing to where it had been for her to sit. She jumped up and sat on the tree with him, they both paused and stared out over the valley ahead, the twin moons bathing it in pale, ghostly light.

"Do you know what happened to Icaria?" She pondered, wondering if he knew of the lair and its fall.

"We do. Athias sent word." He turned to her, his rifle still resting on his lap. "You know Athias well too, I can tell. How has he been these last few days? The magic of Nhivilaurn has a grip on him, and it claws deep the more he uses it."

"He's secretive, you know?" She looked to him, sleeping, and Calden nodded. "It is hard to know how he is, but he is determined, as much as he was before… you know."

"A pain he will carry with him always."

C'k'rian looked over to Bejarn as he sat up against a tree, sharpening a small knife. She noticed a horse on string around his neck.

"The horse?"

"Made for his husband, the day he died." He saw her expressions drop. "Bejarn is as kind a soul as one could ever meet. He used to navigate the harshest seas and the most hostile rivers, always choosing to save lives rather than take them. As the fighting got thicker and Ziath began to take more and more, Bejarn took to the Veins, sheltering refugees from one end to the other, his husband and their daughter too. One day… an ambush… he escaped but narrowly and his family did not." Calden's voice trembled, with anger or sadness, C'k'rian was unsure.

"What's your story?" She asked hesitantly, wary after hearing about Bejarn.

Calden sat up straight and peered into the moonlit valley.

"Roran lost a village of people he cared for. Bejarn lost his family. I was a soldier, a spy. An assassin for the Emperor. Would you believe that, to start with, the Emperor seemed like a good man, we were led to believe that this world was full of evil, that magic lingered here, and it was dark. He told us we would be liberators, saving lives of those afflicted. Before long though I saw it was a twisted conquest we were on, not against. I was drafted into the shadow guard; master assassins sent out to destabilise and destroy. I would not take the lives of a farmer; he would not send Ziath seed, and this was punishable by death. After that day I branded myself a traitor and deserter and left. I was picked up by Bejarn while travelling as far away from the war as I could and shortly after, we found Roran. We've been together ever since."

"You did the right thing." She said, quietly.

"Not soon enough. I should have left as soon as I arrived."

"Arrived? You're not from Brineth?"

"No, of course not." Calden was surprised. "The Emperor and his armies came from far, far away. Across the Eastern sea and beyond that.

Our world was dying, something of Ziath's doing with his living beasts of smoke, poisoning the water and the soil."

"Sorry, I just presumed… You know the world so well. I often forgot that many are not from here" C'k'rian clutched at the letter Tristan had given her, deep in her pocket.

"We three have travelled the world all over. As far north-east as to have seen a dragon as close to me as you are now, as far South-West to have met the Cacaru Tribe. This world is beautiful. Athias is bold to think he can unite the old kingdoms but a fool to think it will work."

"It might."

"Yes, it might, but I've seen the Emperor's armies first-hand. They're on a scale unlike anything else, and if he succeeds in his plans…" He stopped suddenly, as though he had said too much.

"His plans? What are his plans?" C'k'rian spoke sharply, sitting bolt upright.

Calden sighed, knowing he had said too much.

"Athias told us not to tell but you're going to find out anyway." He brought out a piece of bread-cake from his pocket and snapped it, offering her half to which she accepted. "One of my missions as an assassin was to pay a visit to a student of science. He wanted to know if it would be possible to harvest the rare crystals found here and use them to make a device, a device that brought death faster than any man ever could. Athias sent word in the letter he sent that he and a party at Icaria had found plans for the Emperor to build something… Something terrible."

"You think it could be this 'device'?"

"I do."

"Tell me. How many have you killed? How many in your service and after?"

"At least a hundred." He said, calmly.

"And this 'killing machine', how many people would it be able to kill?"

"More than that. In a matter of minutes."

C'k'rian shuddered, looking to them all. A mixed group of soldiers and creatures, all joined through the enchanted sword that sat in its sheath by the tree where Athias lay.

"Do you know of his life before the war? Of the sword that he carries close at all times."

Calden smiled and sighed,

"I don't think anyone knows much of him, nobody but Rayna." C'k'rian looked stunned at the mention of the name, "Ah yes... I know of Rayna. Anyway, you should get some rest, we leave at sunrise."

C'k'rian sighed and stepped down off the log once more, she returned to the others and swept up a pelt. The night was cold now in the absence of a fire, she sat up the pelt and pulled another from the now small pile, she tucked it under her legs and lay down, facing Bejarn as he slept, hat over face, under the lantern's yellow light.

Athias felt his mind wander in his sleep, linking with Gralnor who flew high above a cold, stone tower. Slabs of grey glistened with rain as it drifted down from the sky. Gralnor landed on a balcony, peering inside to see a man towering over a table, examining a map while a woman poured a cup of fine wine at the mantelpiece of a great hearth. Ziath was lean but muscular with broad shoulders. The hair on his head was black with tints of grey, his jaw was sharp as though it had been carved from marble and he had thin, dark lips. His ears were pointed, and his dark blue eyes were stippled with shards of grey. His cloak was a deep red and his brown, leather armour gleamed in the light of the fire to his right.

"What would you like to do, Lady Migra? On this wonderful night?" Ziath spoke to the lady ahead of him, looking up from his map to gazer longingly at her.

The lady was barely twenty years old with a sleek, thin figure and golden hair. She was wearing a low-cut silk dress that draped over her shoulder and clung to her hips and thighs.

"Take me to see them. The great beasts." Her sharp tone was tipped with ice.

Emperor Ziath and Lady Migra made their way down to the cells that the lay in the dungeon beneath the palace. Gralnor followed, fluttering down, and peering in through a grate. The cells were filled with coughing and moans, an armed soldier was standing at every cage, a black cloth over their mouth. As Ziath entered the first corridor the guards stood to attention and saluted, relaxing as he waved his hand. He took Migra by the hand and slowly walked towards the cages. She looked in at them all, an expression of pleasure on her face, much as a child would have after been given a new doll, those inside were tightly packed together, with as many as six sharing each bunk.

"What are these for?" She held out her paper fan and pointed towards the collars around the necks of some of the people in the cages.

"Ah, yes. A design of my own. The collar stops the creatures from transforming or using their wretched disease. We take them off only when they are in arena."

"You must let me watch a fight! When is the next one?"

"Tomorrow morning, my dear. You shall share my box." He pulled her to him, and they kissed.

"Maybe you could get me... a collar." She whispered into his ear, gently licking down his face and biting her lip. He grinned and continued the walk down past the cages.

"That could certainly be arranged." He pulled on her hair a little and dragged his nails over her shoulder.

A group of guards were playing cards and roasting a small duck at their station, opposite was a group of small children inside a cage. Their beds were nothing more than slabs of stone, they were each chained to the wall and shared a bucket for the toilet. A bowl of sloppy stew was on the floor, two of the children had marks of it around their mouths and on their hands.

"Disgusting." Ziath said, the guards laughed and wafted the smell of roasting bird towards the cage and banging their hands on the table. He drew a thin blade from his sleeve and sawed-off tiny piece of meat, he threw it into the cage and the four children pounced upon it. They clawed and bit each other, trying to get to the meat. He turned to face the guards and Migra, laughing and pulled his pistol, firing it into the cage. The dull thud of a slumping body echoed through the cells.

"Shall we?" Lady Migra beckoned to him and they continued down the corridor, the guards continued to laugh as they walked away.

"It's getting late, dear. Take me back to your chambers?" Lady Migra requested.

"Certainly. My lady." He bowed to her, smiling. He slipped up a collar from the guard station as they left and stowed it away in his cloak.

Gralnor perched once more, this time atop a gargoyle outside of the emperor's chambers, peering in, Athias watched.

Ziath's chambers were ghastly. Only a dozen candles stood lit, casting a dim light while creepy shadows beckoned from the corners. Enormous chairs, accompanied by a table topped with fine wines stood facing a four-poster bed with red and black curtains, covered in pelts and thin sheets. Lady Migra poured two glasses of wine as Ziath lit a fire in the hearth. She beckoned to him and, as he drew close, pushed him down into one of the chairs after taking his cloak, shoulder, and chest armour off. She handed him the glass of wine while drinking her own, downing it in one. Ziath placed the collar on the table with the wines and her eyes lit up, she slipped her coat off and it fell, slowly, behind her. She let her dress down and stepped over it, walking slowly towards the bed. Ziath's eyes were stuck to her hips and he took off his clothes, following with the collar. She was waiting for him, bending over the bed and he approached, placing the thick, iron collar around her neck and closing it. He grabbed a bunch of her golden hair and pulled it back and she moaned a little, he then stood directly behind her and gently bit down over her spine. Migra gripped his strong thighs as he pushed her down harder before climbing onto the bed and pulling her on top, she straddled him, and he raised his hands to her face, and she moaned. She pushed his hands down either side of his head and arched her back.

"Oh yes." He spoke with a trembling voice.

She bit his hands and pushed them down again beside his head before reaching under the pillow. The knife narrowly missed Ziath's face, slicing his cheek. In a split second, Ziath pushed her off him and punched her in the face. Ziath stood and dragged her from the bed, she cradled her nose while swiping left and right with the blade, frantically trying to fend him off and as he dragged her towards the fire, she sank the blade into his thigh. He howled and threw her across the room, marching to and standing over her. He tightened his grip around her wrists and snapped the bones under his muscular hands. The knife fell with a clang as she cried and he kicked her, sliding the knife away under his foot. She coughed blood, her jaw fractured, warm liquid dripping into her throat. He wiped the blood from his thigh and pressed the burning fireiron to it, wincing as he wound closed. He wrapped a robe around himself and proceeded to the door, outside two guards were standing, rifles at the ready.

"Fetch the Caedras, tell them to clean this up." He opened the door slightly so they could see the carnage that lay inside. They bowed and nodded before hurriedly leaving.

Ziath pulled a hooked spear from the wall and marched over to Migra, who looked up to him, trying to speak but barely managing a drool. Ziath stood over her and plunged the spear into her chest, pulling down on the handle and ripping her body in two. The Caedras arrived minutes later, they were healers and professors, they dealt with all the problems within the Palace. They wore black cloaks and robes; their faces were covered completely bar their eyes and they wore thick leather gloves, while their bags were filled with potions and tools.

"Would his majesty like me to look at that wound?" One of the Caedras said to Ziath as he sat on the edge of the bed and observed their efforts to clean up the blood from the walls and floor. The body had been taken away moments before, it was to be food for the hounds. Ziath was off somewhere else, planning and plotting. The Caedra coughed, getting his attention which brought him back to the room,

"What? Oh, yes go on then. Pour me some wine too."

"Certainly, your majesty." He poured a cup of wine and brought his bag to the bed which he unzipped and pulled a magnifying glass from, a pair of tweezers, a candle, and a small metal dish.

Ziath sipped on the wine as the Caedra lit the candle and examined the wound closely, peering at it from many angles in the light.

"Your majesty closed the wound, but a thin stretch of blade remains in the leg. I need to remove it…" He stammered.

"Well get on with it then. I haven't got all night." Ziath growled.

"Yes, your majesty. Of course." He squeaked, frightened of the towering man before him.

The Caedra picked open the wound with the tweezers and found the shard of metal. Ziath held out his hand and the Caedra dropped the metal in it. He patched up the wound with the wax from the candle and stitches before leaving, while the other of his order still frantically scrubbed at the bloody slabs. Ziath stood up and left the chambers, his guards outside had doubled in number and stood to attention, saluting as they had before.

"Your majesty. General Nirvo wishes to see you." One bowed as he spoke.

The general stood as Ziath entered the room; a circular council room, with eight chairs and eight windows behind them. He approached Ziath and shook his hand.

"Your majesty! What of your leg?" His voice was bold and thick.

"The Syndicate send assassins to lay with me. It is truly a desperate act for them."

"Your military might has driven them all but underground, now they work the coward's thread!"

"Very well spoken, General." Ziath smiled. "So, what can I do for my finest warlord?"

"It is what I can do for you. Our spies have learned of a hidden crown, an ancient artefact of vast power, and a Vayshanaa too." He paused, unsure of how to press on, "Another thing, great leader, is the northern realms are unruly, they are uniting, uprising almost."

Ziath began to pace around the room, his face deep in thought.

"Send your finest cloaks." Ziath muttered, "Arhn and his brother, tell them to hunt him down and kill this sorcerer. The others in his party too, for I assume he does not travel alone." A nod from the general confirmed the guess. "We will send troops to this unruly north. We will crush them, burn them." Ziath's face lit up with malice, the flames of candles dancing in the dark canvas of his eyes.

"Where are we marching to, great Emperor?"

"We will take the brigades to Nhorrin Dam and press forward. Send word to General Vorskar, tell him to accompany his company to Scaran."

"Certainly, your most humble of majesties."

"We will leave at sunrise. Prepare your legions."

The general saluted and bowed, marching from the room. Gralnor jumped from the windowsill and up into the cold air, rising higher with every beat of his wings, he soared into the clouds and became lost in the thunderous grey.

Chapter Fourteen
The Drowned

Some magic is still relatively unknown, even to those who have studied it for eons. I do not think anyone will ever know the full extent of its power, its reach. I do know, however, that even those who practice it, are perhaps even more afflicted by curses. – Calitreum, The Fundamentals of Magic, Page 626.

Athias awoke with a jolt as a gunshot cracked over the peaceful morning, the sun was rising, and a flutter of birds flew overhead.

"Sorry!" He heard Calden's voice.

The rest were already up and packing away their belongings, chatting to each other. Swivelling around, he hoisted himself up against a tree, gripping the rigid bark for balance

"You alright?" Bejarn asked, gently.

"I'm fine, just need a minute."

"Alright, I'll carry you if you want. It'll be like old times." He chuckled.

Athias took a sip of water and pulled an orange stick from his bag, he snapped off a quarter and ate it, putting the rest back into his bag.

"You don't have to eat that, you know? We still have boar from last night."

"Vakra is fine, thank you though."

"Suit yourself."

"Where's H'Khara? Roran?"

"They'll be back any moment now, Roran took her to get clean water. You'll be thankful for the next leg; we won't come close to another source for a few days." Calden said, entering the clearing, a winged rabbit dragging behind him, he began cutting the wings off and stowing them in his satchel.

Roran and H'Khara emerged through the treeline carrying several deer-hide flasks, the occasional drop of water leaking from each. The six of them took a flask and stowed it away in their bags. Athias stretched as he stood upright, and strapped Spectre to his back. Calden bolted the bayonet back onto the rifle and flung it over his shoulder while the rest collected their belongings and Bejarn scooped leaves and mud over the fire. The company head off, out of the forest and into the valley ahead. The journey north would be long and dangerous towards the Veins. Once plentiful trading routes, the rivers were now mostly deserted, and Bejarn's ship, the Drake, was anchored only a day's march from their current location.

"How far is the dam?" H'Khara inquired to Bejarn.

"About two hundred miles by sea." He chatted back. "There's enough tar on board to fuel it for most of that."

Athias and Calden helmed the company, striding with purpose at the front, away from the others. Calden was drilling holes in a small piece of wood as they walked, looking up from it occasionally as they changed direction a bit or to Athias when they talked.

"Have you thought about what you'll say to her? Rayna, I mean, providing she hasn't moved on by the time we arrive."

Athias looked to the flute that was taking shape in his hands and back to his own, they bore scars of old, some from blades in battle and some from creatures. He thought back to when he last saw Rayna, her eyes bright while the rest a shadow.

"Nine years. I don't know what I'll say, not entirely anyway."

"I'm sure it'll be as mysterious as ever." Calden quipped, smiling.

The landscape was rocky and harsh, long grass, some up to their shoulders, covered the hills for miles while jagged rocks and huge boulders were scattered across it all. As the hours went by, their steps were caught by the sun, casting a peaceful gaze over the hills ahead and small creatures such as hares and foxes bounded through the grass, and birds fluttered overhead. A light breeze brushed over their skin and the grass swayed.

"It's beautiful here." C'k'rian said in awe, looking around her.

"Beautiful and yet, treacherous to those who mistake it. If we respect it, it will see is through." Roran pronounced to which Calden, Bejarn, and Athias all nodded in unison.

"I heard stories of Nhorrin Dam back in Acre Farm. Is it as large as they say?"

"It is as much a city as it is a dam. Miles across, almost a mile tall." Roran fed H'Khara's imagination and watched as her eyes lit up with every passing word. "We will restock there; it will be safe for now."

"Is it not under imperial reign?"

"It is not." Athias chipped in, the group walking close together now as they trailed through the tall grass. "As far as we are aware, the tyrant, for all his resources is unaware of the Syndicate's influence there. It's not unruly and he gets a sizable donation to his taxes. All in the effort of keeping him at bay, though, I am unsure of how long this will last."

"War *is* inevitable." Calden nodded in agreement. "The war to determine if we, those who resist, can survive."

The group journeyed all day through the grass and over the rocks, they traversed ravines and rivers, and crept through troll nests quietly. It was tiring work, but they made it to the Drake by sunset, an old imperial vessel, moored carefully in a cavern. Bejarn and Calden entered the cavern, and shortly after, the bow of the ship appeared slowly, while Calden teetered on the loose rocky path, stopping to secure the creaking bridge to the ship and bringing it in when they all had boarded.

"Imperial ships have less hassle here. In fact, the biggest worry is if you fall overboard." Pointing as he spoke to the waters, a murky green. "Snakes live in these waters large enough to swallow a bear whole, so be careful."

Two small guns sat either side of the paddle wheels that splashed with a soothing sound, propelling them steadily through the murky waters as a thin mist rolled across it.

"There's a few rooms in down below. Nothing exotic but with fresh water and beds, so they'll do. You'll each find a uniform on the bed or in the wardrobe of the room, put them on. If we are stopped for any reason, our story is that we're a trawler, heading to the dam to deliver much needed building equipment before returning south. Understood?" Bejarn spoke with a stern authority, a side that Athias had almost forgotten he had.

Everyone nodded and went below to claim ownership to a room. Bejarn turned and head down into the engine room where he began shovelling crystals of tar and throwing timber into the engine, which already roared with fire. The ship started to move, slowly, it edged away from the shore and out, into the current of the river. Downstairs in the rooms the company had begun to make themselves comfortable, they would be aboard the ship for at least one night, maybe two and Bejarn was right, the rooms weren't anything to get excited but they had featherbeds, a basin, and table, more than most were used to. Fresh air soared in from a small open window above the bed, and from the ceiling hung a lantern, lit by candles, which bathed the cabin in a dim light. Athias had changed into the uniform he had found on the bed, the breeches and shirt were uncomfortable at best; they were itchy and cheap, the fabric irritated his skin. The boots and the jacket were tight, and Athias played with the straps and buttons to try and make it fit better. If it meant they arrived at the dam in good shape, then it was a price he was happy to pay. He had stowed Spectre along with his bag under the bed and hung his cloak over the chair and left to go next door. H'Khara was inside and she too had put on the uniform. She was rolling the sleeves back a little to reveal it fit her better than him, but she looked down at the bold red and dull cloth in disgust.

"It'll only be for a few days, at the most."

"I know." She smiled, "It's okay, never thought I'd be wearing one of *their* uniforms is all."

Calden was making rounds too, checking that everyone had found a room and settled in. He spotted Athias doing the same and approached.

"You should get some rest, Athias. Rorarn and I will help Bejarn with the ship through the night. There's not much, respectively, you can do."

Athias returned to his room and sat up on the bed, pulling the covers over himself. It was much colder on the Veins, with no hills or rocky formation to stop the chilling wind. Steam was towering out of the chimney at the back of the boat as Calden worked at an incredible pace, joined now by Roran and they both took turns to shovel mounds of tar-crystals into the billowing fire which licked the shovels as it fed the flames. Bejarn stood at the helm, rain pouring from the skies, cold water splashing over his face and hands as he gripped the wheel, and it trickled down his sleeves.

Athias closed his eyes and drifted off into sleep where he dreamt of a young boy, running through the reeds, he smeared water over his dark skin which reflected the bright light from the sun. Athias walked behind the boy, watching over from above. The day was hot with not a cloud in sight, the boy ran and jumped and picked handfuls of river-flowers before scattering them in the warm air. A woman sat ahead, and he could not see her face, but she had a willowy figure under her leather cloak and hood, with mud specked boots and trousers. They were just out of reach of him, the boy was running and Athias tried to run faster, trying to reach him, but they remained just behind his fingers. He was crying now; the boy and he lay in the woman's arms who was clutching her own face. There was screaming and the sun had been replaced by the moons which glared down, side by side. Athias looked down to his own hands and they were burning, while a harrowing scream seared the air and singed his ears. The mud where he stood began to flood with red and he looked up to the boy and the woman, slowly, as though his head was heavy. Athias awoke with a bolt, he was laying on the floor and covered in a thick, cold sweat.

Peering through the window he saw nothing but mist, still, as it lay across the river. He could hear a gentle lullaby, soft voiced and melodic. Up on the main deck, he was met by Calden and Roran who were standing at the top of the stairs, looking to the side where Bejarn was staring out into the mist, listening to the song.

"There's someone here for you, Athias." Calden spoke as Athias approached, turning to reveal Gralnor on the side of the ship.

Athias smiled, holding out his arm and the bird hopped onto it and scampered up to Athias' shoulder where he cawed and sat.

"How long have we been sailing?" Athias asked, quietly, feeding Gralnor a pinch of seeds from his pocket.

"Almost six hours, we're well underway." Calden replied in the same manner. Both of Calden and Roran had dirty faces, they had smeared the soot and chalk on their faces as they had tried to clean it. Glancing to him, they saw his own sweat covered face, "the nightmares again?"

Athias nodded,

"They've been happening more frequently in recent weeks."

"On this river they will be more vivid, they will seem real, you will feel stronger emotions. Those who have lost will see their loved and hear their loved. You can hear the music, yes? The voices as they sing?"

"I can."

"The Drowned. Souls of loved ones who died upon this water, they now live as their purest selves, laying across the depths and singing to those they miss. Their music awakens the deepest memories."

"Is he alright?" Athias nodded at Bejarn who was staring into the water as they glided over it, his eyes transfixed on the ripples.

"No. Not really. He'll be able to see them as clear as you can see me now, as clear as the night he lost them. He'll be able to touch them, they will appear real to him, but we are here to make sure he does not follow them."

Bejarn stood as still as a statue, his eyes transfixed upon something in front of him. He held out his hand and turned it over, so its palm was up. He flexed his fingers and tears gushed from his eyes. They fell into the water and onto the side of the ship.

"I love you" Athias heard him whisper.

The Drowned sung their choir of gentle melody. The music found its way into Athias' mind, his heart sunk, while his eyes brimmed with tears. Suddenly Bejarn climbed onto the side of the ship and held his arms out, appearing to hold something, flexing his fingers as though entwined in someone else's.

"No!" Calden shouted and darted forward, tackling Bejarn to the floor. "Athias, fetch some water from the helm!" He pointed to the raised deck. Roran reached into his coat and pulled out a small bag, from inside he bought a small pot of shining powder, and he tipped it into the water, mixing vigorously. They handed it to Bejarn and encouraged his sips until it had all but gone and Roran lay his head down onto the ship's decking, while Calden fetched a blanket and coat, which he lay under Bejarn's head.

"The drink will take effect in a few minutes. It calms him, suppresses the memories temporarily but they will return in a few days." Roran said, looking to Athias who stood over them, looking down at Bejarn. "I'll take the wheel for a while, let him rest." Calden sat with Bejarn, pressing a small cloth to his forehead every so often.

The next day passed slowly as they journeyed up the Veins. Bejarn sunk back into his normal, chipper self, although weary as he steered them around the shallow waters and rocky shores. Progress was slow even with the paddles that scooped through the water. They caught glimpses of other ships from their lanterns, and harbour towns along the stony shore but the mist was thick, shielding them and the rest around them, it rolled down onto the river off the mountains to the East and carpeted the land for miles at a time. Their breath scratched their lungs as they inhaled large gulps of icy air, the ship's deck frosted over, and ice seeped into the cabins through the windows. The company took turns around steam heaters while wrapped in blankets, and at night, they huddled together in the same room, one person warming the covers and pelts every few hours before swapping with another. It would not be long now until they reached the dam and they were all in longing need of it.

"Last time we were here it was the dawn of Autumn, and I thought that was cold… but I would gladly go back to those times." Bejarn's teeth chattered while at the wheel, his skin was icy white.

"It's not even that bad, really." Roran jested, shivering a little.

"Not for you, man-cat. Some of us didn't choose to live in the mountains for all our lives."

"Maybe not, but here we are, in the cold. I am fine and you are not." He smiled to H'Khara who sat opposite him while they all played cards steam heater, the warm cards were pleasant in their hands. "I'd say my lifestyle choice has one-upped yours."

"I'd say you're not wrong. Anyone for some caher?" H'Khara, Roran, and C'k'rian raised their hands and Bejarn stood up and left the room for a few minutes before returning with a tray of steaming, fruity wine, "fresh brewed this evening."

"I'll take one to Calden." C'k'rian said, throwing her cards into the pile in the middle, "wasn't my game anyway."

She took her cup and filled up another, heading above deck. Calden was draped in blankets and wore thick, fur-lined gloves, while at his shift on the wheel. A slight roof stood above the wheel, protecting those who stood there from any rain falling directly down, and a small heater stood in the corner, powered by coal just like the engine.

"How are you doing?" C'k'rian could already see the answer across his blue cheeks.

"Oh, you know… surviving."

"Got you some wine." She raised the cup and placed on the rail next to him.

"Ah, Bejarn's caher wine. Hopefully, it's better than the last batch." He smiled, the fruity smell tempting him, "you not bothered by the cold?" Calden nodded to C'k'rian's blue skin, barely showing any signs of frost.

"When you spend most of your early life beneath the surface of icy cold water, the other cold places of the world barely bother you."

Calden nodded his head, shrugging as the thoughts added up.

"There are only two seasons where I am from, neither of which are particularly cold." He took his hands from the wheel and picked up the cup, smelling the fruity, spiced liquid.

"Can you tell me a bit about it?" C'k'rian was curious, she had always longed to learn of the world, for it surely could not just be Brineth where life did indeed, live.

Calden sipped the ale, it was fruity, and the spices filled his nose and throat, warming it.

"I am from a series of small islands, known to our people as Narthyin. It was beautiful, once. Warm sun swept over the land every day from morning's first light to night's shadow. It was a sandy place, for the most part, with pockets of grassy mountains and lush, tumbling waterfalls. The population was small, maybe a few thousand in total and we lived happily there before it changed, before *he* changed." He took a large gulp of the warm wine.

"Who?" C'k'rian asked, intrigued.

"He was a good man once. A kind man, as hard as that is to believe now. A long, long time ago." Calden dodged answering the question outright but C'k'rian had figured out who Calden had meant and she looked at him with glowering eyes.

"I don't believe you. The tyrant that rules this land?"

Calden pressed on, unhindered by her stare.

"I met him once. I was fourteen years old and training to join his army. My father was sick, and old, but he bought me to the capital. A beautiful place it was, I remember the sweeping marble homes that spread for miles and the golden statues, eyes bright as gems. As I was training to join the military, my father could stay in the barrack homes, and here he was treated for his illness; an unfortunate case of lung poison, which got worse with age." Calden gulped down more of the wine, he felt the warm spices warm his whole body, "a few days into our stay, my father's illness worsened, and he fell, right in the street. New spread to Ziath's aid, who was nearby and Ziath himself brought my father to his own palace hospital to treat him. Ziath operated on my father, and saved him, giving him a few more years to live with his son before he died peacefully."

C'k'rian stared blankly into his eyes, taking occasional sips from her cup. She opened her mouth but closed it, unsure what to say, but her eyes no longer burned at him.

"It never gets old."

"What doesn't?" C'k'rian received no answer but followed Calden's eyes forward and up.

She turned and the cup slipped from her hands as her eyes met with what stood before them. Out of the mist, the looming towers of Nhorrin Dam stood.

Chapter Fifteen
Nhorrin Dam

What a place, where chaos and peace find space together on their own dance floor. Nhorrin Dam is a home, and the beings that gather there, live there, they are its blood. – Calitreum, History of Old, Page 281.

Seven monstrous towers loomed out of the mist, atop a gigantic wall which stretched to block the whole of the river's width: miles across. Each of the towers were large enough to house a thousand souls at least, they stood, immense monoliths of stone, connected by dozens of bridges and ropes on smaller towers that sprouted off from their larger kin. The top of the wall, where the towers stood, was almost fifty metres from the water's level, and then descended into the stretching city below, reaching as far down as nearly ten times that. Nhorrin City sat at the base of the wall, a sprawling mass of makeshift buildings, stacked atop one another. The city was a labyrinth of scaffolding which enslaved the city; buildings and towers, balanced precariously over ledges and on rocks, were masked by it and lost to it. Cranes made of hastily fastened wood, strung by ropes and wires, were dotted throughout the city and added to the forest of architectural nightmares. The Drake approached the great stone towers and the wall ahead, reducing speed. The group of them stood atop the deck now, back in their old clothes. Athias watched as H'Khara approached the side of the ship, staring up at the structure approaching.

"Jarn Nhorrin began work on the dam almost four-hundred years ago. He and a company of adventurers decided to map this great, beautiful world. They created a small home atop the great falls that this once was." Athias gestured his hand, pointing to the dam as it stood, now tall and vast, water cascading through the filter systems. "Jarn Nhorrin said that they should build a dam across the falls to control the amount of water that fell, and therefore make the land around it safer. They stripped their ships bare and used them to begin the dam's wall. The mast pole and flag still stand at the top, embedded in the stone, as they have been all these years."

H'Khara barely said a word, she just gasped, her eyes transfixed upon the growing shadow that approached.

"Maybe we'll even meet the Lady of the Mist." Calden approached from behind, to H'Khara's other side, and her head turned away from the dam, a look of awe across her face.

Athias pulled a coin from his pocket. It wasn't a normal coin, and nothing could be bought with it. It was bronze and flat but engraved with symbols; old runes perhaps, H'Khara thought to herself.

"The Lady of the Mist. A title given to her by the souls in this land, for if you're lucky enough to tell the tale of her deeds, it will be a silhouette you have gazed upon. A shadow in the mist. It is her and her rangers, known as 'Shadows', that keep this land safe. They patrol and guard, and fight injustice."

"Amazing..." H'Khara muttered. "Do you think we'll see her while here?"

"Some know how to find her, some do not. Many say that she is but a myth, while others swear by her as law in these lands." He flipped the coin up and H'Khara caught it, turning it over to reveal an image that seemingly danced upon the metal, an arrow slung from its bow.

Bejarn's signals were matched and the checkpoint gate opened. The checkpoint was merely a singular tower and wooden wall, sitting a few ship lengths from the dam. The checkpoint was as much for approaching ships as it was for stopping creatures of the river from entering the dam's filtration system, an act which would spell their end. The Drake slowed, its engine extinguished, and it glided forward through the checkpoint gate. Once the Drake had been moored, the company travelled in land, following the wooden path towards the wall. At the wall, they were directed to the lifts that took workers up and down from the city and back, and as the lift doors shut and the gatekeepers began winching it down they stood for a moment, looking out into the stretching city.

They surveyed the landscape ahead and looked in awe at the shapes below, as though every building in the city had been constructed from a different idea of what a building should look like. The hulls of ships, mast poles, sails, and cannons had been hurriedly cemented and tied down to form shapes, and the ships had been stripped bare to create homes and workshops of varying craft, while make-do streets; bridges and pathways of stone and rope connected them all. At the bottom of the cliff they were greeted by a handful of construction workers led by a woman, she wore a rusty chest plate and shoulder armour. She held out her hand to which Athias shook,

"Welcome to the dam, my name is Licara. Have you been to the dam before?"

"I'm Athias, this is H'Khara, C'k'rian, Roran, Bejarn, Calden." He bowed slightly and pointed to the group one at a time, "Some of us have been here before, and some not. Which is the best inn that you would recommend, it's been sometime since I have been here, and I'm sure a lot has changed."

"Ha, I'm sure it has." She smiled and chuckled, "Things change here every day. The Waters of Warr is the best, although many will argue it's not. If you're looking for work while you're here, towers one and three are looking for webbers." Licara smiled, nodding to the towers on the wall.

"Thank you." Athias nodded and the builders departed.

"What's a webber?" C'k'rian pondered, looking to the group.

"A webber oversees construction of a particular sector" Roran replied, "there's three hundred and eighty-two sections of the dam and each webber oversees from as little as ten workers to as many as fifty. You gotta be a good person to be a webber; calm and collected but morally strong enough to do and say the right thing; keeping your workers motivated, being fair and strict. It's not for everyone."

"You seem very well informed?" She enquired.

"Roran spent a year on the dam's construction teams before I met him. We met here, after all, all those years ago." Bejarn chipped in from behind them.

"How long has it been under construction, how long exactly?"

"Nobody knows for sure but well over three hundred years. There are documents here signed by the Old King's great grandfather, who visited shortly after its construction."

The group proceeded into the city. The city was a cauldron of salt-water fumes and fantastical smells of bread, honey, and meat. Tastes lingered on the tip of their tongues as they passed by market stalls and workshops alike, while children ran through the jungle of hanging, writhing ropes and across the perilous thin-wooden bridges. They jumped and bounced through, while adults went about business beneath them in the markets, selling and trading, bartering and buying. It was poetic and yet, chaotic, in the same fantastic breath. The people seemed free here, they danced with every step, nobody was afraid here; not the vadoran playing a game of Prison with his friends under the market stall drapes; not the trinata selling spices and bread from his stall, his scales glinting in the white sunlight; not the haerie as she flexed her glimmering wings; not the Coaran who transformed back to a young girl, while others clapped.

"It's beautiful…" H'Khara whispered while grinning. A child ran to her and planted a flower in her hair before running off with his friends again.

"It is. It's home to all who need a new one." Athias replied, he smiled at people as he passed and they were offered plates of bread and salt, cups of wine, and rolls of cloth.

C'k'rian stopped as tiny droplets of water splashed onto her cheeks. She tilted her head to stare up and above her was a towering maze of fabric-lined homes, the hulls of ships with rope traipsing across, pipes and valves criss-crossed around the cranes, while bridges and mills' water-wheels wound down into the ponds around them and up, overhead journeying to the rivers behind the city.

"H'Khara?!" A voice of surprise billowed over the crowd who went on with their lives as if nothing had happened.

The group stopped and turned to see a woman run and tackle H'Khara who fell back into a pile of cloth. Athias and Roran went to draw their weapons but H'Khara raised her hands up to them,

"Wait! It's okay!" H'Khara hugged the woman tightly who kissed her cheek. "Everyone… This is Gh'ael. She was with me at Acre Farm."

Gh'ael had long golden-brown hair and sky-blue eyes. She had a slender build with curved shoulders and hips, she wore a loose shirt, but her trousers clung to her and she had fair skin with a light purple tint.

"I thought I would never see you again! Once you escaped, they sent the Corrin Brothers after you!" The woman said to H'Khara, her eyes brimmed with tears. "How did you survive? The brothers never returned."

"Athias saved me" H'Khara gestured to him and he bowed his head, "he killed the brothers and travelled with me here. Who else made it out?"

"From Acre Farm? Haven't you heard?" She turned and whistled sharply. Shortly afterwards, a dozen figures ran forward. They came, more and more of them, men and women, boys and girls, all sizes, ages, colours.

"A group of soldiers attacked the camp, they had rifles and so we thought maybe they were other imperial soldiers, but they flew the banner of the raven. They freed us and accompanied us here."

"Athias, others, meet my family" H'Khara gestured to the coarans that stood around her now.

There were several handshakes and greetings of the group, while H'Khara beamed with joy at being reunited, and in the company of great beings. She turned, but hesitantly, looking back to Athias who nodded.

"Go, be with your family. I will find you later." He turned his head and whispered to Gralnor who woke from sleep atop Athias' bag and, stretching his wings, jumped into the air to keep watch from above.

"Come on, let us go find the Waters of Warr." C'k'rian addressed the group and they pressed on into the bustling noise around them.

The Water of Warr was a magnificent spectacle. It was primarily made of parts of the Warr, an old vessel named after the town it was built in. The flipped hull topped the rough foundation to make a ceiling while various windows had been roughly slotted into whatever spaces were available. Timber beams held together with paste and plenty of nails stood as walls, rough and uneven, while odd parts of the mostly rectangular building stuck out at hazardous angles. Ropes and tubes ran the length of the roof and down, round the inn, into the ground or out across it. Across the top of the hull though ran a torrent of water, it cascaded over one end to create a waterfall and pond where horses and people alike drank from and many, coloured buckets on a rope pulley dipped into the water, and out again, before being taken all over the city. A small river ran around the inn, the only access was across a thin bridge, lowered from the other side to where they were. A tall, thin man dressed in a long purple cloak, with a long white beard and pale, wrinkly skin sat on an upturned bucket next to an old well outside of the door. Tied to the old winch on the well was the chain that controlled the raised bridge. He stood up as they approached the crossing, leaning on a stick that looked as old as he did, and he stumbled, slowly, over to the bridge which rest a mere metre away from his seat. He stretched his back which cracked in several places and then yawned, resting on the stick again before dazing towards the group.

"One moment please." He fumbled inside his cloak's pockets with spindly, frail fingers, withdrawing an old key, a boot, and a piece of parchment. "Here they are." He coughed. "Welcome to the Water of Warr, inn and place of gathering." He stopped to look at them as they stood, bewildered, staring at him.

"Are you sure this is it?" C'k'rian whispered to Athias.

"He is quite sure, madame. Quiet." The old man coughed again, and words tumbled forth. "Thirteen Corpins, it'll be."

Athias reached into one of his pockets and pulled out a small bag, he plucked out thirteen small, bronze triangles and extended his hand. The man beamed, revealing all his few teeth that shone gold in the sunlight before shuffling back to his bucket and lowered the bridge. It lowered down with a gentle thud and the bridge keeper sat, falling asleep. The group hastily crossed the bridge and Athias dropped the coins in the old boot and took the key, he unlocked the door and they strolled across the threshold into the inn where they were met with shouts and stomps down the corridor ahead, descending down into the ground a little. Stairs shot off to the left and right of the path every few metres before they came to another door which they opened, and inside they were greeted by a burst of sound; merry music from a string quartet who danced along in the corner. An enormous fire roared in the centre, surrounded by chairs laden with all types of being, a drink in every hand. They stomped and clapped in time with the music and drank their sweet ale. A haerie stood behind the bar, short with a pointed nose and jet-black hair. She was wrapped in clothing that resembled leaves, decoratively traipsed over her with wings that shimmered in the light of the fire.

"Afternoon! What can we get you?" She has a sweet, smooth voice.

"Do you have any rooms? And some food?" Athias replied, gently.

"Of course! Always got rooms 'ere! How many you need?"

"Five if you have them."

The haerie's wings fluttered as she flittered over to a book behind her. She skimmed over the pages with thin fingers. She stopped and fluttered back to the bar, her feet just half a metre from the ground.

"We do indeed. My name's Chael, pleasure to meet you all!"

"Pleasure." Athias said, smiling.

"That'll be three galts, please. Food and whatever your choice of beverage is included in the price."

"I got this." Calden chipped in, holding out three golden coins. He dropped them into Chael's hand, and she nodded.

"Your rooms are just up there" she pointed to a set of grand stairs to the right of the bar. "Right to the top and then turn left, the five rooms on the landin' are yours."

Athias nodded and smiled,

"Thank you, Chael." He said before leading the group upstairs.

C'k'rian went into her room, eager to get some proper rest. The other four stood outside of their own but conveyed in hushed whispered, quickly.

"We have a contact here, located in another sector. We'll get to work and be back soon." Calden nodded to the other two, Athias nodded in thanks and opened his door, hearing the three head back downstairs after dropping their bags off.

The room was cosy. A small log burner was at the foot of the bed which was covered with autumnal throws.

In the corner, opposite the bed, was a small counter with a jug and some cups, next to this stood another room, empty but for a bath, mirror, and basin. A bronze pipe was jutted from the wall and wound around the hanging lantern in the middle of the ceiling, finding its way to the bath. The timber slats that made the walls and floor had been nailed together in a hurry, most of them different sizes, though all were a rich auburn colour. Athias flung his cloak onto the bed and placed Spectre down between the bed and a small side-table. The bed sagged a little under his weight while he took off his coat and shirt, proceeding into the bathroom, he soaked up the warmth from the floorboards as he took leisurely steps towards it.

He examined himself in it a mirror that stood opposite the bath, he traced his fingertips over the scars on his back, the wounds deep, like canyons scarred the hills. The scars ran from his hips to his shoulder, jagging across the spine, and he had wounds on his chest, shrapnel from an exploding wall. Athias picked up the sponge on the top of the chest and ran some hot water over it before squeezing it out and dabbing it along the scars, they still stung at times, all these years later still. An arrowhead upon a small chain around his neck shimmered in the light. There was a knock at his door and C'k'rian spoke out.

"Can I come in?" Her voice was hesitant.

Athias snapped to the present,

"Yes, of course. Sorry, I was elsewhere." He opened the door and she crossed the threshold.

The pair of them walked to the bed where he sat and offered her the same, she did. He poured two cups of wine from the jug and returned, sitting next to her.

"Is everything alright?" He asked, "you look... distant." Aware that he had just looked the same.

"I have some questions. Calden... Calden told me about the Emperor's plan, the engine he is building. I want to know why you are here. Why you came back? Was it to fight against the Emperor again or was it for something else?"

Athias gulped down fresh water from a cup. He looked to her, sincerely, then to Spectre, and then to the arrowhead necklace. He slipped a shirt on from his bag and sat on the bed with her.

"You remember the story that Hathael told us? Of the world and the tree of Nhivilaurn?"

"Yes." C'k'rian nodded.

"Nhivilaurn provided the world with magic, as Hathael told, but also the Vayshanaa with their magic. The five of us draw magic from the tree and channel it through our own ways, our own artefacts." Athias' voice was hushed, as though the very walls around them would take notice.

"Yes, I've heard the stories, I've seen you fight. Yours is Spectre, the Sword of Time."

"A week before I met H'Khara in Porthna, I had a vision. I discredited it as a dream but then the next night I had the same one, down to exact details. It was a vision of a crown, hidden behind a bird's wings and buried. Then in the Weeping Woods, on our night with the Third Battalion, a visioness approached me, telling me of a prophecy not yet carved in time but one that was waiting to happen, one of a powerful crown."

"What was the prophecy, will you tell me?" C'k'rian's tone was tipped with intrigue.

Athias sighed. He opened his mouth again and paused but then, begrudgingly, continued,

"The sixth will be revealed. The hidden crown uncovered. Placed upon their head they will climb the thousand steps and raze all upon it. The secrets of the world. They will come undone" he paused, seeing her eyes light up, "They will stand upon the frozen fire and bring forth the wrath that swarms beneath. The world's skin will peel and burn, life will fall to ash and dust and the roots of energy will rot and die."

C'k'rian sat back, even more stunned than before. Athias looked shaken up, his mind was wandering, imagining the worst. C'k'rian still had questions to be answered though,

"Is that all of it?"

"Close enough." Athias was tired and it showed in his voice, not just of their travels but in a darker, deeper way.

"So why are you back? Is it to find this crown or is it to help us win our lives back?" C'k'rian became agitated, her hand trembling a little.

"I must find and rally the Vayshanaa. We must find and destroy the crown before this *sixth* finds it and destroys us all." Athias paused as C'k'rian stood up, walking briskly to the door. "I want to rid Ziath of this world as much as you, but this crown could be the undoing of all…"

"I thank you for telling me, Vayshanaa, but I am in this war for the Syndicate above all else. We thought you had returned to help us fight." Her voice wavered, a mess between sorrow and anger on her tongue, "If you must find your masters of magic, so be it, but it won't be with me."

"C'k'rian, wait, I am here to help you fight but if this crown is found by the sixth…"

C'k'rian slipped from the door, letting it glide shut behind her, carelessly.

Athias sat still in silence, poised on the edge of the bed, clutching the arrowhead tight in his hand. He locked his room door and slipping the shirt and his other clothes off, head into the bathroom.

Chapter Sixteen
Bright as Day

A Vayshanaa is above all else in magic. Those who are adept in magic train and learn, they rise to become masters through sheer will, but you must be chosen to become a Vayshanaa, for it is as much a gift as a curse, to become one so close to magic, and it is a burden for those who are close to them. – Calitreum, Athias' Entry, Page 430.

Athias sat in the bath, submerged in the hot water, steam rising around him. He had not felt comfort like this in weeks, maybe months; the liquid brushed over his sore muscles and over his scarred shoulders. He scooped handfuls of steaming water and splashed his face while scrubbing down his thighs with a gentle bristle. He had lit a few candles around the bath, the scent of jasmine and lavender glided over the warm air and he played with the water, pushing his hand down into it and then lifting it up; watching the droplets dance over his skin, urging to return to the larger body. Athias mulled over his thoughts, letting his mind relax completely, and he found himself rewinding the droplets, sending them back up over his hand. He got out of the bath and wrapped a fresh towel around him, heading back into his room where a tray of bread, cheese and some grapes had been delivered up to. While drying himself and eating a slice of fresh bread there came another knock at his door.

"One minute." He finished the bread and plucked a few grapes before ambling to the door.

Peeking through a sliver he saw Calden leaning on the wall across from his room. He shut the door and quickly threw on some clean clothes before opening it fully and Calden walked in. Athias gestured at the bread and cheese but Calden shook his hand.

"I just came by to say that we found her. She's a few streets over at the Sleeping Giant."

"Okay, give me a few minutes."

Calden nodded and stepped outside. Athias sat on the bed, he sliced some cheese and ate it with more bread, finishing it off with the grapes. He stared at Spectre, standing in its sheath, between the table and the bed. He

stared at it for a few minutes before getting dressed and joining Calden in the hallway, Bejarn and Rorarn beside him. He locked his room, glancing to C'k'rian's room and thinking of trying to talk to her again but then turned, attaching Spectre to his back.
"Expecting a fight? Bejarn questioned.
"Yes." Athias said.

The streets were filled with people, all those who worked on the dam during the days came out at night to dance and eat, while sleeping took place at different times for everyone. Many banners were placed along the street, and multiple colours and shapes caught their eyes as they walked. Darkness flittered in and out of the crowds as beings danced around the fires, and over the cobbled paths. The four kept to themselves, hoods up and cloaks wrapped tight as they stepped forward cautiously, and they kept to the shadows of the alleys. The Sleeping Giant was a quiet establishment and although welcome to all, most who took up refuge here were of the frightening affair; ex-soldiers and gladiators; barbaric warriors from the Askiara settlements at the top of the world; the silent and beautiful, but deadly Visyans, their fire-lit eyes leading many men astray. The Sleeping Giant's many rooms were for the weary on their travels and more importantly, stories of the Shadows' banner-carriers resting here were commonly told. There was no gatekeeper here, just an enormous black-oak door as tall as a mammoth of old at least.
"Fitting." Athias said, speaking quietly. He stood back and looked up at the black-oak and brick walls.
He nodded to the others and they nodded back, lowering their hoods with him. He pushed the heavy door forward and Gralnor cawed from above and soared down, resting in Athias' hood. The door creaked as it opened and the four marched over the threshold. A short hallway led into a vast hall with a gigantic hearth at the back, while four lines of smooth, stone tables ran the length of the room and a bar, bustling with life was positioned at the far end. There was no warming music to greet them in this establishment and their footsteps echoed around the hall, the boots clanging against the slabbed stone. Dozens of small candles were hanging from the dirty brick walls, barely illuminating a man's length around them. Cobwebs ran like mazes of silk over dozens of statues of once-famous

warriors and creatures from their tales, and shadows beckoned from the darkest corners untouched by light or warmth. Sure enough, over on the other side of the room was a banner unlike any seen before; an arrowhead laid over a triangular bar. It seemed to flicker even though there was no breeze. Around the banners sat dozens of cloaked, hooded figures.

"Shadows." Bejarn muttered, while Calden went to get four ales.

The Shadows were wrapped in thick fur black, hooded cloaks, casting their eyes in shadow. Each of them sported a long bow; slung over their shoulders, and each sat with a quiver of arrows upon their backs, the arrowheads a distinctive jade colour. Calden returned and they sat, Athias and Bejarn looking out at the tables while Calden and Rorarn with their backs to the Shadows.

"Can you see her?" Rorarn whispered.

Athias stood up and lifted the sword from his back, placing it on the table, sheathed. Then he removed his cloak, Gralnor still nesting inside the hills of fabric.

"Time to find out." He said, a note of curiosity in his voice.

He stepped out from the table and marched towards the biggest group of the cloaked archers. His metal tipped boots clanged against the smooth stone floor, turning heads with every step.

"There's talk here, of rangers in the mist, those who serve a woman. Those who protect the roads, the rivers, and the shores."

"What is it that they say of this woman?" A voice spoke out from the gather of cloaks ahead.

Athias stopped in his tracks and turned to face the woman, sitting at the head of the table to his left.

"That she is a warrior, sworn to the people and the land, and they are sworn to her."

"Sounds like a myth, a good song perhaps." The voice grew louder with confidence.

The whole hall was silent now, bar the flickering flames that licked the logs as it engulfed them.

"Perhaps." He took another step forward and the cloaked figures ahead of him moved off from one, who remained sitting.

"I think I knew a woman like that once." The voice was clear as sunlight as Athias approached the figure ahead.

He stopped, suddenly, and felt a small blade at his throat. He turned his head gently and noticed a hundred arrows, sitting in their bows, pointing at him.

"It can't be." A familiar, smooth voice whispered in his ear.

He turned, slowly, hands held up at shoulder-level, to see a face looking back. Her eyes were as blue as the morning sky and her skin, dark, was smooth like clay. She wore leather armour, lined with fur inside, and it clung tightly to her body; her ample bosom covered by white shirt. Short silver hair streaked with black hung down by her shoulders, in a long plait. He felt the blade leave his throat as her eyes widened when she investigated his. Athias held out his right hand, the palm flat and Gralnor jumped into the air and soared over.

"It's me, Rayna."

Gralnor cawed at Rayna who smiled, a tear trailing down her cheek as Gralnor nuzzled his head between her thumb and finger.

"Eyes as bright as day." Rayna whispered.

"Skin as cold as stone." Athias replied.

As she spoke these words, the bows around them lowered. Rayna looked up and into Athias eyes who leaned forward and kissed her on the forehead. A tear rolled off Athias' cheek and splashed into the stone floor, Rayna brushed his cheek, smudging the tears and holding his face while Gralnor cawed softly.

"Come. Come to our home." Rayna whispered, signalling to the Shadows who all slung the bows over their shoulders again.

An old iron mine lay just east of the city. Here, the sprawling scaffolding thinned before being replaced by families of trees and earthy mounds specked with boulders, some as small as dogs and others as large as buildings. Many ill-experienced adventurers seeking treasure and more had lost their lives in the earth-rivers, shifting the landscape with the seasons. The old mines, resting in the caverns below the woods had been restored not long ago and lanterns hung on old mining equipment from the timber-swept ceilings, while small streams of fresh water trickled through the caverns. The fires of an old forge still burned, bathing the helter-skelter of creaking paths up and around the cave, the lanterns, and the sheets of cloth that sprawled over makeshift beds in a flickering light.

Calden, Bejarn, Roran and a handful of Shadows were sitting around one of the many tables, they were playing a game of Prison, while currency was limited around here, they still bet portions of what they had. It was clear that the Shadows, now de-cloaked, were from all over; dark skinned and light, human and not, Rayna took anyone that she saw talent in and trained them up use the landscape to their advantage. She and Athias were sitting alone, on a separate table underneath a small lantern while Gralnor was fast asleep on top of a dusty shelf above them. Many other Shadows walked the mines, some grouped to make arrows, while some merely slept while there was no mission at hand.

"I win! Cough up ha!" Bejarn's friendly voice rang out over the room and various sighs and grunts followed before the others at the table pushed in their cards into the middle of the table, some with coins on and others bare.

Athias looked over to see Bejarn performing a sort of dance as he gloated before turning back to Rayna. She had barely taken her eyes off Gralnor since they had arrived here.

"We searched for a year to find you, over the mountains to the east and the vast ice fields to the north. I never thought to check here, foolishly, and I should have known. A place where people are always in need of help." He shook his head, chuckling a little to himself.

Rayna reached forward and pressed her lips against his.

"You made your way back to me eventually, that's what matters, and you brought him with you." She smiled to Gralnor who cawed, happily.

Athias smiled, a tear in his eye, stroking the beautiful bird. Suddenly, a jolt of fire shot through his mind and heart and he pressed down on the table, causing it to splinter. He shook his head, surprised, and looked around.

"I… I'm sorry. I don't…"

"Come with me." She took him by the hand and led him away, her voice soothing, into her private quarters.

The private room had been a mining bunk but the beds that were once pressed together had been thrown out and replaced by a large bed, a desk, and shelves. The floor was covered in rugs and pelts, unlike the tunnels, and there was a small log-burner pressed into the clay-bed wall. Rayna led Athias to the bed and sat him down on the soft mattress which pressed down under his weight. She stood over him and removed his shirt, examining his body, tracing her nails of the scars.

"I have some medicines. Some leaves and powders that will revert the wound back to untainted skin."

"No. It's a reminder."

"A reminder? It's not your fault what happened."

"It is." A jolt of power coursed through him, and a bolt of lightning left his fingertips, crashing into the wall and breaking off stone.

"You listen to me, it's not your fault!" Rayna fell to her knees, holding his hands down, imploring to him.

"I could have protected him. I… I should have…" Athias' voice began to break, cracking.

"Our son would not be angry with you."

Tears gushed from Athias' eyes, they poured down his cheeks, crashing down into the thick rug at his feet.

"He loved you, Athias! He loved you and still does!" Her voice was kind and sincere, but his head fell into his hands.

The cups on the desk and the books on the shelves began to rattle and tremble, flying from the shelves but hovering in mid-air, rotating. The cups filled with wine fell and the liquid floated in circles around them each. Rayna jolted to the door, bolting it down. She turned back and felt frozen in her tracks, a force pushing down and against her like the current in a sea. Mustering all her strength, she turned to Athias and saw him sitting bolt upright on the bed, staring ahead with a fire in both of his eyes. Time stood still, wavering, the contents of the room trembled around them and the poles of the bed frame cracked.

"It should have been me." His voice was unhuman, eerie and echoing.

"Athias! Don't listen to it! He loved you!" Rayna shouted through the ringing noise, it clanged in her ears and echoed around her mind. "What did you sing to him?! Do you remember?" Still he sat, motionless, trembling as the noise around them grew louder and louder until it seared her ears. "Eyes as bright as day" she lay her hands on his shoulder and pushed herself down to his eye level. "Skin" she sighed and panted, "as cold as stone!"

The books fell from the air and the liquid of the cups splashed down. Rayna fell to the floor as the weight upon her ceased and Athias collapsed.

Rayna quickly stood up, her ears ringing and ran to the cupboards, she mixed two vials and then hastily returned to his side where she poured the liquid into his mouth. She unbolted the door and Calden burst through.

"It happened again, didn't it?" He asked, panting.

"Yes, unfortunately it did." She peered out into the cavern where there was a multitude of smashed cups, while many were jumping to their feet. "He will sleep now, let him rest."

Athias heard the last of her words before his mind fell quiet.

Twenty-Six Years Earlier

Athias was jolted awake by a rumbling sound that shook the ceiling and the pillars around the room. Paintings slipped from the walls and the stone coughed clouds of dust from the cracks as the bricks rattled. Tutor Abbrath rushed in holding a cloak and boots, he was silent as he threw the covers from the bed and made sure the window was bolted firmly.

"Up! Get up. Now!" *He pronounced; his tone was scared.*

"What is it?" *Athias sat up, slipped on the boots and cloak before standing.*

"Ziath has found us, he is here, his ships will land any moment now."

The hallway's candles and lanterns flickered with every rumble, shaking the walls and doorways. Hastily the pair made their way down to the temple where several other tutors were standing, waiting, with their own students; Tutor Vilcor was with a young person, a similar age to Athias, called Eifig. Tutors Vilcor and Abbrath greeted, bowing to each other, and muttering the old tongue words. Tutor Vilcor flicked his thin, spindly fingers up and pressed his palm to a wall behind him, and the bricks melted away to reveal a curtain. Tutor Abbrath pulled Eifig and Athias aside quickly, he handed Eifig a small, black box with decorative silver lining and gave Athias a long flat box, almost the length of his own height.

"Be strong, care for each other. Eifig, you are going to the Askiara Mountains, you will be taken in by Finhaal, our brother of Creation. Athias, you will be taken in by Hathael, our sister of Life. Go now, Athias Hyaran, Vayshanaa of Time. Go now, Eifig Landrin, Vayshanaa of Emotion."

Athias and Eifig went first through the doorway. Looking back quickly they saw the tutors standing in a circle, rivers of light flowing from their hands and into the wall as they mumbled words together. Athias had learned, years ago, what they would do if the Temple was in danger, as it was now. The Castle of Haurtyn, home to the Order of Vayshanaa, was as magical as the earth-rivers of the east or the kingdom below the sea.

Eifig and Athias pressed forward into the darkness, the passageway had been home to nothing but spiders and frost mice, who had seeped in for shelter against the battering winds. At the end they were greeted by a stone slab engraved with symbols, and Athias recognised the middle one, it was the Order's founding symbol. Eifig rummaged in their pack, removing the small box they had been given, and opened it to reveal a ring; made of smooth, polished stone, embedded with a clear crystal. Slipping the ring on, it shimmered, casting their fingers in a pale light. They pressed the ring against the stone ahead and the same light shot through the carving from the middle to the corners of the slab which then split in half and each part preceded into the wall around. Athias and Eifig were greeted by another tunnel, winding round to the right but these walls were bright; light was at the end accompanied by the sound of ice-tipped rain peppering the stone and the smell of salt from the waves that crashed into the island. Once upon the black stone beach, they saw a small sloop at the docks, swaying with the rocking waves, its sails shining with a silver glint in the light of the moons. They each in turn clambered down the slippery rocks to the beach, the pebbles glimmered in the light. The castle behind them rumbled again and the rocky foundations shook a little, the faint sounds of rifle fire flitted over the wind and the roar as creatures, released from the shackles of enchantment in the castle, hurtled forwards to fight back. Battle had commenced.

"Over here!" *A distant voice shouted over the rising storm.*

Athias and Eifig looked to the ship and a figure with a lantern stood upon the docks, holding on tight as the wooden pathway shook and swayed.

"Go, quickly!" *Eifig said to Athias, letting them pass.*

"We have to get you out of 'ere!" *The man bellowed; A cracking sound followed his trailed words as the jetty started to give way.* "Quickly! Onto the ship!" *He gestured to another figure, clad in furs, who ushered them onboard.*

Athias and Eifig ran below deck. The small ship had sloped walls and a low ceiling, but it was war, out of the icy rain. Benches ran the length and were topped with fur blankets.

"Please, sit. Get warm. We will bring you some food when underway." *The other figure, a lady, guided them to the benches.*

An almighty crash ripped through the air and the ship shook as the waves in the storm splashed even higher in this moment. Athias ignored

Eifig's shouts and ran above deck where he was greeted by an icy wind, pressing against him with all its might. He peered through the shards of water as they descended from the skies to see a stone hand, larger than the sloop itself, rising from the depths.

"By Zohya's words..." The captain muttered to himself in shock as a gigantic figure emerged from the water, and it stood, waist deep in the sea, towering over the castle.

The gigantic titan swayed, looking down at the Haurtyn those attacking it. Cannon balls raced into its face and shoulders, sending cracks down its smooth stone neck. It raised its arms and the enormous hands closed. Athias gripped the rail, looking on with tense eyes. The titan, protector of the castle, slammed its arms down. Its mountainous fists crashed through the castle with such an almighty blow.

"No!!" Athias shouted, confused, and the captain grabbed him, shielding his view from the island.

"Look away, boy! Look away!" The captain shouted through the raging storm and Athias buried his face into the man's cloak.

His cheeks were numbed the by water-soaked furs, and although he covered his ears, still he heard and felt the crash of the titan's ship-sized fist punching through the rocky island. Another figure emerged from the sea on the other side of the island. The figures, the protectors, raised their arms, one last time before slamming them down onto the castle which now stood, but a shimmering ruin. Athias pushed the captain aside and looked out at the island sinking into the sea, a few small towers standing still. The figures crouched down once more and the water washed over their smooth skin, soon they disappeared completely, beneath the surface. The storm raged on, the furious winds blew into the sails of the ship and it soared forwards into the mists.

Chapter Seventeen
The Story of Nhorrin

Jarn Nhorrin was a good man, it was an honour to welcome him as he travelled to the Realm of Naer, to speak with him, and to sing with him. – Calitreum, Calor's Entry, Page 440.

Athias awoke with heavy eyes. Across from the bed were a series of bookshelves and cupboards, a small table stood next to the bed and upon it was a basket filled with straw, a familiar face was resting on the edge and as Athias sat up, Gralnor cawed quietly. His head was ringing, it felt as though he'd been hit by a bolt of lightning, his skin felt numb and his vision was blurred. The door opened and Rayna stood before him, clutching a bowl of stew and a cup of water.

"Athias, you should be resting." She hurried over to the bed and placed the bowl and cup down before pushing Athias back onto the bed, sitting him up.

"Did you know I'd be up today?" Athias nodded at the stew.

"We've been making it up for you and bringing it in the last few days every morning and evening, just in case." She spoke softly, pausing to kiss his head.

Athias smiled. He sat up straight and took the bowl of stew, briefly stroking Gralnor.

"Any word from H'Khara? Is she safe?"

"Don't worry, Gralnor took us to her last night, she came back when she heard of this. She wants you, when better, to meet the rest of the Coarans."

"I will go now."

"You will do no such thing. Your mind is jumbled, the fracture with in is growing stronger and stronger. Do you even remember what happened?"

"I… I remember pain."

"You almost destroyed this place. Your mind is tearing between love and guilt, and the Abyss' grip grows on you more and more. You must rest, for now."

Athias knew not to fight her on this. Rayna was stubborn, she always wanted what was best.

Athias looked around, not noticing the unfamiliar glint of steel.

"It is safe," Rayna looked to him, longingly. "You must take some time away from it every now and then. I lost you once, I won't lose you again." She finished before getting up and leaving.

Athias smiled and sat up, taking the wooden bowl, and smelling the hot concoction. The wood warmed his skin as the numbing faded, feeling his grip returning. The stew had lumps of meat, of which type he was unsure and did not care. It was smooth to the touch of his tongue, warming his cheeks and throat, a delicious mix of vegetables and meat dusted in spices and root powder. Athias picked a leaf and fed it to the raven who was awakening from his own slumber, before placing the spoon down and drinking the remaining stew, gulping down the spicy broth. The oak of the bedside table was reassuring under his fingertips; the gentle bumps from the rough cut of the tree, and the coarse fibre left a rugged memory in the nerves. Athias stood up slowly, stretching every limb, and took his eye patch from the table. He carefully marched across to the bookshelf, examining the books, rolls of parchment and maps. Rayna had been busy while stationed at the dam, securing ports and towns all down the Veins, while holding skirmishes and interrupting supply trains. There was a scramble of knocks on the door and Athias felt his strength come back to him,

"Come in." His voice was gruff, he coughed to clear it.

Bejarn, Calden, Roran, and H'Khara bounded in. Their faces lit up with beaming smiles when they saw him standing ahead of them. H'Khara ran and hugged him briefly before turning, bashfully, and walking briskly to Gralnor to stroke him.

"You worried us there." Calden said.

"It felt like the mine was going to collapse, luckily however, we're so far from anyone else in here that it didn't effect anyone else. We put you to bed and took shifts on the door." Rorarn informed.

"Thank you… I'm so sorry for what happened. I didn't know I could lose control like that anymore."

"Well you're in good hands now. I knew it was getting worse, we all did, but we should have seen the signs earlier on." Bejarn nodded.

Athias looked to H'Khara, sitting on the bed with Gralnor on her lap who stretched his wings and yawned.

"Oh, she knows. Rayna sat her down and told her about the connection to the Abyss and Spectre, how it draws on the ancient magic, allowing it to channel your power but also brings you closer to danger." Roran continued.

"Right." Athias shrugged, looking embarrassed, ashamed.

"Athias, I could never feel anything over then admiration for you. You saved me from the Emperor's clutches, I could never fear you. Rayna told me because I am travelling with you." H'Khara spoke up, she spoke softly.

"Where is C'k'rian?" The word of travellers prompted him.

"Oh... well..." Calden shuffled his feet.

"Is she okay?" Athias voice was panicked.

"She's fine, we err, we just hoped this wouldn't have come up so quick."

"What do you mean?"

"She left. She came to see you that first night, she wanted to be alone with you. After a few minutes she came out and said that she had to leave, that there was something she needed to do, something to get, and that we should never run from who we are."

Athias hung his head, the last words they had shared hung in his mind like poison.

"This place is wonderful, Athias." H'Khara said, breaking the silence that grew longer after Bejarn's words. "Will you come with me to see my people? The family I had at Acre Farm?"

"I will. Of course." He smiled, pleased for the subject change, bowing his head. "Would you like to go now?"

"If you're not too tired!" She beamed at his response, "Oh good. I will go ahead and tell them you're coming."

She scampered from the room, Gralnor following. The others turned to him, a serious expression on their faces again.

"So, what now then?" Roran said "Your plans didn't end with finding Rayna."

"I need to go north, to find Eifig and Finhaal. They have soldiers too, soldiers that will be needed when Ziath eventually comes."

"What makes you think he'll go north or come here? He's ruled over Brineth for years and not enforced his claim."

"That is exactly why he will come soon. He has a new weapon now. A weapon that will enable him to crush the Syndicate if they are not united." Athias finished.

"When do we leave?" Bejarn said, boldly.

"Not today. Go, enjoy yourselves. You have all earned it."

They nodded and smiled, leaving the room and Athias turned back to the bed, making it up.

"You take it easy today. Please?" Athias recognised Rayna's voice, she ran her hands over his back, over the scars. Her skin was rugged and coarse like his own, but it felt relaxing.

He turned to her and kissed her forehead. It felt good to be back with her again. They had always made each other feel like they belonged together, they had fought side by side and loved each other side by side. Rayna reached up and kissed his cheek, her hands on his chest. She ran her fingers over his muscular chest and abdomen, tracing his nails over the ridges.

"I missed you." She whispered to him as she pulled away.

Athias pulled her closer and in turn, ran his hands over her shoulders. She was athletic and strong. A fierce woman. He kissed her neck and cheek, and then she leaned up and pulled him in to kiss his lips. She bit them playfully and wrapped her arms around his neck. His lips were one of the only smooth parts left, unburned, unscarred. Rayna lifted Athias' eye patch and looked deep into the enchanting colour that swirled and danced but Athias' brought it down again, he looked away from her, ashamed.

"Don't. I can't lose control again. I... I'm breaking."

"Then let me fix you. The Abyss calls on you often, yes? The roots of Nhivilaurn crush your bones and pull into the centre of the tree? Well let me be the beckoning call to guide you away from it." She ran her palms over his stubble, and he held each wrist.

"I won't let you come to anymore harm on my watch. I fell deep into the Abyss when I left. It caught me and dragged me deep." His voice wavered.

"Whether you like it or not, Athias. I am going to help you." There was that stubborn voice he had remembered.

She lay her head against his, taking in a deep breath. Athias felt all the tension in his mind release, and his body relaxed. It had been a long time since he had felt truly relaxed.

"You should get some clothes on. H'Khara has been talking about her family of Acre Farm for days, we'll all be thankful when you've finally been and met them." She chuckled to herself before kissing his hand and leaving the room.

Athias cleaned up and put on some new clothes, they were white, or tan, and clean. The fabrics were soft and warm, it had been a long time since he had worn anything that felt as comfy as this, for life on the road was anything but. His other clothes, his armour, and bag would be cleaned in the hot springs. Making his way from the room, he saw Rayna readying for another skirmish.

"An Imperial battalion has been spotted a few miles from the town." She was briefing the Shadows who were equipping their bows and tightening their gauntlets. "Pack light, we need to move fast, and remember, we need one alive." Rayna spoke out to them all as they slid knives into their boots, flexed their bows, filled their quivers with arrows and began to paint charcoal onto their faces.

Many nodded to Athias as he passed, and Rayna made her way through the crowd to take his hand.

"I'll be back by sundown. Please, enjoy yourself today, eat the delicious food, laugh with your friends. My rangers will interrogate the one we bring back." She kissed him on the cheek before returning to the gathering before her. "Alright. Let's go, Shadows!"

The Shadows walked past, through the mines and out into the frosted sun. Calden, Bejarn and Roran were sitting at a table, chatting among each other. Athias recognised the hilt and pommel of Spectre protruding from some cloth on the table. He walked over and Calden clocked his line of sight, he stood up and raised his hand to Athias who stood still, confused.

"We've been asked by Rayna to look after Spectre today. So, you can get out there and feel less of the burden, enjoy yourself. We got a few days before we have to move."

Athias looked concerned.

"I know you've carried it for years, every day, but you gotta let us do this. Just this once." Roran said and Bejarn nodded behind him.

"Alright. Look after it."

"We will. Like it needs looking after, ha."

He heard their laughing as he left to meet H'Khara who was standing outside the mine, balancing precariously on the roots of a tree that shielded the secret entrance.

The path towards the city was thin and winding, it took them through rocky boulders the size of houses and across fields of purple flowers, and yellow reeds. Athias and H'Khara exchanged stories and songs from their lives and cultures as they marched forward with a spring in their steps. H'Khara turned to Athias,

"Can you tell me about Nhorrin, about how he died? I asked the other three and they gave me a skimmed version of him and his story, but I want to know the full story?"

"Of course. Nhorrin was said to be a proud and friendly man, he welcomed many from all around to join him at the dam, to work on it and live by it. He and this family of found explorers, outcasts, and adventures, they mapped the land around this structure for many miles. They ventured out each week to gather supplies and map the landscape, seeking to draw venturous diagrams of the rivers and mountains, the forest, and caverns. On one trip out, Nhorrin stumbled upon another settlement of strange folk who wished for nothing but for Nhorrin to leave them. Nhorrin could not leave them in such a state, their huts had flooded, their clothes were torn. He brought them back to the dam and showed them a fair, honest life. But their tribe's leader, who had not been with them, returned to his home to find his people gone and so he tracked them to the dam. He attacked Nhorrin and threatened to destroy the dam for it was merely scaffolding at this time, he threatened his tribe should leave or they would die there but they did not, and so he set about his sabotage. Nhorrin found him and confronted him, and the pair fell into the rivers below, going over the falls. Nhorrin's people never knew to this day if they tripped, or if Nhorrin sacrificed himself for them."

Chapter Eighteen
An Old Love

I know little of love but for a love of the forge. Though once I saw a lady, a lady of fire and smoke, and she burned me, but I loved her so. – Calitreum, Finhaal's Entry, page 443.

Being away from Spectre was a blessing, it was good to walk without the songs of many dead men bound to his spine, his mind hadn't been freed of the burden that came with it for as long as he could remember. A huge flock of birds flew overhead, hundreds of them, dancing through the sky with each other before soaring down into the forests around the city and as they drew closer to the settlement, which sat just outside the main city, they were greeted by pleasant harmonies; singing and drums. Athias and H'Khara came around the corner to see dozens dancing, while others were cooking, fishing, erecting tents and making boats, in human or animal form alike. Gh'ael rushed towards H'Khara, picking her up, embracing her and squeezing her tight, she paused and looked to Athias when putting H'Khara down.

"So good to see you, Athias." She held out her hand and Athias took it firmly. "You saved H'Khara's life, you are our family now as well as hers!"

"I did what anyone should have done." He smiled, nonetheless.

"Yet, nobody came to her aid but you." Letting go of Athias' hand, she locked foreheads with H'Khara, before beckoning to them both, "Come and meet everyone."

The pair walked into the encampment and many heads turned with grinning faces or whispering to each other. Was this the stranger that saved H'Khara, their sister? A large group of them walked to Athias, taking his hand in theirs, in turn and whispering to each other, Athias caught the passing line or word.

"It's him. It's the one who saved H'Khara."

"He's here. The sorcerer."

"They're all so grateful to you, for H'Khara, for what you did." Gh'ael bowed.

"I only saved one of you, not all though."

"Ah but it is not just the act of saving our sister, here, it is that you stood for something other than yourself. Dare I say if any had been in that inn, in need of help, you would have stepped in; one or ten or a hundred."

Athias smiled, unspeaking, although his expression confirmed it. Gh'ael smiled back, sipping from a cup, H'Khara held out a tray laden with cups to everyone, and many took one. Athias took one too and sipped it, it was nettle tea but had a fruity, soothing smell.

"Will you join us tonight? It is a celebration of life."

"I would love to but what of the others in my party?"

"H'Khara has already seen that they are invited." She chuckled.

The sky was mesmerizing that night, filled with specs of white amidst deep purple and blue, and the moons were white as ice, staring down at the world from up high. Gh'ael had travelled into the city with dozens of others, bringing baskets of bread and word of a celebration open to any who wish to attend, as were the ways of old. The coaran species had always been one for ceremonial tradition, and it was unclear throughout history if humans had in fact been the first race or if it was the coaran who came first, either way, the coaran celebrations and traditions passed down from generation to generation over thousands of years were almost the most colourful, and spectacular of events. An enormous fire stood proudly in the palm of a gigantic brick, carved like a hand, with a different animal at the end of each finger. A group of musicians played variety of wooden instruments and drums atop a stage and the music carried down over the benches, and to the water where it danced over the water in time with the ripples from thrown stones.

Soon the settlement was filled with many species; haeries; trinata; humans and coarans; even a giant or two from the caverns of forgotten mountain passes. Many were dancing by the water, while others by the fire, including H'Khara and Roran, two that Athias could see were happy to be with their own. Athias had enjoyed the day of honest work, with friendly people. He had enjoyed getting to know them, learning their names, hearing their stories. Bejarn and Calden left to get food and Gh'ael stared out at the dancing, Athias noticed her eyes upon H'Khara and Rorarn.

"They look very happy together." Athias' voice was calm and quiet, the first it had been for some time.

"They do. I am happy for her." Gh'ael said, smiling.

"I'm sorry, do you…"

"What? Oh no! Ha-ha! You thought I was with H'Khara? No, I am paired to another." She flicked her head to the side, towards the stage.

Athias turned to see a tall woman with light brown skin, dancing with the musicians upon the stage, a cup in hand.

"She's very beautiful."

"She is. Her name is Nachaya. We met in Acre Farm."

"I'm sorry. I'm sorry for everything you and your people have endured… and fly?"

"We were freed because of people, humans like you. Humans willing to fight against the oppression. I want you to know that when the war for survival comes, the final fight, us… all of us will stand with you and your people." Gh'ael gestured to the people around her.

"Can I ask how many of the coarans here are third echelon?" Athias could only imagine the amount of help a dozen creatures like H'Khara would be.

Gh'ael stood up, she held her hand up towards the entrance to the settlement.

"In Acre Farm there were about fifty thirds, then about another two-hundred between first and second echelons. They all want to fight against Ziath and they all will." She paused, spinning around. "Ah, right on time!"

Athias looked to the entrance and saw Rayna standing by the entrance. A black dress covered her sublime figure, while her body sat inside a corset, and a red sash swirled behind her. The dark leather of her boots soaked up the fire's warmth and she was wearing a necklace like his, an arrowhead of stone on string, while she wore other bracelets on her forearms. The black silk dress resembled a wraith gliding over fire and Rayna's dark hair flowed like waves of jet-black water and her eyes glimmered like gems on the ocean bed. Athias felt his heart leap at the sight of her, as she walked towards him, staring at him. She took him by the hand and led him towards the fire where they began to dance in time with the music, taking a faster pace now.

"Rayna… you look stunning."

She moved close to him, taking his hand as they walked together into the crowd where many nodded and clapped, and they danced, perfectly in time, as they had done before, a long time ago.

"I love you, Athias."

"I love you too." His voice was at peace.

They kissed in the middle of the dancing crowd. Athias became oblivious to the world around them, the only living things surrounded by swaying shadows, while the ground beneath their feet drummed. Rayna took Athias' by the hand again and led him to the woods that surrounded the settlement. They chased each other through the arching roots, around boulders and over the earth before stopping, and Rayna took Athias' hand, placing it upon her shoulder. He removed his top and looked into her eyes while she traced her fingernails gently over his skin. His heart soared up into his mouth and beyond, into the sky. When she stopped, he kissed her again, pressing his lips against her neck and cheek, brushing his hand up her thigh and turning her so she was facing the tree, he picked her up and wrapped her legs around his waist. He became lost in the sensation, his heart beating like the drums of war. Rayna whispered to him as she removed his cloak, and he kissed down over her chest as he pushed forward into her. Music from the settlement skipped over the air of the cold night and danced around them as they moaned, embracing in each other's arms. The grass shone silver from the moons' glare and the water licked at the pebbles of the bed while music was overtaken by the trembles of the earth, and the creature of a thousand dancing footsteps. Fireflies sprung from the grassy roots around Athias and Rayna, floating up to caper among the swaying branches in the cool night. Athias felt something surge through him, not power, not strength, but tranquillity.

Athias and Rayna awoke from under Rayna's dress, they lay in the warm earth of an enormous tree; its roots sheltering them from the cool breeze that grazed across the rough wood. They dressed and head back into the settlement, eyeing H'Khara and Roran stumble from a tent, laughing while Gh'ael and Nachaya were laying together, curled in each other's arms in the shell of a boat-turned-shelter. Calden and Bejarn were sleeping still, resting against the gate, side by side, a mug still in hand. Athias stretched as he strolled, still waking up from a deep, dreamless sleep, and H'Khara spotted them, bashfully turning to Roran's chest, burying her face in it, before joining Rayna on a walk down to the river for water. Roran was greeted by Calden and Bejarn who hugged him and smiled, and they beamed to Athias who arched his back, feeling the spine crack. More and more people began emerging from their homes of the night and trickled back to the dam, slowly. Gh'ael told them not to worry about cleaning up, as was coaran tradition to clean up the earth of their celebrations, to make it clean. Bejarn and the other two said they would be back soon but were going to venture into the dam city for the time being and H'Khara said she would stay at the settlement for now, while Athias and Rayna returned to the dam, accompanied by a group of Shadows who had accompanied Rayna the night before. The walk back to the mine was peaceful, sounds of construction leaked from the dam but birds were singing in the trees overhead and the gusts of air wound through the plants beside the path. However, just as they reached one of the secret entrances to the mine a ranger appeared, hands bloodied, a look of desperation on her face, and Rayna's expressions changed from at peace to concern, following the ranger inside.

Athias followed at an arm's reach, and Rayna signalled to the guards who opened a heavy iron door just inside the entrance, they waited for her and Athias to cross the threshold before swinging it shut once more. Athias heard the heavy locks bolt down behind them. It was dark and musty inside, an old storage room once used for timber, steel and coal. The walls were smooth and the ceiling high with tall shadows hanging from high; the room lit only by a few sparse candles hanging from the ceiling. At the centre of the room, tied to a chair, secured to the floor with rusting, heavy bolts, was a man. He was bloodied, bruised and scarred. Beneath the patches of dried scarlet blood was pale skin, although half of his figure was draped in shadow, while the other was fractured; dark, dry blood had seeped from his nose, broken in several places; his right eye was blackened and the bone beneath had dented; blood had run from puncture wounds in his shoulders down over his fingertips; his right knee was broken, twisted and contorted; and several teeth lay scattered on the floor at his feet. He was a broken husk, wheezing with every breath he took and coughing on every breath out. To his side was a small table laden with tools and instruments of all kinds, and a bucket filled with steaming water, now a shade of red. A ranger approached the man, tilting his head back into the dim light so he could see Rayna. He grinned showing less teeth than more, his lips split and cracked.

"He smiles?" She spoke curiously but was cut off before saying anything else.

The soldier spat blood onto the floor as he talked, his jaw a scarred wreck. He spoke in a high, sneering voice.

"He comes. The Great Emperor comes north! He will bring his legions to wash away the filth that plagues this land, from the waters he will come, from the land!"

Rayna sighed, she brought forth a knife from her boot and marched round behind the man. She sliced the blade across his pale skin and sharply walked from the room, the sound of a gurgle and trickling blood behind her.

Chapter Nineteen
Death

Life and death have tangled together, more than once. They have danced across meadows and swam through lakes. They have tempted those who could not be and have beckoned the weak and foolish to their claws, more than once. – Calitreum, The Fundamentals of Magic, Page 648.

Athias and Rayna looked over a map of the dam, the city, and the rivers that left it. The mines were busy around them now as her rangers gathered supplies and weapons, making sure to count every arrow. Athias pointed to parts of the map, measuring distances.

"We need to evacuate." Athias' voice had returned to it's deep, imposing state.

Rayna pulled him aside, out of earshot from the rest,

"I agree but we have to do it our way, we've been building and preparing this city for a time such as this for years."

Rayna turned to four Shadows, waiting for her.

"Each of you, take two of our kin. Ride out across the lands and then return by nightfall and tell us of what you have learned. Fetch me Ru'i."

The Shadows left, one returned with a young man before bowing and leaving again to fulfil her order.

"Ru'i, my dear, can you send the birds to the inns of the city and their owners. As we talked about before?"

"How many of them?" The young man asked tentatively

"All of them." Rayna spoke boldly.

He nodded and scampered away.

"Bejarn has contacts that can send ships. I will find him"

Rayna and Athias kissed quickly before splitting ways. Athias rushed to the room he had awakened in and whispered to Gralnor, picking him up and placing him on his shoulder. He then retrieved Spectre from the forge and his clothes from the drying rack above the steam grate, his green and brown cloak, gauntlets, and boots. He grabbed some food from one of the tables and took a swig of water from a cup before leaving the mines. He lifted Gralnor up and the bird took flight, towards the city. As he looked back towards the dam, he saw streams of black-cloaked people heading down the hills and into the city as well, and he spotted a familiar person walking among the long grass at the base of the forest he and Rayna had been in the passing night.

"H'Khara." He called out to her and waved, she stopped, and he made his way to her. "I was just on the way back to the settlement to look for you." He said as he drew near. "I've got something for you."

"Oh yeah?" She sounded curious.

Athias pulled the cloth-wrapped item. He handed it to her, and she looked puzzled.

"Thanks?" She held it in both hands, it was long, almost three feet long.

"Unwrap it, ha-ha!" He laughed. He was anxious of the events that were to unfold, things would change very soon, however he wanted to keep her calm.

H'Khara unwrapped the cloth to reveal a short sword. A shining, silver blade with black leather strips around the hilt. The blade glinted in the light, it was freshly forged, the steel had set only hours ago.

"You said you wanted a sword, right?" He joked.

"I did! Thank you, again. Will you teach me how to use it? Just a few strikes!"

After trekking through the woods, they discovered a small crater, perhaps an old mining pit. Athias put his bag down and helped H'Khara down into the pit with him, the earth was a yellow colour. H'Khara was stood opposite him, clutching the blade in both hands, the tip was pointing down. Before Athias drew Spectre, he approached her, hands raised,

"First, you're going to want to hold it like this." He stood to her side and raised the flat of the blade was to her side, pointing up. Then he moved behind her and slightly adjusted the angle, so H'Khara was holding it across her body and head. "The sword is light but strong, and it should normally be used with one hand but for now we'll stick to two." He then took a few paces back and lifted Spectre from its sheath. The blade slid from the sheath cleanly, making a smooth noise that seemingly clung to the air around the frosted steel. He stood directly opposite her, poised in the same way that he had shown her, Gralnor returned from his flight and perched upon a branch above them, his caws echoed through the forest.

"Now, I want you to lunge at me from your right and watch how I parry it, then you will parry me as I return to same strike."

H'Khara went to strike, taking a step forward as she did so, and he parried. They reset and repeated a few times.

"You have good footwork which is the key element to becoming a blade master."

H'Khara smiled and lowered her blade and Athias went forward to strike, she flinched as the blade stopped an inch from her face.

"Never let your guard down, even when training. It'll become second nature to you this way."

"That's correct, child, never lower your guard. Not for a second."

A cold, deep voice washed over them and Athias spun around looking for the source.

"It's true. A warrior *never* lets their guard down."

Another voice but this one was high pitched and thin, it latched to their eardrums as would a burst of fire to a tree.

"Who goes there?" Athias spoke into forest, his voice collected.

"Shadows lingering on the end of your fingers."

Like a breeze, the thin voice danced through the air and birds cawed around them.

Athias slid Spectre back into its sheath and gently lowered H'Khara's blade. Athias looked around, peering into the shadows of the thick trees which stood still like soldiers on watch.

"You have nothing to fear from us. This is a free place." Athias said, calmly.

He was greeted by laughter. High-pitched, manic laughter which echoed around them, beside them, it crawled upon their skin and through their woven hair.

"You think this place is *free*?" The voices entwined, cackling, while the laughing continued.

Athias went to the vision of Gralnor who took flight and circled the trees while remaining below the tops. He looked down through the raven's eyes and saw... nothing. No shadows, not heat, just cold and slithers of sound. Athias signalled to Gralnor who flew away and then Athias returned to his own sight.

"What's happening?" H'Khara was scared and nervous.

Athias spotted something silver fly towards them and raised Spectre swiftly. The small knife clanged as it hit the blade and flew off to the side.

"He has his tricks!" The first voice spoke.

"He has his magic." The second hissed in return.

"What does the sorcerer have without his tricks, his magic, his wit? Is he nothing?"

"Say those who work from the darkness, those who practice in blood ritual. I know who you are. If you want to know what I can do, if you want to know who I am. Why don't you come and find out?" Spectre's blade shimmered in the light.

"Gladly!" The hissing voice coiled around Athias' ears.

"Death comes for you, man of magic!" The second shouted.

Two figures jumped from the shadows ahead. They were tall and lean, enthralled in thick long, hooded cloaks that swirled as if in a strong breeze but there was none, and they bore shining talon-tipped gauntlets, a breast plate each and linothorax with spiked shin braces and sandals. Standing tall Athias spotted the ancient design upon the grey-steel breastplate; mountains entrapped by waves and engravings of a beast's teeth were etched into their masks that sat over their jaw and nose.

"Cloaks." Athias spat.

"What?" H'Khara's voice was timid.

"An ancient order of assassins, all but dead and gone."

Athias thought back to his books while a child, and to the stories he heard of the Cloaks, Ziath's answer to his own order. Deadly killers, savage and ruthless, virtually unmatched in combat.

"Yes, we are not that much different, are we, Vayshanaa? Arhn and I, Verith, to you, were just discussing."

H'Khara threw the sword into the earth and fell to the ground, transforming into her wolf form, the transitions were easier now and painless and as she mastered her ability, her size grew too, now she was almost as tall as Athias.

"The Spectre and the Wolf." Arhn began to pace to Athias and H'Khara's left. "What a *marvellous* sight." His voice was cold and dead.

"You are but a plague upon this world, dark-skin." Verith continued, his voice was more snake than man.

"Yet, Mother Zohya will welcome you and I all the same unto the realm of Naer." Athias brought Spectre up as soon as the last word had left his lips.

H'Khara roared and the grains of dirt upon the woodland floor trembled as she dug her paws into the ground, leaping towards Arhn. Athias swung Verith who raised his knee, deflecting the sword with his brace before jump kicking Athias in the shoulder, sending him rolling down a dip. Athias and Spectre slid down the dusty slope, the Cloak didn't let up as he jumped after them, swiping at Athias again, this time with his talons. The Cloaks' practiced day and night for almost all their lives in the arts of combat, they were agile and nimble, trained to develop their own fighting styles. Athias heard H'Khara roar up the slope and felt the ground quake. He ducked as Verith lunged at him, like a tiger would pounce on prey but he raised his sword to meet the talons. They scraped down the blade and sparks flew but left no marks, Athias pushed forward and stomped on the Cloak's foot, his knee and then slammed the hilt of Spectre into his body. Verith flipped back, using his hand to spring as balance, his cloak billowed in the cool air; the rips in the fabric giving it an eerie look. Their eyes met and Athias launched another strike, Spectre clashing upon the gauntlets, sliding off, and then into the clutches of the talons. The Cloak sliced down Athias' fingers on the hilt and blood seeped from the wound. Athias wiped the blood, it stung as he smeared it.

"You're fast but not fast enough, Student of Time." The Cloak said, calmly, as he patrolled around Athias who was panting.

"Vayshanaa." Athias channelled power through him once more, letting loose a burst of force which rattled the trees behind him and flung dust into Verith's eyes.

He went in for an attack but before he could swing Spectre down, he was disorientated and dazed as he felt a punch to his body, another to his knee, a slice across his shin, then a whirlwind as he was grabbed by the hood and thrown over the Cloak's body. Athias ignored the pain and clambered to his feet, just in time to dodge the next blow much to the surprise of the Cloak. Athias met the talons again with Spectre, forcing them down before bringing the sword up. He punched the assassin in the neck and sliced across his calf with Spectre to which the assassin let out a small grunt. He retaliated in kind; taking a handful of powder from a pocket on his belt and blew it. Athias could only watch as the smoke surrounded him like a curtain, and claws like that of a bird's talons swiped through the swirling sand-like mixture, cutting across Athias' arms, hands and chest. Athias dropped to one knee, Spectre in front of him, he whispered an enchantment and plunged Spectre into the ground. As the sword pierced the rocky earth, the shadow-sand dispersed, fading away.

"No more tricks. No more hiding." He said as he returned to his feet, wrapping his shin and fingers in bandages quickly, stopping the blood from spilling.

The Cloak dropped his belt and took a pace back. He reached up and removed the mask and shoulder guard and slid off his torn cloak, Athias followed suit, pulling the straps of his armour down and standing straight while the steel thudded into the earth, covered by the cloak. Athias stepped forwards, he dug his feet into the earth and waited for the assassin to make his move. Verith adjusted his wrist braces and extended his bloodied hands, standing like a raven before grabbing its prey. There was nothing but silence for a split second and then the assassin jolted forward, ducking under a swing of the sword, slicing down Athias' shoulder with his claws, and Athias flinched, swinging round to catch the assassin, bringing Spectre up swiftly with a flash of steel. The Cloak dabbed his wound and licked the blood before dashing forward to meet Athias where they met with blade and talon, deflecting and parrying, steel clanging, echoing in their ears. Athias felt pain in his wrist and the sword fell from his hand, kicked to one side by the attacker. Athias leapt forward, spearing Verith and punching at his face, and elbowing his nose, breaking it. He let out a howl of pain and fell to his knees but not before springing back onto his feet and slicing up with both talons. Athias coughed and warm blood slithered over his lips, looking down to see a gaping wound in his chest while Verith stood back again, admiring his work, wiping the blood from his nose. Verith retrieved Spectre from the dirt and leisurely stroll towards Athias, kneeling, coughing.

"You were too slow, *Vayshanaa*."

Athias heard it before he felt it, the breaking of his bones as the sword's blade glided through them. Blood spurted from his mouth, trickling down his cheek. It started to rain, and the cold water washed down his face. The world around him began to blur as his lungs and throat filled with blood and the warm, the searing fire, spread through his arms and shoulders. He closed his eyes and felt an inferno around him, an inferno of cold, seeping into his skin, silencing him.

He felt nothing yet this could not be death, could it? He thought to himself. He reached to his face and felt nothing but suddenly light appeared ahead of him, warping towards him at great speed. A tree came into vision, zooming towards him faster and faster.

"No. No!" He screamed as the monstrous, twisting oak flew towards him as he sped towards the light.

He fumbled for something, anything, to stop him from colliding with it. His heartbeat climbed and he reached for his sword. It was gone. He reached for his legs. They were gone. The tree burst into full view as he seemingly escaped the tunnel of darkness and then he stopped, abruptly, and was standing before a single tree among rolling hills of white ice. He walked, now distinctly feeling his feet upon the ground although unable to see them and approached the snaking roots that wound round the ice ahead of him, around him. A glowing figure appeared from within the darkness, a figure he recognised.

Tristan looked different to that of when Athias had said his goodbyes on the bridge. He walked with Athias into the tree and began climbing a set of smooth stone steps, reaching up into seemingly nothingness. His voice too was different, it sounded distorted as though they were underwater.

"You shouldn't be here. It's too soon." His voice rippled around them.

Athias turned to look at him but he faded from view, disappearing completely like a breath of air in the wind. A door stood ahead of Athias now, which opened, quietly. Across the threshold were two great chairs, thrones perhaps, they stood alone but for an open fire in a room of crystal floor, and Athias could see no end to it as it stretched for miles in every direction, into shadows.

"It is glad to meet you, finally." A voice of velvet glided over the air.

A woman walked through the door and sat herself in the chair opposite him, while another knelt in front of the fire. The woman opposite had dark skin, peppered with silver, and hair that flowed from her head like smoke.

Athias felt his heart drop as he recognised her from the statues in the temple of his childhood.

"Mother Zohya."

"Athias, my master of time. This is Nhivalium, you are sat with me in the very first tree that combines our worlds. From Naer at the top, to the realm you joined me from at the branches, and down, deep into the Abyss below us, in the roots."

"I died though. I felt the blade, my blade, it took my life. Should I not be in the Realm of Naer?"

"You cannot cross into the Realm of Naer until another has been chosen to follow in your steps and carry your sword. It is a fate unique to the Vayshanaa, and I need my Vayshanaa more than ever as a storm is growing."

"The Forsaken Crown." Athias sighed, he was tired, even in this place.

"Yes, the Forsaken Crown."

"The crown itself, what powers does it hold?" Athias leant forward, eager to learn.

"Powers beyond any of you, my Vayshanaa. Powers that will transcend and twist the fabric of our realities, it could destroy them, and destroy our world. While you will not wear it, you must be the one to find it."

Athias looked puzzled, unsure as to why it had to be him.

"For you are the Vayshanaa of Time." The other woman by the fire spoke out before he could ask why. "You are the only one of us who can enter the grove under the spells placed upon it, the only one of us with enough control over the very magic that guards it."

Mother Zohya pressed on.

"I created it for those of the world, should the Eternal Giants return, that much is true from the stories. However, what the stories do not declare is when the giants I defeated did not return to seek vengeance I had to ensure it would not be uncovered by accident."

"Where does it rest?" Athias felt his thoughts swirl, even before he finished asking.

"The crown lays in a tomb within the Gaerlwood Grove. A place of mystical power. The crown is protected by the memories of those that find it and that is why you and only you can venture to it, for it is your control over time which will protect you." A flash of information showed Athias the grove; a circle of trees hidden deep in the northern mountains. "Go to Hathael and give her this," she showed him a roll of parchment as they escaped the vision.

"Can I ask, why can you not just come to our realm and show us?"

"I am bound to this and the Realm of Naer, as was the reason I made the Vayshanaa. I was too weak to walk upon the physical realm and so when I made the first masters of magic, it was with a promise that I could never step foot in the world I once belonged to."

Athias nodded, a question he had longed to know, and asked so many as a child had now been answered.

"I will. Will I be returning now?"

"You will and your sister, Calor, too. The Vayshanaa of Death." She beckoned to the lady by the fire who came and stood before them.

"I will find the crown."

"I know you will. We will meet again, in the Realm of Naer." Then Zohya snapped her fingers and Athias was jolted through a tunnel of flashing crystal and light before returning to his damaged body where he knelt, wheezing.

Verith stood over him, Spectre in hand.

"You were too slow…"

His voice was cut short as a shadow, seeping like water, cascaded around him, and consumed him. It dispersed, leaving no sign of the assassin. Athias felt blood trickling from the wounds on his back, it was agonising, and Calor crushed a piece of stone, drizzling the dust over Athias face. It was a searing pain, a fire that shot through his veins and into his mind. Next, an icy cold spread over his bones, battling and replacing the heat. It travelled from his neck to his toes and and Athias felt pain no more, he looked down and saw no wounds, no blood, he tore open his shirt to reveal nothing, no wounds. Athias simply looked to Calor with a confused expression, admiring her jet-black, crystal-like skin with shimmering white eyes and her torn, hooded cape that moved like the flame of a candle, disappearing into the air, and reappearing again.

"We all have our gifts." She simply said before helping him up to his feet.

Suddenly another body flew down and landed next to them. Calor flinched and withdrew two short swords; blades of moving black smoke but Athias signalled it was alright and they looked to the body. It was bloodied, with many bones protruding from the skin. H'Khara appeared on the edge of the mound and roared, shaking the trees. Athias looked to her and smiled, relieved she was alive, and she began her transformation back to human form.

"Athias!" Rayna's voice was heard from behind him and Athias turned to see her, Gralnor perching in her hood and a handful of Shadows stood with her, their bows drawn, scanning the environment. Her face was stricken and frightened, she was panting and out of breath.

"What is it?" Athias asked, standing now, slightly obscuring Calor from vision.

"The Emperor…" She panted, resting against a tree to balance.

"He's here." Calor whispered.

Chapter Twenty
Prepare for War

War. It follows some, and it flees from others, though I have never met those that fall into the category of the latter. – Calitreum, A Vayshanaa's Oath, Page 11.

Just as Athias and company entered the city, deep and loud horns blew out across the dam, loud, rumbling like an avalanche. H'Khara had gone to Gh'anel to start the evacuations, while Bejarn, Calden, and Roran had headed towards the docks at the smaller river behind the city in an attempt recruit the sailors into using their ships for the evacuation, unwilling to rely purely on the aid that Bejarn had called upon for it had been years. The Shadows stood ready at the outskirts, preparing to follow the orders relayed by their commander. The horns sounded again and the beams of iron and steel of buildings around them shook.

"We're out of time. Gralnor, here." Athias raised Spectre to the sky and Gralnor soared overhead, aligning with the sword.

Athias visited Gralnor's sight as the bird flew high until the clouds were but hanging over him. He gazed out over the monstrous mouth of water ahead to see the ships of Ziath's conquest, the very same ships that had brought Ziath to this land before. Gigantic steel and iron steamboats, pressing over the water like tar would across earth. They stretched for as far as Gralnor could see, streamlined and brutal, laden with cannons and other ordnance of war. On the roads leading to the forests that stood on the cliffs around the dam marched troops, gathered in strict formation, a scarlet banner at the head of every legion. Every soldier was wrapped in a rich brown cloak fastened tightly under a cuirass, marching with a rifle held at the waist and pressed into their chest; a shirt of red, while a scimitar or rapier hung, sheathed upon their ranks. Every half-second came a quake from the beast of ten thousand footsteps.

"All Mother…" Athias' trailed off into a murmur, returning to his own eyes.

"How many?"

"It is as it was before when he brought his armies to these shores. Thousands, tens of thousands."

"We cannot stand against that in full, and yet, we must so that those who cannot fight will live to do so another day."

Athias nodded,

"Agreed, can you send your Shadows to delay the troops' advance, to the north-west?"

"Calor, will you take my Shadows north-west. Buy us time? I know we do not know one another but you are a Vayshanaa, yes?"

"I would be honoured to lead and fight with them, soldiers of mystery after my own heart. I will do this, Rayna, daughter of Treha. I will bless their bows and their eyes with death." Calor nodded.

"Your words are strong. Thank you. Take the Third Shadow and give the order for the rest to enter the city, search for those who need assistance and then make their way to defensive positions."

Calor bowed her head, her hair flailing in the breeze.

"I will find you afterwards!" She shouted back to them riding towards the mines where the Shadows had been preparing.

Athias and Rayna galloped off into the city, the horns blew again, and the entire city trembled. The pair of them raced forwards, passing hundreds as they poured into lines leaving the city, hundreds and thousands hastily grabbing cluttered bags of possessions before meeting others at pre-prepared checkpoints, children were crying, adults were shouting, it was a disorder known too well by many of this world. As the pair of them reached the heart of the city, Shadows could be seen in pairs, running into the city and climbing high into the scaffolding, on the search for those in need, while others stayed on the ground and began to lead the lines, the crowds, out towards the docks behind the city.

Athias and Rayna arrived at the dam's base, jumping from their horses, and stepping into one of the many lifts that ran the length of the wall, powered by steam furnaces, that were surely running low on coal. Athias worried that the thick, steel coils would cease to move as they started ascending. As they slowly rose, the sprawling mass of buildings came into view, the whole city still stood as a harmonious mess. The disturbing reality that it could all soon be, but a memory shot into their minds. Higher and higher they climbed, and as they approached the top it became apparent quite how tall the dam was, the towers atop it were almost brushed by cloud and as they stepped out onto the walkway, they were met by a strong breeze, pushing them back, howling as it flew over the dam and trickled out into the city. The people below, the thousands of them, they looked like ants from up here.

"My lady." A webber clad in fur and leather bowed to Rayna and held out a scroll. "We received this not moments ago, it's from Ziath himself."

"May I see it." She asked, and the webber handed her the small roll of parchment which she unravelled and read aloud to Athias.

"Inhabitants of Nhorrin Dam.

If you do not yield, I will burn and flail every child, man, and woman. This is my country, prepare for nothing but fire and death."

At that moment Calden stepped off another lift with forty or so other men and women, all bearing a rifle equipped with scope and bayonet, while, Roran appeared off another with almost a hundred Shadows in the other lifts combined.

"Where do you want us?" Calden asked, gesturing to all around him.

"Set up at intervals across the wall, make sure the towers are cleared out." Athias instructed.

Calden nodded, taking to the towers with speed, the Shadows behind him

"Roran, did you manage to recruit any of the Askiara tribe?" Rayna asked.

"Bejarn is with them now, they're at the base of the dam, preparing."

"We also found the Minute Council, and they are readying too. Weapons are sparse but they will stand with the city." Roran said.

"Times are truly desperate if the Minute Men will join our cause." Rayna spoke with an ounce of surprise.

"Evacuations are well under way, but the attack will come before everyone is out. Rayna, I brought these Shadows who could be spared, where are the rest?" Roran asked.

"They've gone to establish a defensive line among the ruins in the north-west forest. We will pray that they can hold their line, if they cannot, a flood of soldier will wash into the city. I've already sent a handful of my Shadows to the lifts that you arrived in; they'll be sabotaged."

"Ah, a familiar yet all the more unwelcoming sight." Bejarn stepped from a lift, looking out to the Veins as his eyes were greeted by thousands of chimneys, gushing coal smoke into the sky.

Bejarn peered forward and reached into his coat pocket, pulling out a small sight-glass and put it to his eye.

"What is it, brother?" Calden asked him.

"Raise your scope, directly ahead. South-west. Tell me what you see." Bejarn replied and Calden did so, raising his rifle and looking through the crystal-glass scope.

"No… it can't be." He said, his voice trickling off into a mumble.

"What is it? What do you see?" Athias asked, Rayna looking at them too.

Calden handed him his rifle, encouraging him to look.

"They were called 'Spires'. I only ever heard of their design in passing, extending tower-like structures, capable of holding hundreds at a time, with hundreds more in the body." He sighed, all hope fading from his eyes. "He's going to siege the dam itself, not just march legions into it from the side." Calden spoke in a bold voice.

Athias lowered the rifle and looked stunned.

"Is there anything we can use to delay the approach?" He asked.

In the background, at the base of the towers, the construction workers were now pouring from their quarters.

"Well… There's the cranes at the outer-checkpoint, we could collapse them from the base, and they would block the ships… but… "the webber trailed off.

"But what?" Calden asked.

"It would have to be done from the base, there's no other way. Whoever did it would be stuck on the crane platforms after they fell."

"They'd be stuck with no means to escape from the ships. A certain death." Rayna whispered, shaking her head.

"I'll go." Calden spoke out over the silence.

"No." Athias said as quick as Calden had spoken. "We need you up here, you're one of the best sharpshooters we have."

"We'll go." Two Shadows stepped forwards. "If you will have it, Lady of the Mist?" They asked Rayna.

"Bereh, Nateth. I would have it but only if you are sure, I will not make any go."

"It would be an honour to die for you, my lady" Bereh spoke, bringing down her hood and scarf, and keeling in front of Rayna.

"As it would for the people of this world." Nateth followed suit.

"Very well. We need to drop the cranes here." Rayna pointed to where the checkpoint sat, "The Spires, if they land, will then have to head for this part of the wall, which is still under heavy construction." She said, calmly.

They bowed to her and she smiled before greeting them when they stood up and hugging them.

"Fill your quivers, sharpen your knives. May Zohya guide you." She gestured to the webber who had greeted them and the two of them went to her, before marching to the workshop that overlooked the veins.

"We will have to hold the damn for as long as possible, rest assured Ziath won't bombard us with his gun batteries, at least, for he would not fear knocking the dam through. He will however, no doubt, use mortars to terrorise the city. Go, make barricades out of whatever you can, get ready to fight them in the streets, fight them from the air, and on the ground. Use the sprawling maze of this city in whatever way you can, any vantage point, if you see a way to get an edge, take it. Those legions marching towards this city are deadly in size, but each soldier is weak individually and they do not know this city like we do. Aim for their necks and they will fall as fast as man!" Rayna shouted over the gushing air.

Everyone began moving at once. Taking lifts down and up again bringing supplies to the top or taking them down. Calden took his sharpshooters into the city to find the best spots, and then back to the dam where he told them to spread out along the wall, keeping their eyes on the roads towards the dam. Roran went down into the city and began organising warriors from all over, giving them weapons and armour, while Bejarn went down too and emptied buildings of furniture and materials they could use to build barricades.

"They're ready." Calden said, handing his scope to Athias again who took it and looked out at the legions on the roads, a singular man at the front, signalling up with the banner.

Then a singular horn blew from within the fleet, echoing over the water. It was sharp and shrill, like bird song. Then came a cry, a shout of all the soldiers in unison and they stamped their feet in time as thousands of birds flew up from their nests in the trees on the roads and Gralnor flew above them still, watching all. Athias looked through his eyes and saw Calor setting up positions in a series of monastery ruins, she had blessed the arrows of the Third Shadow; they would pass through bodies like spectral shards. Ortharlia became alive upon Calor, the cloak of death readying to send many into the next realm. Gralnor cawed again, a long-drawn-out cry as the ships began to move forward, their chimneys chugging black smoke and the wheels churning, propelling them forward, while legions upon the winding roads began to march, a beast trailing back for miles and miles.

"There's no stopping what's to come now." Rayna spoke from in front of Athias, looking out at the water and the ships ahead.

Her voice was tremulous, a fear in her eyes as she stared out across the approaching destruction.

"Give us a hand over here!" Construction workers gathered around a wheeled platform, it was covered by cloth and stuck in the doorway of a workshop that sat adjacent to a tower.

Athias and Rayna rushed over and helped pull it free, the top of it scraped the ceiling and caused a partial collapse. They then pushed it, with the help of workers and Shadows, to the edge of the dam's walkway, resting it against the lower wall. With a sigh they pulled the cloth from it to reveal a catapult of sorts.

"There's several of these along the dam's top. We built them for disposing of large amounts of debris if we should ever need them. The range isn't great, one hundred metres or so but we can use them. Bring up the crystal powder and rocks from below!" A webber shouted before joining his workers in a lift and going down with haste.

Catapults were placed into position and small fences were raised atop of the lower walls that ran the length of it. It became a battlement, like that of a tremendous castle, partially unfinished. Archers and sharpshooters paired up across the length and carts of rocks were placed by the catapults, the workers and webbers each taking turns to lift them and douse them in crystal powder; a highly flammable dust that clung to the moisture on the rocks ready to burn. Athias kissed Rayna and left to find Calden. Calden was inside one of the workshops, he was surrounded by men and women; some old and some young, he was holding a rifle in the air and instructing them all, Athias ducked behind a couple of haeries and sat in the shadows, watching.

"This is standard arms for imperial soldiers. Use any weapons at your disposal but in case you find one of these or take one of our own, here's how to use it." He said in a bold, loud, but calm voice.

The wind outside was loud, and it rattled the wooden walls, it slid under the rickety door and twisted through the floorboards. Calden was a soldier and natural leader, even with the screaming wind he had captured the attention of all in the room and there was over fifty. He held up the rifle and showed them how to load a shot and how to aim, even giving his own personal tips which went away from what a trained instructor would say.

"Now, go down into the city. Station at the barricades and find a weapon. Be ready." The room was suddenly alive, chairs and tables scraped as the audience stood up and made their way to lifts.

Some picked up a rifle on the way out and a small pouch of ammunition, it was sparse but there was enough to go around. The last person left and Calden sat down, cleaning his rifle for a last time before the battle. He took an apple from his pouch and bit into it, the juice dripped over his lips and over his fingers, and he sat for a moment in the silence, eating. Calden chucked Athias an apple, confirmed he knew that he had been watching.

"You're quite the natural speaker." Athias said before taking a bite from the apple too.

"Maybe I'll become the new mayor here." He chuckled, wiping his fingers on his coat.

There was an almighty rumble and crash below them, the pair of them rushed to the window overlooking the city and saw a tower of smoke rising from the city where a building once stood. The pair of them ran outside and saw mortar shells rising with a puff of smoke from the ships ahead, they trailed smoke as they whooshed over the dam and then plummeted into the city the other side, causing explosions and deafening booms. Athias grabbed a rifle from one of the racks beside the catapults and looked through, horrified, he saw tens of enormous mortars, wide enough for a bear to sleep in. The sun had begun to fall, sliding smoothly through the sky towards its slumber and the ships beyond the dam were falling into shadow.

"Steady!" Calden shouted to the mismatch of archer and sharpshooter dotted along the wall.

"Load them up!" Bejarn shouted and the construction workers began rolling the rocks in the dust before placing into the launching bucket.

"Torches!" Calden shouted with fire in his voice.

He lit a torch and waved it towards the wall of the dam. Another torch lit and then another, more and more spaced out, while some dropped their torches into iron baskets, lighting fires. Rayna appeared again, wrapped in full leather body armour and with a masked face. She signalled to the Shadows on top of the dam who all, in unison, stepped forward to the wall and slotted an arrow in their bows. Rayna dipped her arrow into a fire which battled the raging winds. More shells passed overhead, crashing down into the scaffolding city.

"Steady… steady now!" Rayna shouted. "Athias, my love, go down below and find Roran. Take the Askiara and go to meet the Third Shadow, they will pull back soon."

Calden nodded at him and the lift started to lower. For a moment all he could hear was the wind, clawing at him as he escaped its reach and then, suddenly, sharply he heard Rayna's voice from above.

"Fire!"

Calden's voice echoed hers with a command of his own and then came the crack of rifles as sharpshooters released a wave of shots and the unmistakable sounds of catapults released their payload. Athias looked up again and took control of Gralnor who had been flying above all this time. He saw Rayna's first arrow of fire rise high and the two Shadows at the crane cut the wires, unbalancing the weights and the cranes collapsed in on themselves; throwing concrete, iron and timber across the bay of the checkpoint as the entire thing fell apart. Ziath's Spire Ships hit the debris and faltered. Athias heard the cheers from the dam as the ship began to buckle, the timber cracking, and more cheers as the rocks from the catapults on the dam landed into the fleet. Some ships went down instantly while others caught fire which halted their progress, at least temporarily. Gralnor turned to the north-westerly woods, Calor stood among the Third Shadow, switching between her spectral, smoke-like and human forms. She would jump up and disappear among the branches only to land for a split second in the legions' lines, dispersing a wave of black-smoke that grasped at the soldiers, pulling them into the earth, or unleashing a handful of jet-black knives that sliced through flesh and bone like paper. When Athias reached the floor it was apparent the city was in turmoil; more and more shells plummeted into the buildings and roads around him, and instead of a peaceful scene the city now mirrored a warzone; iron pipes and girders were protruding from mounds of unearthed concrete; buildings lay in ruins as they had collapsed, surrounded by fire; water pipes had burst and the cold liquid was gushing into the streets. Ahead of him, on the main road towards the dam was an enormous barricade made of anything that could have been gathered, lumps of concrete and iron poles, furniture and wagons. Similar barricades stood across the city and many types of being stood on watch upon them, ready for the inevitable. Athias was greeted by Roran and people of the Askiara clan.

"This is Grithord, he will lead the clan alongside you. They are with you." Roran shouted over the destruction unfolding around them, holding out his hand to Athias who shook it.

Athias caught glimpses in his eyes of Rayna's Shadows sifting through debris for anyone in the fallen buildings, or up above, running across the ropes like agile spiders, heading for vantage points or following the screams of children.

"Grithord. It will be a pleasure to fight alongside your people!"

"Likewise." Grithord grunted and bowed his head, holding his two axes across his chest.

The Askiara mountains birthed some of the most ferocious warriors; trained from a young age in the arts of warfare and old magic. Their weapons and armour were tough, much stronger than steel, made of a rare metal ore that birthed a light and incredibly durable material. The Askiara clan's ruler was mysterious, not even Athias' trio of knowledgeable friends and travellers had seen him before, although the stories of his skill in the forge were unmatched. The warriors donned grey, ceramic lamellar armour over the top of chainmail made from the ore found in the rocks of the mountains, and this too was worn over fur-lined clothing. A top their heads were horned helmets, and each man and woman was armed with a spear and shield, while axes and swords hung from their hips. The warriors ahead of Athias all had ice-white beards, the woman had blood-red hair, and both were painted with charcoal.

"We must go to the old monastery. Allies need us." Athias spoke to Grithord hastily, just as there was a lull in the barrage of the city.

"With me, Askiarans!" Grithord shouted to the soldiers around him who lifted their spears and shields, cheering with him.

Chapter Twenty-One
The Sacrifice

Magic seeks us out. It is not our choice to see it or to use it, but with it, we can do incredible things. Magic is the blood of this world, it flows through it, giving and taking life, restoring, and keeping balance. Magic seeks out those that can use it, and those that cannot, one way or another.
– Calitreum, The Fundamentals of Magic, page 603.

Athias and Roran led the warrior clan through the city and out, up into the westerly winding tracks. Gralnor cawed from above again but this time it was higher pitched, almost shrill, as if in pain. Athias saw, as they were approaching the monastery, they were greeted by the Third Shadow, who were in full retreat towards the city with the imperial soldiers not far behind. The Third Shadow came into view as they ran from the trees across an area of stumps once trees in full before the dam called for their timber. Athias raised Spectre towards the forest,
"Form a shield wall! Get in front of those Shadows!" Grithord nodded, whistling to the clan who sprinted forwards waiting for the Shadows to pass them.
"Get up to the dam, they're going to need all the help they can, take whoever you pass." Rorarn growled, glancing behind to see the small plumes of smoke rising from atop the wall.
Calor stopped by Athias as the Askiara clan closed the gaps and locked shields, some crouching, some standing, their shields overlapping like a rising tidal wave.
"We tried, brother. Many are with Zohya now, they fought well."
"Now we will fight again." Adrenaline was pumping through Athias' veins.
He noted that she was not out of breath at all if anything she was as calm as when she had healed him in the forest. A whistle blew from the treeline followed by fast drums and when peering through the gaps in the shields, Athias saw the lines of imperial soldiers marching forward. A three-line formation, rifles ready.
"Archers ready!" A member of the clan shouted, "on my command."

Archers of the clan slotted arrows into their curved bows and Calor cast a blessing of smoke-like magic across the line of arrowheads, and when it returned to her, they shimmered like a liquid. They aimed high, ready to release. The imperial soldiers took their formation; the first line crouching, ready to aim; the second line standing, rifles ready; and the third line behind the second, ready to swap with it. Athias knew that they would have a split second to charge if to take minimal losses, a split second of which he would have to use his powers. A whistle blew again followed by a crack as the rifles released their first rounds. Smoke puffed from the rifles and a few members of the clan fell but the shield wall maintained its structure, the shields holding strong. Another whistle blew, followed by another crack as the second line of rifles fired and this time a few more of the clan fell.

"Archers. Now!" The clan's archers released a volley of arrows that found their mark, plunging into the line of soldiers, burrowing deep into their flesh and their skin turned black as obsidian.

"Think on your families, not of their loss, but of their honour for your deeds this day." Grithord chanted through gritted teeth.

Athias followed this up with the same spell he had used back at Icaria, throwing Spectre forward like a spear and into the ground ahead of the riflemen which blasted them in cold light, pausing time momentarily. The clan's warriors advanced, keeping a loose shield-wall formation. Their speed increased and the warriors hurtled forwards as archers let loose another devastating volley. Athias sprinted with the soldiers, they were slightly uphill, so this advantage had to be taken quickly. Time returned to normal but the riflemen were caught off guard as the Askiara threw their spears into the lines and then jumped, taking their swords and axes from their belts and smashing into the riflemen formation, and breaking the strict lines like a torrent of water against a cliff. Blood splattered across Athias' face, Calor jumped to her wraith-like form and flew through their lines like before, and axes and swords rose and fell. Many of the riflemen were firing at will, terrified as the snarling faces of the legendary Askiara clan hissed at them and shouted war chants. The clan started to spread out from the initial clashing point, breaking down the lines further, they fought with the ferocity of savage beasts. Roran had buried his blades deep into soldiers somewhere and had since transformed into his own beast-like form, pouncing between the lines of riflemen fast and swift, ripping off arms and biting through necks with his powerful jaw, other Coarans had that joined turned into their animal forms too; wolves, bears, the powerful and sturdy bricic; a cattle-like creature with giant horns a-top its head.

Athias cut through the barrel of rifles like a knife through butter, he looked around to see steel clashing amidst puffs of white smoke. Ahead of him he saw a familiar face which made his blood boil. A thin man wearing a snug-fitting officer's uniform, with short, shaved black hair and a pointy, crooked nose. Tristan's killer stood before him. He held his pistol close and smirked as the trigger squeezed, a warrior in front plummeting into the mud. Athias pulled his sword up and charged forward, pushing past friend and foe until his eyes met Karr's and for a moment, Athias' heart jumped in his throat and his mouth was dry. Athias rushed, sword poised, and Karr raised his pistol again, pulling back the second lever. Athias ducked, the iron ball whizzing past his face. He sliced through the barrel of the gun with such force that the polished wood barely splintered, he followed it up by slamming the hilt of his sword into Karr's bony face, and the thin, goblin-like man fell back grunting.

"Quite a swing there, boy." Karr's voice was sharp, he sneered, wiping blood from his lips as he drew a sword of his own.

The scimitar was gold and recently polished. An elegant design, with a gentle curve on the sharp blade. Even though the fighting was thick around them, Athias noted the sting on the air as the blade shimmered.

"Today's your last day, murderer." Athias' spat.

"Murderer? No. Liberator."

"Enough." Athias pulled back Spectre and lunged forward.

The two blades crashed, sending sparks flying. The vibrations coursed through Athias' fingers as Spectre's smooth blade hit the scimitar's cross guard. Karr grunted and pushed back but his lean build was but a blade of grass to Athias' stature. He flicked the blade up and sliced at Karr's neck, nipping through the skin. Karr swung wildly back in a panic, launching a fist into Athias' ribs but buckled in pain as his fingers cracked. Athias closed his free hand around Karr's fist and twisted, releasing a howl from the legionnaire's throat. The fighting was thick around them, riflemen pushed forward, through the trees, and smoke poured from the barrels.

Steel clanged and wood splintered, and warriors fell left and right. Athias, determined, pressed his own attack, a rage of unfathomable depths rising in his heart; hot blood pumping through his veins as he heard Tristan's last words in his mind. Spectre in his hand, seemingly fighting of its own mind, with light spinning off as it flicked up and down with finesse in Athias' hands. He clasped at the hilt with two hands and with a swift swing, cut through Karr's arm, slicing the hand clean off. Karr let out a howl of pain and gaped at his stump, blood spewing, rolling over the earth beneath them.

"No…" Karr cried, a wounded beast.

He looked up to Athias in fear and went to pull a knife from his boot but Athias kicked his hand away, and it crunched under his boot, Athias felt every break. He bludgeoned Karr's bony face with Spectre's hilt, shattering his jaw. The man slumped, twisted around his own shadow, and spat teeth from his blood-filled mouth.

"Know fear." Athias shouted, pulling Karr's head back, just as he did his own eye patch, and staring him in the eye.

The memories of Tristan's last moments surged between the pair of them. Tristan's sadness passing over them, Athias' fear of losing his friend, and the hatred he had felt for what he had done. It washed through Karr's mind like a hand through water, and it burned, searing the mind and flesh behind his eyes.

"Y… you." Karr stuttered, spitting more teeth from his husk of a mouth.

"Me." Athias whispered, sliding Spectre into the sheath upon his back, the world around him second to the view in front of him.

Karr went to try and speak but gagged as Athias' placed three fingers upon his bloodied tongue and three from his other hand against the top of Karr's mouth. He pulled and pushed on his hands, and Karr screamed. The sound of Karr's cheeks ripping apart as he pried the lower jaw from where it sat were but a harmony to the rage he felt. Blood gushed over Athias' arms, pouring down over Karr's uniform and still Athias' pulled, pulling the jaw cleanly off with a snap. For a moment Karr sat there, howling, in what seemed like silence around him. Then, with a crack, Athias' discharged the pistol lying on the floor and Karr's body fell back, contorted and disfigured, crashing into the dirt.

The ground began to rumble and tremble. Around him groups of riflemen and warrior alike were sent flying into the air and landing, sprawled out across the earth as dust and pebbles settled around them. Athias looked past thin line of riflemen and saw cannons. Gigantic, smooth, iron forged beasts. Towers of smoke poured from the black barrels, a tunnel from which devastation soared. They fired again and brought havoc upon the fighting soldiers, the riflemen started to fall back as the cannons were brought forward, pushed slowly over the rigid roots and grainy dirt. With them marched more lines of riflemen who crouched, cannons to each side, took aim and fired. The clang of steel was dwarfed by the crack of rifles and followed by the shattering scream of cannonballs soaring over the air and into the ground around Athias.

"Fall back! Back to the city!" Grithord bellowed.

Calor and Athias ran with the warriors, picking up wounded over their shoulders. Calor blew smoke into her palm and then fed it to the ground. Behind them, the roots from the dead trees sprung into animation, coiling themselves around the wheels, dismantling the cannons, and dragging the gun-crews into the mud. The rigid roots of cracked wood moved like liquid-smoke and then solidifying again.

"That'll give us a few minutes." Calor said, unsure though, as the riflemen behind were already lightning torches to burn the roots.

As they reached the scaffolding covered buildings Athias caught glimpses of the roots slinking back into the earth, swallowing the riflemen beneath. They made their way into the city, through the outer barricades, and towards the Sleeping Giant which had been turned into a designated field hospital. Using Gralnor's eyes again Athias looked to the top of the dam as the Spire Towers approached the wall, they were minutes from touching down on it. The legions to the north were digging into the earth, establishing a gun battery line ready to blitz the city, and to the east, the legions were at the lifts, though they fell fast after the Shadows' sabotage.

"Calor, arrange for the wounded to be taken to the docks, there are some ships still that have not left. Get as many on as you can and then hold one for us."

"I will." She nodded as Athias and Roran ran from the inn.

They sprinted through the city towards the lifts that went up to the dam. The faint sound of rifles firing from the top drifted down to them. At the lifts they found Bejarn and a handful of other people.

The lift started to rise before they had shut the door, the lift-crew desperately pulling on ropes to raise the lift quickly. There was an explosion from the top, it was sudden and swift, fire roared through the air; as terrifying as magnificent.

The Spires were sure to touch soon, Calden and his sharp shooters were taking careful shots down to the ships below, trying to take down certain targets on the ships deck but it was not enough. Looking out over the Veins Athias saw fire; the occasional destroyed ship, and hundreds of bodies half submerged in the water around them. Helplessness began to rise in his heart, his eyes watered and ears rang. The Spires drew closer still, Rayna and the Shadows on the walkway pulled back from the wall, preparing to fight the hordes of riflemen as they would pour from the towers' gaping mouths. There were tens of them, spaced out along the length of the dam, and in each were a thousand riflemen ready to purge those in the city. Rayna ran to him; she was out of arrows and her facemask was scarred with dust and splinters of wood.

"We have to go, now!" Athias shouted, the city will fall!

The Shadows made their way to the lifts, pulling every being with them as they went. snapped back to it and ran to Calden who was kneeling with Roran and Bejarn.

"We have to go! We need to leave here; the defences have fallen." He shouted over the roaring fires and whooshing of mortar shells passing overhead.

The three nodded to each other and began to help him with any wounded, putting them in a lift. Athias stepped inside and heard the door shut behind him, bolting.

"What are you doing?" He scrambled with the door, trying to pry it open but the old iron would not budge.

"Someone has to stay, make sure they don't follow you straight down." Roran said.

"No! We need you all." Athias started to reply in protest but was cut off by Bejarn.

"Have you heard the story of Nhorrin, Athias, our old friend?" He shouted over the creaking towers that were now mere moments from touching down.

Rorarn snapped off his pendant and gave it to Athias, through the bars.

"Give this to her, to H'Khara." He smiled and the lift began to tremble as it lowered.

"May the Mother be with you, dear friend." Calden nodded.

They disappeared as the lift slowly made its way down. Athias heard the almighty crunch of stone as the towers arrived at the dam and then the creaking sound of bolts and cogs turning as the landing bridges prepared to fall. Athias jumped to Gralnor's eyes who circled above and looked down at the three, preparing wagons of the crystal powder, creating trails of it between, before jumping into hiding spots. In one swift motion the Spires' landing bridges smashed down onto the concrete wall of the walkway and the soldiers began to pour out. As hundreds upon hundreds of the riflemen marched onto the walkway, spacing out and edging forward carefully, examining the barrels and the powder, Bejarn rose from his hiding place and pointed his pistol towards one of the many barrels. Athias did not hear the shot as Gralnor flew down to join him but a series of explosions ripped through the air. Fire gushed across the walkway and poured over the dam; sliding down the wall towards the city before being sucked up again and screaming through the pattering rain. A tongue of burning orange jumped high into the sky and licked over the dam. An enormous plume of smoke followed as a charging stallion of heat ripping through the air. Athias dropped to his knees, tears cascading from his eyes as a moving body of molten stone from the walkway glided over the walls and down towards the ships attacking it. As the roar surpassed, all Athias could hear was the creaking iron lift and his own gasps of sharp air. The lift creaked to a stop at the bottom, touching down. Rayna ran to greet him, pulling Athias to his feet.

"Athias?" She asked him softly but felt his tears trail down over her neck.

He opened his palm to reveal Rorarn's pendant.

Rayna pulled on Athias' hand and they, with the rest of the survivors, made a break for it.

Chapter Twenty-Two
The Breach

It is said that when Mother Zohya tore down the giants and created the world from their skin, their muscles, that she carved out every river with powerful magic. She is a goddess, after all, a goddess and a saviour, our saviour. What magic that must have been, to open the world up and fill it with water, and to create such marvels, and such horrors. – Calitreum, Story of the Vayshanaa, Eifig's Entry, Page 449.

The trading docks of Nhorrin Dam were normally peaceful. A flock of birds or two would fly overhead, their bodies cast in shadow against a setting sun. The several piers that stretched out over the shimmering would be laden with barrels of wine, cages of fish, crates of stone, and piles of timber. Today, as the evening light dimmed, the piers were laden with thousands of tired, frightened beings, eager to escape. Lightning flashed across the sky and thunder followed moments after, rumbling over the mountains and down across the rivers. Cracks of gunfire trickled over the air as they fled the city, while louder roars of cannon fire followed, masking the cries of those falling into the clutches of death.

Long lines trailed back from the jetties as those fleeing took their turn, one by one, ready to board the scrappy fleet of ships that had arrived. The possessions of a lifetime cramped into the hands of a family or less, some were tired, having been on the run from the Emperor's reach all their lives and some were distraught that their lives had been uprooted yet again. Guards sporting the banner of the golden raven dotted the harbour, they stood in proud pairs throughout the harbour and on the road into it, and a Syndicate ship could be seen off in the distance, watching over the mouth of the sea.

"The Syndicate must have sent these from Eirshen. They must be holding the fortress there." Rayna mumbled to herself.

"Then that's where we'll go" Athias replied, swiftly.

He climbed upon a cart and surveyed the bay. Many ships had already set off, filled to the brim with souls, and others had abandoned reason, hastily encouraging many on at a time. On the longest jetty was the largest ship, its high sails shimmered in the pale light as the sun began to set and rich, clear water caressed the hull while the ocean's temper was calm. Hundreds more were marching up the boarding bridges, crossing onto a would-be home for the day. Everyone told a different story, some in families and others alone. Athias wondered what someone might think was his story. Peering across the crowds he spotted Calor, she was standing over H'Khara, tending to her wounds.

"This way." He jumped down and beckoned to Rayna who grabbed his hand and followed him through the sea of people frantically trying to escape.

At the dam behind them all, buildings were collapsing in a shockwave of smoke and dust, and seeing this devastation unfold not a mile from them, people were getting increasingly agitated and restless, all pushing forward to get onto a ship. Their murmurs grew louder into disgruntled shouts while their gentle swaying evolved into pushing and shoving. Many voices shouted over the crowds, children started to wail, and animals started crying.

"This place is going to get dangerous before long." Rayna said to Athias in a hushed tone as they briskly walked through the crowds, picking up the pace.

Another ship docked and lowered its bridges to the jetty and people started to march up, each person a little quicker than the one before them. Rayna and Athias signalled to Calor who caught their eyes and started to prepare the brigantine for departure, lowering the sails and tightening the ropes. Athias clambered over the side and Rayna jumped with a few of her rangers from the jetty to the deck. The ship was already over the capacity of people it should have been. A gunshot cracked through the air and was met by screaming, as the crowd turned stampede rushed to the ships while Athias and his company could but watch. There was another sickening crack of rifle fire and tens of people fell before reaching the boarding bridges. Athias and Rayna ran to the side of the ship, stricken with shock as they witnessed riflemen stand up and reload before moving forwards, another line marching in, and another, more and more. They walked around the docks and pointed rifles towards the crowds of innocents. The rifles spat shards of iron and steel into the crowd who were still frantically trying to escape, and shrieks and screams was all that could be heard between the rifles. Athias went to jump overboard, to swim back, but was pulled back by Calor and Rayna who looked to him, dead in the eye.

"I'm sorry, Athias." Her voice was strangled, she turned her back to the docks and the screams followed her.

The remaining ships had cast off, putting as much distance as they could between themselves and the harbour. The riflemen edged forwards, spearing many on the floor with bayonets, and more shots followed, into those who had nowhere but the water to go. Athias looked on as he saw a few warriors left, pulling pistols and knives from their waists, charging forward before falling to the floor with a puff of smoke. He looked on as his heart dropped, watching those few left, swimming frantically towards the ships. He stared in a wretched agony to the jetty where a father cowered, sheltering his son from the onslaught; Athias could make out a shivering body before a final wave of shots were released and he, like the boy in front of him, fell to the floor.

A man rode into the harbour slowly atop a silver horse, his red cape flapped in the wind and his breastplate glinted in the last of the suns light. The Emperor himself. Ziath slowly directed his horse into the bloodied docks and dismounted before walking to the end of the jetty and kicking the boy off, into the water and staring out at the escaping ships. Athias' skin tightened over his knuckles as he gripped the bannister.

"Come. Please. There is much to discuss between here and the Breach." Rayna whispered to him; all was quiet apart from the gentle rain between the thunder in the skies, and Athias stared at the Emperor who stared back at the ships sailing away.

Athias looked up and whistled. Gralnor dipped from the clouds and swooped down, landing on his shoulder. His feathers were soaked from the rain but Athias noticed a tear in the bird's eye too. Rayna hung her head, taking his hand and walking with him into the ship's cabin where Calor, the captain and H'Khara were standing. H'Khara was leaning upon the centre table which saw a map sprawled across it, she was still recovering from her battle earlier and Athias noticed bandages wrapped around her waist and chest, sticking out past the tops of her shirt which had been ripped to remove the sleeves, and her leg had been braced, in a rush. She winced a little every time she went to take weight off the table and as she sat down in a chair brought to her by the captain. The captain then went to stand at the door, locking it as Athias and Rayna entered, then she lit several lanterns that swayed gently in time with the rocking water. Outside the rain poured down, splashing into the deck and the clouds turned from pale grey to black as ink. The cabin was warm but everyone inside was stricken with a cold that twisted into their hearts and throat, clawing into their skin and spreading, relaying over and over what their eyes had seen just minutes before.

"Athias, this is Captain Ha'lai. She's from Eishern and was sent personally by an old friend of yours, supposedly." Rayna gestured to the captain.

Ha'lai was wearing a weathered leather coat with a collar that towered above her ears and trailed low, swinging by her boots. She nodded her head to him and held out a scroll of parchment. Athias took it, nodding and shaking her hand.

"Thank you. Thank you for coming, for saving us."

"It is an honour to help against Ziath." Her voice was strict, a woman of the military perhaps.

"Well… What do you make of it?" Rayna asked tentatively, eyeing the parchment.

"I'm not sure but it's definitely from Eishern. Are we heading there?" He asked the captain.

"Aye, should be in port by tomorro' night with good wind"

"Ziath will follow. Maybe not directly to Eishern but his army sails along the Blackstone-shore. They'll find their way to the Forts of the Breach soon enough." He paused for a few moments, thoughts racing through his mind.

"What is it?" Calor asked, making Athias jump, forgetting she was there.

"Ziath will send his legions after us, by land and sea. Beneath the Forts of the Breach are tunnels, tunnels that spread far into the mainland, towards places of security. When we arrive at the Eishern we should reinforce the garrison and prepare for an attack while sending the rest through the tunnels, there are some old castles in lands so inhospitable that Ziath will be forced to send his full army straight at it with no chance of surprises from any other direction."

"It could work. The Askiaran clans would welcome those people to their homes, I could send a letter to Eishern to inform of this plan,"

"The Askiar hold Eishern?" Rayna was surprised.

"Yes, didn't you 'ear?" Ha'lai looked around, bewildered, but was met by plain faces. "Twenty nights ago, the clan came and liberated the forts. Thousands of 'em drove back Ziath's numbers there and then joined with Syndicate ships."

"Captain Ha'lai, send a bird ahead of us. Inform them that reinforcements are on the way."

"Aye." She bowed and then left the room.

"Can I have the room with H'Khara, please." Athias' voice was solemn, and the rest nodded, leaving slowly.

The ship swayed in the water, rocking gently side to side. The timber beneath his feat creaked slightly as he trudged over the pelt rug atop it. Athias dragged his feet towards H'Khara who looked at him with a confused expression, every step forward felt as though he was pulling a tremendous weight. He was dreading the conversation that would unfold when he sat down next to her, H'Khara was still resting, leaning on the table, and clutching the sword he had given her early that morning. Athias dragged a chair to her side and sat opposite her, he lay Spectre down on the floor and removed his hood, his wrist guards, and gloves.

"Please take my hand." He could feel sorrow brewing in his chest, his teeth started to chatter, and his heart felt heavy.

H'Khara sat up, she was alert now, aware of the sadness in his voice.

"What… is it?" She stuttered but he did not say, she could see the sorrow unfolding in his eyes. "Athias? You're scaring me now."

Athias took her hand in both of his and cleared his throat.

"Roran." Athias said and H'Khara began to cry.

"No. No, please don't say it." Her voice was taut and shrill. She tugged at her hand, trying to pull free but Athias would not let go.

She stood up and pushed him back, barely wincing from the pain, but he still would not let go as she started to cry. He went to hug her, but she started to transform. The chair behind her began to splinter, it broke as she kicked it. Claws emerged from her fingertips and hair lengthened down her back, she shouted and screamed, taking a swipe at Athias who blocked it, the claws scraped down his arm, drawing blood but he fought her off and brought her closer to him. He wrapped his arms around her, his size dwarfed hers and he sheltered her, as a bear would for her cubs. She punched his chest and squirmed.

"I'm so sorry. He was a good man."

H'Khara stopped fighting abruptly and rest her head against his chest. She mumbled something into Athias' cloak, pressing her face into it, he could not make out what the words were. The claws sank back into her fingers and her hair returned to normal. She began to bawl, a river of tears stained her cheeks and fell, a waterfall of tears splashed into Athias' cloak. He picked her up and carried her across the ship, into the officer's cabin, placing her down onto a bed where he covered her with a pelt and sat on the corner.

"He wanted me to give you this." Athias took the pendant from a pocket and dangled it by the chain, she opened her palm and as he placed it down into her hand, H'Khara closed her fingers around it, bringing it close to her chest as tears fell onto her fingers.

"I'll come back in a few hours. Please, try to rest." Athias croaked, his mind tired and pained.

He left and closed the door slowly behind him. As the door slid shut, he coughed and a single tear escaped from the fortress of his eye, trailing down his cheek and becoming lost in the darkness of his cloak. Calor greeted him, a look of sadness over her own expression.

"I'll watch her. Go and be with Rayna." She hugged him but withdrew quickly, it was an awkward embrace.

Athias smiled briefly and head to find Rayna in their room. The captain had been kind to them, giving them as much room each as she could and her crew were hard working and loyal, just over a dozen men and women crewed the Snarr; named after the type of black, icy-skinned octopus that was found in northern waters. Athias looked from the ports on the side as he travelled through the lower deck and it had started to snow. The occasional flake fell slowly from the sky and an icy chill swept over the valley. They had been given a bed and steamer, a small heater that evaporated water to warm the room, and the floor was covered by pelts. A small lantern hung from the ceiling and another two were on each wall to his right and left. Rayna was sitting on the bed, she had taken her boots, mask, cloak and gauntlets off, and her bow was hanging on the door next to her quiver.

"Come sit with me." She whispered and lay her hand on the bed next to her.

Athias hung Spectre up on the hook too before removing his own boots, cloak, and leather armour, setting it down with a thud on a chair. He went and sat next to her and the bed sagged a little under the extra weight. He looked defeated, and stared at the steamer with brooding eyes, consumed by grief.

"I should have brought them with us, I could have convinced them. Now they're gone." He murmured, slurring his words.

"No, you couldn't have. Athias, my love. You can't save everyone, none of us can. I see the fear consuming you, fear that you'll fail me, or fail yourself."

"I lose everyone. I am a curse, a curse bound to this world. I lost our son, Tristan, Calden, Bejarn, Roran. They all died because of me."

"You've not lost me." She kissed him on the cheek and turned him to face her, "They were brave people, bold and daring men, they gave us the time we needed to escape. They made up their mind before the battle started."

"I love you." He whispered to her.

"I love you too." They pressed their foreheads together and sat in silence for a moment.

"Will you tell me a story? One of the those you read to me after Galin was born. The ones you told to me all those years ago, about the Heroes of Old."

Athias took one of the pelts from atop the steamer and lay it over her, it was warm to the touch and she lay down, curled up beneath it. He poured a cup of wine from the jug on the bedside table, it was silky smooth, probably from the exotic ports of Rargnos where the sun never set, or so the stories said. He sat down on the bed and began to tell the tale and Rayna began to drift off while the ship rocked gently, smiling as her hand lay in his.

Chapter Twenty-Three
Secrets and Stories

Eirshen and her sisters all built castles upon Islands of the Breach. They became known as the Stone Sisters; looming monoliths of shimmering grey rock, built by giants from the Rocky Mountains. These giants, though much smaller than those that Zohya had faced, were no less brutish, and their strength and size made short work of the castle, and all its tunnels, that would otherwise have taken hundreds of years perhaps. The King, Dramatha, he visits Eirshen's Castle regularly, his son was born there, and he was buried there. - Calitreum, History of Old, page 303.

Eirshen was as beautiful as it was daunting, said to reflect the heroine herself. Athias had read of its magnificence from the pages of the Calitreum while with Hathael and at the Temple before that. Eirshen and her sisters had travelled to Brineth long ago, by their words in the Calitreum, it could be assumed that they were among the first to travel here, the first to see it when it was the most beautiful. He slipped down from the main deck, where the tall towers of Eirshen's Castle had appeared round the bend, downstairs, he found Calor was sitting, telling stories to a group of children. He hung back, listening as intently as they did.

"The stories say that Calliu Eirshen and her sisters came when the giants still roamed, descendants of Zohya's enemies. It is said that they were drawn to Eirshen, they obeyed her and served her, and when Eirshen's own people demanded that she forsake them, to return home, that she could not for she had fallen in love with one.

"Eirshen built this castle for giants, for her and them to live together. When Eirshen's people came to Brineth, demanding that she leave this land, she refused." This was met with a gasp, louder than one when she had told of a human loving a giant. "They besieged the castle but to no avail, it stands upon an island of black stone, with treacherously sharp edges, and slippery surfaces. Eirshen's castle has enormous, thick walls and high, advantageous towers.

"The outer wall's gate is three times as tall as any man or woman today. It is made of strong oak, a hand's length in thickness, but the main gate stands almost two times that, this one is made of thick oak and iron bars, it requires a gate-crew of eighteen strong to open from the tower above with a series of winches to be pulled in a secret order. The castle of Eirshen was, as far as assaulting efforts went, unbreachable. So, her people left, and Eirshen saw that her sisters also took giants for lovers, something drew them to each other as a race, you see. Calliu and her sisters, they each built a castle upon one of the larger islands in the Breach, and these castles still stand today, protecting Brineth from any who wish foul deeds upon it from the sea."

Athias walked onto deck as the towers of Eirshen appeared in full, towering high. Its structure stood tall against the backdrop of clouds and sea even though it was over a mile from the mainland. The would-be fleet of assorted ships spaced out across the river's water, spanning the distance of a few hundred metres in every direction. Ships of all types from magnificent, cannon-bearing galleons to small longboats. The snow had fallen all through the night, covering the mountains of the valley in a crisp, white carpet. The roaring winds had calmed sometime in the early hours of the morning and now the ships sailed forward with a gentle push from the breeze. Athias strolled up to the helm where Captain Ha'lai stood, it was uncertain if she had been there all night, but it was apparent that she was used to this weather. She had turned her collar up and tightly fastened the thick, long coat around her.

"Are they expecting us?" He asked her.

"'Ey should be, we'll strike the colours when 'e draw near."

"Can I get you anything? You look like you've been here all night?" He looked around at the ships, the longboats had disappeared. "Where are the Askiara?"

"'Ey landed on the shores and are makin' their own way to Eishern, 'ey got people in the hills, you see."

Rayna appeared on deck, wrapped in blankets. Although she claimed to like the cold, it was something else to be in direct line of the wind that soared in off the sea. She stood at the side of the ship and looked out over the water; her head tilted upwards as she clocked the towers from Eishern and she gasped as Athias appeared behind her, his arms around her.

"It's something isn't it?" There was a flicker of awe on his voice.

Although surrounded by other islands, Eirshen stood out like a sword among strands of straw. The Breach itself was magnificent, peaceful, and beckoning with flocks of birds flying overhead, waves lapping at the cliffs, sighing as it did so. The remains of two statues stood tall at the Breach, signalling a safe passage to all those leaving the mainland and heading out into the ocean, the statues were joined in the middle; two hands joined while their others held shields taller than the crow's nest of their ship. As the fleet began to draw close, they signalled a colour change in their flags. Several of the ships veered off and towards the other forts but the bulk of the ships headed to Eirshen. Captain Ha'lai brought the ship close to the island that Eirshen sat upon and slowly sailed it towards the docks. The docks were made of slabs of grey stone, found at the bed of the ocean beneath the cliffs of the island itself, and each metre of it glimmered a little as the water splashed over it from the sea. The docks were mostly deserted apart from a few guards in the towers that overlooked the port and a solemn, cloaked figure ahead of them. Whoever it was stood perfectly still as the howling wind attacked them, their cloak billowed around their feet. They stood still again as the ships unloaded and men, women, and children filed past. Many looked at the figure but diverted their gaze as they were ushered by the guards up towards the bridges and stairs to Eirshen. Captain Ha'lai nodded to the figure who nodded back, slowly, and then returned to the ship.

"Com' on, we'll take it to the caves." She said to her crew who began the preparations for the ship. "I'll 'ave a bite with you inside later, do you play Prison?" Ha'lai shouted as the ship turned ready to sail around the island.

"We do! Until then and thank you for everything." Rayna promptly replied.

Ha'lai bowed her head as the sails dropped on the ship and she began to ease it from the port. Ahead, the figure still stood, perfectly still. Athias began to approach the person and the person began to walk forward, their body wrapped in cloak, it was hard to distinguish boot from cloak.

"Vayshanaa of Time, Vayshanaa of Death. I've been expecting you." A voice carried from the figure; a voice that sounded oddly familiar.

"Eifig? Is that you." Athias asked.

The cloak crumbled before them, fluttering up, like falling leaves into the breeze.

"It is me, old friend."

The same voice continued but it was closer, Athias turned to look behind them and there they were, standing a few feet from them.

"Eifig!" Athias shouted with pleasure, his excitement rang out over the howling air which died down just as Eifig pulled their hood down, turning their right palm over, as though the storm had been on strings at the end of their fingers.

"The Vayshanaa of Emotion. As I live and breathe." Calor sighed with relief.

"Excuse me, Miss? How did you do that?!" H'Khara stepped forward, limping on some crutches. "

"Mx, if you would please." Eifig kindly asked.

"This is…" Athias started.

"This is the wolf, H'Khara, yes."

"Sorry! Mx, how… how did you know that?" H'Khara squealed, excited.

"Emotion influences everything around us. It influences your mind and mine, it influences weather for that is alive with magic, and it influences the very fabric of our reality." Eifig paused, enjoying H'Khara's dumbfounded expression.

"Eifig is very powerful, let's say." Athias chuckled.

"Come, we have much to discuss from your letter." Eifig smiled, leading the way up to the great castle.

The keep was warm and welcoming, hundreds of fires dotted the main hall and tables stretched out from end to end. It was clear that if it had not been built by giants, whoever had, loved the theatrics for each hearth could have seen a mammoth sit comfortable inside. The tables had been added over the years, maybe quite recently, Athias thought to himself as they passed through its doors. The hall was filled with all different beings that had travelled from Nhorrin Dam; they were all refugees again after many years of peace. Athias, Eifig and Calor just stood there and looked to them all, huddling by the fires, drying their soaked clothes, and rolling out bedding. Soldiers from the fort were taking pots from the kitchens to the middle table and handing bowls filled with steamy, thick, stew to those now resting around. H'Khara spotted Gh'ael and other Coarans, and Rayna spotted some familiar faces. They each made their way into the crowd, becoming lost in the bustling, environment that had lit up with voices. Eifig's appearance had changed as any person's would when they grew up but Athias could still see the young soul he grew up with, back then they had pale white hair and now it was a faint purple, platted and extending well past their shoulders; it was well learned that those who dabbled in the school of emotion would become a changed person. Eifig had the same sandy skin and bright green eyes, eyes peppered with gold dust, they had a sharp nose and pointed ears as did all who were born amidst the misty reeds of Nriac to the east. They were incredibly beautiful. Athias remembered the feelings he once had for them when they were just students at the temple. They used to meet in secret at the top of the library and study from the shadow texts.

"You're conflicted, my old friend?" Eifig said quietly, turning to Athias.

"Your connection to Nhivaliurn is stronger than ever." Athias replied, looking to the ring on her right hand. It shimmered a little, a flicker of red and purple light danced from its jewel at the top.

"As is yours." Eifig whispered before the pair of them turned and hugged.

They turned to Calor; her cloak of shadow flowed like a river even though there was no breeze. "I've heard of another, the one who was not taught. Calor, am I right?"

"You are. Three Vayshanaa under one roof, it has been a long time since..."

"Four." Eifig cut in and Athias stood back, confused.

"Who else is here?"

"Come and see." Eifig extended their hand, and Athias took it as they left the hall.

The corridors were narrow but still warm and well lit, a lantern every few metres and fires at the end of each pathway, sending heat up and down. Calor followed Athias and Eifig who made their way from the hall and up into the maze of rooms, corridors and towers above it, each ceiling untouchable, high above, while many fabulous paintings hung on the walls they walked past. Eifig brought Athias to a set of double doors that led to private rooms, these were bedrooms, each with a long table and huge hearth so warriors close to the commander of the fort could plan away from prying eyes. Eifig gestured to the door and Athias knocked with no reply but Eifig opened the door themselves and gestured again but this time for Athias to head inside. Athias took a foot over the threshold and turned to Eifig who simply smiled.

"We will wait in the hall for now, come down and get something to eat when you two are ready. Then we will begin our plans in preparation for the Tyrant."

Athias was confused but stepped into the room all the same, Eifig shut the door behind him and Athias heard Eifig's footsteps fade, while Calor's made no sound at all. The four-poster bed was made up; furs and pelts untouched and yet a fire roared in the hearth, flames licked the stone walls and smoke poured upwards. A decorative lantern spread hung from the ceiling, dozens of candle lanterns placed on stag's antlers, and several ancient paintings hung on the walls, some dating back to when Eirshen had walked these rooms. A raven cawed and flew in from one of the windows. It cawed again as it looked to Athias, tilting its head, and jumping from the window-ledge onto one of the tall wooden chairs. Athias went and stood by the fire, it had started to rain, and the water was pattering on the balcony, bringing a cold breeze with it. As Athias leant down to warm his hands up there was a flutter behind him.

"Hathael." He said, smiling but hiding his face from her.

"My boy. It's good to see you… or the back of you at least."

Athias turned and looked at Hathael and smiled, kneeling, and bowing his head. Athias had always showed respect to Hathael, she was after all, the closest thing to a mother that he had ever known, that he remembered at least.

"Come here, Athias." She beckoned to him and stood up to meet him, chuckling.

"I thought I might never see you again." Athias said through her thick coat as they embraced.

"When you almost died and ventured to the Nhivaliurn itself we all saw a vision, all of the Vayshanaa. We glimpsed the crown and felt the power it holds and while you may be the one tasked with retrieving it, you will need our help with what comes next." She had a kind voice; it was sweet and comforting, it always had been.

Although he felt grief, he also felt a flicker of warmth in hearing her voice.

"Rayna is here, I found her. I think she would be pleased to see you."

"I would be pleased to see her as well. The Vayshanaa must talk, there's four of us here now, yes?"

"We must. There is only a short time to prepare for what comes next."

Athias took Hathael by the arm and the pair walked downstairs to the hall. Hathael clung to her staff with every step. Eifig turned to greet them, clutching a scroll, they smiled but there was a flicker of remorse on their face. They followed her to a room that overlooked the harbour, windows carved from the rock of the island looked out over the seas and the island together. Calor stood up when the other three arrived and shook the hand of Hathael who smiled, genuinely, as they did so. Calor then placed a pot of stew into the hands of Athias and Hathael before sitting down again to observe the map that was stretched over the table, it was not whole; the corners had been ripped, hiding whatever had once been shown there. Eifig strolled around to the other side of the table and unrolled the parchment in their hand, pinning it to the top of the map.

"Ziath has sent another force into the lands and they are making their way through the eastern towns. We… I sent scouts, envoys, to these villages to inform them of the coming attacks but they must have been intercepted." A tear rolled down Eifig's cheek and their ears drooped a little, "Ziath's legions have been told to give no quarter. They raid and rape as they go, burning the towns, while the bodies of a thousand Coaran children now hang from the trees of Kch'tar woods."

"How many soldiers?" Athias barked.

"From what our scouts did manage to relay, several thousand. Armed to the teeth…" Eifig paused, more words poised on her tongue. "The scouts reported back of steel beasts of war, and threats from the sky, 'airships' they said, in their report."

Athias finished the stew, throwing the bowl into the fire which cracked and spat sparks.

"You knew of this? Of this machine?" Eifig agonized, "I sense it, I sense a secret in your mind."

Athias leant over the fireplace, staring into the vicious fire.

"Put your ring away, Eifig. Yes, I knew of the machine, or part of it. I was with the Syndicate at Icaria when we tried to destroy something a source and friend called an 'engine'. They said it would be powerful enough to power great beasts of war."

"Were you going to tell us of this?" Calor addressed Athias formally but Athias did not answer, he simply stared into the flames, thinking over the events of that day. "What are we to do?" Calor turned back and addressed Eifig and Hathael.

"Finhaal marches to meet them as we speak. Though I do not know if he knows of these beasts." Eifig's voice waned.

Athias turned when hearing this.

"Finhaal... how many soldiers does he have?"

"Six thousand. His most determined, bound by blood to his order."

"That's not enough." Athias returned to the table to observe it, looking to the mountains and back.

"It'll have to be." Eifig tried to be strong but their voice faltered, glowering at Athias.

"I have a suggestion." They all turned to see Rayna in the doorway.

"Rayna" Athias began but she cut him off.

"Look." She sighed, a long, heavy breath. "We have another ally, someone with three-thousand strong soldiers."

"Who else is out there who has not joined us already? There is nobody else." Eifig's voice cracked.

"There is one more who has yet to enter this war." Rayna marched over to the table, she pointed to a mountain range, known to the locals as the Dolthraag. "King Dramatha's second legion, the Rhalnarg, they were sent there to guard the path, but that was not all they were told to guard."

"What do you mean?" Hathael turned, curious and intrigued.

"They've been protecting the King's daughter."

"I'm sorry? Daughter? He had a son; I saw it written in the Calitreum myself." Eifig asked.

"A son, yes, that is what was written. A son that died on the battlefield along with his father." Rayna paused, pointing to the ford on the map, not far inland from where they were. "He did have a son, but he also had a daughter. Kaelon was her name and she was born here, in this very castle. She went with the second legion to guard the Dolthraag passage, making sure that royal forces could not be flanked. A cover up no-less, for it is certain that the Emperor knows not of any passage at all."

The room was silent. All that could be heard were the flames that licked the wood in the hearth, cracking the logs and spitting burning arrows of orange ash, which quickly faded in the cold air.

"H… how? How do you know?" Athias turned to her, his tone ringing of surprise.

"When you disappeared, the King gave me a message to go to the pass… to find her. He knew he was going to die and wanted me to be the one to tell her."

The rest of the room was silent still, they had all seemingly crept back into shadow, out of sight and out of mind. Athias took a deep breath, filling his air with lungs. Then he snapped back around to the group, with everything returning to his senses.

"Would Kaelon fight with us?" His heart was beating furiously.

"With absolute certainty."

"Am I missing something? Kaelon, the second legion, they only number at three thousand. How are they going to tip the scales?" Eifig asked.

"Three-thousand ordinary soldiers would do no such thing, you're right. Not even three-thousand Blood-Born from the Askiara clans would tip the scales. The Rhalnarg however, they are more than soldiers. Three-thousand knights, elite with spear, sword, and shield alike. Their armour and sword blessed by magic."

"So, what's the plan?" Calor urged. "Ziath's legions he sent from the dam ahead of the rest will surely be here soon."

"Rayna, take Gralnor and go to the passage but first gather a handful of Shadows that will stay. Us four will go with the Shadows, and Eifig's chosen soldiers to join Finhaal on the battlefield. The rest of the soldiers will go with the refugees to the mountain city, the fight at Scaltian Fields will not be the last." The other Vayshanaa nodded as he finished.

"What about your plan who hold this fort against the legions that followed us from the dam?" Rayna challenged, while making the effort to sound friendly.

"Plans change all the time in war. Especially when new information is presented." A smiled flickered briefly across his face.

Rayna walked out onto the balcony and whistled. Gralnor landed on her shoulder not moments after and she walked back to the door, stopping briefly to kiss Athias gentle on the cheek before leaving the room.

"What about the crown?" Hathael investigated.

"When the battle of Scaltian Fields is over, Finhaal will send his soldiers back to the mountain city to prepare and then he will join us in retrieving the crown before we journey north to his domain too. Like I said, I will need all of your help to break it from where it lays."

A horn blew out, it rattled through the corridors and echoed from slab to slab. It was eerie and high-pitched, signalling an approach. The four of them hastily made their way into the hall again and clambered onto a table to address those huddled together.

"I know you have come far but now you must travel again. This castle is strong, maybe unbreachable but we cannot take that chance. It can be attacked from many angles and we are against a foe with surprise after surprise. You will take to the tunnels. It will be a long journey, but it leads to the safest place, possibly the best chance we have against the Tyrant!" Eifig shouted, addressing the room. They whispered to their ring and clenched their fist, pointing to the candles hanging above which burst into butterflies of fire and fluttered towards a hearth at the top of the hall, which slid back to reveal a passage.

Eifig jumped down and led the way towards the barracks where Eifig's guard; a company of Askiara Blood-Born had taken up residence, among them were a few Shadows too. There were no-more than two hundred in total. Upon entering, the soldiers stood up and to attention.

"Gather your armour, your weapons, then meet us by the main gate."

The soldiers began to rush around, picking up weapons and armour, and then followed Athias and Eifig out into a courtyard to see Hathael and Calor preparing a ritual. Calor drew a circle on the floor with marsh-bark, a chalk like substance, while Hathael began to mumble a string of ancient words, her hands clutching the staff steady.

"It's ready." Hathael said quietly.

Athias marched into the centre and drew a blade from his belt, slicing across his palm and squeezing so the blood dripped down onto the stone slabs, which burst into fire the moment he stepped foot outside the circle, and the flames followed him to the edge.

"With me." He shouted over the fire and it roared as a mountain did when falling.

He closed his eyes and stepped into the fire, vanishing, shrouded in smoke. He felt a cool breeze upon his cheek and his bleeding palm stung, the smell of salt lingered on his nostril. He opened his eyes to see grass at his fingertips, pale green and tall, and snow, in a valley, spreading far as he could see, deep into a mist. He heard voices behind him and one by one the soldiers joined him, many looking amazed. Calor then appeared, then Eifig and then Hathael who plucked a piece of grass and whistled with it to her lips. The fire erupted but collapsed in on itself, disappearing. Ahead of the company now stood the city of Myal and the Scaltian Fields, draped in snow and ice.

Chapter Twenty-Four
Creation

Magic takes a toll on us, those that use it. I have learned too, however, that it can be used for such beauty, such elegance. It can create, and with certain tools, those creations can be both mighty and inspiring, and dangerous all the same. – Calitreum, Story of the Vayshanaa, Finhaal's Entry, Page 422.

The city was all but deserted, only rats and foxes patrolled the streets now. The walls in part had long since crumbled, and the gates torn off their gigantic hinges. It had not lost its beauty, however, the ancient structures stood tall and proud. Red, smooth stone had been crafted with excellence to create curved buildings and streets. Athias and the others passed through the open gates and into the main courtyard, where he made his way up onto the walls and Eifig joined him.

"There they are. The Scaltian Fields." Eifig sounded calm, at peace. "Finhaal will be here by nightfall, he'll lay a trap to intercept the legions coming this way."

Athias turned and looked down at the others and the soldiers.

"What's he like?" Athias asked, abruptly, over the quiet air.

"Finhaal?" Eifig queried to which Athias nodded. "He's something that can't quite be contained. He trained me after the temple fell, as you went to Hathael. He is brilliant and mighty, yet kind too when it calls for it. His magic… I've never seen anything like it, never seen anyone with that level of mastery, so precise and fine."

"I would read about him at the temple, and while with Hathael, about his craft and his creations. I couldn't believe that someone like that was real, even after everything, and I never thought I would meet him."

"Do you think we can win? Against Ziath." Eifig faltered.

Athias paused, he was unsure of what to say.

"I'm not sure it's as simple as that." The others jumped to see Calor, moving silently; shadows shrouding her feet.

The three looked out over the fields again. They were all searching for signs of Finhaal while equally absorbing the beautiful landscape as they gazed over the horizon.

"I'm going to rest, wake me when there's any news." Athias left the battlements and went into a tower.

He took a blanket from his bag and rolled it out over the old bed frame which creaked as he rested upon it. It was uncomfortable but not the most unpleasant Athias had ever slept upon, so he removed his coat and pushed it under his head.

"How long was I asleep?" He mumbled.

"Only a few hours." It was one of the Shadows, Athias recognised him from the dam.

Athias splashed water over his hands from his flask and then massaged his face. Blood magic was tiring, more so for those that 'pulled the lever' as they say. Athias stood up and looked from the tower to see Calor, Hathael and Eifig all gathered on the wall and joined by a handful of the Shadows, while the Askiara clan stood to attention in the courtyard, keeping out of sight. Calor looked up and gestured to Athias to come and join them. He then looked out over the snow-covered fields to glimpse a faint outline of movement, the shimmer of silver armour in the moonlight.

"Is it him?" Athias directed his question to Eifig who nodded.

"It is, wait here. I will go to him." Eifig descended to the courtyard and pulled up her hood before walking through the archway and into the grass that pierced through the blanket of snow.

Athias, Calor and Hathael climbed down to the courtyard and began their wait. The sound of snow crunching underfoot returned not a few moments later, though this time it was thousands of steps, rather than one, and then Finhaal appeared in the archway. The stories of Finhaal's prowess were far from true, for he was far more; a strapping, broad-shouldered, burly man standing at over seven-foot-tall with piercing blue eyes and pale skin. His beard, silver-white fell to his waist and swayed gently in the breeze. Finhaal's muscles bulged, standing rigid as mountains with veins like rivers coursing through his tremendous body. Finhaal's armour was perfect; sleek steel that glistened in the moonlight. An elegantly designed helmet: smooth metal with a nose guard and sweeping guards over his cheeks, with huge horns protruding from the side, twisting to face forward. His right arm was covered by smooth, overlapping strips of enchanted steel that ran into a gauntlet while his left was bare and Athias examined his form; appearing as though sculpted from ice-covered rock. His enormous body was hidden under a series of steel plates, beautifully constructed, laid over thick fur and leather. While his shins were as thick as a grown man's hand from finger to wrist and his thighs were twice that, they too were cast in steel and fur, while a ripped tunic hung from his waist to his knees.

Finhaal held Caereth over his shoulder, it was the biggest weapon Athias had ever seen to be help by just one person. The handle, almost five-foot-long, was made of iron-ice; a combination of iron ore and ice-steel - a steel clad in rock-hard ice with black leather wrapped tightly around the grip, and the head was a mixture of stone and steel. Purple crystal ran through it like veins, deep into the body, handle, and grip alike. There was only one person alive who knew how to craft such a thing and Athias was looking directly at him. Finhaal marched through the gate and placed his hammer down in front of Athias who looked up to him.

"You must be Athias." His voice was deep and echoed strength. "I've heard much of you. Time is a hard creature to control, brother." He held out his hand, gripping Athias' forearm who returned it, nodding.

"It is an honour to meet you." Athias knelt, bowing his head.

"Get up, brother! I have longed to meet the Athias that Eifig learned by at the temple, I have longed to meet my brother of Time." He picked Athias up and beamed at him.

Eifig stepped through the gates next, they smiled at Finhaal and then to Athias,

Many of the Askiara that came with Athias' party greeted others that had just arrived, embracing in strong hugs and laughs. Finhaal's soldiers wore specially forged armour, sleek and light, but strong, a mixture of chain, plate, and fur; mirrored in Finhaal's own aesthetic. Each carried a spear, with a large circular shield on their backs and many had bows underneath the shield too. Many men and women, some young and others old, stood ready to prepare.

"Come, the others are here." Eifig said, happily, beckoning to Finhaal.

They led him into the courtyard and Calor and Hathael marched down the road towards the gates.

"Hathael! Is it you? My it has been too long." Finhaal's burly voice ringed with delight.

"Too long, and you've not aged a day I see." Hathael greeted him and they hugged.

Eifig gestured to Calor,

"This is our sister, bound by death."

"Sister. Death is an art form." He bowed, kneeling briefly to her.

"Please, creation is the most beautiful of arts." She smiled and shook his hand.

"Four become five, eh? When was the last time all of the Vayshanaa stood together?" Eifig pondered.

"Three hundred years ago, or just before." Finhaal looked to Hathael who nodded.

"The world will be better for it." Finhaal said with pride.

"I'm sure. However, there is something more pressing we need to discuss." Athias was cautious, he knew that Finhaal's devotion to his people was of paramount importance, but he was pleasantly surprised by Finhaal's reaction.

"Ah. Yes, we do. The vision, the crown." He bowed his head. "Come! Let us go inside, start a fire and talk of this crown." He led the way up the street and into an old building.

The temple was circular and domed, a small hole was at the top and centre of the dome; shining light into the room that was reflected and amped via pools of water. Mother Zohya stood at the centre of a table that had been built around her knees. Athias remarked upon her face, it was hugely different to the real Zohya but of course, the people living here probably never saw the real form of Zohya and envisioned how she may look. A warrior. Strong, fast, beautiful. As they had entered, they had passed under two other statues, warriors again with spear and shield, there was something puzzling about them; the way they looked to the statue in the middle. Finhaal lay Caereth down behind his chair and sat down first, each sat at a point around the table to create an even circle among themselves.

"Firstly, I have some more news regarding the battle to take place." Athias prompted.

"Oh yes?" Finhaal was curious.

"I was informed earlier that we have another ally. Dramatha, sent a legion to guard the Dolthraag passage years ago and they have been there ever since, but with them is his daughter."

"She was born after his son, and kept secret, so that she would be safe." Eifig chipped in upon seeing Finhaal's confused expression.

"Rayna… an ally who was with us at Nhorrin Dam, has travelled there. She will be riding with Kaelon, and the Rhalnarg will be coming with her." Athias paused. "They're roughly a day's ride from here."

"Well… Good. My scouts indicated that Ziath's legions are close. We'll discuss strategy later, when they've returned. First tell me of the crown?"

"I need all your skills, all of your abilities and power, to help me retrieve it. Time is but one river that flows into the ocean of our magic." Athias sighed.

"It's true." Hathael spoke, she had a heavy voice, and it wavered. "The magic of the world is fracturing… Nhivaliurn itself is splintering and the Abyss grows stronger. If we do not find this crown, the magic of the world could die all together."

"Do we know what the crown does? Did Mother Zohya tell you?" Eifig sounded doubtful.

"She did not but it's a risk we have to take because it's that or let the world burn." Athias warned.

Finhaal stood up and began to stroll round the table. He paused briefly at Eifig, placing a hand on their shoulder who took it before he walked circle back to his seat. He then made his way back to the hammer, picking it up and resting it over his shoulder.

"I will join you to find the crown and protect it. We're all brothers and sisters here, a family of magic. We may be all the world has to survive." He had decided, there would be no going back now.

"Thank you." Hathael was the one to speak, smiling to him.

"I must go and await my scouts."

Athias stood too, respectfully and waited for Finhaal to leave before sitting back down. Calor now got up and began to stroll around the room, admiring the statues by the doorway.

"They look sad, don't they? Why would they be sad, standing in the presence of Zohya."

"Envious maybe." Hathael whispered.

"Maybe" Calor spoke quietly but her words flew over the quiet room. "Or maybe they were jealous, much like many people who have walked upon this world."

Athias turned to her. He looked concerned.

"What plagues your mind?"

"I've been alive longer than any of you, I've seen countless wars, in the claim of peace, in the name of sons and daughters, I've seen what comes from them. What if all that comes from our victory in this war, another war, is jealousy, like all the rest."

"We do not exist to make that call, we fight so that others can be free, so that they can decide what sort of world they want to live in. Where has this come from?" Athias' voice was steeped in caution.

"The crown. What power lurks with in it? It is stronger than any of us, we must be weary of it."

Could Athias note a hint of admiration on her voice, surely not. He was silent for a moment but nodded, deep in thought.

"Come, let us go to the gates." Hathael advised.

Back at the wall, one of Finhaal's scouts had returned but the atmosphere had changed completely, he was covered in scars and bloody, two hands hung from his belt and he was panting. Finhaal was tending to the man, handing him a cup of water, and tending to his wounds. He picked the scout up and carried him towards a gate-house building.

"With me. Build a small fire, fetch a blanket." His voice was loud and stern this time.

Several Askiara warriors followed him inside and began constructing a fire, while another, a shaman, came in too with a blanket. Athias and the others stepped inside and waited by a table while Finhaal lay him on the blanket, next to the fire. He then held a bucket over the fire until it began to bubble gentle. He sat next to the scout and ripped cloth from a blanket, he scrunched it up and dipped it in the water before squeezing it out on the scout's cheeks and neck, wiping the blood away gently, before untying the string from his belt where the hands hung. He passed them to the shaman and nodded, the shaman bowed, leaving the room. Finhaal addressed the others, as if he knew they would ask of the hands.

"They belonged to the other scouts and will be given back to their partners, so that they can be buried. In absence of the body, so that that they can turn the lock, and enter into the spirit world to be greeted by another body so that they can live in peace there."

The scout began to talk, his voice was husky and quiet.

"Orthana. They're at Orthana. They have beasts of smoke, and steel!" His voice was strangled and dry.

"Go on. Easy now... You're safe here."

"They took the others, but I snuck in. I saved them from the pain, and I took their hands. I was chased, to the Faourds, where I lost them."

"I caused a distraction and I killed them, I saved them from the pain. Then I took their hands before leaving but I was seen, and they chased me, attacking me. I lost them at the Faourds."

"The Faourds aren't far from here. A few hours." Finhaal looked to the others.

"You did well, son of Zohya, son of smith." He stood up, pressing a thumb against the man's chest as he did so, "make sure he is cared for, take him to the monastery at the back of the city." He spoke to the shaman and soldiers around him who all bowed, kneeling to him. "Come, we must draw up plans. They will be upon us much sooner than anticipated." Finhaal beckoned to Athias and the group.

Outside he marched to a horse, one of many that came with the army. He took a roll of parchment from one of the satchels on its saddle and unravelled it, holding the corners down with rocks. Down from them was Myahl and the Scaltian Fields, the Faourds next; a series of rivers that criss-crossed, and then the fort of Orthana and forests behind it that led to a series of villages.

"Ziath's legions come from Orthana." He pointed to the fort, "they'll be here in a matter of hours, by what the scout says. It's not the battleground I would have chosen but it's what we have. I will take half of my warriors and hide in the long grass, Athias I want you to take those rangers that you arrived with, along with the few-hundred cavalry we have and go with them atop the ridge that you arrived on, await for my command, and take Calor with you."

"I will make good use of it." Athias said

Hathael knelt, pointing at the forest just by the Scaltian Fields.

"I will, with your permission, take some warriors and wait in the forest. My magic works better when amidst natural life."

"Of course, my old friend. You may take a thousand. The other four thousand will wait in the city, ready to join the fight upon my signal. If worst comes to worst, and our new ally does not arrive in time, we will need to pull back to the city."

"Ziath's legions come with machines of death. Mechanical giants, they say, as tall as rearing stallions. These should be our focus, for they will deliver the strongest blow." Eifig addressed them to which Finhaal stood up and nodded in agreement.

"What of any airships?" Athias asked, the name still bitter in his mouth.

"Hmm?"

"It is true, they do have mechanical giants, beasts of steel and smoke. They also have a threat from the skies, so the reports say, the hulls of ships strapped to gigantic, fabrics, powered by heat and propelled through the sky."

"If they come, I will deal with them. As you have seen, although briefly, the weather is manipulated by emotion. I will do what I can to disrupt them, but it will take all of my effort, and I will be out of the fight below."

"These and the machines will be our primary focus. Use your magic wisely, do not tire yourselves out, and protect those who fight alongside you."

"We should dig trenches, away from the walls. If our archers can fire from them but their rifles cannot hit it, their machines will be drawn out. While you hold the line, I will ride with your cavalry to take out the machines and any artillery battery that they set up. Then you will bring your forces back to the second trench and Hathael will have her way and we, from three sides. We have to make the most of this landscape, we need our men more than Ziath does." Athias pointed across the map, tracing his nail from one position to another.

Finhaal looked to him and smiled, grinned even.

"Let us prepare, Vayshanaa, friends of old."

Chapter Twenty-Five
Emotion

Each spectrum of a Vayshanaa's power is vast and plentiful. Each are powerful in their own magic, and skilled beyond measure, but none more so, in my mind than that of Emotion. Embasha, the ring that channels emotion and passion, is the gateway to true power. I have seen many take it in my time, and with each I have seen wonderous things. Wonderful things, certainly, but powerful. – Calitreum, The Fundamentals of Magic, Page 628.

Athias knelt in the long grass atop the very ridge he had arrived at earlier that day. A cool breeze brushed over his cheek and the long grass swayed. Behind him crouched the Shadows that had accompanied him here, and behind them, in the outskirts of the forest, around two-hundred cavalry sat. Hathael had long since disappeared into the forest, no doubt she was casting spells and enchantments. Athias sat upon the ridge, among the grass, and looked out over the Scaltian Fields. He was both curious at what stories this land held that had never been told, and sad too, for he knew much blood would be spilled in the coming hours of the night. Calor came and sat by him, she had just finished her watch duty turn.

"Beautiful night. Doesn't seem right, a night like this, given what is to happen soon."

Athias did not answer, his mind began to wander. It was true, what Calor said; the moons rose slowly from the depths of unknown where they had spent the passing hours sleeping, with each passing minute, more of the valley was illuminated by their presence as they watched over the lands; a pair of gigantic silver eyes, staring down at them. The long grass became a forest over a body of snow. Athias had heard many stories of the moons, some said they were an unknown god looking down on a piece of bark that had been plucked from the tree of Nhivaliurn itself. Others said that the moons were in fact decorations on the underside of a gigantic bird's wings that soared over the world. While some said they were reflections from the ancient mountains that now lay in the vast ocean.

Whatever the truth was, it was undeniable that they were the most beautiful things anyone had ever seen.

A bird suddenly flew overhead, black with striking blue feathers, a mountain bird. Athias whistled and the archers around him and Calor slunk away into position. He looked through a sight-glass, he pulled from his belt, and saw Finhaal marching through the trench, talking to his warriors. The ground began to tremble as a growing rumble approached. Pebbles at their feet began to shake, and dance. The shout of commands trickled over the still air, and the ominous beat of the drums that accompanied each legion carried over the deep mist.

"Knock your arrows." Athias hissed.

The first arrows were dripping with a black tar-like substance, a reserve of oil had been found in an old inn cellar. Although their faces were covered, he could see their nervous eyes.

"One, two, three, four." The officers' voice became louder and deeper, and the quake that followed upon every footstep sank deeper into Athias' mind.

Figures wrapped in shadow burst through the mist, like a knife cutting through a curtain. The legions pressed forward, more becoming clear through the mist with every passing step. They were neatly compiled, marching in rectangular blocks, hundreds of them at a time. The drums were loud now, each tap in time with the steps of legions; they were pristine, a collection of exact copies walking side by side. A rifle in arm, over the shoulder, with beaming cuirasses over red cloaks. The legions were marching through the valley, at the bottom of the ridge where Athias, Calor and the Shadows stood, waiting.

"Draw." Athias whispered to those beside him who drew back their bowstrings, the rest noticed and followed suit.

The legions were below them now, marching forward still towards the forest. He lifted his hand up ready and the Shadows tightened their bowstring. The column of soldiers trailed back far but four legions now stood ahead, separated from the next four by some forty feet.

"One, two, three, four!" A command again accompanied by the drums.

"Now!" Athias shouted, "Loose!"

Arrows were slung from their bows. Coursing through air, they swiftly found their mark. Soldiers fell and stumbled, the screams and shouts of men and boys carried over the air. Finhaal signalled to his soldiers as a horn blew, and another from the forest. The legions huddled together, trying to take up a firing position but uncertain where to aim.

"Loose!" Athias shouted again over the billowing horns.

This time the arrows were alight, each Shadower sparked flint over the arrowheads and drew the bows back tightly again before firing. The flames licked at the arrow heads, and then erupted as they made contact into their targets. The fire leapt from cloak to rifle, chasing the dripping oil from before.

"Fire at will!" Calor shouted now, signalling the engage.

The Shadows turned their attention to the legion on their right. They peppered the legion with arrows and more soldiers fell, clutching their knees and necks as arrows soared straight through the bone. The legions behind them stopped, turning and positioned to fire, aiming into the long grass on the ridge.

"Down. Now!"

Athias shouted as sounds of discharging rifles was followed by bullets soaring overhead. Many hit the dirt or snow, sending white and brown dust flying. A few found their mark. A handful of Shadows let out a cry as the fell, slumping into the ground.

Another sound trickled over the air, growing louder with every passing moment. Harrowing screams and yells from deep in the woods. Hathael stepped out from the treeline ahead with the Askiara behind her, their war cry ringing over the air. She raised her staff, the raven eye-like stone glowed at the end, and the spindly wooden fingers around it pressed tight. Her free hand also shimmered, emitting a purple glow.

Then came an almighty roar from within the forest. Another followed, and another. A bear appeared beside her, nestling her head against Hathael's elbow. Then another came, a pack of gruffons poked their heads through the Askiara shields, proud beasts with enormous bone horns running from their snout to tail; magnificently clubbed, more bears, wolves and stags emerged from the forest. Hathael slammed her staff down into the ground and purple light coursed through the soil, up into the trees, illuminated like veins on fire. The Askiara began to walk forward as the legions turned, re-positioning. They began to sprint, the beasts around them roared and followed, uniting man and nature. Roots grew fast from their trees and wrapped around legionnaires, pulling them into the soil and hundreds of birds flew from their perches, up into the air and then diving down towards the riflemen. The burrowing animals, thick snakes, and dust cats, emerged from the ground and sprung at the legionnaires who aimed their rifles forward but sat in confusion and fear, unable to pull the trigger as beast and man hurtled towards them. Athias saw legionaries fly up into the air as the Askiara hit, joined by the creature companions, many torsos were cut from their legs, many arms were flung away from their bodies, while the birds caused confusion and terror; plucking eyes from sockets and scraping talons over fingers.

Another horn blew and Finhaal emerged, sprinting forward with his band of warriors into another legion, knocking the rifles to the side with their blades. Eifig jumped over the rifles completely, axe in one hand, small blade in the other. Finhaal and Eifig were in the thick of the action. The Shadows were peppering the legions with arrows, firing over the line of Askiara, whose shields had been specially plated to resist rifle-fire. Athias noticed the Blood-Born tearing through legionnaires, a tremendous war-axe gripped in hand. Finhaal and Eifig fought passionately beside each other, complimenting each other's fighting style; Finhaal was strong and calculated, crushing entire soldiers with his hammer, while Eifig was fast and furious, throwing knives as she leapt. They raised Embasha, their ring, as a plume of smoke erupted from a firing line and the bullets turned into butterflies, soaring up into the misty air.

A deafening roar of sound pierced the air, it sent shivers down Athias' spine. He grabbed the sigh-glass and peered away from the battle, into the mist. The machines. To call them beasts would be quite accurate. Marching with the legions that approached, mechanical bodies, with limbs, and a seat where sat a rider. Pipes ran from the back to the shoulders and legs, pumping liquid through its body while smoke poured from a pipe behind the head, poisoning the sky, and the boot-resembling metal at the bottom of each leg delivered a dull thud as each walked forward. The machine's metal plating was sharp, jutting out at all angles, while its fists were enormous, and a series of rifles were clustered together on one. Turning back to the valley, Athias was met by chaos, steel clanged and small puffs of smoke scampered up into the air. Athias itched to enter the fight himself but stayed back, relaying orders to the rangers by his side, focusing his attention on the oncoming fight.

"Aim for the divide. Behind the legion!" The Shadows dipped their arrows into pots of oil and fired, and each landed, forming a line behind the legions engaged with Finhaal.

With another command they released another volley, and the fire-tipped arrows plummeted into the oily grass, creating a line of fire that separated the incoming monsters of steel with the fight ahead. It would not burn for long, however, as snow had begun to fall. Athias whistled, and when Finhaal turned, Athias signalled towards the fire. The Askiara began to move back towards the trench while the Shadows finished off what was rest of the remaining riflemen.

"We're up." Athias turned to Calor.

The Shadows grouped and made their way back towards the forest that swept round. When they entered the treeline the Askiaran riders approached, staying back so to not be seen on the ridge. Calor mounted a horse but Athias waited by the edge, peering through the sight-glass. The machines were making fast ground, marching out ahead of the legions which followed a few dozen metres behind. He waited until the last possible moment before mountain his own horse. They edged forward and began to walk their horses down the ridge. After a few minutes they began to canter, picking up speed and forming two lines of a hundred each. They reached the base of the valley and began to pick up speed, heading towards the mechanical giants that loomed in the mist ahead.

A sudden rattling sound cut through the air and was followed by cries of riders and horse alike as bullets soared through the air, knocking riders from horses, or sending the steeds crashing down into the snow. Athias raised Spectre up from the sheath on his steed and the Askiara lowered their spears. They began to gallop, reaching full speed as they approached the steel beasts which raised their rifle-fists and fired furiously. More and more riders fell from their horses until almost a hundred had fallen. The riders passed the trench where Finhaal stood, a look of determination swept across his face and he clambered up from the dirt. He lifted his hammer high, clutching the grip. The hammer shone bright with white light and he slammed it down, grip-first, into the ground while shouted something that Athias could not make out but suddenly a construct appeared around his sword, his arms, and his horse. The same construct, seemingly made of white light, appeared around the Askiaran horses, bodies, and spear. The bullets from the mechs collided with the riders but melted upon contact. Athias was close now, he could see the panicked eyes of those in the mechs, bewildered as to why their bullets did nothing to the approaching attack. Athias saw again, as Finhaal next struck the ground with the head of Caereth and a bolt of the same light surged through the ground, lifting the soil around it, and a pillar of snow-covered soil rose up from underneath one of the mechs, sending it flat on its back with a deafening crash. The riders grouped, into an arrow, before smashing into the mechanical contraptions ahead.

Athias was flung from his horse as one of the mechs swung, catching him with the enormous fist. The constructs around him faded, fizzling out. Athias clambered to his feet, watching the battle around him briefly. He saw the bodies of dozens of horses behind him and ahead, with the others pulling back. He knelt upon Spectre and clambered to his feet. He was alone now, facing down a mech ahead. Athias remembered back to his training, and back to the Calitreum, how magic could be used in more than one way.

"Arkan'darina!" He felt the words trembled upon his lips, and felt magic course through his muscles, enhancing his strength, his senses and speed.

A mech faced him down, it was enormous, almost three times his own height. He clutched Spectre close and charged forward, his fleeting footsteps carrying him forward as fast as a bronze-cat. To his side charged wolves, racing into the corners of his eyes from behind. They howled and Athias' hair stood on end, he raced with them, springing over bodies and over mounds of rocky soil. The mech's rifle barrel began to turn, making a whirring sound as bullets slid from the box on its shoulder into the clip. Athias sprung forward taking tremendous leaps towards the mech, jumping from rock to wolf and onto the steel-plated beast itself. He clutched Spectre tight, scaling the plating with no time for thought. He slammed the sword down, between the thick armour plates and felt a fissure, and a hiss followed as black liquid spurted from the pipes beneath.

Before he could attack again, roots leapt up from the snowy soil, wrapping around the iron plating and pulling it off the inner shell until the pilot was exposed. A wolf jumped up onto him, ripping his head off. Athias nodded to Hathael who raised her staff up again and more birds soared forward, cawing in unison, as they crashed into the legions. Around him animals fell as the mechs open fired again but Finhaal chanted, slamming his hammer down again, raising a wall of earth and ice between the remaining creatures and his forces, and the mechs. When the wall crumbled, they launched another attack on the mechs, destroying the armour plating and cutting the fuel pipes. Now that the mechs were destroyed, the full force of the legions was pressing forward. Almost ten-thousand more legionnaires in battle formation. They had lost many soldiers at the start of the battle but when the Vayshanaa's plan to tackle the mechs first was into effect, the rest of the legions formed up and now they were in firing lines, pressing forward, shooting, and then pressing forward again. Finhaal chanted again, as bullets pinged off his steel armour, and raised the hammer to deliver one final strike to the ground and a wall of ice, covered in constructs of its own leapt up between the soldiers and the Vayshanaa.

    A whirring sound replaced the rifle fire. Athias looked around but saw nothing yet it grew louder still. An explosion came and he looked back to see dust flying and rangers sent coursing through the air.

    "Up there! Look!"

    The Vayshanaa peered up and a ship began to pierce the clouds, and another, and then slowly an enormous dirigible balloon appeared from above, attached to each ship where sails would have stood. Tiny figures were dropping things over the side and shortly after, more explosions sounded, and dirt leapt from the ground into the air.

    "Go!" Eifig shouted to them, the wall ahead began to crack.

    "Pull back!" Athias shouted out as animal, ranger and Askiara fell around him.

    "Back to the city walls!" Finhaal joined, picking up one, then two injured warriors and began carrying them back to the city.

    Eifig walked forward, looking up to the ships and the clouds. They dropped their weapons and nursed the ring in their hand, whispering to themselves as they strolled forward. The whirring sound travelled across the air and another crack of rifle fire echoed with it, the wall ahead cracking further as Finhaal's constructs began to fade. Eifig looked to Athias who looked back, nodding, carrying an injured soldier over his shoulder. He heard the words on Eifig's lips as he, and the others ran back towards the city.

"Mirran Elren'darieshen!" The words were old, even by Vayshanaa tongue, Athias recognised their meaning for he had read the words with Eifig when they were children, high in the library, in the forbidden texts. "Vara Vel Mirran! Mirran Elren'darieshen!"

Racing back to the gates Athias turned, Finhaal too, to see Eifig as they stretched their arms out wide, the ring glowing furiously. The sky above darkened and a rumble of thunderous sound crept across it. Athias looked on in awe as Eifig began to levitate, rising into the air and sparks leapt from the ring. He could not hear her words anymore, but the clouds dispersed, scattering into wisps of white. Eifig continued to chant and Athias could hear the faintest of shouts from aboard the gunships as confusion and disorder crept in. The clouds had all but disappeared and the black night sky loomed above, starless, and empty. Lightning flashed across it, slashing into the black canvas. Then again, coursing across the starless sea above, as the moons looked on in envy. The snow turned to hail, peppering those on the ground and causing Athias to shield his eyes as he looked out to see the hail, all but swirling around Eifig as they rose higher still. A bolt of lightning stuck the first airship, piercing the dirigible balloon and the ship entirely, as an explosion rocketed through the air. Another bolt plunged down and stuck it again, and another into the second ship. Eifig shimmered white as ice and the ring illuminated the ground beneath them. Thunder roared and hail struck down with tremendous force, sparking with electricity as more lightning whipped down and stuck both airships as one. The ships lost control and crashed into another before hurtling down towards them.

The wall that separated Eifig from the legions crumbled and Athias caught a glimpse of figures in the mist behind the legions. The airships crashed down with an almighty sigh, sliding across the snow and grass, racing into the lines of legions, as smoke and rigging trailed behind. Eifig collapsed on the ground and Athias peered forward as he rushed towards them. More and more silhouettes approached from behind the legions.

They were tall, a line of castle towers moving forward. Athias heard the horns blow and neighing of horses. Something in the sky caught his eye and he glanced up. A white raven drifted over the sky, before soaring down.

Athias and the others looked on as the Rhalnarg appeared through the mist and smoke, sitting proud on their horses, knights in shimmering, immense armour. They hurtled into the legions, and their formidable lines swept over the legions as a wave did against pebbles. Soldiers were crushed beneath the hooves of their great stallions. The legions panicked, turning, and firing without order, their iron spheres merely bounced off the glistening armour of the riders atop the horses. Their horses were covered in armour also, impaling soldiers upon horned helmets. Askiaran warriors helped Eifig, carrying them back to the city while the other Vayshanaa blew their own horn and warriors dashed forward. The Rhalnarg's sturdy lances pierced straight through the cuirasses, leaving legionnaires speared above the ground, blood spurting from their open mouths, their fingers fumbling around their neck in a desperate attempt to loosen the breastplate. The few that did hold their position were slaughtered. A knight stopped next to Athias, Gralnor perching on their shoulder. They raised their visor to reveal Rayna. She got down off the horse which neighed and hoofed at the ground, seemingly unbothered by the battle around it. Rayna hugged Athias who stood, blood splashed over his face and armour, blood dripping from his sword. He embraced her firmly, letting out a sigh of relief.

"How did you get here so fast? He croaked, panting.

"The Rhalnarg have studied the Eastern mountains since they arrived there, they know of its secrets, its hidden paths. We rode all day, stopping only a few miles from here to rest. We began riding again not long ago again, we saw the lightning, the air-ships?" Her voice was soft but pleased.

"Eifig. I always told you emotion is the strongest magic." Athias panted, as steel and iron crashed around him. "We need survivors for questioning." He added hastily, seeing so many riflemen fall before they could get a proper look in.

"They know, we talked before arriving. Kill all but a few." She nodded again, climbing up onto her steed again.

Gralnor jumped down onto the horse and then onto Athias' shoulder, rubbing his beak against Athias' face making a low gurgling sound.

"I missed you." Athias whispered and Gralnor cawed, happily.

The legionnaires had all but been slain. The ground around them was strewn with bodies; animal and man, the snow now amassed with crimson splatter, dented brass-iron armour poked out from the carcasses and tattered cloaks lay where they had fallen. The airships lay as smoking wrecks, the ship hulls splintered and bloody. A handful of legionnaires had been caught and tied together with thick rope. Athias, the other Vayshanaa and the warriors began to cheer too, many animals roared and cried too before returning to the forests as the magic upon them began to fade.

"The battle is won" he paused, looking up at Rayna and knelt, bowing his head. "Many thanks, you must be Rayna?" He was inquisitive.

"Finhaal. Athias talked about you often." She replied, kindly.

"Many legends will be told of this day. How you and your friends saved us, let them show who won the day out." He smiled, returning to his feet.

Another rider stepped down from their steed and marched to Athias. They were slightly smaller than the others, shorter and less stocky. They held out their hand to him.

"Athias. I've heard much of you. I heard the stories of when you served with my father." A woman's voice, unfamiliar to Athias' ears.

The woman lifted her helmet and earthy-brown hair cascaded down over her shoulders. Her skin was pale with flecks of silver, mirroring a beach at sunset, and her eyes were green, light as spring-time grass. As she held the helmet underarm, the other knights got off their horses and knelt around them.

"I am Kaelon Reame, first of my name. Daughter of Dramatha Reame, third of his name. It is an honour to meet you."

Athias and the others dropped to their knees immediately. Athias took her hand as he did.

"My Norjiin." Every hair on his body stood up. He spoke in awe.

"I haven't been called a Norjiin in some time. Up. Please. All of you." She called out to everyone around her. "For now, I will send Rayna ahead to the city to find carts for the wounded and then we can get back. We have much to discuss about this world."

Chapter Twenty-Six
The Grove

The Calitreum was made by the first Vayshanaa, although back then it was multiple books instead of one; a story from each. It grew to become one single, large, account of magic and souls that used it, as well as beings that walked our soil, and the great cities that came from civilisation. However, that is not to say that every single aspect of our world comes to life among these pages, some things remain buried, unmentioned. Some things deserve to stay that way, out of sight, out of thought. – Caliterum, A Vayshanaa's Oath, Page 23.

Snow was falling fast and thick now as the two companies readied themselves to leave, as to not be slowed or trapped in the city, it had already brimmed over the tall blades of grass outside the walls. The sun was above the horizon now, though still low, it cast a brilliant, warm light over the sky. Rayna, Kaelon and the Rhalnarg were to accompany the Askiara back to their home, deep in the mountains, and prepare the defences against Ziath's approaching armies. He would be bringing everything he had. While Athias and the other Vayshanaa were to take horses and head for the Gaerlwood Grove. Many had slept the remaining hours of the night after the battle, though a great deal had been monitoring the wounded, bandaging them up as best they could. The Vayshanaa had interrogated the prisoners, gathered from the battle and they had learned that Ziath's full invasion force was journeying up the northern coast, a forty-thousand strong army of ships laden with soldiers, steel beasts, airships, and other artillery. Kaelon and Rayna would take the warriors and reinforce the Askiaran city of Rurnaeiir, which spread deep into the mountains and was protected by a magnificent fortress known as Frosthorn.

"Take Gralnor. He missed you." Rayna whispered to Athias and kissed his palm before pressing it against her cheek.

Athias smiled, stroking Gralnor gently.

"I'll bring him back with me, I promise. Be careful out there, while Ziath's legions are gone from the countryside, his spies still linger. You'll need to take the old roads and move fast if you're to get there before his fleet."

"I will see you upon your return. Long may we stand."

"Long may we stand" Kaelon said from behind her, "I will get this army to Rurnaeiir, Vayshanaa, I promise. You make sure you bring your weapons and your magic to us."

"We will. We will repay you and your knights for what you have done for us this day." Finhaal spoke out while Rayna helped Athias up onto his horse and then returned to her own.

"After you. I insist." Kaelon raised her hand to the gate and the Vayshanaa passed through, heading east from their current location.

Athias peeked over his shoulder as they rode and saw a column of riders and warriors exiting the city heading north. Their armour glistened in the rising orange tint of the sun's light. Athias and the Vayshanaa rode fast into a gallop, heading into the thick forests.

"Have your wits about you! These parts are filled with ancient spells, illusions, and spirits. Those who lost their path, they came here and never left." Finhaal's voice was gruff and stern.

The paths of the forests were rocky, peppered with earthy soil and strewn with long, writhing roots that had long since been forgotten. Blades of untamed grass ventured from their border along the path out into the way, towers of green, casting shadows down to the insects that scuttled beneath. The treetops were thick, masking the company from the warm sun as they ventured deeper into the myriad of trees standing idly, unmet by eyes of weary travellers for years. Athias saw flashes of children behind the trees as they raced through; running and playing in the roots, crying out each other's names and laughing. In the same flash, they were gone, replaced by glimpses of thorn covered vines wrapped around branches. A breeze whispered through the trees, narrowly slithering between the thick trunks, and soaring over the snake-like branches at their feet. A murmur followed. A brief sigh.

"Help us…"

The words clung to Athias' ears, singeing the tips of his hair as it chased him.

"Help us… we're lost…"

A giggle followed, high pitched and playful. That of a child. The thick grass susurrated underfoot with every step the horses took and Athias peered around, catching fleeting glances of children. Some were standing still, staring at him, waving as if slowed in time, while others ran through the trees, laughing.

"Stay close now!" Finhaal's harsh voice broke through the illusion.

Athias steered his mind away from the children in the grass, away from the horrible things that had happened in the forest eons ago. Athias had heard but snippets of the horrific crimes and blood magic sacrifices. Although the sun was now climbing into the sky, only shards of occasional light peeked through the dense forest and as the companions rode further into the trees, drawing closer to the mountains, the temperature dropped further still. Snow could not pierce the exterior of treetops, but a chilling mist rushed through the grass, and over the path; it was thick like smoke, and cold, unforgiving. The blades of grass turned brittle as a cast of white-ice covered everyone, and the once earthy-soil had become hard. The companions rode for hours, passing haunting burial sites and old, ruined temples, ancient settlements now awash with icy crystals, and deep crevasses beckoning with mysterious promise. They rode in silence, they were cold, shivering with every pace forward; their thick cloaks battling the harrowing chill.

"We're close now. We should rest up before continuing." Hathael's teeth chattered as she called out.

"Agreed!" Eifig's teeth chattered so loud they could all hear it.

They came across a small clearing and dismounted. Hathael went to the centre, looking around.

"Yes, this will do nicely." She muttered to herself.

Hathael then went to her horse and removed her staff, Dr'arenth, from under the saddle. She patted her steed and returned to the centre where she placed the staff down and began an enchantment. The staff stood straight as a dim purple light coursed through it, from the crystal, and down into the ground around. The trees around the clearing began to sway as if taking deep breaths after waking from a long sleep, their branches began to shudder, and their roots broke through the icy soil. The others stood and watched in awe as the branches and roots began to grow upwards and outwards, building a thick enclosure around their clearing. Athias unloaded the tents off the horses and began to construct them, they may only be stopping for a few hours, but they would need rest and it was too chilly to sleep out of cover. Eifig and Calor tied up the horses and covered them with their coats, feeding them and taking the saddles off so they too could rest. Finhaal began to make a fire; he smashed chunks of icy rock with Caereth and the magic, flowing through his hammer, shaped them into shards of glass-like crystals. He picked them up and then smashed down on the icy floor again, creating a small crater which he scattered a handful of the crystals over. Placing his palm upon them and whispering an enchantment, a purple light, like that which Hathael had summoned, shimmered in his eyes and coursed down through his fingertips, igniting the crystals which burned without sign of falter. Athias finished with the tents and pelts, so went to his bag and removed a shoulder of meat that he had stowed, wrapped in cloth. He was cold but felt the icy claws around him start to melt away as the fire's warmth spread throughout the clearing; hitting the enchanted walls and climbing up as did waves which splashed against a cliff, masking the entire enclosure in a pale but warm light and thawing the frost. The five companions sat around the fire as the meat roasted, drinking ale that Finhaal had brought, and retelling stories of the world and their lives in it, eating the salty, chewy meat. Athias' mind wasn't really with them though; it had begun to wander. What challenges would lay in wait for him at the Gaerlwood grove? What would it take to remove that crown from the ground where it lay?

"Athias what do you think? Athias?" A voice cut through the sharp images in his thoughts.

Athias snapped back to see the others looking at him, Finhaal was holding out a goblet to him.

"Sorry, what did you ask?" Athias' replied distantly.

"The forests, they're beautiful in their own way, wouldn't you think?" Finhaal said softly, aware that Athias' mind was wandering.

"Absolutely." He took the goblet and gulped the ale. "Sorry, I'm tired."

"Ay, we should get some rest; the grove is barely an hour's ride as Hathael was telling me. Get some rest, all of you."

"I will but first, I must visit the bridge." Athias said in a low voice to which the others offered a faint smile, nodding.

"Be careful, we need you to be at full strength."

Athias returned to his tent and drew Spectre from its sheath. He carried it away from the tents, the others looked to him and nodded. Athias peered at the sword, looking up and down the shimmering blade. Then he spoke the words once more.

"A bridge standing taller than any peak, a spectre stood upon, it ready to speak."

The blade sunk into the earthy floor and a flash of white passed his eyes. Athias let go of the sword and looked up.

Ahead of him, in the near distance, were the towers of the bridge before Zohya's realm once more, the Realm of Naer. Sure enough, ahead of him stood tens of figures. Glimmering shadows of white and purple, and Athias approached them each in turn, speaking to them, listening to their final goodbyes. He recognised each one, every soldier he had slain in previous conflicts, he remembered them all. It was his duty to see each soul taken by Spectre, see them and hear them, before they crossed over into the next life. Some final conversations were filled with regret, others with joy, it was not for Athias' to judge. Only to listen and to teach. When he was done, he marched back. Each step seemingly drew him no closer to the sword, standing in the glimmering floor as proud as a tower watching over the rocky shores at sea. Upon returning to it, he twisted Spectre and one by one, the beings on the bridge faded from view as Athias was taken back to the present with a flurry of flashing lights. He arrived at the exact moment he had left, the others were still looking at him, the smiles on their faces still lingering as he looked up. A tear rolled down his cheek as he drew Spectre from the ground.

Athias sheathed Spectre and lay down on his pelt, his head propped against his bag. He ran his fingers over the fluffy fur of the bear skin he lay upon, the spices from the ale lingered on his tongue and the heart beating at tremendous speeds in his chest began to slow. Before deciding to sleep, Athias sat up and lay his hands out, on his lap. He straightened his back and began to hum as he closed his eyes. He stopped, as his heartrate relaxed, and he felt magic coursing through his veins.

"Venartium Calitreum."

His voice was deep, and he opened his eyes just as a weight pressed on his hands. The summoning spell had brought the Calitreum into his hands, he flicked through the tremendous book, resting it on his legs due to the immense weight. He rummaged in his bag, setting down a pot of ink and a quill beside him. Gralnor swooped in and nestled on the pelt next to him, who stroked the bird's neck and it made a low, gurgling croak as it relaxed. Athias flipped through the pages to the latest entry, separating it with a line of ink and then began to fill in another entry. He wrote for a few short minutes, adding an entry to the History of Old section, and another to The Vayshanaa's Oath, about magic and its toll on him. It was this book, after all, as Hathael had reminded him, that would teach all further Vayshanaa and those who studied magic. Athias dried the quill and slotted the ink back in his bag before meditating again and releasing the book back into where it hid, in a reality between ours and the next, in the flow of magic itself.

Athias drifted off to sleep, comforted by the gentle neighs of the horses and cracking of the fire. He turned and tossed all night, his hands clenched the pelt he lay upon, drawing it up and releasing it as though he was controlling the waves of an ocean. His mind was plagued with wary thoughts. He stood in a temple of Zohya, the one that he spent most his young life in, though the walls were charred, and the statues defaced. A young adult stood before him barely a teen himself, huddled in the corner, watching over a sleeping child; dark skinned and green eyed, the green of Athias' own. He picked the child up and covered his face.

"Athias." A voice whispered through the temple hall, soaring up and gliding through the statues like smoke.

Athias spun round to catch it, hoping it would land upon his ear.

"Come home… Athias…"

Athias looked around but the voice had no master. The rest of the dream blurred into a stream of colour and he jolted awake. It was dark still, the fire had reduced to embers, emitting a low, red glow. Athias sat up, getting to his feet, Gralnor slept peacefully next to where he had laid his head. He wandered over to the fire, sitting down next to the hissing embers and ash. They fizzled slightly as he prodded them with the tip of his boot, cracking with veins of crimson, charred with white and purple; the remnants of Finhaal's magic lingered. He felt a flutter and Gralnor landed on his leg, looking up at him, Athias stroked the beak of the bird who nuzzled against Athias hand.

"Oh, you're up. Good." A gruff voice echoed around the enclosure. "That's one less to wake."

Athias turned to see Finhaal, bare chested, emerging from his tent. His chest was burly and muscular. Several scars rest upon his skin, on his abdomen, his shoulders and chest, and round from his back. Athias thought to himself, what manner of thing could have made scars like that on a man so muscular, so powerful? He watched Finhaal ruffle the tent where Eifig lay

"Come on, up now. We have to make good time." This was greeted by a sigh from inside.

After a short time, everyone was awake and up. Readying themselves for travel, Hathael set free the magic that had guarded them that night. As it returned to normal, the icy chill seeped in and frost spread over the floor, the branches, and the leaves, returning them to shards of glass. The company mounted and wrapped themselves up as best they could. As they walked their horses from the clearing Athias looked back briefly, pondering on the dream he had witnessed. The group set off to the path once more, heading deeper into the thick, cold, forgotten woods, though today, the path faded completely, and the group were left to navigate the harsh soil wrapped in roots.

"Look there, ahead." Eifig's teeth were chattering profusely, she pointed forwards with ice-white fingers on the edge of turning purple.

Athias followed her finger forwards to see three trees standing close, resembling a triangle with one ahead and two behind. They were standing tall and proud; a light seemingly descended from the treetops to illuminate them however when looking up, all to be seen was darkness and thick branches. The trees' skin was brown but splashed with silver as though someone had poured an enormous bucket of paint over them from the top and it had crashed into a pattern. Veins of crystals ran up the trees from the roots; the stones like turquoise daggers, and the soil around the roots was warm. The Gaerlwood Grove.

"We're here." Athias said quietly, peering around, making sure they were alone.

He dismounted and the others with him. The horses immediately lay down on the warm soil that surrounded them, spreading from beneath the Grove, and the icicles on their pelt-covers began to thaw. No trees came close to the Grove from any side, even the branches turned away from the Gaerlwood trees as if bowing in honour. Athias walked around the three trees, looking closely at them, trying to find a sign. From all angles the trees looked the same, a triangle bathed in light, and when returning the others looked puzzled.

"I…" Athias opened his mouth but couldn't find the words, he felt ashamed that he did not know what to do.

"You must enter the Grove. You must walk between the trees and face the trial." Hathael's words fell lightly on Athias' ears. "A trial of time, it will be."

"How?" Athias asked, bewildered.

"The trees, the crystals upon them, the soil around us; it talks to me. I can see what it wants." Hathael marched to his horse and pulled Dr'arenth from under the saddle bag, "There are spirits here." She addressed them all now as they all looked to her, "They will try to stop us; the magic here is as alive as the rest, though, here, I sense pain and torment. We will fight them, the guardians, giving you your time, my boy." Her words were kind, they warmed Athias' chest and heart greater than the warm air that seemingly circled the grove itself.

Athias marched to his own horse and placed Spectre's sheath upon his back, tying it in place. Finhaal went to his and lifted the hammer from its place, while Hathael whistled and the leaves fluttered, the horses got to their feet and bolted off, back towards the path.

"Go now, Vayshanaa of Time." Finhaal nodded.

Athias approached the trees and as his feet crossed the threshold he heard the soil behind him rumble, a quake shook the ground around them all and he turned to see patches of icy earth ahead of him falling away, sounding like the scrunching of parchment under hand. From the ground game black, spindly arms with claw-like hands; shadows of liquid-like darkness.

"Go! Now!"

Hathael shouted over her shoulder as they spaced out, protecting the Grove from each side. She began an enchantment, digging Dr'arenth into the ground and raising the roots around them into lines of spears, while Finhaal smashed his hammer into the ground as he mumbled a spell. A light that covered the four companions readying to fight: creating armour and cloaks, sleek and strong. The spirits jumped from their resting points and sprinted towards the Grove from all sides; they were rabid, there was nothing in their eyes but bloodlust. Calor jumped into her wraith-form; masked in a cloud of smoke. Eifig kissed her ring and raised her fist to the sky and Athias examined the leaves above them, morphing into sharp daggers, which fell fast, down towards the floor as though fired from a bow. Gralnor cawed loudly and sprung into flight, circling the grove, a trail of white dust traipsed behind him, a protective line. Athias wanted to stay, something clawed at him, pulling him into the grove but something equally pushed him back. He gripped the crystals embedded in the tree's bark and pulled himself forwards, mustering all the strength he could dare to call upon. He pushed his way into the centre of the three trees and all was silent, suddenly, and he looked back to outside the Grove and there was nothing but white light pressing on his eyes.

Suddenly he was falling, the soil beneath his feet plummeted and his heart jumped into his throat, but it was over as soon as it began. Athias was presented with a door made of the crystal-embedded bark that the trees around him had been made of. He cautiously pushed, and the door opened without resistance. He pushed the door ajar and walked inside.

Chapter Twenty-Seven
Time

Magic is a dangerous thing. It takes a toll on all who use it, but the magic of time is something else. In all my years of teaching, I have seen the same in them all, the students of Time. I have seen great power, and great loss, none more so than in their memories of old. – Calitreum, The Fundamentals of Magic, Page 628.

Athias was standing in a small home; a clumsy table with knives set upon it stood in the room ahead of him. Candle lit lanterns hung from the clay and wood walls, and a small fire sat in the corner inside an iron casket. A woman with bushy brown hair and dark skin was bustling through from the kitchen area, she was carrying large iron pot with stew inside; its pleasant smell passed under Athias' nose. He stood in the corner against a slim bookshelf that had only a handful of covers on, the pages of which were tattered or creased. It appeared that she could not see him even when he waved his hand in front of her face, he wondered where he was, wondering at the significance of the room.

"Come and eat, boys." She had a lively voice; it rang around the room.

Two boys came running around the corner, one was holding a wooden horse and the other a ship. They were playing, making sounds and grunts. One was older; maybe twelve, while the younger was about five. They put their toys down on the table and took a bowl from the pile their mother had brought in after the stew. She marched round the table, passing through Athias where he stood.

"Mum, mum. Look at what we made!" The older boy took a figure from his pocket, a few twigs and flowers tied together to resemble that of a human.

"That's very pretty! Where did you make that?" Their mother beamed.

"Down at the Shairns' house, by the river, with the bear children!" He blurted out, obviously referring to a family of coarans.

A man entered and flung his coat over the chair, he gave the woman a kiss on the cheek and put his boots by the door.

"This smells lovely, Arin. Thank you." He took a bowl too and ladled stew into his and his children's bowls, "What did you two get up to today?" He asked the boys.

"We went to the Shairns' house, we sat in the water for a bit and then made this with the bears!" The older one showed his father the figure.

"Very impressive! You'll be quite the builder when you're my age. Maybe you'll be even better than I am." He whispered and laughed.

The younger boy smiled and ate his stew. Athias looked at him curiously, and in an instant the room changed, and the young boy was now sitting with his father on the floor, they were keeping warm by the iron casket and playing with figures of knights in armour.

"My head hurts daddy. It feels hot." The boy rubbed his forehead, his eyes squinting.

The father picked him up and put him on a chair at the table and went into the kitchen, he started making a lotion out of honey and herbs. He kissed his wife's head as she entered.

"His head again?" She asked.

"Yes, but we're just going to make a lotion and nurse that ache right away." He smiled at the little boy.

"Should I send word to the temple?"

"No, no it's fine, we have more time." Their voices had turned into hushed whispers.

"But they warned"

"Just a few more days, please, with our son." The man pleaded to her and she nodded, walking through the backdoor.

The man stared after her, longingly. Meanwhile Athias watched the child, he began rocking on his chair. Tipping back and forth slowly. The chair fell back entirely, and the boy smacked his head on the floor. He started crying and his father rushed to him, scooping him up in his arms and cradling him. Athias felt a searing pain in his mind and as he looked back to the boy he screamed.

"It's okay, it's okay. Daddy's got you." The father whispered, trying to sooth the child's tears.

Time stood still; a ringing sound burst through Athias' ears. The father froze, his muscles twitching as he tried to move, taking drawn out steps forward. The ringing grew louder still and flowers on the table began to float, up and out of the vase which started to crack. Arin returned, sprinting through the door and the father turned as the spell broke. He looked frightened and confused but kissed the child's head as a tear rolled down his cheek.

"Daddy?" The child welled up and his father hugged him tight.

The father erupted into flames. He screamed and fell to his knees, passing the baby to Arin. Stallions of flames jumped through the room, spitting fire to everything in sight. The child's older brother sprinted in from outside, but a bookshelf fell, entwined in flame, barring him access. Arin kissed the baby on the head and whispered to him, before marking a symbol on his hand in a lotion from a small bottle in her pocket. She passed him to the older brother Athias stood among the flames which lapped at the books on the shelves behind him, he was untouched by their burning grasp. The flames roared as the building around them started to crumble. The mother, Arin, was knelt, behind a burning bookshelf which had blocked the door. She saw the brother looking on in fear, seemingly immune to the heat although he was merely in shock.

"Go! Get out of here! Take him to the temple, the one we talked about! Please, promise me you'll find a way there!" She screamed, the ceiling cracking as beams of wood fell through.

The boy nodded, a tear on his cheek. The house shuddered as flames licked the walls, spreading up through the gaps in the ceiling to the next level. Athias felt dread set in, pulling at his heart, wrenching it around, and every hair on his body stood on end. He knew where he stood. He moved closer to Arin on the floor as the boy fled. He looked to Arin as she kissed her ring and the structure began to give way.

"Mother..." Athias whispered. He knew she could not see him, nor hear him, but he brushed his hand over her hair.

The house fell on itself and the flames roared, like an ocean storm. Athias watched his older brother pick himself up. He wrapped little Athias in his cloak and disappeared into the crowd of people that had gathered around the writhing flames, licking the wooden beams that once supported walls. Athias tried to follow them through the crowd, he pushed his way through the seemingly lifeless figures but they had gone and he was met only by a darkness where the ground had fallen through, as though his house was an island of which he could not leave.

Athias turned back to the house and it was gone, the people too, and ahead stood a bridge that passed over a river of stars. A tower came into view as he stepped forwards, examining the mystery around him with each foot passing the other. The tower: made of shining, black stone, soared high. He went to knock upon the door, but it vanished and then suddenly, without warning, he was inside it and the door was bolted behind him. Small fires burned in brackets on the walls, casting a menacing trail over the stone, shimmering with every sigh of flames. He heard crying, a child. It was wailing and the noise spread eerily around and down the smooth walls of the staircase next to him, attempting to push him away. Athias climbed the stairs and the crying grew louder, the flames danced higher with every bracket he passed but the temperature dropped with it. He came to the first landing and the door was open, inside was his brother again only older now, by a few years and he was no longer holding the little Athias. Instead it was with someone Athias did remember... Tutor Abbrath. He and Athias' older brother talked over the crying child. Athias crept in, although it was almost certainly unnecessary for, like before, he was sure he could not be seen or heard. His suspicions were confirmed when he walked past Abbrath and the man did not even flinch or turn. Abbrath's hair was brown with flecks of silver-white and his skin was far less weathered compared to that of when Athias had to leave the Temple.

"We will watch over Athias, but won't you stay, Torjn? There is room for you here, you have journeyed for over a year to reach here, after all." Abbrath's voice was seemingly distant, as though he was speaking from underwater.

Athias' heart filled with emotion as he heard his brother's name. He had all but forgotten it, as he had the memories of his mother and father.

"Our mother thought we had more time. More time to be a family before he came here. He should have no memory of me, of our parents, of his life away from this. I love him, always have and always will, that's what's important."

The child, little Athias, kept crying until Abbrath wrapped him in his cloak and carried him through another door which shut gently behind him and then the floor began to slip away, as if being dragged down. Athias jumped and ran back to the door he had entered in, closing it firmly. The staircase was now in silence except for the sound of flames flickering ahead. Athias pressed forward, climbing the smooth stone steps and came to another door on another landing.

This one was iron, with rigid bolts across it. He carefully unfastened the bolts and pushed against the door which creaked open slowly as it dragged across the floor, scuffing, and scratching it. Inside was a meadow that spread further than the eye could see, and a hot spring ahead of him, where Rayna sat, cradling a baby. The warm, steaming water washed over her arms and legs as the baby rested against her chest. Athias saw himself there too, they were both smiling.

"Our son. He has your eyes… Have you decided on a name?" Athias was peaceful, stroking Rayna's hair.

"Galin. Like the river song." Rayna smiled back and left a light kiss upon Athias' lips and he grinned, sinking down to lay next to the spring beside her and stroke the baby boy's brow as he slept.

From a few metres away, Athias watched on, tears brimmed in his eyes, but he held them back. Then his memories changed again, and the peaceful scene was stripped bare, ahead now was his younger self again, a few years after the previous memory. He watched on as his younger self knelt in the mud his hands soaked in blood, his own cloak in tatters with gaping wounds across his back, and he cradled a child. Besides them was the body of a creature. A Murkin; powerful and relentless, proud once, with two enormous jaws and a thick shaggy coat. Its body had slumped in the mud with Spectre protruding from the neck. Athias, observing, went and sat down by the creature, the fur felt like burning paper as he went to brush it. He looked over at his son in the arms of his younger self and remembered the tears as they cascaded from his eyes, splashing into the mud.

His younger self cradled Galin's head. He kissed his nose, his slashed cheeks and chest, rocking him gently back and forth. Athias, looking on at this memory, felt anger burn in his chest and heart, and his blood boiled as tears cut rivers in his cheeks. He marched towards the body of his son, wanting to hold it again, one last time. With every step he took though, his younger self and Galin became further away. He began to walk faster and then broke into a sprint but Galin became further still. Behind him was the door he came through, still as close as when he had first entered but he turned away, determined to reach his son. He watched, from afar now, as his younger self picked up Galin in his arms, plucked Spectre from the beast, placing it on his back, and left. He faded from view as though travelling through a waterfall that masked his steps, and the ground around Athias began to rumble and ripple, as though every frantic step he took was a stone thrown into a pond, shattering the cold and calm illusion. Athias sank down against the door behind him and slammed his fists on the cold iron and pain shot through his fingers and palm but he did not care, tears cascaded from his eyes, soaking into his cloak. They splashed into the floor, swallowing the dirt as it rumbled, taking it away forever.

Athias hammered his fists against the door and it swung open, Athias toppled out and lay flat against the smooth stone, his chest rose and fell unevenly as he panted, his heartbeat racing and a sickness in his throat. He traced his fingertips over the lines, the gaps between the stone slabs, his son's laughter echoed in his mind, bouncing from memory to memory, the few he had of him. Dragging himself to his feet, he journeyed up the stairs once more and came to another door. A fire in a bracket opposite burned, yet no sound escaped from the flames, even as he stood inches from it, and he felt no warmth on his face.

This door ahead of him now was warm to the touch. Athias turned the simple handle and pushed, it opened swiftly and smoothly, seemingly weightless, and he crossed the threshold into a candle lit room where Rayna stood over a table with a mysterious cloaked figure. They looked directly at him when he entered and he felt his heart drop but through him came another, carrying something cloaked in her hands, the body of a child. This was not Athias' own memory, surely, he thought to himself, straining to remember. Rayna was between Athias and the table, he could not see, but he had noticed a familiar nose from under the thick black hood that the man was wearing. It was crooked slightly, the shadow cast from his hood shielded all his face bar the nose and Athias remembered it but before he could place it, Rayna spoke and filled in the dots for him.

"Master Abbrath."

He cut her off, however,

"Tutor, please. I am a teacher before a master."

Athias stood still, he felt rooted in place and a cold swept across his face, then down over his arms and legs. Tutor Abbrath survived Ziath's assault, he thought to himself. Why didn't Abbrath try to find him? Is he still alive? The questions began to sear through the canvas of his mind, smoke filled his eyes and it burned. His heartbeat began to rise, faster and faster.

"Tutor Abbrath, thank you." Rayna's calm, smooth voice snapped him back to reality. Her words washed across his face like a splash of cold water, "When was the last time you saw Athias?"

He sighed; he was upset. Something Athias had never witnessed other than on the last day he had seen Abbrath, and that was different, still to this.

"Not since I sent him away. Not since he had to leave and we were attacked," he suddenly stood up tall, his back straight and shoulders wide, "but we will find him once more, we will bring him back. The world is not yet ready to be without the Vayshanaa."

Rayna stepped aside and Athias' gut clenched, Galin lay on the table. A mask lay across his face, as was the custom for Rayna's culture when death took them. Abbrath shook his cloak from his pale, spindly hands and flexed his fingers, dipped his fingers into a bowl of orange paste, and flecked it across Galin's body.

"What can I do, Tutor Abbrath?" Rayna spoke softly.

Galin's hand was in hers and a tear rolled down her cheek, a single tear, strong and beautiful.

"We are almost ready. Go next door and get Ror. He will be sleeping. Are you sure you want to do this?" Abbrath inquired.

"My little Galin... I would do anything for him."

Rayna bent down and softly kissed Galin on the forehead of his mask and then she made for the door, taking slow strides as she let her son's hand fall away from her own. Tutor Abbrath began to chant as he ran his fingers over Galin's skin. Athias watched on, still rooted in place, he wanted to touch Galin again, hear his laughter again. One more time. Abbrath swung his hood down completely and took the back of Galin's head, throwing the mask into a fire.

"Vinic Traul'nic. Cindar eletalvet." The fire roared behind him as he scooped up a handful of flames, they danced over his skin, leaping from finger to finger like spiders swinging on web.

"He's beautiful." Rayna nodded to the Raven and Abbrath nodded back.

A raven sat atop her shoulder. Abbrath held out his hand to Rayna who took it without faltering. The fire engulfed her hand, yet she did not flinch, and her skin did not burn.

"Do it now!" Abbrath shouted, the fire raging in their hands masked almost all sound as it flickered from orange to green to black.

Rayna scooped Galin's head in her own free hand and kissed his forehead again, and then she pressed her nose to his as she and Abbrath lowered their hands to his body. There was a flash and the fire coursed over Galin's body, covering it in a blanket of flicking light. Abbrath let go of Galin's head and held his hand over the flames, his palm out flat, facing down, and lowered it. He let go of Rayna's hand too and threw Ror, the white raven, into the air above the fire. Time seemed as though to stand still over the duration of what happened next. A blue-white spectral figure emerged from Galin's body, it was Galin, but before he died; he bore no scars, no marks at all. Ror flapped his wings in slow motion, hovering above. Abbrath guided the spectral figure up and towards the raven which blinked and cawed peacefully, and the figure was drawn inside the body.

Suddenly, as it happened, all the candles and fire went out and the parchment littered around the room moved gently. Abbrath lit a candle, whispered, he was hushed and manic. As the room lit up, Rayna came into view too.

"Did it work?" She fretted.

There was no word from Abbrath, but instead came a cawing noise and as she held out her hand the raven, Ror, landed in her palm and scampered up her shoulder to her face. His feathers were now a silver-white, instead of black as before. She turned to look at him and he pressed his beak against her nose, making a low, gurgling sound, as Rayna exhaled and her breath ruffled the feathers on the bird's face.

"I think we have our answer." Abbrath smiled. "Galin and Ror are one and with Ror's body, Galin will fly high, re-born of magic. What will you name him?"

"Gralnor, I think." Rayna whispered, stroking the raven and smiling. "He will find Athias, I am certain of it.

The room began to distort, as though a pebble had been thrown into a picture painted on water ahead of Athias. The view in front faded away, gushing upwards as part of a reverse waterfall and suddenly he was falling and he saw flickering images unfolding around him; three women, silver haired and golden-brown skin, sitting around a table; the women again looking down over a cliff and pieces of the world he knew passed by like shards of broken glass; the crown as it was buried, tossed into the earth and soil piled above it; a war raging of magic as masters came together to fight others; a set of armour and a shield on a stand in a smooth rocky case; Abbrath's face became shrouded as he turned away and he whispered.

"He will find Athias and bring him back, from the Abyss, and from his fears. Athias will know it is his son, once more, with him." Tutor Abbrath bowed his head.

"Thank you, Tutor Abbrath. What will you do now?"

"I will wait, and I will study, there is much more to be done." He stopped abruptly and turned to look directly at Athias, who stood behind him. "Come home." His voice was deep and toneless.

Athias landed on the very soil that he had entered the grove to find. He heard the fighting outside the group of trees, Finhaal's definite grunt as he swung his mighty hammer and Eifig's cry as they jumped from root to root. He felt a warmth coming from beneath the soil and began to dig with his hands, the grains of sand-like soil slipping past. As he dug further, he reached a point where no matter how much soil he scooped, more took its place. Athias drew Spectre from its sheath and held it, blade pointed down into the hole. He whispered the words of old,

"A bridge standing taller than any peak, a spectre stood upon it, ready to speak." And he pushed down with all his might into the hole.

The soil dispersed, flying out in all directs as light flashed across his eyes. He saw a montage of images; the crown being made and buried, three women looking over a cliff, Spectre, and the other weapons of the Vayshanaa all standing side by side. It was over soon, and Athias looked down and saw it, the crown. It circled around the tip of Spectre's blade; shining as though polished not that same day; the smooth bones that made it were of ivory colour, and the fine metal that wound its way round was elegant. He stepped out of the triangle of trees and saw hundreds of shadow-like figures, the same that had begun to attack when he left, collapse, and seemingly melt into the ground. Finhaal, Eifig, Hathael, and Calor stopped and turned to him, their faces scared and bloody.

"We were beginning to think you'd never return. Those… things… they wouldn't stop coming." Eifig stared out at the woodland as the creatures faded into the ground with a hiss and a whisper.

Athias looked perplexed.

"You were gone two days." Finhaal placed his hammer down and sat, slumped against the roots, breathing heavily, "Do you have it?"

Athias was stunned. Two days? He thought to himself, it felt like hours; he had not slept, or had he? Athias brought the crown into view, taking it from inside his cloak and sliding Spectre back down into his sheath. Gralnor cawed and flew down, landing on Athias' shoulder and nuzzling Athias with his beak.

"The Forsaken Crown." Finhaal whispered in awe.

Chapter Twenty-Eight
Where It All Began

Haurtyn Castle was built by the first of our order. They cast their fine magic and forged the great castle, and the temple with it. It is said that giants and mammoths helped lift and pull the enormous, decorative stones, though I am not sure of this. It bears the mark of magic, and I can feel every path of the Vayshanaa in it. It is a place where magic lives, and magic learns. – Calitreum, Architects and Archives, Page 79.

Athias rode alone now. He had given the crown over to Finhaal before leaving their party as they journeyed to Askiara Mountains and Finhaal's fortress where the fighting had surely already begun. Athias had told them of the vision he saw before he returned, of Abbrath, and how he could not rest peacefully again if he had not been back to the place where this all began.

The sheer icy cold that had wrapped them in chill when they had ridden into the forest only a few days before was leaving, as though a fire had been set beneath the soil and thick roots. Athias noticed the occasional flicker of bright reds and orange, the leaves returning to their natural colours after eons in the dark and cold. Athias pushed his horse, they were not far from Haurtyn and a spell drove Athias on; a blend of excitement and nervousness as thoughts dared to dance across his imagination. The forests thinned as he pushed on, jumping over fallen trees and racing through the undergrowth, and as he did, the trees were replaced by boulders and stony soil. The rocks were uneven and charred, as though a dragon of old had flown over and cast its fire down upon the land.

Ahead emerged a narrow path of trodden earth, it formed a rough trail that led up, as many riders had travelled over in time before. Athias slowed and trotted up the path, carefully minding the horse as pebbles fell away under hoof, scampering down into a nest of jagged rocks. Athias felt a cold breeze on his face as he neared the top of the trail a few hours later, after he navigated the broken bridges and precarious crevasses, and now, above him, he could only see clouds; how they swirled above him. The unmistakable caw of birds grew louder and the gentle sway of waves lapping against cliffs, sure enough, emerging over the top of the path. He looked out over the sea ahead, the murky waves were marbled grey and silver and sitting amidst them were the ruins of the once magnificent Haurtyn Castle. He remembered the storm that he endured as they fled as children, scampering up on deck to watch the great titans beneath the waves emerge, he remembered the crack of cannon fire and the clash of crumbling rocks as they slid into the sea.

It stood now, crumbling. The great bridge that had joined it to the mainland was all but gone, now only a few towers stood alone, like drooping flowers. The temple and the castle itself were shadows of their former self, walls and floors collapsed, statues defaced, and bare to the elements. A flock of birds flew overhead, circling above the ruined castle and cawing, their song skimmed over the air like a light stone over water.

Athias dismounted, looking down at the cliff and seeing nothing but sweeping stone and sharp drops. He removed the saddle, taking Spectre from it and offering his hand to Gralnor who jumped upon it. He placed Spectre on his back and Gralnor nestled inside his hood, then he turned to the horse.

"Thank you, be free now." He whispered and the horse neighed, gently, before trotting back down the path.

Athias turned, facing the daunting task at hand of journeying down to a small jetty where a single boat lay, rocking gently with the waves. His heart shuddered in its place with every step forward, judging the sturdiness of the rocks beneath his feet for they were old and battered. Athias' sharp eyes jumped from crack to crack, measuring the worth of his slow but sure journey, though he could not share the guilt of abandoning his party who would now be close to the fight. He trailed his fingers over the smooth stone beside him, a constant reminder that he had not fallen yet. Gralnor cawed and jumped from his hood, hovering above Athias as he fell. Thoughts scrambled through his mind as the pebbles beneath his boot crumbled and shards of dull-blue rock scampered around him as he slid, faster and faster towards the jagged spears below him. Athias rolled over as he slid and his hands tensed, he tried and failed to grip onto the tiny crevasses that he passed, he could smell the salt of the water as it crashed into the cliffs beside him, showering him with cold droplets. So he reached up and edged Spectre from its sheath, and as he fell from the slope and seemingly hung in mid-air for a split second before hurtling down towards the rocks, he plunged the sword into the wall that he desperately reached for. Spectre cut into the stone like a calm hand reaching through a waterfall, but he was still descending too fast and the coarse rocks loomed below, littered with the carcasses of small animals that had also ventured beyond their safety.

Athias pressed the sword in further, he tried to speak, to utter a spell but the wind rushed up to meet his open mouth and battered him, drawing the breath from his lungs before he could mutter. He focused and shouted out in a frantic burst,

"Paraviel'ael!"

His momentum slowed and the jagged, spear-like rocks beneath halted in their advance towards him gradually, as the magic gripped the sword and slowed his fall. Athias felt his left shoulder stretch as his right hand flew from the hilt and a bead of sweat ran from his brow to his chin, leaping off and splashing on the salt-wet stones beneath. Athias, panting, let out a long sigh of relief as he found his footing; his toes just reaching the stones below, and he pulled Spectre he balanced himself, pulling Spectre from the rocks, and ahead of him lay the jetty.

The boat was old, just like the poor wooden construction it was tethered to. The oak slats were damp and soft, and the hull of the boat had many chips scattered beneath Athias' feet, swaying in a small puddle as the boat leaked with a hundred pin-prick sized holes. Gralnor marched up and down the boat, cawing his distaste at their vessel. The waves were choppy, and the boat rocked with every pull of the oars, propelling Athias slowly closer to the rocky beach ahead, one he remembered all too well. The events of that night plagued him almost every day, the dread in his heart which weighed him down as he left the only home he had remembered as of then, a place where he learned and loved so much. The storm from that day still rattled in his mind, he could hear it, he could feel the cold rain scraping away at his skin, but today the water was calm, the boat rocked but only as it swayed in time and motion with the water. A thousand pebbles lay sleeping ahead and the cool air rolled off the glass-like water and caressed the shining flints and smooth tones. Athias stepped from the boat as it landed amidst the wet sand and polished stones, he took a few steps forward and then removed his boots for a moment. He stood in the quiet, listening to the birds above and the water ahead, digging his feet into the pebbles and letting the cool discs wash over his skin, they were cold but soothing, it was a surreal peace in this war-torn, ravaged world. Athias slipped his boots back on and made his way up the gently sloping beach, reaching a crumbling staircase that headed upwards towards the old gate-bridge of the castle.

He stood before the old gates and reconstructed it in his mind; the ruined statues of warriors that stood beside the gates, their tall shields masking their whole bodies, each clasping a spear, a lantern attached. Now the gates were nothing but fractured splints of wood that lay, littered across the inner hall, surrounded by chunks of stone and crystal, it was wet, too, as the rain and the sea had washed over it all Athias walked through and into the courtyard, then into the grand hall, it had once been a proud, beautiful building. White crystal had decorated the thousand hearths from which filled the space with a warm, enriching glow and a dozen enormous stone dragons were carved into the ceiling. An oddly poetic symmetry; forgotten beasts in a forgotten place. Athias took one of the many short stairs from the hall and pressed on deeper into the old fortress, he saw glimpses of his younger self, as a boy, running through these very halls and the tutors stopping him, showing him instead, to the library. He had been here with many students, and wondered where they all were now, if they even alive, many had died he was sure of it, as was expected in their harsh reality. Athias came to the Temple of Zohya, a few of the statues depicting the great goddess, the All Mother, were cracked but none had fallen, they stood around the room embodying the stances of all living things: the creator, warrior, a kind stranger, the fearless monster, a praying father and loving mother, and a sleeping child. Lines ran from each statue, small trenches that were once filled with water, gently running towards the centre of the room where the water dropped down back into the sea.

"You came." Athias turned sharply and drew his sword instinctively but turning, seeing, he let it sink back into the sheath.

Abbrath stood before him and Athias did not wait. He ran to Abbrath, squeezing him tight in a hug. Abbrath's palm lay flat across Athias' back and the other was placed on his cheek, Athias looked down at his old tutor, his old friend and smiled.

"You're alive... I can't believe it." Athias grinned a nervous smile.

"I am, my boy. I am so sorry you had to wait this long to find out." Abbrath looked up and down at Athias and smiled, "Look how you've grown, more than I could ever imagine. How is the sword serving you?" He gestured to the sword which rose a little out of the sheath once more.

"It is ever faithful." Athias whispered, holding the blade out, the blade twanged in the air.

The two stood there for a moment, in peace, before Abbrath pulled away patting Athias on the shoulder while smiling.

"Come, my son, I have much to show you and little time to do so."

Athias followed Abbrath from the temple of which he seemed to be eager to leave. He was in silence as he took short, fast steps from the room and led Athias down a secret passageway hidden behind a statue, one Athias had never ventured into and he had been through many, his cloak trailed behind him and Athias hung back behind it as to not tread on it. Athias fell silent too, he felt like a student again; excited but a with strain of nervousness licking the back of his throat. Athias glimpsed old paintings that had been splashed over the stone. The paint upon the walls had faded for the most part, some designs were nothing but scrapes of red and brown left upon the cold rock as they journeyed further down into the temple, they depicted battles of old and ancient, legendary heroes. Athias stopped at one, a woman costumed in leather armour, holding a sword high, a sword with an unmistakable grip.

"Was this...?"

"The first Vayshanaa of Time, yes. Orlana. Legends tell nothing of her but of the ferocity she inspired." Abbrath's voice croaked in the cold air and Athias could now hear the gentle waves lapping around them, they must be deep into the rock of which the castle stood atop now.

"Why didn't I learn of her?" Athias asked, noticing the frost tipped breath that soared into the air as he spoke.

"Come. Please." Abbrath sounded sad now or was it nervous? Athias could not deduce it.

They reached a heavy door. Iron and stone moulded together in an arching shape. Abbrath placed his hand against it and muttered words under his breath, a mist escaping upwards. The door awakened, criss-crossing across itself and retreating into the stone and then the door itself shuddered, sinking slowly into the arch surrounding it. The room inside was circular with one seamless hearth that ran the circumference, although no flames licked the walls and instead it burned in embers. Huge banners ran down the walls from the top to halfway down, out of reach of the heat from the crackling wood. They were of the first families of Brineth, the founding families that grew from the seeds of the Great Creation. Athias had been so fascinated by the banners that he hadn't even noticed the lady sitting in one of the black stone chairs.

"Rayna?" He was in disbelief.

There she sat. Upright and alert in her chair, her eyes bright but mixed with sadness.

"My love…" She sighed, her words fell from the dark lips and fluttered to the ground. She looked to Abbrath, "I don't know how to start… How to begin."

Athias looked between the two frantically.

"Start what?" His voice was desperately confused.

"You've been lied to. Mislead and led away from the truth. It happened right here, for years, in this very temple."

"What are you talking about?" Athias muttered, failing to give weight to the words coming from his former mentor's mouth.

"The Vayshanaa were built upon a lie."

Chapter Twenty-Nine
A Tale of Three Sisters

The price of betrayal is blood. What, however, is the price for one that does not bleed? – Calitreum, Gilen Abbrath's Entry, Page 427.

Abbrath felt his heart's beat rise and strike inside his body like lightning against an anvil. He was cold, he was hot, he felt heavy, as though his own body resisted the commands from his mind.

"My dear. My love." Rayna stood up slowly. "It's true."

Athias looked to her, a shock of disbelief carved into his face.

"How can it be a lie? What are you saying?" His questions raced around his mind, darting from one thought to the next.

"Athias, please, come and sit." Rayna whispered, taking his cold hands, and guiding him to the chair, gently nudging him down.

"The Mother Zohya lied from the very beginning. I didn't believe it myself, either, not to start with. Tell me. While retrieving the crown, did you see three women looking over a cliff?"

Athias stood still but nodded. His hands were clammy with cold sweat, he felt as though the air around him avoided him, a statue.

"How could you know that?"

"Let me tell you a tale. A tale of three sisters." Abbrath shook his sleeves from their rest.

"Zohya did indeed slay the Eternal Giants, ruling over what came before, but she wasn't alone. She battled against them with two others by her side, Ciarth and Hyara. They were her sisters.

"After the war was won, they worked together to create Brineth and the other islands we know; Rothnord, Cayhorth, and Rargnos. It is said in the history, she was injured in the battle with the giants and that's why she could not walk upon the surface and so created the Vayshanaa to 'create' the world for her.

"But in fact, she was injured when she turned on her sisters. Zohya wanted to create life to rule it. Her sisters opposed this, seeing this as no different from the very evil they had slew together. Zohya created the five Vayshanaa and used them into forging life on Brineth in the image of

Zohya. Ciarth and Hyara created two more Vayshanaa in secret, bestowing them with other artefacts of power, just like your sword, Eifig's ring and the rest. Zohya learned of their creations and attacked them, slaying her own kin but not before they were to cast ancient magic upon her, binding her to the godly realm. A war waged on Brineth, a war of magic, as Zohya's creations fought her sisters'."

"What were her sisters' creations of?" Athias sank back, absorbing as much information as he could."

"The Vayshanaa of darkness and light, but they were defeated and with them gone, Zohya convinced her five champions to create the crown as a gateway for her return. The Vayshanaa did so, forging a crown of power and beauty, but once they learned from their slain kin's letters that Zohya would seek to rule them, they hid it, burying it in a grove of cursed time, sacrificing memories of their own. It is this, which is why you and each Vayshanaa of time that has come before you, has sacrificed memories of old, and it is also this, which is why you alone could retrieve it.

"Zohya could see the crown but she could not reach it."

"She has been manipulating the Vayshanaa, hasn't she? To get us to retrieve the crown?" Athias sat upright.

"She may have even brough Ziath to our shores as to unite you all together." Abbrath stared into the embers around him. "In the morning after you escaped, Eifig too, and the magical protections had faded, I was shown a vision too. A vision of this chamber, which Ciarth and Hyara built for their Vayshanaa."

Athias looked stunned, massaging his hand over his forehead. Abbrath cast a spell on the table beside the chairs and a crack ran around the side; it was a box, not a table.

With a swish of his hand the top came off and Athias stood up to look inside. His heart dropped and his eyes widened. In the stone case lay a set of beautiful armour; black and smooth with silver lining, mirroring the appearance of a dragon; and a bow, long and eloquent, with splashes of gold across the crystal-like wood.

"What are their names?" He whispered in awe.

"The armour, Shadowfire and the bow, Sunpiercer. The protection of darkness and the weapon of light." Rayna said calmly.

"How?" He started.

"Abbrath sent me a message too, it was cryptic, and only that I should not tell you, but I should come here. I journeyed here after we arrived at Eirshen and Abbrath told me everything."

"There is another thing." Abbrath's voice was stern now, like that of a strict teacher, he had been years ago. "We have been told that the Vayshanaa may not die before a successor has been chosen by them to take on their role. This is a lie. The magic may choose to jump to another, if that one is willing to take on the mantle." He paused, "I am sorry, my boy."

"There is nothing to be sorry for." Athias had accepted the story to be truth, how could he deny it?

"You must take the armour, and Rayna the bow. You must return with the Vayshanaa and summon Zohya with the crown." He held his hand up to Athias who had opened his mouth in protest, "and then you must kill her. She is powerful, yes, and she will grow more so in given time upon our realm but in the few moments that she walks upon the physical reality she will be weaker, for the magic will fall around her."

A raven cawed and Gralnor flew in, landing on Rayna's shoulder. Giving Athias an idea.

"Come with us."

"I would only slow you down my boy." Abbrath sighed.

"Not if we take night's passage." Athias looked to Gralnor who flapped his wings and cawed playfully, a smile seemingly flickered across the feathers on his face.

"Have you ever been to the night's passage? It's a legend." Rayna Said.

"I've been there. Once." Athias was quiet and the others knew of which time he referred to.

"We need all of the Masters. We need you, Vayshanaa."

The words filled Athias' heart and chest with warmth and his arms felt relaxed, the tempest in his chest soothed.

"Oh, my boy. I have had the pleasure of knowing and teaching you, one of the greatest." Abbrath insisted with an urge of kindness, "I will come with you. I have been in this temple for many, many years. It is time I walked upon the land once more.

He embraced Athias again and Athias leaned into Abbrath's arm and when he departed, he felt a new sense of strength from within.

"Is it possible to bind the armour to Gralnor?" Athias asked.

"It is, if you give me a few minutes, I will perform the enchantment. Rayna, please, take the bow from the case. Get a feel of it."

"I will be back momentarily. I want to say a proper goodbye to the temple." He turned his head back to them both as he approached the door. "I didn't get to last time."

Athias patrolled around the great hall. Tracing the flat of his fingers around the now wet but smooth stone and gently pushing stones, the pieces of statues from above him, around with his feet. This place had been everything to Athias. A home, filled with family of all types, bound by their willing to learn the ins and outs of magic. Athias walked around the hall, touching every bit of smooth or coarse rock alike, he went full circle and found himself back at the small corridor entrance which led back down to the secret chamber.

"Goodbye." Athias mumbled under his breath, a smile flickered across his face.

He walked back to the chamber and found Rayna flexing the bow in her hand, no quiver atop her shoulder or on her hip, and yet as she pulled back the bowstring an arrow appeared, glimmering as though being patched together. When she relaxed the bow, the arrow faded from view again. As he walked into the light of the embers she looked up and smiled, and Gralnor cawed and jumped onto his shoulder, nudging him with his long beak. Abbrath sat before them both and stood up upon Athias returning.

"Are we all ready to go?" Athias asked.

"We are." Abbrath replied and shook the sleeves from his wrists.

"Take my hand." Athias said to Abbrath who clasped it.

Athias pictured the rocky, icy riverbed just east of Finhaal's mountain castle, where the sheet of white was peppered with grey rocks and ash-like earth that peered through gaps in the thick snow.

Gralnor hopped off Athias and took flight, circling around the room, gaining speed. raised his hand, fingers outstretched and Gralnor extended his talons as he spread his wings and slowed. A brief second of pain shot through Athias' fingers and then there was a flash of white, then dark, then they stood upon the frost-stung ground, snow around their feet and a cold chill at their necks.

The mountains echoed with the sound of war, the distant booms of cannon fire and the unmistakable cracks of rock falling. Athias began to march forward, jumping across the small streams and ascending the Rocky Mountains, their tops secluded by cloud.

"Come, the night's passage, takes us behind the castle."

The path was narrow and the ground shook gently beneath their feet, while the causes of these tremors grew louder with each passing minute; the unmistakable snarl of cannons relinquishing iron shot; the war chants of soldiers as they most probably moved from one trench to the next, closing in on the castle. Athias had seen his fair share of fighting, of wars, it tired him, and with every step he took his heart wavered knowing that soon he would be among the thick of it again. Upon reaching the peak of the ridge they saw more mountains, sprawling out across the horizon ahead with a glimpse of a castle in the distance. The old stories told that the mountains were prisons for the children of the giants that Zohya had slain, Athias had believed the stories so long, often failing to get to sleep for hours until the glimpse of dawn approached.

Beautiful, they were. A criss-cross of rock and earth, layered snow and icy shards, light from the sun seeped over the triangular titans and across the valleys in their stead. Gralnor cawed as he soared overhead, flying high into the clouds and down again, swooping and gliding, and the four of them pressed forward, crossing ancient bridges and navigating fields of boulders the size of small homes, and crevasses falling far into the depths of the known world. They reached a natural clearing above a ledge on one of the mountain bases and looked down at the battle. The sun flickered in and out of thick clouds above them, bathing the castle in an occasional streak of orange. Finhaal's home; Frosthorn, was a tremendous castle built upon the ridge of a mountain range which stood like a sleeping dragon. The city of Rurnaeiir spread deep into the caverns and tunnels of the mountains themselves.

The castle was immense, with several parts; walls with their battlements running through mountainous caves and then swirling round to extend past and over frozen rivers; towers and turrets were constructed as part of the mountain face and the keep and various buildings stood at a variety of heights over the rocky surface as though being held up by dwarves at one and giants at the other. Frosthorn had many halls built into the caves and it sat, overlooking a harbour that once brimmed with trade vessels every day and night in the summertime but now was filled only with the Emperor's mighty warships which had cleared a path through the thick ice with their rams. Athias peered down and saw many tiny beings running up and down the battlements, archers firing arrows, while down below, he saw catapults atop platforms on the walls launching jagged rock into the surging army at the base of the mountain where lines of men armed with rifles and pikes edged forward, running through trenches, makeshift walls, and tree stumps, slowly pushing forward towards the gate-bridge. Plumes of smoke drifted high from the gun-batteries, and steel beasts, like they had encountered at the Scaltian Fields loomed next to them. Mounds of earth erupted as the projectiles landed, many crashed into the walls, though little did much damage for many a spell had been cast over these walls.

As Athias and the others crossed over a thick blanket of snow, approaching the castle, two knights rode out to meet them.

"It is a Vayshanaa." Abbrath gestured to Athias before he could speak.

"Come, quickly." The knight held out her hand to him and then to Rayna and both climbed onto the steed, stripped of its armour to reveal a tan-colour hair.

Athias climbed onto the other and together they rode back to the castle.

"How's it looking?" Rayna shouted over the galloping thud of the hooves on snow which danced up behind them.

"We are doing all we can, but it is only a matter of time before they breach our gates. The emperor has brought it all to the fight, including the Gravestalkers."

"If they break through the gate, we will be there to meet them." Athias spoke with a loud, strong voice, but his mind was clouded with doubt.

The Gravestalkers were a force he had wished never to meet again. Immense warriors wrapped in bone armour, with large, serrated swords. Athias had met them face to face at the Battle of Vinharven, the bloodiest of conflicts in the invasion, where he and Tristan had led the king's forces against the oppressors. The battle was fresh in his mind as though he had fought it just yesterday. He had witnessed these Gravestalkers cut down lines of knights, striking through a man to cut him clean in half.

"This way, please." The two knights dismounted and led the three of them, with Gralnor now on Athias' shoulder, through a winding passage, thin and low.

With the horses behind them, they pressed through the passage as swiftly as they could, and the bells of the fortress chimed louder with every step. Through the passage, they slipped over a bridge that stood over a crevasse of darkness, and then through a small gate. The knight signalled for the bridge to be raised as Athias and company sprinted through the courtyard and up the stairs.

At the top warriors rushed past, talking of reinforcing the battlements. The knights knocked on a door, turned to Athias and bowed, and then left to return to their lookout. The door opened fast just as a rumble came and the floor shook briefly. Finhaal stood there and behind him Eifig, Calor and Hathael around a circular table. Athias, Rayna and Abbrath entered the room bathed in a gloom by candles and fire, and ahead of the table was a window overlooking the approaching army. Upon seeing Abbrath, Eifig looked astonished, and a tear of joy seeped from their eye, trailing down her cheek.

"You're alive..." their voice trailed off as she stood, dumbfounded.

Chapter Thirty
The Siege

There are castles and there are fortresses, and then there is Frosthorn. A magnificent monument of architecture and engineering. Equal works of magic and labour built these great halls, grand works of spell casting, and stone laying, built the high walls, in a land where ice does not melt, not even to fire. Inside, a labyrinth of beauty, halls and corridors that span miles into the heart of the mountains, and the forge, of course. The forge where bursts of cold fire once forged my sword, and power with it. – Calitreum, Story of the Vayshanaa, Orlana's Entry, Page 424.

Athias stared out over the siege ahead of the castle as it unfolded, the conversation between Abbrath and Rayna and the rest was blurred, as his attention was drawn to the legions marching closer towards the gate-tower, slowly moving a wheeled-ram forward and stopping occasionally for the arrows from the battlements to hit their barricade. Athias heard them all behind, the words washing over him as though distorted. The words came back into focus as Athias drifted back to the room and those around him, the words stung at his ears, at his mind and at his very memories. He turned back to them, addressing the whole room.

"We will need significant time to make this work. I would like to suggest that Abbrath and another go to the Forge Hall and prepare, while the rest of us mount an organised defence of the castle."

"I agree, I will take Calor if it suits her. Her talents will be most effective." Abbrath tried to hide the tremulous tone, realising the events that were about to take place were no longer stories or distant thoughts.

Calor nodded to him and the others before leaving the room and Abbrath followed, his cloak sliding across the slabbed floor. Athias and the others now grouped together, peering over the map on the circular table between them all. The rocky floor was a dusty grey, mountains were a foot high from the table surface and all the rivers and lakes of the world were a blue-green crystal that had been embedded into it. Athias looked down at the castle on the map and the surrounding area and the little wooden flags placed around it.

"How many strong do we have in the castle?" He asked surveying the layout and the positioning.

"About elven thousand, including the Rhalnarg who are on the lower wall and in the gate courtyard. Kaelon is with them and their horses are in the grand stables at the back of the castle, embedded into the cave." Eifig pointed to various locations on the map.

"And how many, by your counting, are out there? Approaching us." Athias asked again, counting the flags himself but knowing they were but a rough estimation of the units.

Another boom followed his words and smoke rose from the gun battery, the cannon balls, slung from their guns, flew out and hurtled into the walls of the castle-city. They hit with a dull thud, denting the stone, cracks starting to form.

"Close to triple that, if not more, excluding gun batteries and those mechanical beasts we encountered on the Scaltian Fields. The Tyrant has brought his full force to fight. The Gravestalkers will soon be ready to storm the gate and then the fighting will be bloody."

Athias stood back, looking over the battlefield. A sense of dread filled his heart, for the more he looked, the less ways out he saw. The main gate of Frosthorn was tall, thick iron but it would not hold for long once the Gravestalkers made their way to it, up over the long bridge from the frosty soil at the base. He peered over the courtyard and gatehouse, and his view became transfixed.

"What is it?" Eifig asked, noticing his eyes darting from one place to another and a perplexed thought crossing his brow.

"What if we let them in." He paused as Finhaal, Eifig and Hathael looked to the map and then to him sharply.

"What are you suggesting? That we just open the gates and let the hoard of bloodshed fall through?" Finhaal's voice was gruff, defensive.

"I am suggesting we lure them into a trap. There's no way we can win this our force against their force, they will overpower us one way or another, especially if they break through the gates stopping us from raising a physical barrier. We need to be clever, and we have to make them think we're not."

"So, we raise the gate, let them into the area between the two gates and drop the gate again?"

"Exactly. A trap sprung but all of us in part." He nodded Hathael, who had been remarkably silent in all this, and she nodded back.

He looked to the others who looked back, concerned. "If anyone has any other ideas, I'm all ears, but we don't have long, and we need to hold them off."

"Once the gate is not an option, Ziath will focus his commitment to the walls. It will be a vicious push, with ladders and grappling hooks. He will make the climb and it will be bloody." Finhaal's gruff voice was now levelling out as he too examined the map and the fortress city.

Athias and Finhaal marched down to the gate house, accompanied by a few dozen archers. They had briefly spoken to Kaelon first, and she, and her knights were readying to leave. Rayna had joined them above the gatehouse wall, she had brought a sturdy line of Shadows, creating an archery formation of almost two-thousand strong. Rayna flexed her new bow as she stood on the outlay, while arrows still reigned down in the occasional barrage from the higher walls, where Eifig, organising the warriors there, preparing for the climb. They signalled to the catapults and few ballistae, dotted over the walls and towers, ceasing their fire.

Athias and Finhaal stood inside, the signal had been relayed and the old storm cover had been lowered, over the gate. A thin wooden shield that had protected the iron from the icy waters that once, an era ago, had spread out over the land with the tide. While this was down, the gatehouse crews had raised the main gate, and stood ready to release it again.

A horn blew and Ziath's Gravestalkers chanted as they began to push the wheeled ram forward. Athias opened one of the small window hatches on the cover to see the massive device slowly edging forward; as tall as a mammoth and long enough to shelter thirty men on either side, and the ram itself was cast-iron, heavy, strong.

"Archers!" Rayna's voice echoed over the rumble of the thick wooden wheels as they pressed over the stone of the bridge. "Nock your arrows! Draw!" All was silent bar the creaking wheels. "Loose!"

Athias looked out to see a barrage of arrows, thousands of them. He watched as the arrows peppered the ram and the pike men behind it and he watched on as tens and tens of the them fell off the curved bridge ahead, urging the ram forward. Athias noticed the ranks of riflemen way off in the distance and an officer behind them, he couldn't make out any words but soon smoke erupted from the ends of the rifles and an almighty crack echoed as the rifles and cannons unleashed their shots. Athias heard shouts and cries and crashes as the cannonballs smashed into the battlements above and he heard the clang and thuds of archers falling from their posts into the courtyard behind them. Athias closed the hatch and nailed wood over the top of it as the ram edged closer.

"Loose!" Rayna shouted again and the twang of arrows, flying from their bows together, sounded like a bird ruffling its feathers.

A smaller horn blew from inside the castle, high on the walls, and the soldiers around Eifig's positioning unleashed their flurry of arrows and shot from the few rifles too. They were targeting the lines of rifles, causing as much chaos as possible. The gate and gate house began to tremble, more and more with every passing second, Athias' heart was beating stronger and stronger. He could feel each beat, each pulse of blood, and dust fell from the archway above the gate ahead. Tiny pebbles and pieces of brick on the smooth stone beneath their feet began to dance up and as the ram edged closer, grunts of those with it followed. The few shards of light that came in from around the gate itself became black and the stone-brick of the walls shook harder, and harder, and then stopped. The ram stood outside the pretend gate and Athias could hear the shallow breaths of the Gravestalkers attached to it, the ram snarled with the sound of one hundred soldiers breathing through their thick, steel helmets.

"One." A gruff, deep voice shouted over the quiet. "Two." A creaking followed and the sounds of chains sliding back over wood. "Three."

"Heave!" One-hundred deep voices shouted in unison as they pushed the ram's cast-iron head into the storm cover, which shuddered and cracked.

"One. Two. Three!" The same voice as before, gravelly now.

"Heave!" The shout came again, and the ram battered the gate.

The wooden cover creaked. Small cracks started to jolt from the wooden beams. Athias heard Rayna shouting distantly, as his attention became focused on the gate, and the flurry of arrows launched from their bows again. The cover shuddered again and bent inwards. The voices outside blurred into snarls and growls. Athias drew Spectre from its sheath, and Finhaal made ready his hammer, and as they did, the cover flung open and off their hinges towards them.

"Vorins'a!" Finhaal shouted and in the blink of an eye, a wedge comprised of orange light stood before Athias, head to toe. The storm cover hit it and spun off to the side, shattering on the walls around them. Athias turned and bowed his head to Finhaal who raised Caereth high in two hands.

The gatehouse was dusty, brick and splintered wood lay to the sides of them all and outside was shrouded in shadow. Then, as suddenly as the gates had flung back, a stampede of grey and silver charged forwards into the gatehouse accompanied by a roar. The Gravestalkers poured in, charging towards Athias and Finhaal, bloodshed in their eyes.

They were monstrous. More beast than man, clad in jagged bone armour, their swords shimmered in the dull light. They were all tall and built like mountains, brandishing broadswords as tall as a grown man and red glowed from the eye slits in their helmets. Athias rushed forward and brought Spectre up and it clanged against a falling sword. He flicked it out from under the thick blade and stomped upon it before pulling Spectre's handle upwards and cutting into a limb. The second gate raised, and Blood-born warriors rushed in, encouraging more Gravestalkers into the trap. Athias ducked and dodged, Spectre met blade after blade. He turned and blood splashed across his face as an Askiaran warrior fell, cut clean in half. Athias brought Spectre up and sparks of lightning shot from it as it crashed against another blade. Athias struggled against the attacker. He was faster and far more skilled but what did that matter against such ruthless opponents? Every strike his sword landed just thudded into the armour, hard as iron, somehow. He needed to cast the spell. They were to be over-ran if not, but he could not escape the clutches of the fight. A fist caught Athias in the cheek and he fell to the floor, Spectre slid from his hand and as he coughed, he inhaled brick-powder.

He felt his cloak being pulled and scrambled to reach Spectre, but it tumbled through his fingers. He was pulled around and lurched forward towards a red glow of a helmet. Athias pulled a knife from his boot and pushed it into the helmet slits, through which mist-like breath escaped. He was met by a rough howl and fell back, picking up Spectre and jumping to his feet as he brought the blade up precisely, pushing with his might as the blade sunk into the chest of a man. For he was just a man. Athias fell back and began to mutter spells beneath his breath, spells he could barely hear over the screams and shouts and the clang of steel. Finhaal was in the thick of it, he crashed Caereth down onto a helmet, twice, three times, and blood seeped through the thin slits as his ferocious warriors lunged their spears and sheltered behind shields.

"Voron Icaya. Voron Orona. Voron Icaya." Athias repeated the words over and over. "Voron Icaya lae mene!" He shouted and felt the sword charged with magic.

Athias plunged the sword into the stone floor and cracks of burning white light coursed through the stone beneath the fighting. He waited for them to pass under all those gathered and out of the arch where the ram stood.

"Finhaal! Pull back now!" He shouted and Finhaal raised his hammer above the heads of those around him before smashing it down into the ground, his eyes closed, words jumping from his lips. Finhaal ran back and his Blood-born followed. Athias pulled his sword from the ground. For a brief second nothing happened and then the spell erupted. Light blasted up from the stone, pausing time briefly, and the hundred Gravestalkers, tightly packed, were dazed and confused. Finhaal whistled upwards and with a cheer, the front gate sped down, slamming into the strong stone. Athias joined Finhaal and the second gate fell too. Archers opened hidden windows in the gatehouse and peppered the Gravestalkers with arrows. The thudding sounds were followed by grunts and shrieks of pain, which seeped from behind the thick iron door.

Athias jumped to the mind of Gralnor who flew above the clouds and then down to Hathael who hid beneath the gate bridge. Gralnor swooped down and flew under the bridge, cawing, and Hathael nodded. Gralnor flew up again high into the clouds and Athias returned to his body as he heard it, the bridge began to crumble as it was deconstructed by thick roots buried deep in the rocks. Rayna looked down Athias, concerned, and she shouted something that he could not hear. Figures jumped over the wall where she stood. Slender figures with dark armour beneath black cloaks, the occasional glint of silver shining from their masks. Cloaks.

"Rayna! Look out!" Athias shouted and began to rush the stairs to the wall as the Cloaks began to tear through the Shadows and other archers on the wall before they realised what was happening.

As Athias reached the battlements a dozen grappling hooks flung over and scraped against the stone. The ropes tightened and then ladders rose, thudding against the rock. Athias looked over the wall and saw tunnel entrance and hundreds of soldiers pouring from them, like water from a spout. A bell rung on the higher battlements as more ladders were carried through the tunnels and raised against the walls and then were masked by the red cloaks of those who began to climb them.

"Finhaal, go to the top!" Athias shouted down and Finhaal began to sprint up to the walls accompanied by those that were alive after the gate skirmish.

A dreadful whirring sound leaked across the air again, and he looked up to see more airships approaching, small explosions peppered the courtyard and walls as explosive barrels hurtled down from the sky.

Athias was too busy thinking what to do and was met by silver talons, narrowly missing his face. He raised Spectre and the blades slid over the frosted steel. He raised the sword and carried the talons, bent over the blade, up before kicking the Cloak away from him and rushing towards Rayna who was still firing arrows but now focusing on the ladders. A boom of cannon fire shot overhead and smashed into the over-head battlements. As the old magic started to fade, the protection with it. Athias cut down a red cloak in front of him, splitting the rifle he held clean in half, the sting of blood splashed over his lips and the copper smell signed his nostrils. Hathael made her way into the courtyard after returning from outside, the Shadows with him drew their bows and shot with deadly accuracy up to the walls, red-cloaked legionnaires fell from the wall and into the courtyard, arrows piercing their necks above the cuirass.

Bodies hit the cold, grey stone with a thud and blood spewed from their veins. Hathael signalled them to join their kin on the walls while she made her way up, into the towers. She spoke to two Shadows, signalling ahead, and they ran up. Athias glimpsed the two rangers raising a ballista, pointing it up, towards the gunship and firing but the bolt missed, crashing down into the rocky earth below. They began to adjust it as Hathael left to find Calor and Abbrath. The fighting atop the walls was furious. The archers began to turn away from firing arrows to fight those that climbed up the ladders and as more archers turned away, more made the climb. In the next few minutes, thousands of red-cloaked legionnaires had climbed over the battlements, which began to overflow, forcing fighting down into the courtyards and up the inner ramps and bridges inside the walls. Athias heard a caw and looked up, then looked towards where Gralnor was pointing. The Rhalnarg were galloping across the thick ice and snow but the forces of Frosthorn had no way to distract the rifle lines. He on-looked with dread as the artillery, the mechanical beasts, and the rifles began to reposition; turning to face the charging line. Around him a vicious conflict grew larger and larger, as a sea of red with splashes of black, covered the entire castle. He engaged in combat with those that rushed to him, although his mind was off with the Rhalnarg, each beat of his heart trembled in his chest.

Down in the courtyard, H'Khara and the other coarans that were able to fight had joined the fray; dozens of bears, wolves, and even gruffons and small drakes the size of a pack of wolves. They roared and growled, tossing soldiers aside and ripping their limbs off, then came the howls and cries of pain as the animals were speared on pikes or took numerous shots from the rifles in a messy onslaught of blood and steel. A crack whipped across the air as well as the faint rat-a-tat of a whirring machine gun. Athias looked over the battlefield to see smoke pouring from the cannons and then ahead of them horses dropped, falling into the ice-burned earth, and disappearing in a cloud of dust. The ballista exploded as barrels of sparks landed, and the wood and iron shattered in a burst of flames.

The ground beneath Athias began to growl as though a dragon had awoken beneath. A roar from the mountains passed over the castle and spread down to the bay, growing louder and stronger, and the earth at the base of the walls danced up and down. Fear gripped Athias' mind. An avalanche? Would they be safe? Boulders of ice began to hurtle down from their resting place on the mountains, atop the castle and cracks began to appear in the rocky soil. Looking over to the bay, the warships began to sway, and bells rang from their decks. Athias ran as fast as he could to a watchtower and ascended the steps to the top. The ice surrounding the ships began to rise and fall, smashing into the ships as they tried desperately to turn, having spotted something in the distance. His ears rang and his bones shook. The ships in the bay crashed against one another, denting, and puncturing the iron hulls, many fell into depths, and the black waters were pulled back, pulling many ships with it.

Athias pulled out a sight-glass, the clang of steel and crack of rifles, a distant blur now. Through it he saw horror. A wave, as tall as the castle towers. It rushed towards the earthy, stony, icy shore; a stampede of castle-tall stallions.

"Brace yourselves!" Someone from below, perhaps another in a high tower, shouted out.

The waves lowered and rushed into the bay and the ice slid, and spread out onto the shore, crashing through the attacker's trenches and gun battery, and seeping into the cold soil. Then came a whale to the surface, its fins wrapped in steel armour, and a rider sat in a saddle. The rider stood upon the whale as the shaking ground came to pass. Athias whispered to himself as he gazed through the spyglass,

"No..." His voice fell away in awe.

C'k'rian before him. Standing proud, clutching Ocean's Roar in hand. The Stormbinder; a shining black trident that glistened as the droplets of water fell. Her tattered leather clothing was gone, and instead she had donned black armour; a chest and arm plate adorned with purple strikes and lining. While her trousers had been replaced by a golden-studded, black pteruges, and black shin-guards were strapped to her blue skin. Atop her head was the Maelstrom Crown, the ancient crown of the ocean worn by Queen Haruorn from Vadoran before the city had sunk. She raised the trident and bolts of lightning struck the airships, while waves rose around her, passing her, and from the water's shielding clutch came soldiers. Thousands and thousands of blue-skinned, shield-clad warriors rushed from the sea's embrace into the trenches and soldiers in them. C'k'rian let out an almighty war-cry and charged head-on into the fight. In this same moment, the Rhalnarg collided with the gun battery and Ziath's forces were caught between steel and sea. Athias looked to Rayna and the pair of them fought their way down to the courtyard and then up towards the Forge Hall, knowing there would be no other chance to perform the ritual. Eifig and Finhaal were already at the doors when they arrived.

"Who was that? Down there, in the bay." Eifig was amazed.

"The Queen of Vadoran." Athias spoke quietly but with words filled with wonder.

The battle raged on and the sound of ten-thousand war cries carried over the air, which was filled with the stench of copper: blood and rust. Athias pushed open the door into the castle's cavern-halls and the others rushed through, Gralnor soared down and through the doors before Athias heaved the thick stone shut. The fighting outside diminished from their ears entirely.

Chapter Thirty-One
The Forge

I have seen many great items come from the forge at Frosthorn keep. The Vayshanaa each carry with them, a weapon, created from the icy steel. There have been others too, some lost and some not. It gives life, the creations born from it are alive in some way, maybe as alive as I am now.
– Calitreum, Stories of the Vayshanaa, Finhaal's Entry, Page 414.

The halls and corridors inside were enormous, miles of elaborately carved stone, the walls glistened with crystals and ice-white marble. The Forge Hall was a place that Athias had always dreamed of seeing it and thought it would remain mere dreams for all his life. Such stories he had heard of it. The group took great strides into the mythical hall where the first Vayshanaa had held the first council of magic, a council long forgotten as time took a hold on the world. A dozen dragons ran the length of each wall; enormous beasts of marble wrapped in crystal fire, licking the stone around their talons.

Athias imagined the feasts here long ago, charred boar and spiced rum, spread out across tables a plenty, and a phantom taste lingered in his mouth as he imagined it. The fighting outside had faded completely as they pressed forwards through the tall doorways and down another corridor, this one curved gently, winding its way around the enormous towers of rare crystal embedded in the mountain rock. The company came to a decorated set of doors standing tall, almost as wide as the Grand Hall's thick stone gate. Finhaal pushed the door open, it slid gracefully over the stone floor, and he led with Athias, Eifig, and Rayna following, and Hathael was ahead of them but Athias looked to the walls and was left stunned by what he saw.

The walls here were so elegantly carved; entire landscapes and battles engraved into the dazzling but smooth stone. The hall was illuminated by candle-less lanterns and great, stoic fires. Marble, grey-stone, and brilliant gemstone were entwined from the ground on which they walked up to the high, curved ceilings. Statues of the first knights stood proud around the room, equally spread down the long wall while behind them, carved into the rock stood beauty: icy mountains, their heads in the clouds, and winged dragons of old soaring above. Wolves howled in packs; the raging sea lapped at the mountains and grumbling volcanoes. As the four led by Finhaal entered the room all of the creatures on the walls turned their heads and roared, howled or cried, and only stopped when Finhaal approached to which they all bowed their heads before continuing their life upon the walls.

"You made these? All of them?" Rayna approached Finhaal who stood facing the wall, the gemstone water flowing under his hand.

"I crafted the stone, I fed the magic to from the forge, yes." He was humble even in these times.

Athias noticed that his voice was heavy though, sadness crept in at the idea of the halls, and all the life within them, being torn down.

Behind them stood he forge itself. Athias had been so enthralled in the stonework he had completely forgotten, in that moment of peace, of the forge and what they must do now. The Nightfall Forge sat upon a dais of jet-black stone, each edge was cut, and sharp. The forge was perfectly circular, and the thick stone leapt up from the floor of the dais, curling and running up until it bent over on itself and ran back down into the orange glow that shimmered with a white tinge. The forge sat in the middle of the hall, joined by grooves which from each corner of the room. Each groove was filled with molten rock and metal and they each fed into the furnace.

Athias stood at the side of the forge and dazed into the bubbling, brewing storm of fierce reds and warm oranges. Across from Athias sat an anvil and workstation with many fantastic weapons strung up on hooks. He felt a low buzzing on his back and, when gripping the hilt, felt Spectre humming. He drew Spectre from the sheath and inspected the frosted steel as it glimmered; the silver-grey of the blade twinkled with an orange glow.

Abbrath stepped out of the shadows and Calor behind him. His faced flickered with a faint smile, while she looked on,

"Spectre was created here, and it knows it. It feels drawn to the forge and the fires, that stir in its molten belly."

"I feel drawn to it too. I can feel the hot stone on my skin, nursing me." Athias replied softly, but loud enough that everyone else heard.

"Are you ready to proceed?" Calor spoke with a no-nonsense look about her. She was nervous but eager to start what must be done.

"I am." Athias nodded his head and looked to the others.

They all nodded individually and Athias looked back to Abbrath who sighed and let down his hood to reveal a grey-haired ponytail and scarred skin.

"Very well. Give me the crown and gather around the forge."

Athias handed the crown over and looked up to Gralnor who cawed, swooping down from the statues on the ceiling. As the raven began his descent, winding round the room and Abbrath placed the crown in a harness, the others took their positions around the forge.

"When the crown dips below the surface of the molten steel, it will open the gateway, and Zohya will arrive. Are we ready?" Rayna looked around, sincerely.

In the moment that Gralnor flew over Athias' head, he raised Spectre up and the raven's talons skimmed the steel. There was a flash of light and then Athias emerged, clad in the Shadowfire armour, a helmet upon his head with guards from the ears to his lower lip, while the neck bore spikes, that which a dragon's would have. Athias' chest was covered in black and silver, and the armour ran smoothly from one plate to the next, down from his neck and to the gauntlets on his hands.

"Ready."

Athias and the others watched on as the harness, a cradle in chains, edged its way to the centre of the forge. It had to be dropped exactly so that the magic could disperse evenly into the molten rock and metal. Finhaal picked up Caereth and held it over his shoulder, ready. Eifig polished the Embasha, before pulling daggers from their sheaths and Hathael stood, poised with Dr'arenth, though she was leaning on it, tired from the fight already.

Calor and Abbrath raised their hands up and began to channel the magic, shrouds of black smoke covered Calor's arms, and her cloak, Ortharlia, billowed around her. Abbrath's hands shimmered with green sparks. The chains creaked and clanged as they shuffled forward and then, suddenly, they dropped fast, and the metal clinks rattled as they cycled over. The crown hit the surface of the bubbling liquid and sat for a second, fizzling as it slowly submerged in the heat. Athias felt his sweat on his fingertips, he felt Spectre humming as the crown began to sink; a circle of mountains sinking into an orange sea. He raised Spectre up, so the blade was across his face, and felt a hissing which grew louder and louder. The crown began to fracture. Cracks shot through the materials entwined together and a glow of purple began to shine from the cracks.

"Easy now…" Athias muttered to himself.

The peaks of the crown were all that remained now, and the forge began to bubble furiously. Bubbles erupted as large as human skulls, and then came a rumble and a hiss. The crown sank completely below the orange and reds and then came a scream, piercing and harrowing. A scream which brought forth a searing pain in Athias mind. From where the crown had submerged came a white light, and it shot through the liquid, coursing through as though it were rock. Beams of light broke from under the liquid, and swords of light shone through, cracking the ceiling and walls that were touched as they rotated up and over a circle forming in the middle, before erupting completely and flooding the whole hall in brightness. Athias shielded his eyes and was thrown off his feet, landing a few metres away.

Athias picked his head up and looked to the forge which was now solid and upon it stood a woman. She was different than before. She had shimmering; obsidian skin laced with burning orange trails; like veins of fire beneath the dark soil of a volcano. Her hair, a molten-red, flowed down over her shoulders. Her lips, like the eyes, were ivory and smooth, and a wisp of smoke fell from her mouth as she took a long breath. She looked around to the hall, to Athias, and the others ready to oppose her.

"Oh, my children… You stand, ready to welcome me. It has been a long, long time since I have felt the air upon my lips, the smell of steel and fire."

Smooth, black armour clung to her curved, poised figure. Her shoulders and arms bore beautifully moulded armour plates, smooth metal, slotted into place and engraved with silver and grey.

"Dressed for war, traitor?" Finhaal got to his feet and spat.

"You look old, Finhaal. Tired." Her voice echoed around the hall, her eyes glimmered.

Athias looked directly to the goddess before him. His armour caught her eye and she turned to him as he edged his way towards her.

"We know the truth, Zohya. We fought, for thousands of years, for a lie. Your lie."

"Maybe so. But some of you enjoyed it." She smirked.

"What are you talking about?" Hathael started to say but Calor disappeared into a shroud of smoke beside her, and Athias could only watch as Hathael was flung across the room.

"To arms!" Finhaal shouted and swung Caereth into the smoke but Calor dodged and shrouded Finhaal before picking him up and throwing him too with long, skeleton-esque claws.

Tutor Abbrath muttered a spell and the hall was illuminated in green light, Calor fell to the floor, smoke swirling around her. She launched an attack at Abbrath who blocked it with a shield and her claws scraped down the magical barrier.

Meanwhile, Zohya pulled two jet-black axes from her back and swung them at Athias who ducked but felt the blades skim across his cheek as he turned his head in a split second. She swung again, calculated, and swift. Athias ducked again and raised Spectre up parrying. An arrow plunged into Zohya's breastplate and she looked down, smiling, before pulling the arrow and snapping it. Athias looked behind him and saw Rayna forming an arrow, and another, launching them from Sunpiercer.

"You'll have to do better than that, my dear." Zohya had a honeyed voice. It was smooth and calm but eerie, and she rushed forwards, brandished the axes but Athias jumped in the way and deflected the black metal blades.

The hall began to shudder and shake as black crystals emerged from the forge's molten liquid. A tower of shiny, black shards, growing taller and wide with every second. They burst through the floor around the forge, and through the slabs of stone, covering everything slowly as Zohya rushed forward. She launched a barrage of strikes and swift cuts and Athias did all he could to avoid and block them. He caught the two axes as they came down and scraped over his right eye and cheek, slicing through the skin.

"Argh!" He let out a grunt of pain and channelled his power through Spectre, "Arkan'darina!" As he screamed, he felt his strength and speed increase, his muscles flexed under the skin.

He struck Zohya's arm and then, ducking under the axes, slashed at her leg. Rayna released a barrage of arrows and each found their mark upon Zohya's arm and shoulder, but the arrows bounced off the armour. Zohya caught Spectre in her hand and took it from Athias' hands before swinging an axe upwards and into his stomach. Athias felt a fire in his chest and then a searing pain. He looked down at the armour, mostly intact, with the axe blade lodged in his stomach. It dripped with blood.

"No!" Rayna shouted and pulled back an almighty arrow, firing at Zohya who buckled as one, finally, pierced her shoulder plate.

Zohya forced Athias to his knees before charging at Rayna and kicking her. She flew and crashed into the wall, slumping at the bottom, while Sunpiercer fell from her grip. Zohya returned to Athias, looking down at him as he looked on at Calor as she flew up high and sprayed Hathael and Finhaal with attacks. A flurry of claws, smoke, shadow-daggers, and screams. Abbrath lay on the floor behind Zohya.

"Oh, Athias. How does it fit, the Shadowfire? She was a beautiful creator, my dear sister Ciarth. It suits you, but I will take it from you if I must." She lifted him up to his feet and towered over him, standing at least over half his total height more than him. "Come. Let me show you something." She tipped his head back and stared into his eyes, an ocean swirled in her ivory eyes; clouds of cascading water, spiralling, enthralling him.

All around them fell silent abruptly. Athias got to his feet, he no longer felt the pain in his chest. All was paused around him, all but Zohya who stood with her hand held out but Athias refused to take it. They began to walk around the hall. Passing Rayna who lay peacefully asleep, passing Abbrath who was covered in bloody scars, and Calor who was motionless in the air above Finhaal and Hathael who were shielding their bodies from an onslaught of shadow-knives descending from the smoke around Calor.

"Look around you, Master of Time. What do you see? Conflict. Pain and conflict are all this world has come to know." Zohya waved at the surroundings. "Look back at your life, your own life, what has been consistent? Pain. Suffering. War." The hall vanished around them and instead Athias was looking at a paused battlefield. A wash of shimmering steel and black cloaks, blood-soaked grass, and a thousand banners obscured by towers of smoke drifting from ten thousand rifles. "I know you can see the amount of suffering the world has endured. I know you hate it, just as you hate your own suffering, Athias." The words drifted smoothly from her lips to his ears, they were comforting, almost sincere. "I wish to end that. To end it all and to start again. You could join me, we could all work together to create a new world. Long has it been since I walked upon the physical realm, long has it been since I shaped the elements to my will. You could join me, Master of Time. Become a ruler of time."

The whispers clung to his ears, finding way through to his brain and he stopped for moment to listen rather than to just hear. Could it really be so simple? An answer to his suffering, to the world's suffering? Before he could process the thoughts however a familiar voice cropped up in his mind,

"What would you do if Ziath had never invaded?" Athias looked around and saw nothing. He was clutching Spectre and all around him shone, a crystal-like white.

The white around him started to fade as did the words, distorted, as though through water. A scene began to form around him. Athias was stood between two men, each sitting against a rock, a small stream running between their feet as they talked to one another. "What would you do, if Ziath had never invaded, if you had never met me?" Tristan was sharpening a knife on a whetstone and Athias, his younger self, was fiddling with some leaves and grass before looking up to his old friend. Clutching Spectre, Athias marched to the side and looked on at himself and Tristan. This was a dear memory, one that had fallen into the darkness of his mind, but now he remembered clearly. "Rayna and I always talked about buying a small vessel and visiting one of the other isles. We would laugh about raising Ror in a land of sand and stone instead of the murky, once so beautiful, forests here. We would find a patch of land somewhere where the smooth sand would join a sloping, earthy mountain scattered with thin trees, and we would build a house and a farm, overlooking a lake. Rayna wanted to build a mill by the streams."

Athias remembered those words as though he had just spoken them. He could taste them on his lips, they were sweet and joyful. An idea was all it took to spark joy in even the darkest of minds, and it had been a dream, they would joke about it, sure, but the desire had lingered. And then the world took a turn of its own and brought a plague of destruction with it, extinguishing the hope. Then came a handful of words from Tristan one more.

"If the world were freed of Ziath, it would grow beautiful again. Cut out the rot and the wound will heal."

With those words the wisps of colour began to fade once more, back on themselves this time, dripping away as though someone had splashed a bucket of water over the fresh paint. He appeared back in the present, not a moment had passed since Zohya had declared her intent only now Athias heard the whine as the words pressed against his ear. He felt the singed skin they left behind and the icy claws that dragged over his cheeks from standing in her presence. The facade that her words presented began to crack.

"So, what will it be?" Her hushed voice slithered around him in the air.

"No." He spoke sternly, "You are the rot."

Athias focused and brought the paused time to an end. The flurry of movement around him startled Zohya and he jumped up on her thigh, slicing down into a thin gap in the armour with a small knife.

"NO?!" You dare defy me?! I who created the seeds from which your race began. I who shaped the mind of a once-gentle ruler to come and wash you away." Zohya dropped Spectre to the floor and picked up her axes which were embedded in the stone, their corruption spread with black tendrils from the blades. As she brandished them, sparks flew from the blades.

Abbrath had climbed to his feet, helped up by Gralnor who circled around him, deflecting the shadow-knives from Death's hand. He nursed a red glow within his hands and muttered, still protected by Gralnor's aura.

"Darin Vinco-qurl!" He billowed as he stood and red vines shot from the floor, wrapping themselves around Zohya's feet. "I call upon the Abyss. Nurse me. Feel me. Feed me!" He shouted and a storm began to brew inside the hall. Lightning crashed across the ceiling and thunder brewed. Zohya tried to chop at the vines which manifested faster with every slice, spreading up her body, crimson with blood. "I call to you Ciarth and Hyara, bless my hands with almighty wrath. Bless Spectre with the poison of your betrayed blood, let us avenge you, let us free you!" And then there came a scream as lightning struck down upon the ground around them, a thousand bolts of black sparks punching the ground. "Go, Gralnor, go and get H'Khara, bring the coarans. Let us finish this!" and Gralnor cawed before soaring from the hall, ducking, and diving through the lightning.

"What is this?!" Zohya shouted. You dare call upon my sisters?!" Her tone was harrowing, and her voice pierced the brittle air.

Athias felt the power of the Abyss flowing through his veins as it filled inside him. Spectre flew to his hand and he felt it, the force of a thunderbolt in his hands and the wound in his stomach closed. He felt in tune with it and with everything else in the space around him, he could feel Abbrath's life force dwindling as he acted as a portal for the Abyss. He could recall every memory he ever had and the emotion of Rayna down to the fiery surge in her heart. He could feel the magic as it took a physical structure from Finhaal's power and the emotion from Eifig's ring bounced from stone to stone in the room as they turned the smoke from Calor's shadow into water, or the knives into butterflies, and Calor was drenched in rage. Zohya broke free from her shackles and charged at Athias. He could feel her power, her rage, her speed.

Sword and axes collided mid-air and sparks lashed out like claws, reaching out around them. Rayna pulled back the bow string and arrows imbued with sparking, shimmering magic. She delayed Zohya, firing arrows linked by magic wires, tying the goddess to the floor. Athias swung furiously, swift, and strong, while Zohya parried and countered. The pair forced one another back and forward, showing finesse and skill, the likes of which Athias had not felt for many years. Athias ducked, leaning back as the axes brushed over the hairs on his face and then lunged forward, shaving the obsidian skin on Zohya's face. The door swung open behind them and H'Khara burst through with a few other coarans, following Gralnor who cried out as he flew into the room. Blood was seeping from a cut on H'Khara's shoulder. Athias briefly glimpsed them in the corner of his eye as sparks were flung from Spectre ahead of him. H'Khara began her transformation as did the other coarans and they pounced into the fight, Athias looked on as he saw the gigantic wolf disappear in a blast of light. He noticed Rayna sliding under falling rock and unleashing magical arrow one after another. Across, behind the forge, Calor jumped into her wraith-like form and picked Eifig up before throwing them down into the ground and catching a blow from Finhaal which temporarily stunned her and Abbrath worked his healing magic upon them all.

"Gralnor fal, vror." Athias whispered as he struck Zohya's thigh, slicing up and across the back to which she grunted.

Gralnor cawed and soared down towards him and he held up Spectre briefly which Gralnor's talons touched. Gralnor sliced at Zohya, fluttering around her head. Athias struck against the axes once more and they seemingly froze in mid-air, Zohya's arms too, but she broke free, shattering the time barrier, like a snake shedding her skin. Zohya threw an axe and Athias ducked before jumping forward and lunging, catching her shoulder and feeling the lightning from the Abyss course through the sword into her. Behind her Athias heard a shout of pain and looked under her arm as Abbrath fell to his feet, Calor emerged from the shadows behind him, blood dripping down a dagger as she smiled and Athias felt pain grip his heart as the wound opened again and he heard Gralnor cry out behind him. He turned and his heart sunk into the blood-filled stomach. Rayna lay, slumped against the wall, the thrown axe stuck in her chest. Blood bubbled from her mouth as she gasped for air. Athias turned to Zohya who smiled, wiping dirt from her own face.

"You could have stopped this all. You could have prevented her suffering, sorcerer." Zohya smiled menacing, taunting him.

"Enough!" Anger gushed from his lips. Adrenaline coursing through his throat, the pain from his stomach held at bay.

Athias held Spectre in both hands by his stomach, the blade flat against his face and the frosted steel shone, silencing all noise around him. Zohya gripped her axe with two firm hands, the blade extended like liquid and hardened, forming a mighty war axe. Zohya swung the axe and Athias slid on his knees, under it, before jumping up behind her and slicing the blade across her back and she howled. She turned, faster than he thought and the blade of the axe slashed across his left arm and into his chest.

He spat blood onto the floor and clashed Spectre against her axe, he knocked it to the side and swung Spectre up, cutting clean through her armour and dragging across her chest, leaving a trail of shining silver in her skin. Zohya clasped the axe again and swung it once more, with the force of a stampeding mammoth, and Athias lunged forward putting all his weight behind the blade. There was a flash of silver followed by streaks of purple as the blade plunged into Zohya's heart and the black axe blade plough violently into Athias chest, forcing him to his knees.

"Athias!" H'Khara's kind voice screamed over the carnage.

Athias and Zohya knelt in front of each other. Blood spurted from his lips, down over his smooth skin. She winced and pushed the axe further into his chest. He felt his bones splinter and the blood in his body spurted from the open wounds, but he pressed on Spectre with all his might. Zohya's eyes filled with a darkness and Athias coughed, splattering blood across her face. He smiled as Spectre pressed into her, hilt deep, and purple light burst from the blade which protruded from Zohya's back. Zohya fell back against the blade and Athias whispered to himself, looking up at Gralnor,

"I love you, my son. We both do." He looked to Rayna and then his head hung.

H'Khara rushed to him, changing back from the wolf and skidding on the blood, falling beside him. She tried to pull the sword from Zohya's body, which was cracking, turning to ash. Finhaal, Hathael and Eifig joined her and pulled the axe from Zohya's grip, before resting him on his back.

"Get them to the Fountain of Runes! Follow me!" Finhaal created a stone of magic beneath them, and, lifted them gently before leading them from the room with hurried steps.

Calor's ivory body lay slumped against the ancient forge which was now crystallised. A white mist seemed to drift from her body, up into the air, trailing off in different directions. Gralnor landed on Spectre and the sword disappeared as the bird took flight once more.

Chapter Thirty-Two
The Spectre & the Raven

The Calitreum is more than a book, it is a living thing. It draws power and life from the ink on its pages. The book re-orders itself as time goes on, sorting the stories and the entries on its pages. It does this so that the story can keep on being told, so that others can learn from it, indefinitely.
– Calitreum, The Fundamentals of Magic, Page 601.

A great pyre ship sat alone in the cool night, bobbing in the bay gently, tethered to the rocks and the moons gazing down at the crowds that gathered to see it off. The battle at Frosthorn had ended and passed two days prior and the many hours that followed were a solemn affair: gathering the many thousand dead, burning, and burying them. Ahead of the crowd, on the silver-grey shore stood six individuals wrapped orange and black cloaks.

Large fires burned, dotted around and among the crowd in large iron caskets. One by one the robed individuals strode forward into the cool water which splashed against their shins and each strode out and up onto the ship, they gathered around the pyre in the centre of the main deck where Athias and Rayna lay together, one hand in each other's and the other by their side, palms flat. Each of them had been washed and cleaned, their wounds neatly sewn shut. Their eyes were closed, and they were dressed in decorative robes: green with embroidered white and black decoration. The skull of a mammoth sat at their feet, a gold, engraved token was placed in each of their palms and their arrowhead necklaces were each laid flat over their chests.

The others gathered at the edge of the ship, speaking out to the crowd.

"Tonight, we send two servants of life and magic to you Ciarth and Hyara, may they find peace inside the great tree of Nhivaliurn, may they feast with you in the great halls of Naer. May they find life anew in their death and watch over us all." The speaker lowered her hood and Hathael's face was revealed in the light, offering a flicker of a smile as a tear rolled down her creased cheek.

"May they find life anew." The other five echoed.

"Now we say our goodbyes before you, Ciarth, and you Hyara. Guide them out to sea and take them in your embrace." Hathael handed the book to Kaelon.

The Rhalnarg stood on the shore, in neat curved lines around the bay. Their silver armour glimmering in the moonlight. The crowd was awash with many colours from the Vadorans, with their smooth blue skin and golden armour to the Rhalnarg in their shining silver steel, and the Askiarans with brown leather and fur, and the rest.

"Brineth will know their loss. Brineth will mourn their passing and then it will flourish as their spirit lives on in Nhivaliurn and their blood and bones will become food for new life, a part of the world evermore." Hathael spoke quietly and the ship swayed gently, creaking pleasantly.

The others nodded and Hathael stepped back.

"We met not that long ago but I came to call you family. You saved me from the clutches of evil, you showed me another world. I am honoured to have been a part of both of yours." H'Khara spoke out, battling the brimming of tears in her eyes as she looked down at the pair.

She stepped back, Hathael stretched an arm around her.

"You were a son to me, Athias, you always will be." Abbrath was teary too "Rayna, a fire in the darkness, a rock in the river. Never will I forget you, your life, or your son." Abbrath looked up quickly and he glimpsed white feathers dive behind the sails.

The ship was silent now. The sails rippled in the light breeze and the timber creaked underfoot.

"May I have a line alone with them?" C'k'rian was quiet, her voice was dry.

"Of course. Light the pyre when you're done and then join us on the beach." Hathael smiled and led the others from the ship, down into the splashing water again.

C'k'rian walked round the pair, lying peacefully

"Rayna, I never knew you, but you were the light in Athias' life and for that, I thank you. Athias… I have so many things I wish to say but I will leave you with something short. Never have I met anyone to come back from so much pain, never have I met someone so fascinating." She took a few slow steps around the pyre, round to their feet and looked up at them. "We will chase the tyrant back to where he sleeps, we will break him and burn out his shadow. The land and sea are united again, you showed me, in your own way what I must do... may you find the peace you always sought." She turned to leave the ship, whispering to herself, "Sleep well. My old friend."

C'k'rian took the torch that rest on a bracket of the small bridge which led down to the jetty and tossed it onto the pyre.

The fire licked at the kindling and spread over the dried grass. C'k'rian stepped from the bridge and pulled it back, it splashed in the water as it fell clear of the ship. Abbrath signalled to Finhaal who lifted his hammer to cast a spell, flowing his hand over the stone before placing the handle down upon the shore. A light drifted out as the base of the handle sank into the pebbles and at the base of the ship, in the water, small horses appeared one by one. They carried the water forward which in turn carried the ship, pushing it out from the shore as the fire began to grow. The logs began to crack and the fire flickered, casting a dancing orange light up above the ship. An unmistakable raven soared overhead, crossing over the ship back and forth, his white feathers shimmering in the light. Gralnor cried out as he peered down to see Athias and Rayna resting, the fire engulfing their bodies. The rest of them stood upon the beach, watching as the ship's sails tighten with a strong breeze and picking up pace as they sailed out into the bay.

"The world will know their loss." C'k'rian fought back tears as they brimmed in her eyes.

"The world will know their loss." The others echoed.

Kaelon stepped forward from where she stood and turned to her knights, she slowly raised her sword from its sheath and pointed it high into the sky where the rare silver shone in the light of the moons.

"We will avenge those who fell here. We will fight for every drop of magic that courses through this world and all others from here to where the moons rest beneath the world. This land and the next will know their loss, it will know and feel and mourn the loss of all who died to protect it."

One by one the knights raised their swords and spears to the sky. Then came dozens more from behind them, and then hundreds.

"The world will know their loss!" The gathered crowd shouted.

C'k'rian began to cry. Tears gushed from her eyes, splashing over her skin and crawling into the shadows beneath the pebbles. Abbrath swirled his hands around in silence and two spectral forms appeared in front of them. Athias and Rayna looked at them before looking to each other, they held their hands out. H'Khara nodded to the rest of them and they stepped forward, each of them placing a hand on the spectral figures who smiled. Their hands felt real, warm, and smooth to the touch. Through they saw the ship gliding effortlessly over the water, the sails catching air in their cloth nets. The fire spurred on, climbing the mast poles, and eating into the timber.

The two figures smiled and nodded their heads. C'k'rian, Eifig, Hathael and Finhaal all mumbled their goodbyes and Abbrath offered a slow nod. The two figures, holding each other in hand, turned and marched into the sea where the white, mist-like form dispersed and the ship, far out ahead of them became engulfed in flame. The sound of the masts falling into the sea could barely be heard, and the water flooded into the hull, dragging the ship down into the depths. Over the next hour the crowds fell back into the walls of Frosthorn where they would feast, retell stories and dance, in memory of those that fell, and before they prepared to continue the fight. One by one Athias and Rayna's closest companions fell back inside too, each saying their final goodbyes in their own way, but C'k'rian and H'Khara stayed by the bay. The pair sat on an earthy ledge, their backs to a small fire which sat in an iron casket, thawing icy grass around them. Their legs hung over a ledge and their feet skimmed the water which lapped gently, and they stared out to where the ship had sunk.

"What of your parents, and your kingdom?" H'Khara questioned, staring out at the open sea ahead, how it spanned hundreds or thousands of miles, she did not know.

"My parents forced me to leave as a child, they sent my brother after us and I killed him. My parents wanted nothing more than to sit on their thrones and let the world fall into the sea around it. They're now gone, they rest, and the sea is better off for it." C'k'rian plucked grass up from the freshly thawing ground and tossed them into the water. "Many of my people cannot come above the surface, but I will find a way to change that, so we can all be united once more." She scooped up a handful of soil, warm from the hot iron casket and she held her clenched palm out over H'Khara who held out her hand, she emptied the soil into H'Khara's palm.

"What of your plans, where will you go now? Ziath's grip on this world is weak and soon he will be gone from it, one way or another."

"Athias had a saying, I heard it on the first night we met. Kalvae vau'lomo dellata. He said that it meant to raise your sword for those who cannot. He may be gone but his words are not, and they were not lost upon me." She scattered the soil over the water beneath their feet. It settled briefly before falling through the veil. "There are still those out there who cannot fight and need help. I'm as much in this fight as I was the days after Athias saved me."

C'k'rian nodded and smiled.

"Very well. I will teach you, like I said I would. I will train you in the art of the sword, the spear, the knife, and the fist. And how to dance. Footing is as important to a warrior as is the sword."

H'Khara hugged her abruptly a tear in her eye.

"I miss him already."

"We will miss him for the rest of our lives." She smiled as H'Khara rest her head upon her shoulder, a tear in her own eye.

One Month Later

Over the passing month, the world saw many victories for the resistance. Their numbers had grown exponentially as they had lifted the reign of terror over tens of cities and towns. They had fought battles in the mountains, in the streets, on the long marshes and out at sea. The updated banner sporting a white raven over a gold hand was carried, hung over walls and homes, and planted in the ground by the thousands. Many prison camps had been liberated and work was well underway for monuments made of iron, marble, and frosted steel, which were to be placed along the Earth Road: the road connecting many major cities.

A hooded man, Abbrath, sat inside a clump of ivy trees by a small fire where dry leaves and sticks crackled. A rabbit roasted above the flames. The trees sat upon a small hill which overlooked a stream that ran down towards a village where the sign for an inn could be seen swinging gently in the wind. The Horn and Crow it read. Rain pattered around him, but he was shielded by the thick tops of the trees and he turned the rabbit slowly while unpacking a roughly carved wooden plate from a bag he had taken from his horse, a healthy black mare with splashes of silver.

"Is there room for one more at your fire." A peaceful voice carried across the calm. Abbrath knew the voice and he turned, smiling, and was greeted with another smile.

"There certainly is, especially for a familiar face." His tone was gentle.

A woman walked with her horse to a tree beside Abbrath and tied her steed up. She reached into her cloak and pulled out a carrot, feeding it to horse who chewed and settled. The woman, cloaked, swung a sheathed sword down from her back and lay it on the floor among the leaves before laying down a blanket and sitting across from Abbrath.

"Abbrath, my dear friend."

Abbrath looked up from the Calitreum, which he had summoned, preparing to write.

"H'Khara. It is a pleasure to see you again." He smiled and H'Khara lowered her hood. "How does it feel to be back here? This was the place, wasn't it?" He gestured down to the small town at the base of the hill and the marsh behind it.

"It was. Athias found me in the inn down there. I thought I would be scared but I feel nothing for it, nothing other than a drive to free it from the red cloaks' grip."

"And we will, and it will be soon. Shadows are taking up positions among the reeds as we speak. How is the sword treating you?" He nodded towards Spectre in its sheath laying among the crisp leaves.

H'Khara drew it from the sheath quietly, with a steady hand and held it out over the fire. The frosted steel glimmered in the fire.

"It sings its own song." She tucked it back into the sheath "I'm learning, slowly, and I can feel Athias' presence upon it as I do."

"He would be so incredibly proud of you. I can think of no-one better to have taken his place as a Vayshanaa. The first Coaran to become one." Abbrath lifted the rabbit off the fire and divided into two, passing half to H'Khara who began to dig into it. "The powers bestowed upon you will take time to master. Just as those you were born with did. Gralnor will assist you though, he always will. My own powers are proving hard to learn too, for death is a fickle thing."

A raven cawed, soaring down from the treetops and fluttering above the fire. H'Khara held out a small piece of rabbit and Gralnor snatched it up before landing upon her shoulder. He perched there, eating the tender meat. Abbrath and H'Khara ate their portions and scuffed dirt over the fire to extinguish it.

"Let me ask you something. Do you know why Spectre's name was changed, all those years ago?"

H'Khara shook her head.

"No, I barely remember Athias telling me that it had a name before."

Abbrath smiled, he always did love to tell a story.

"The first Vayshanaa, Orlana, found out about Zohya's secret. Orlana was gifted in the arcane, maybe the most gifted a mortal being has ever been. She reached out to Ciarth and Hyara, and she found a way to bind a small piece of their souls to the sword itself. The sword carries with it, the spectres of Ciarth and Hyara, and so the name Sciraria was lost and Spectre was found."

"They've been with the sword ever since?"

"Yes. In a way. Though only a small part of them, and their full power upon it could not be known until a gateway connected us to them."

"That's why Athias felt such a strong connection to the Abyss, isn't it? It was their mark on the sword, dragging him closer."

"You do learn fast, I see him in you, in that regard." Abbrath smiled.

"Where did Orlana come from? It wasn't Brineth, was it?" H'Khara was as curious as ever.

"No, it was not. She came here as a child, before that she lived on Rargnos."

"I should like to go there, when all this is over. Maybe Eifig will join me, I know they too wish to see other lands."

"Have you thought of a name for your book? The one you have been writing ever since you met Athias." She shot him a glance, "It took a lot for Athias to miss things."

"I have. The Spectre & the Raven." She stood up and returned to her horse, untying it.

"Very fitting." Abbrath nodded, a loving smile on his face, writing in the Calitreum as he did so.

"I will see you down there, my dear friend."

H'Khara mounted her horse and left the thicket of trees, looking down into the town that stood, although barely, below. She looked at the red banners and makeshift barricades at the entrances, and the figures as they hustled from one point to another like ants. A ray of sun passed over the marsh through the thick, grey clouds before hiding again and thunder rolled in across the horizon. H'Khara took one last look back towards Abbrath and then up to the sky as she pulled her black hood up and fastened Spectre to the saddle. Droplets fell upon the horse's clean hair.

Rain. It was always raining here, or at least it seemed that way.

Acknowledgements

I started writing this book in the second year of my degree, shortly after my father had passed away, suddenly. I struggled at university for this reason and I wanted to get away from it all but I could not. So, I turned to writing, and I turned that grief into motivation to write this story, the story of Athias, a character who is grieving. I feel that I projected a lot of my trauma onto him as a character, I have read that writers often project parts of their lives or their characteristics onto protagonists or antagonists. Completing this book would not have been possible without a few people. Three of my friends are the reason that I managed to finish the first draft of this book: Rowan Hearty, Will Barrett, and Ben Littlejohns. Without their support and encouragement, coming to see me and helping me learn how to process my grief, this book would have never made it past the halfway mark.

The second draft of this book, the one which came to be what you have read would not have been possible without Emily Foster, a courageous woman who stuck by me through multitudes of career changes and setbacks, and always encouraged the changes in the story.

Thank you to them, and to you, reading this now. The world of Brineth may return, yet.

Printed in Great Britain
by Amazon